Praise for *Nine Tailed*

"Urban fantasy readers will adore fox spirit at the heart of this fast-romance."

"Jayci Lee has gifted us with the best kind of romantasy—a wild ride with a sexy, protective hero, a spunky protagonist, a fast-paced plot sprinkled with the perfect amount of sexual tension, and world building so layered and rich you can sink your teeth into it!"
—Lexi Ryan, #1 *New York Times* bestselling author

"*Nine Tailed* is a wild, scorching, compulsively readable romantasy that delivers it all—characters who leap off the pages, fast-paced adventure, romance with all the feels, and a fascinating, magical world to die for. You won't be able to put it down!"
—Abigail Owen, #1 *New York Times* bestselling author

"Fast paced, heartwarming, and heartbreaking—my new fave fantasy romance! *Supernatural* meets K-drama vibes, immigrant globe-trotting immortals, and an epic battle between destiny and fate. *Nine Tailed* stole my heart with an explosion of fireworks and a wonderfully compelling gumiho. A stellar start to what promises to be a swoon-worthy series. I cannot wait to get my hands on the next one!"
—A. Y. Chao, *Sunday Times* bestselling author

"An absolute thrill ride! *Nine Tailed* is brimming with action, humor, and smoldering tension. Lee spins a fantastically original tale filled with cool magic and swoony romance you don't want to miss."
—Juliette Cross, author of the Stay a Spell series

KING
FORETOLD

OTHER TITLES BY JAYCI LEE

Stand-Alone Novels

Give Me a Reason

That Prince is Mine

Realm of Four Kingdoms

Nine Tailed

A Sweet Mess

A Sweet Mess

The Dating Dare

Booked on a Feeling

The Heirs of Hansol

The "I Do" Dilemma

The Not So Secret Crush

The Enemy Entanglement

Hana Trio

KING FORETOLD

JAYCI LEE

Montlake

Published by Montlake, Seattle

www.apub.com

Amazon, the Amazon logo, and Montlake are trademarks of Amazon.com, Inc., or its affiliates.

EU product safety contact:
Amazon Media EU S. à r.l.
38, avenue John F. Kennedy, L-1855 Luxembourg
amazonpublishing-gpsr@amazon.com

ISBN-13: 9781662533655 (hardcover)
ISBN-13: 9781662520778 (paperback)
ISBN-13: 9781662520761 (digital)

Cover design and illustration by Elizabeth Turner Stokes

Printed in the United States of America
First edition

To my readers. I can hardly believe you are real. Thank you for sharing this wild and beautiful journey with me. It is only possible because you read the words I write.

QUICK AND DIRTY GUIDE TO

PRONOUNCING ROMANIZED KOREAN

Pronouncing romanized Korean words is really hard, even for those fluent in Korean. In *King Foretold*, I try my best to be consistent in romanizing Korean words, following the Revised Romanization of Korean system currently used in South Korea.

The consonants are pretty straightforward. The way you intuitively sound them out in your head will be close enough not to trip you up while you read. But there are a few tricky vowels that you might need some getting used to.

I think these are the most helpful ones to note:

a is pronounced "ah"

ae is pronounced "eh"

eo is pronounced "uh"

i is pronounced "ee"

o is pronounced "oh"

u is pronounced "oo"

The cool thing about these vowels is that they will always sound the same no matter what consonants you combine them with. So the word for *nine-tailed fox spirit, gumiho*, is pronounced "goo-mee-ho"; the word for *the world of gods, Shingae*, is pronounced "sheen-geh"; and the word for *Heaven Lake, Cheonji*, is pronounced "chun-jee"; and so on and so forth.

Now, if I haven't confused you more, go forth and read *King Foretold* with confidence. You got this! Welcome back to the Shingae.

PROPHECY OF THE KING FORETOLD

Cruelty bends the heart of kindness,
Melds a union that should not be.

From the depth of twisted fate,
Born is hope to free the realm.

Beings of light shall not divide,
The will of good, the will of life.

Brave is the king who discerns,
Path of truth from path of shame.

CHAPTER ONE

I sit up with a gasp and scramble for my sword. My hand wraps around the hilt of my hwando, and I sag on my sleeping mat, my shoulders dropping from my ears. I glance longingly at my pillow, but I'll never be able to make the morning roll call if I give in to the temptation. The timid light of dawn is already seeping in through the hanji-pasted windows, staining the near-opaque paper a sweet coral.

Sweet coral? Fantastic. I'm a poet now. *The timid light of dawn* is particularly poignant.

With a snarl curling my upper lip, I kick away my rumpled comforter. But I cringe and freeze when my roommate, Hana, stirs across the room. Not wanting to rob her of a good hour of sleep, I slow my movements and soundlessly extricate myself from my sleeping mat.

I fix the bedding and smooth my hands over the silk duvet to make sure not a single wrinkle remains. In the Kingdom of Sky, even a lowly suhoshin cadet gets silk bedding as long as everything remains immaculate—sharp, wrinkle-free, and spotless.

I slip off my pajamas, fold them neatly, and place them at the foot of the sleeping mat before I change into a fitted dobok, the official uniform of the soon-to-be-dead cadets. With the annual trial on Lunar New Year taking out three-quarters of the cadets, they have better odds at becoming corpses than suhoshins.

I, of course, have no intention of *ever* becoming a high-and-mighty suhoshin. The defining characteristic of the guardians of the Shingae is that they all have sticks up their asses. I would rather avoid that discomfort.

Well, that's not entirely fair. Hailey and Jaeseok are chill for suhoshins. I might even go so far as to say they're cool. The jury is still out on Minju, a historian of the Order of the Suhoshin, since she did stab me in the chest. Even though she only did it to confirm I possessed the Yeoiju and healed me immediately after, I get a touch jumpy when she comes within arm's reach of me.

As for Jihun, he definitely has a stick up his fine ass. I make a *yuck* face and shut down my thoughts on the caliber of the suhoshin captain's ass.

I briskly braid my hair down my back and secure it with a scrunchie Hailey brought from the Mortal Realm. She has no idea *where* exactly— the jeoseungsaja confuses cities with states and states with countries.

You would think having a good handle on geography would be a prerequisite for someone born as a grim reaper. *What do you mean you're not Cindy from Rome? Ohhh. You're Cindy from Rome,* Georgia. *My bad.* Fortunately for everyone, Hailey became a suhoshin instead of someone responsible for harvesting the dead.

I scrub a hand down my face. Talk about waking up on the wrong side of the bed. Or the sleeping mat. I'm in a mood—even for me. I wholly attribute it to the fact that I've been a sappy idiot ever since I fell in love with Ethan.

Because, come on, *sweet coral?* I irritate the hell out of myself. And I'm ashamed of taking it out on Hailey with my mean thoughts. I typically find her difficulty with geography a great source of entertainment, not something to snark about.

The sooner I fall out of love with the Prince of Mountains, the better. For both our sakes. My heart . . . I clench my fist, ready to punch my wayward brain. My stomach—*not* my heart—aches. I must be hungry. I execute a blasé shrug to perfection with no one around to witness it. Maybe I developed acid reflux in my old age. I *am* one hundred and thirty-two. But since I stopped aging at eighteen, I might not be able to play the old-age card.

At any rate, the ache in the vicinity of my chest cannot have anything to do with love. I already decided I can never be with Ethan, so my heart . . . or stomach . . . or whatever is hurting had better get its shit together.

With my boots in my hands, I skulk out of my room, slide the latticed door closed behind me, and head down the hallway toward the training courtyard. The cadet barracks is a hanok, a traditional single-story building with a stone-tiled roof and curved eaves, inside the walled parameters of the Suhoshin headquarters.

The other hanok structures in the sprawling property include an extensive library, offices and meeting rooms, living quarters, and the Donggul, where the Suhoshin trial is held. I have no idea why the shadowy building butting against the jewel-toned forest got nicknamed "the Cave," and I want to keep it that way.

The Donggul gives me the heebie-jeebies. Maybe because only one in four cadets comes out of that building alive. The creepy factor is exponentially exacerbated by the fact that the ones who *do* make it out never breathe a word about what lies inside. And whenever anyone even utters the word *Donggul*, the faces of the new suhoshins spasm uncontrollably. Some suhoshins actually curl into a fetal position on the ground, rocking back and forth. It's not a pretty sight.

Anyway, there's no point thinking about the Donggul, especially since I don't ever plan on darkening its doorway. I hope to be far, far away from the Kingdom of Sky and the Realm of Four Kingdoms by the time the trial rolls around.

I just have to master the Yeoiju inside me before the Lunar New Year—and destroy the corrupt mudang resurrected by the Amheuk, an ancient force of darkness. I mean, how hard can it be?

"Don't answer that," I mutter to myself, stepping out to the main hall, which opens up to the courtyard.

A part of me wishes Daeseong won't emerge from the depths of Heaven Lake for a long, long time—even if it means I have to participate in the trial. At least I have a 25 percent chance of surviving the Suhoshin trial. My odds of defeating the demented shaman are a big fat zero at this point.

We are nowhere close to forging the sword of light, and my attempts to wield the Yeoiju, our only other weapon against Daeseong, have been a study in abject humiliation.

At least no one but sweet and patient Minju, my private magic tutor, gets to witness my shame. She insists on secrecy to protect the Yeoiju, the most powerful and coveted magical item in the realms, and me, its reluctant vessel. Even Jihun, Hailey, and Jaeseok aren't allowed to observe my clandestine lessons.

The only one in our group Minju hasn't explicitly banned is Ethan—probably because he's the King Foretold, the one prophesized to unify the Realm of Four Kingdoms and all that. Or it might be because he hasn't asked to watch my progress like the rest of my friends. I apparently have those now.

Ethan used to be one of them and could've been so much more . . . but he's been keeping a wide berth from me ever since we left Las Vegas and the Mortal Realm. Can I blame him, though? I threw his beautiful love back in his beautiful face. Maybe he's not even my friend anymore. *Shit.* My stupid stomach hurts again.

The only saving grace in this entire situation is that the cadet dobok is black and much cooler than the kind eight-year-olds wear to their taekwondo lessons. Hanbok dresses dyed in the colors of the sunset are undeniably beautiful, but I'll take this black dobok any day. What can I say? Black is my color. It never fails to brighten my day.

I jog down the three stone steps leading to the training yard and drop my boots on the dirt ground. I grin as I pull them on because they happen to be black as well. I find joy in the little things. Laughter barks out of me. I am so full of it.

I walk out to the vast yard, swinging my arms back and forth to wake up my body. The suhoshin instructors are merciless, so I warm up with some deep stretches. After the first day of training, I couldn't lift my spoon to eat my gukbap because I hurt *everywhere*.

Three weeks into the boot camp from hell, I'm in better shape than ever, but that doesn't mean a day of training won't kick my ass. Contorting myself into a pretzel now ensures that I'll be able to limp, not crawl, to my room later.

"That doesn't look very comfortable," a sardonic voice drawls behind me.

I crack open an eye to find a beautiful seonnam standing behind me in a silver dopo—a long outer robe worn by Korean nobility—with a gat tied under his chin. Jihun has his arms crossed over his broad chest and his head cocked to the side like he's studying a particularly fascinating piece of art. Except he's upside down, because I'm folded in half with my legs spread wide and my butt in the air. I open my other eye to smirk at him.

"Stop staring at my ass, Captain," I admonish gleefully, knowing full well he's only taking in my odd position. Then I lift my torso with a straight back, my body hinging at my hips, and rise slowly so I don't pass out from the blood rushing to my brain. But I definitely want to be upright to watch the stoic suhoshin squirm.

"That's asking too much of a male with a pulse, Sunny," he says huskily, and I nearly pitch forward into the ground.

If I were a pearl-necklace-wearing sort, I'd be clutching it right now. We're friends, for gods' sake. Or more accurately, we're two people who tolerate each other out of necessity. *Liar.* I sigh. Jihun and I *are* friends. I have to stop pretending to be the same sullen loner I was when Ethan found me in Las Vegas.

Oh, I get it. I teased Jihun about staring at my ass, so he's trying to embarrass me back. Touché. He had me for a minute. I'm new to this having-friends business, but I'm a quick study. If I mess with a friend, they'll get me back. My lips quirk. That actually sounds kind of fun.

Even so, my cheeks feel warm when I turn around to face him. The captain seems to be sporting some high color himself, but it's hard to tell with the rosy dawn drenching the courtyard. *Rosy dawn?* I cup my forehead. *Enough with the ridiculous poetry.* I'm so tired of being a lovesick fool. Why can't I just . . . stop?

"What's wrong?" Jihun's brows pull into a frown.

"Nothing." Except that I want to run to Ethan. I want to be in his arms so much that my entire body aches from the effort of holding myself back. *Enough.* I grit my back teeth and try to lie more convincingly. "Nothing is wrong."

The King Foretold is destined to kill the one who possesses the Yeoiju. If destiny forces Ethan to kill me, even though he loves me, then I'll do everything in my power to make him believe I don't feel the same way. At the very least, he won't have to kill me knowing I love him back with everything in me. I can spare him that much. If I play my part well enough, maybe he'll come to think of me as the female who scorned his love—someone he hates a little.

"To what do I owe the pleasure of your company?" I turn away from Jihun, blinking back tears, and grab a spear off the weapon rack. "You usually don't make an appearance this bright and early."

He doesn't respond for a moment as his dark gaze takes in more than I want him to see. Before I can bash his head in with my spear to make him stop, he says, "I need to speak to Captain Seo. I thought I'd catch her before morning roll call."

"Be careful," I mutter. "She might give you a black eye if you make her late for her torture duties."

"Do I detect a hint of animosity?" Amusement lights his eyes.

"Whatever gave you that idea?" I deadpan. "The captain and I are BFFs."

Captain Seo Cheyun, the head instructor of cadet training, is the bane of my fucked-up existence. The captain, a seraph like Jihun, is exquisite on the outside, but she's a merciless hard-ass on the inside and works the cadets within an inch of their lives. A part of me respects that, but I get the feeling she has it out for me.

Who the hell knows why? Maybe she's a bigot like the rest of the Shinbiin, who think animal spirits don't belong in the Realm of Four Kingdoms, much less in the Kingdom of Sky.

Even though I keep to myself, the news of a gumiho being recruited as a suhoshin cadet spread like wildfire. I can't step outside the Suhoshin headquarters without being gawked at like a zoo exhibit. The Shinbiin haven't seen a nine-tailed fox spirit—or any animal spirit, for that matter—in over five hundred years. The "younger" generation has *never* seen one.

To be honest, I get stared at inside the headquarters as well, albeit less overtly. The cadets are taught that it doesn't matter which kingdom you're from. It doesn't matter which life force—Sky, Mountains, Water, or Underworld—courses through you. Once you pass the trial and take your oath, you are a suhoshin first and foremost. *Unless you're an animal spirit.*

Jihun walks up to the weapon rack and peruses the deadly choices as though he's picking out an apple from a fruit cart. I arch an eyebrow when he selects a pair of scythes for himself instead of his usual weapon of choice, a longsword.

"An intriguing selection." I lead him to the sparring circle closest to the weapon rack, itching for a fight.

"I'd say the same about you." He nods at my spear, swinging the scythes with loose flicks of his wrists. "Not going with a hwando today?"

"How will I learn if I don't venture out of my comfort zone?" I widen my eyes innocently, but Jihun doesn't buy it for a minute, so I drop the act with a shrug. Then I slide one foot behind me and thrust the spear out, bending my front knee to take a low fighting stance. "I feel like wielding something a little more"—I suck my teeth—"brutish today."

He saunters toward me, the scythes whooshing by his sides in lazy circles. Something about the movement and the sound sends my pulse into a gallop. Jihun's lips quirk for the barest second, like he knows something I don't.

"Do you want to spar or not?" I goad, my skin tightening with agitation. "Or do you need to change out of your fancy nobleman's clothes?"

"Are you suggesting I undress?" He unties his gat from his chin and drops it onto the ground outside the circle. I watch his hand smooth down the front of his robe, and I swallow as heat rushes to my face. Is he still messing with me for my earlier *staring at my ass* jab? What the hell? He already got me back for that. "But I am quite comfortable as I am."

Too heartsick for a friendly tit for tat, I scowl and lunge at Jihun the minute he steps into the sparring circle. I meant what I said about the spear being brutish. The shaft is so thick my small hands can barely wrap around it, and my attack is clumsy as a result.

Jihun blocks with one scythe as grooves form between his eyebrows. "I could easily have disarmed you. You should know better than to take sparring lightly. These aren't practice weapons."

When they commence their training, the suhoshin cadets are twenty-four years old, fresh from their coming-of-age. The Shinbiin come into the peak of their powers in the second evolution of their zodiac animal and become nearly immortal. They heal fast, don't get sick, and age slowly enough to live for a thousand years.

The same goes for me, for whatever reason, even though I'm not a shinbiin. As a consequence, the suhoshin cadets use real weapons—and spill real blood—during training since we heal so quickly. *Fun times.* Did I mention we still feel pain like any other living being?

"You aren't my instructor, Jihun. Stop nagging and come at me." I tighten my grip on the spear and renew my attack.

Since the weapon is so unwieldy, I hold it pointed forward and advance on him with quick footwork. When I reach striking distance, I thrust the spearhead straight at his face, but he effortlessly evades it with a twist of his torso.

"Perhaps I should put these down." The scythes hang loosely at his sides.

"Why don't you stick them up your—"

I barely raise my spear in time to block the downward arc of his scythe. The impact vibrates painfully down my arms, but I don't even have time to grimace as I swing the blunt end of my spear up to fend off his other scythe. The second blow has me skidding back several steps before I dig my heels into the dirt. I risk a glance behind me. Another step and I'll be outside the ring, losing the round.

I arch back and swing the spear in a wide circle, forcing Jihun to retreat. Then, using its heft to gain speed and power, I bring my brutal weapon down on him. He crosses his scythes over his head to stop the spear blade from giving him an interesting haircut.

"Maybe you *should* put those down," I taunt.

He tightens his scythes around my spear, the metal blades digging into the wooden shaft, and rotates his arms in an arc, putting his back into the maneuver. I feel the spear being wrenched out of my hands. I can't let him be right about easily disarming me, so I flip my entire body through the air, leaning into the trajectory of the spear rather than fighting it.

Triumph flares in my chest at Jihun's look of surprise. I drop back down on my feet, our weapons still gridlocked. I meet and hold his gaze with a cocky grin until the surprise in his eyes heats into something sharp and turbulent. I can't catch my breath as my smile melts off my face. *Don't fall for me.* The thought comes out of nowhere, and I stomp it down. Of course he isn't going to fall for me.

"Jihun?" a chilly voice says behind me.

I jump back with a start, my spear clattering to the ground. I shoot a glance at Captain Seo, then back at Jihun. His eyes don't leave my face as he slowly lowers his scythes. I have an annoying urge to fidget under the intensity of his gaze, but I refuse to look away like a shy maiden.

"Jihun," Captain Seo repeats, placing her hand on his arm.

He holds my gaze for a second longer, then acknowledges the seonnyeo with a nod. "Cheyun, I thought I might speak to you for a moment before you start instructions."

"Of course," Captain Seo says with a soft smile. I'm shocked the hard-nosed instructor is capable of smiling.

"In private." Jihun walks out of the sparring circle without a backward glance at me.

I slump with a relieved sigh. That's more like it. I can handle the stern, brooding side of the seonnam. As for his odd, smoldering side, I hope it doesn't make another appearance. I can barely handle my feelings for Ethan. I don't want things to get strained with Jihun. I shake my head. Everything will be fine. He was probably in a weird mood.

Captain Seo turns to follow him, and her wings of wind catch an iridescent glimmer of the morning sun. Before I can fully appreciate their beauty—or traipse down poetry lane—she shoots me an icy look over her shoulder, and a shiver runs down my spine. I gulp as I belatedly realize the significance of her spread wings. She is ready for battle.

I don't know what I did, but I have a sinking feeling that I am her unwitting opponent and I'm in for a world of pain.

CHAPTER TWO

"Again," I wheeze at my enormous sparring partner. My early morning duel with Jihun, on top of the hour of sleep I lost, took its toll. And lucky me, I still have a long day of training ahead of me.

"Are you sure, Mihwa?" Haesan wrings his hands, the smooth planes of his face etched with concern.

My chest heaves, struggling to drag oxygen into my burning lungs. Even in my human form, I'm pretty fast and strong. But I have my limits, and I've apparently reached them. Not that I'd ever admit that. I would rather collapse, vomiting blood.

"Yes I'm sure." I swipe the back of my hand across my mouth, probably smearing blood across my cheek. "And how many times do I have to tell you to call me Sunny?"

"Mihwa is easier to remember than Sunny." The merman rubs the back of his head, his golden barbels flickering by his lips.

Gang Haesan is an in'eo from the Kingdom of Water, and like most of the cadets, he doesn't speak English. Only the Suhoshin travel to the Mortal Realm and speak multiple languages to navigate the human world. The rest of the Shinbiin in the Realm of Four Kingdoms don't need to speak anything but their native Korean because they never leave their precious realm.

"Mihwa means *beautiful flower*, and you *are* beautiful like a flower," Haesan continues, cupping his hands in front of him like he's cradling a blossom. "Yet, you said Sunny means *bright like the sun*, but you always wear such a dark scowl. Your American name should be something that means *stormy*. Then I'd be able to remember it better."

I bite my cheeks to hold back a smile. It's hard to glower at someone who's genuinely kind and earnest. Why does he have to be so endearing? He has got to be the most annoying merman I've ever met. Even his life force is a perfect cerulean blue like the unpolluted waters of the tropical ocean. *So* annoying. I don't need more reasons to like him.

Then I gasp as my gaze ping-pongs around his large form. I can *see* his life force. But how? My spirit eyes aren't open. It doesn't make any sense.

All beings of the Shingae originate from the four life sources born of the Cheon'gwang, the true force of light. And the gi of each source radiates a different color—green for Mountains, silver for Sky, red for Underworld, and blue for Water. In the Mortal Realm, I needed to open my spirit eyes to perceive the life force of magical beings, but in the Realm of Four Kingdoms . . .

The hairs on the back of my neck stand. I have a feeling Captain Seo is giving me the evil eye from somewhere in the training yard, but I don't risk turning around to confirm my suspicions. It'll only make matters worse if our eyes meet, because I'm not in the habit of backing down. Whatever is happening to my magic, I don't have time to worry about it now. I need to shelve it and ask Minju tonight.

"Shut up and come at me," I bark at the merman with the beautiful blue gi. *Damn it all to hell.* I give my head a rough shake, and the color disperses. I might very well be losing my mind, but I'll deal with that later too.

Haesan reluctantly widens his stance, bouncing lightly on his knees, and raises his arms loosely in front of him. I'm still getting used to the fact that he has legs rather than a tail and fins. In fact, other than the barbels and the gills behind their ears, the in'eos look no different from the rest of the Shinbiin.

"We don't have to do this," he pleads one last time.

"Have you met Captain Seo?" I gape at him. "We definitely have to do this."

I take a surreptitious glance around the training yard. At the opposite end of the long courtyard, the cadets not sparring are running through drills under the watchful eye of the junior instructors. My gaze skims swiftly over them in search of Captain Seo. I find her making the rounds through the ten sparring circles, stopping at each to point out the good and the bad. She'll reach our circle soon.

"Come on, Haesan." I beckon urgently with my hand, but the big softy doesn't move. *Damn it.* I have no choice but to strike first.

I launch a flurry of attacks on Haesan. I feint a kick toward his head, anticipating his dodge that leaves his left torso open, and pivot to bury my knee into his unprotected ribs. When he grunts and takes a halfhearted swing at me, I kick the side of his head.

The mountainous merman sways slightly on his feet, and I rush him like a linebacker, angling my right shoulder toward his stomach. If I plow into him hard enough, he might stumble outside the sparring circle, and I can take this round.

My plan backfires when I bounce off his ridiculously muscular body with only a ringing head to show for it. Haesan, who I know has been holding back, reaches for me with lightning-fast reflexes and grabs me before I fall flat on my back. With an apologetic grimace, he lifts me up by the arms and gently sets my feet down outside the circle.

"Sorry, Cho Mihwa," he whispers, releasing my arms when my head stops lolling from side to side. "I mean, Sunny Cho."

What started out as a bad morning is turning out to be an even worse day. I can't seem to catch a break. Ever since we returned to the Kingdom of Sky, I've been hanging on by a thread. I saved Ethan and my friends from Daeseong but almost died in the process, and I'm terrified I won't be able to do it again. I can't lose them. Not now.

Gods. I'm no closer to understanding the powers of the Yeoiju than I was three weeks ago. I don't have time to play suhoshin cadet.

"Why are you sorry? Are you scared my gumiho will toss you around like a toy?" I let my incisors lengthen, and I flash Haesan a vicious smile.

The merman pales but holds his ground, catching himself before he backs away from me. *Shit.* I shouldn't take out my frustrations on him when he has been nothing but kind to me—unlike the other cadets.

Even though we're forbidden from using our magic during training—including taking my fox form—the vast majority of the cadets stay clear of me. They fear me because I'm an unknown quantity. I get that. But I've faced enough racism in my hundred years in America to recognize bigotry when I see it.

The cadets ostracize me because they believe they are better than me. They believe they deserve all that is good and fair in life because they were born the way they are, and I don't deserve any of it because I was born the way I am. They only have to *exist* to garner all the privileges of this realm. But it infuriates them that I dare exist alongside them, fighting to *earn* my share of the goodness and fairness that is just handed to them.

Their deeply ingrained bigotry makes my skin crawl, but I refuse to direct that disgust at myself. I refuse to give in to the instinct to shrink in on myself, to hide from myself, to erase myself. It took me more than a century to embrace the gumiho in me. The Shinbiin can hate me all they want. I will not be ashamed of who I am.

But Haesan is a good male. He's smart enough to fear me, but he didn't back away when I baited him because he didn't want to make me feel any more reviled. I didn't mean to befriend him, but I did. Then I threatened to play hot potatoes with him. I am definitely the asshole here.

"I'm sorry, Haesan." I drop my head. "I didn't mean that. Neither I nor my gumiho would ever toss you around. Besides, my gumiho is me. And I am my gumiho. We're the same person. And you're my . . . friend? So yeah, I wouldn't do that."

I press my lips together to stop babbling. I'm obviously as bad at apologizing as I am at being a good friend. Even so, Haesan's face lights up with a guileless smile.

"You don't need to apologize." He claps me on the shoulder, and I'm damn proud of not crumpling to the ground. The male is freakishly strong. "You were just being you. Speaking of which, what's an American name that means *dark like a storm*?"

"*Stormy*," I grumble in English.

"'Store-mee'?" He sounds it out.

I shrug. "Close enough."

"Well, better luck next time, Stormy." He grins.

"Yeah, yeah." I take his teasing lying down because he's earned it.

But he stiffens, and his smile dies a swift death. I glance over my shoulder, following the direction of his gaze, and stiffen as well. Then I wince because every part of my body feels bruised and battered. Haesan felt squeamish about punching me with his paint-can-sized fists, so he opted to throw me onto the ground during our first two rounds.

"Who gave you permission to stop sparring?" Captain Seo's voice slashes down on us like a whip.

"We finished the three rounds, Captain." Haesan stands at attention.

"Is there a victor?" the captain asks with a straight face, even though everyone in the whole damn training yard knows there's a victor.

Haesan is by far the best in hand-to-hand combat. A few cadets with similar builds have put up a good fight, but he has never lost a sparring round. Captain Seo matched me up with him so my ass and my pride would take a beating, and she knows it. She's been extra nasty to me all day, ever since Jihun came to the cadet quarters this morning.

"Haesan won all three rounds." I try to keep my tone civil. I really do. But civility isn't my forte, especially when Captain Seo routinely berates me in front of the other cadets for my many inadequacies. And I'm pissed at myself for giving her more ammunition to humiliate me. "As you well know."

Captain Seo pivots on her feet in slow motion until we stand face to face. Her expression is set in stone, and there's menace in every line of her body. "And how would I know that?"

The Mean Girls snicker behind me. I don't waste my energy acknowledging them. I have my hands full with the furious angel in front of me, as well as the angry gumiho inside me. The captain picked the wrong day to mess with me.

"Because he's three times my size and weight." I throw an arm out toward Haesan, and he whimpers. "And he's a being of Water, with the might of waves in his veins. Without magic, no one in this training yard can defeat him in hand-to-hand combat."

"Is that your expert opinion, Cadet Cho?" The captain sounds terrifyingly calm. "That no one smaller and weaker can defeat him?"

"It's common sense," I bite out, doubling down.

I've already shown enough disrespect to earn me a week of barracks cleaning. I might as well crash and burn like a blazing meteorite. Besides, the captain can't work me to literal death. This whole cadet farce grants me amnesty, which means no killing me . . . for now.

"Would you agree that Gang Haesan is stronger and bigger than me?" Captain Seo unbuckles her leather belt and drops her twin knives onto the ground.

Fuck. I shoot a panicked glance at Haesan, who turns an interesting shade of green. I'm the one who challenged her authority. She's angry at *me*. I won't let her take it out on my friend. I round on the captain with murder in my eyes.

"Leave him out of this," I growl.

"You've made that impossible, haven't you?" She steps into the sparring circle that Haesan and I recently vacated. "How else can I unburden you of your flawed thinking? As your instructor, it would be remiss of me not to use this as a teaching opportunity."

With his giant shoulders drooping, Haesan walks inside the circle. Captain Seo is taller than me, but she still only comes to the merman's chin. Even assuming her slender figure is made of corded muscles,

Haesan could lay her out within three minutes. Is the captain counting on that so she can punish him for hurting an instructor? I can't let that happen. I suck in a breath, ready to apologize . . . to beg.

"In this circle, I am not your instructor," Captain Seo says in a clear, carrying voice. "We stand as equals. Don't be afraid of repercussions. There will be none unless you fail to try your best. And do *not* insult me by holding back because I am smaller and weaker than you. Is that understood, Gang Haesan?"

"Understood, Captain," Haesan answers automatically.

"I am not your captain." A ghost of a smile crosses her face. "I'm Seo Cheyun, your sparring partner. Ready?"

Haesan nods and takes his fighting stance. "What are you waiting for, Seo Cheyun?"

The cadets, as well as the other instructors, gather around the circle, jostling me from behind, but I don't take my eyes off the fight. The excited murmur quiets into awed silence as Captain Seo and Haesan face off.

Haesan is big, but he's startlingly fast. He's been holding back with everyone, not just me. But Captain Seo . . . She fights like a work of art come to life. She moves like poetry, lithe and fluid, and strikes like lightning. Their fight is an intricate dance choreographed to a symphonic masterpiece—beautiful and deadly, nuanced and brutal.

They punch, kick, block, and spin in a blur of flying limbs and twisting bodies. Haesan lands the first punch, and they break apart, dust swirling at their feet. Cheyun wipes the blood off her busted lip with her knuckles and gives her opponent a nod of acknowledgment. He smirks and beckons her with a flick of his hand.

After another furious burst of fighting, Haesan grunts and stumbles back two steps, barely stopping within the circle. Cheyun stands with her leg in the air for a second longer—the leg that just delivered an explosive kick to the merman's chest—then lowers it with impressive control.

Then they circle each other in loose fighting stances, panting from the exertion. The two seem evenly matched. I don't know who I'd put my money on. This fight might come down to stamina. They can't fight at this speed and intensity forever.

Yet, they spar for fifteen more minutes straight without seeming to tire. They are fucking machines. I'm exhausted just from watching them.

Suddenly, Cheyun moves in on Haesan like a streak of light, heading straight for his center of mass. She is so fast that I would've missed it if I wasn't paying attention. But it's not going to work. I already tried that strategy. Battering into Haesan is like slamming into a mountain. It's going to hurt her a lot more than it'll hurt him.

This will be over as soon as he gets his hands on Cheyun and throws her across the yard. I don't even blink because I'm afraid to miss her spectacular defeat. But—and I don't say this often—I'm wrong.

Cheyun lifts Haesan off the ground with a grunt and throws him over her shoulder, and he flies feet first through the air. In a blur of movements, she slams him down on the dirt and kneels on his chest, pressing one knee against his throat. "Do you yield?"

Haesan gurgles, and she eases the pressure off his windpipe to let him speak. "I yield."

Riotous cheers shatter the awed silence. The cadets jump, whoop, and pump their fists in the air, like their favorite basketball player sank a game-winning three-pointer with 0.01 seconds on the clock. They already think Captain Seo is the biggest badass to ever walk the Realm of Four Kingdoms, and she just handed Haesan, someone twice her size, his ass on a platter. It's going to be nauseating to watch them suck up to her even more.

The captain helps Haesan to his feet and claps him on the back. That probably hurt her hand, and I hold back a snort. But the merman nods and smiles at something she says, and I purse my lips. I'm not obtuse enough to miss the fact that she's behaving like a decent being toward Haesan.

Then why the hell is she such a jerk to *me*? I swallow the small knot of hurt. It isn't bigotry, because I don't feel that slimy mixture of rage and shame when she torments me. It feels like straightforward loathing. *Whatever.* I don't care if she hates me. At least, I don't want to care.

I tense when Captain Seo turns toward me, ignoring her sniveling fans. It's time to eat my words. Hell, I would rather eat a kale salad with no dressing. No, I take that back. There's no need for dramatics. I take a deep breath. Fair is fair. She proved me dead wrong, so eat my words I shall. With Shakespearean flare apparently.

"Come with me." She speaks English to me for the first time in a crisp British accent. Because *of course* she has an upper-crust British accent.

She heads for an unoccupied corner of the courtyard without waiting for my answer. I don't have a choice but to follow. I'm more confused than annoyed, though, because Captain Seo might actually be sparing me the humiliation of a public tongue-lashing.

"How did I take down someone so much bigger and stronger than me?" The captain crosses her arms.

"What?" I blink at her even tone. Where is the tongue-lashing?

"Were you or were you not watching my demonstration?" The captain's eyes narrow with impatience, but she has yet to yell at me.

"Your demonstration?" I blink some more. Had she really been trying to teach me something helpful through her sparring session with Haesan?

"Shall I demonstrate once more on *you*?" she snarls. That's more like it. I understand her antagonism better than whatever that was a second ago. "Last time, Cadet Cho. How did I take Gang Haesan down?"

"You took time early in the round to dissect his fighting style—his strengths and weaknesses." My eyebrows draw together as I play back the sparring match in my head. It happened fast, but I saw it all. "But not too long, because you already knew your own weaknesses. You knew Haesan had you beat on strength and stamina."

"Go on." Captain Seo's expression gives nothing away.

"Haesan's fast, but you're faster," I continue. "When he began to tire, getting a little sluggish and sloppy, you went in for the kill, so to speak. You got close enough to get a good hold on him, and before he could grab you—because you would've been done if he did—you used his own weight against him to unbalance him. From there it was pure technique, flipping him over your shoulder and pinning him down by his throat."

Gods damn it. I'm actually impressed.

"Now you know you didn't lose all three rounds to Gang Haesan because he's bigger and stronger than you." The captain arches her brow. "You lost because you're lazy and stubborn. Wouldn't you agree, Cadet Cho?"

I manage to stop myself from flinching, but my voice breaks as I ask, "What do you have against me?"

"Tell me I'm wrong." Not a single feather on the ice queen is ruffled. "Weren't you too busy being angry at me to focus on your rounds? Too busy fuming at the unfairness of it all to keep your head in the game? To strategize?"

I open and close my mouth. *Fuck.* My cheeks heat with chagrin.

"Do I even need to waste my breath on explaining your laziness? You half-ass your way through every training session." Her gaze bores into me. "Just because you don't intend to participate in the trial doesn't mean you don't need this training. You need it more than anyone."

"How do . . ." My blood pounds in my ears. How does she know?

"Captain Song asked me to provide you with additional one-on-one training." Captain Seo ignores my half-spoken question. "We will begin after the end of formal instructions today. But starting tomorrow, you will meet me here every day, two hours before dawn."

Did Jihun tell her that I possess the Yeoiju? That my objective isn't to become a suhoshin but to stop Daeseong from unleashing eternal darkness on the worlds? He wouldn't have. Jihun would never risk the mission. He wouldn't risk *me*. Unless . . . Does he trust Seo Cheyun? I squint at her. I can't imagine her as an ally.

"Wait, what?" I squawk as an urgent, very serious thought interrupts my mental spiral. "One-on-one training?"

"Yes. One-on-one training. Every day." The captain's expression hasn't shifted, but I can *feel* her glee. She's enjoying my torment. "Is there a problem, cadet?"

"No, Captain." My bottom lip threatens to quiver.

Captain Seo holds my miserable gaze for another second. "You're dismissed."

With a curt bow of my head, I spin on my heels and join the other cadets in the yard. Training is predictably brutal, leaving me little time to lament this tragic turn of events, but I don't forget for one instant that I am going to kill Jihun.

CHAPTER THREE

I thought the one-on-one training with Captain Seo was punishment enough for my earlier "insubordination," but I was wrong . . . again. Not to say the one-on-one *wasn't* punishing. She was relentless and demanding, and my legs felt like wilted asparagus by the time she was done with me. It just wasn't the full extent of my punishment.

I'm on my hands and knees, wiping the floor of the cadet barracks with a wet rag folded into the size of my palm. But the tiny rag and the hands-and-knees method isn't part of some cruel and unusual punishment. This is how everyone in Korea cleans their floors. Or they used to, at least. My mother and I cleaned our small, thatched-roof hanok like this every morning after we folded away our bedding.

"I thought I'd find you here," Hana says, crouching down to peer into my face. "How are you holding up?"

"I'm fine." I thump down on my ass and use my hands to pull my legs out, one-by-one, in front of me. "As fine as a person can be after fourteen hours of training."

"I can't believe Captain Seo made you train for two extra hours. The Mean Girls are saying you needed it because you're hopelessly bad." My roommate crinkles her nose like something reeks, color rising to her round, childlike cheeks. "I'd be offended on your behalf if they weren't so obviously wrong. You're one of the best cadets we have. They're just making themselves look stupid with their lies."

"They don't need lies to look stupid." I yawn, rubbing the back of my hand across my eyes.

"You must be starving." Hana tuts her tongue and takes out something wrapped in a handkerchief from the folds of her dobok. "Here, I brought you some jumeokbap."

"Where d'you get these?" I reach for the rice balls and stuff half of one in my mouth before she can answer.

"One of the kitchen attendants likes me." She shrugs modestly. Hana is a being of Mountains like me, but *unlike* me, everyone finds her sweet and lovable. "I told her you missed your dinner, and she just whipped these up for me."

"They're delicious." I wolf down a second jumeokbap.

"She drizzled toasted sesame oil on warm rice and crumbled some roasted seaweed over it, then mixed it all up." My roommate's face splits into a cherubic smile. It's really hard not to like her. Gods know I tried. "I helped her shape them into those fist-sized balls."

I raise the last rice ball and open my mouth big, then pause to glance at Hana. Being considerate is also not my forte, but I belatedly ask, "Do you want some?"

"No, I'm full." She shakes her head, pressing her lips together as though I might stuff the jumeokbap in her mouth. "I brought them for you."

Hana needn't have worried. I scarf down the last rice ball so fast, it's gone before she finishes her sentence. She gives me an indulgent smile and folds her sage green handkerchief into a neat square. My sappy roommate tenderly runs her fingertips over the delicate lilacs embroidered in the corner before tucking the handkerchief back into her dobok. She once unnecessarily shared that lilacs were her favorite flower. I didn't have an answer when she asked me for mine. I mean, why in the worlds would I have a favorite flower?

"Duna and I are going for a walk in the flower field at the edge of the city. Lilies are in bloom, and they're her favorite."

Duna is my roommate's twin sister. The Order of the Suhoshin normally doesn't accept more than one sibling from each family as a cadet, probably due to the astounding death rate, but the Shim sisters seem to be an exception. I assume it's a twin thing.

"That's nice," I say with minimal sarcasm.

"Do you want to come with us?" Hana continues, taking my words at face value. "Maybe you can decide which flower you like best, then I can make you a handkerchief with *your* favorite flower embroidered on it."

"No, thanks." But at Hana's crestfallen expression—Why is she crestfallen when I *never* say yes?—I rush to add, "I have more . . . chores to finish. Sorry."

"Oh no. You poor thing. I totally understand." My roommate pats my knee, pursing her lips in sympathy. "Duna's going to be disappointed."

I barely stop myself from laughing out loud. Shim Duna, while identical to Hana in appearance, is her sister's polar opposite in disposition. While Hana exudes warmth and light everywhere she goes, Duna is a sullen, taciturn shadow, orbiting her sister and her circle of friends. I avoid interacting with Duna as much as possible, because contrary to popular belief, grumpy plus grumpy does not make happy.

And Duna rubs me the wrong way—something about her sets me on edge—not that I would ever tell Hana that. My roommate loves her twin sister and cares about *me* for some unfathomable reason. If she finds out Duna and I have a mutual aversion to each other, Hana will be heartbroken.

Besides, I wasn't lying about having unfinished chores. I have to rendezvous with a stabby historian for my nightly magic lesson. And it's definitely a chore. My stomach clenches with nerves. How many people am I letting down with my continued failures? Is Ethan disappointed in me? Is that why he hasn't come to see me?

"Don't worry," Hana consoles me, mistaking my sigh for disappointment. "We'll go again when you're free."

"I would . . . like that." I sound halfway convincing. "Well, thank you for the jumeokbap. I better finish cleaning the floors."

"I wish I could help you . . ." She eyes the folded rag on the floor.

"Don't even think about it," I warn. "You won't be doing either of us a favor."

"I guess not," she says with a small pout. "Knowing Captain Seo, she'll probably double your punishment."

"That's right." I give her a pointed look. "Bye now."

"Okay." Hana rises to her feet in one graceful motion. It must be nice to have functioning legs, unlike my sore, wobbly ones. "I'll let you get back to work."

Once my roommate rounds the corner, I struggle onto my hands and knees and fall into the repetitive rhythm of scrubbing and scooting until I've carried out my sentence. When I'm done, I want to lie down right on the hallway floor and go to sleep, but a quick glance out the window tells me I'm late for my date with Minju.

I scramble to my feet and haul ass to Jihun's estate, the only place secure enough for our clandestine lessons. I sneak out of the cadet barracks and move swiftly through the shadowy alleyways. I can't moon shift and risk someone tracing my magic there for obvious reasons, and also because I'm breaking curfew.

When I first came to the Kingdom of Sky, Jihun petitioned to sponsor me so the Council of the Suhoshin would grant me amnesty. Those assholes will punish him for any infractions I commit, so I've become a reluctant rule follower.

Fortunately, Jihun's estate is not far from the Suhoshin headquarters, and I climb over the wall to the eastern wing in less than ten minutes. I slide open the latticed study door too hard, making it shake in its frame, and stand panting in the doorway.

Minju sits at the modern conference table, a solemn frown on her exquisite face. She is nowhere near as uncompromising as Captain Seo, but I'll take the captain's nasty sneers over the historian's quiet disappointment any day.

"You're late, Sunny," Minju chides in a calm, even voice. "You know how important these lessons are. Time is not on our side."

"I know, and I'm sorry," I say stiffly and walk into the study. "For some unfathomable reason, Jihun asked Captain Seo to give me one-on-one training, so I spent two hours after the regular training being berated by her. Then, as punishment for mouthing off at her this morning, I had to clean the floors with an itty-bitty rag . . ."

"Oh no." Minju rises from her chair and crosses the room toward me. "Have you eaten?"

My face crumples at her concerned words. It's been a long day. I sniff and nod. "Hana brought me some rice balls."

"That's good." She leads me to the table by my hand. "Are you hurting anywhere?"

"Everywhere." I have the weirdest urge to hug the historian and sob into her shoulder, but I fight against the disquieting impulse. I'm stronger than this.

Minju gently nudges me to take a seat at the table and sits down next to me. Then she places her hand on my thigh and softly chants an incantation, a silvery light glowing from where her hand meets my leg. My aches and pains disappear like magic—har har—and my body feels like my own again. *I* feel more like myself. I hurriedly shift my leg, forcing Minju to withdraw her hand.

"Thank you," I croak and lock away my vulnerabilities.

I have to remember I'm not safe here. This realm isn't my home, and the Shinbiin aren't my people. As for Jihun and his team—Hailey, Jaeseok, and Minju—are *they* my people? What about Draco, the angsty dragon spirit who reminds me so much of my younger self? Are Hana and Haesan my people? *No.* They're not my people either. I can't deny that they are my friends, but friends come and go. Forming attachments only leads to pain. It's inevitable. I can't forget that.

Case in point, all I got from falling in love with Ethan was constant heartache. It hurts I can't be with him when I know in the depths of my messed-up soul that he's my person and my home. And having him so near makes it hurt even more. Gods, I hate it here. This perfect little kingdom that has no place for me.

Ethan and my friends only make me want to belong somewhere I can't. The more time I spend with them, the more I want to stay by their side. They're changing me, and I'm afraid it'll ruin me. I want to run until I forget everyone, even myself.

An unsteady breath hisses through my teeth. What I want ceased to matter the moment Daeseong reentered my life. There is no running from this. If I run, all will be lost. I will lose *everyone*.

"This realm is fucking me up." I have no choice but to stay, so I might as well ask Minju for her help. "It's . . . messing with my magic. My spirit eyes are acting strange."

"Your . . . spirit eyes?" The historian squints in consternation.

"That's what my mother and I used to call it." I purse my lips. "Maybe you guys have a different term for it up here. You know, it's like . . . Gods, I don't even know how to describe it."

"Try," Minju says in all seriousness.

"Spirit eyes are like . . . like your third eye." I *try* as I'm told. "It's a different kind of *sight*. It's the power that lets you see the gi around you."

"How . . ." Minju swallows. "How do you see . . . What . . . what does the gi look like?"

"What do you mean what does it look like?" I give her the side-eye. "It looks like gi."

"Just humor me, please." Minju focuses her gaze on me with an intensity that tells me I might be missing something here.

"All beings of the Shingae have an . . . aura around them." I circle my hands, urging the words to come. "The aura, or glow, kind of . . . looks like a rainbow. The colors are distinct, but you can still see through it."

"The colors?" the historian chokes out.

"Yes, the colors," I repeat slowly. She is the smartest person I know. Why is she acting like she doesn't know any of this? "You know . . . blue for Water, silver for Sky, green for Mountains, and red for Underworld. You do realize you're acting weird, right?"

"Can you open your spirit eyes right now?" Minju asks urgently, ignoring my question. "Can you . . . see my life force? What color is it?"

"That's what I've been trying to tell you." I throw my hands up, confused as hell. What has gotten into her? "I don't need to open my spirit eyes to see the gi anymore. I saw Gang Haesan's life force with my *physical* eyes earlier. I think it has something to do with this realm. But I'm not sure I can even control the power anymore."

Minju slams her palms on the table, making me start, and pushes up to her feet. Then she paces back and forth, mumbling under her breath. She does this often. It helps her think, so I usually wait it out. But tonight, her nervous pacing only makes me more apprehensive. Before I can ask her to just tell me whatever she is thinking, the historian suddenly pivots to face me.

"What were you doing when you saw his gi?" she demands.

"We were about to spar, so I . . . I kind of zeroed in on him." My eyes widen, and I jab my pointer finger at her. "You're a genius. I need to concentrate on someone—"

"Look at me." Minju snatches my finger out of the air and pushes my hand down. "Tell me the color of my gi."

"I can't." I stare at her, narrowing my eyes. "It's not working."

Then I rear back, blinking rapidly against the brightness. I see her gi. She's a radiant silver, which doesn't come as a surprise. She's a seonnyeo, a being of Sky. Of course, her life force is—

"I see red gi threaded through your silver gi," I whisper, and Minju gasps, pressing her hand to her chest. The red threads of her gi flicker, then flare, burning as brightly as the silver. The twin flames of her life force are . . . beautiful. "You're part Underworld?"

My mother told me beings of the Shingae are drawn to those of the same life source because their gi calls to one another. *Like calls to like.* I had taken her words literally and assumed beings of different life sources couldn't be together. I honestly hadn't thought too hard on it since I was never drawn to anyone.

In all my years, I'd never met any beings of the Shingae who contradicted my assumption . . . until Ethan. He was the first person I was ever drawn to, and he was also the one who proved my assumption wrong.

His mother's jade necklace—which bore the last of the Queen of Mountains's love, tears, and magic—bound his powers and kept him hidden from his father for twenty-four years. When he broke the stone of tears, it unleashed his magic and imbued him with his mother's memories, revealing his past and his destiny.

His magic burns with the silver gi of Sky and the green gi of Mountains. He is living proof that beings of different life sources *can* be together. Minju is proof of that as well. Then why aren't there more beings with dual life forces? Ethan and Minju can't be the only ones.

"You must tell no one," she says, reclaiming her seat next to me.

"Why?" I shake my head. None of this makes sense. I'm so tired of being clueless. "And how is it even a secret?"

"Which question should I answer first?" A mischievous smile curves the historian's lips. She must have learned something new from our little exercise. Knowledge is her addiction, her aphrodisiac. It's nerdy but strangely endearing. "You mustn't tell anyone because it is forbidden. *I* am forbidden under the Code of the Realm."

"What?" I sputter. "That's total bullshit."

"I agree, but marrying someone outside of one's own kingdom has been prohibited for hundreds of years—partly because of the feud between the four kingdoms and partly because it is close to impossible for beings of different life forces to have a child together," Minju explains matter-of-factly. "It is hard enough for the Shinbiin to procreate as is, so the rulers of the four kingdoms decided not to risk the population dwindling even more. It was one of the few things they all agreed on."

"Then how . . ." I trace Minju's outline in the air with both hands.

"My parents married in secret, accepting they would never have a child together." She shrugs delicately. "But here I am. A statistical anomaly."

"You're a miracle," I correct her. *Just like Ethan.*

Minju nods shyly, then asks, "Do you want to know the answer to your second question?"

"My second question?" I scrunch up my nose. "I forgot I had one."

"How is my parentage even a secret?" She practically bounces on her chair.

"Okay. I'll bite." My lips quirk into a grin, her enthusiasm contagious. "How?"

"Because no one can see the colors of my gi." Minju grabs my hands and swings them between us. "When I actively use my magic, I draw solely from the life force of Sky, so people only see silver fire burning in my eyes."

"Wait." I snatch my hands back, needing to concentrate. "Why can't anyone see your gi when you're *not* using magic?"

"Because no one has that power. No one in the history of the Shingae has *ever* had the ability to *see* gi." Minju grips my face between her hands. "But *you* do. Do you realize what that means?"

"No clue," I say through puckered lips. I dislodge her hands from my face with an exasperated shake of my head. "You are making zero sense."

"It makes perfect sense. Don't you see, Sunny?" A triumphant smile spreads across the historian's face.

I *do* see, but I wish I didn't. This power is another reason I'm different from everyone else. It only makes me feel more alone. But Minju stares at me expectantly, so I give her the answer like a good student.

"I'm the only one who can see gi because I'm the only one with the Yeoiju," I say in a monotone. "I'm somehow harnessing its powers to perceive the life forces around me."

"This is a good thing," she says softly, squeezing my hand. The understanding in her eyes makes my throat tighten.

"If you say so." I look down at our hands. After the briefest hesitation, I flip mine over and squeeze hers back.

"I asked Captain Song not to share this with you because I didn't want you to be distracted from your lessons. But . . ." Minju hesitates, and I raise my head. "Daeseong disappeared from Heaven Lake."

"I . . ." A shiver runs through me, and I squeeze my eyes shut, trying to block out the memory of that terrifying battle. "I th . . . thought he was t . . . too hurt to leave the lake."

Daeseong had lured me to Heaven Lake to steal the Yeoiju from me. Even though Ethan, Jihun, Hailey, Jaeseok, and Draco fought at my side, the dark mudang was too strong for us. His nightmare monsters ripped us to shreds.

But in the end, it was the darkness that nearly destroyed us. The darkness that stole our hope . . . our will to live. In my desperation, I somehow harnessed the powers of the Yeoiju. I forced Daeseong to retreat to the dark depths of Heaven Lake, but I almost died in the process.

I thought I had more time. As long as he stayed in the lake, it meant he was too weak to carry out his plans. It also meant I didn't have to go after him since no one can dive that deep without imploding. But if he left Heaven Lake, all bets are off. I have no choice but to face him, whether or not I'm ready. I lock my jaws to keep my teeth from chattering.

"Suhoshin sentries have been watching the lake around the clock," Minju explains. "But the dark mudang somehow got past them."

"Wh . . . where is he?" I force out.

"We don't know. He's gone into hiding again, which means he hasn't fully recovered. But our time is running out, Sunny." The historian takes a deep breath and attempts a reassuring smile. "So it is a *very* good thing that your connection to the Yeoiju is growing stronger. It means you are one step closer to commanding its power."

"Oh goody," I say weakly, glomming on to the fact that Daeseong went into hiding again.

I don't have much time, but I might have enough to master the powers of the Yeoiju. It's too soon to give up hope. I haven't failed everyone. At least, not yet.

A SEA OF BROKEN PROMISES

The Queen of Mountains was kind and generous to her core. She never stopped hoping that her husband would become the king their people deserved. He promised to do better. He promised he would try. Even as she drowned in a sea of broken promises, she looked past his shortcomings and saw glimpses of the good in him.

One day, when the queen was newly with child—so new that even she was not certain—she foresaw that she would give birth to the one destined to unify the Realm of Four Kingdoms. The one destined to unite all beings of Sky, Mountains, Water, and Underworld.

Shaken by the enormity of the revelation, she told her husband about her vision. She needed to share the weight of responsibility. She wanted to share the joy. For their son was hope. But the King of Mountains did not want an heir, much less an heir foretold to be the greatest king the realm had ever known.

Too late, the queen understood that the good she had seen in the King of Mountains was an illusion, a mere reflection of the hope she had placed in him. Too late, she saw in the mad glint of his eyes that the king believed her to be his possession, to keep and to break, but their son was a threat he had to end.

Fate had never been kind to diviners. Those with the gift saw both too much and too little. The Queen of Mountains had not seen that her husband would strive to kill her son to preserve his power. But it was not too late for her to save her son. That she knew. He would endure much pain and loss in his journey, but the King Foretold would rise triumphant.

For she had foreseen it.

CHAPTER FOUR

It's well past midnight, and my trek to General Bak's estate takes longer than I'd like. But I'm exhausted, and my legs refuse to carry me any faster. I look longingly at the moon and sigh. I can't risk moon shifting because my magic might be traced to Ethan.

The night we returned to the Kingdom of Sky, the formidable general crumbled before our eyes when he saw Ethan for the first time. In the general's endless tears, I glimpsed a brokenhearted father who had lost his beloved daughter, only to be reunited with his grandson twenty-four years later. And in the embrace of his grandfather, Ethan found his family again.

The moving reunion, however, was short lived. As soon as General Bak pulled himself together, he began to plan for a war to place his grandson on the throne of the Kingdom of Mountains. In the meantime, the general made Ethan promise to hide his true identity and keep a low profile because there might be spies in the kingdom. He said if the King of Mountains found out that his son was in the Realm of Four Kingdoms, Ethan's life would be in danger.

When I finally reach the outskirts of the general's estate, I stop and take cover in the shadow of a tree. I have no idea which wing Ethan occupies, much less which room. I obviously didn't think this through.

But after everything Minju told me, I couldn't find the willpower to stay away from him. Just a glimpse of his face will remind me why

I have to be strong—why I have to fight—even if I feel more alone than ever.

Everything I knew about my spirit eyes was wrong. No one else can perceive the gi around us. No one else can see the beauty of the worlds saturated in the colors of life. I thought it was a power I shared with every being of the Shingae, something that connected all of us. It always made me feel like I was a part of something bigger, like I wasn't a loner adrift in the worlds. But none of it was true.

I'm the only one. It is my power alone. I'm always alone.

I shake myself from head to toe like I'm covered in ants. I'm not only a poet but a *mopey* poet. This is bad, like zombie-apocalypse bad. If there is anything more pathetic than feeling sorry for yourself, it's feeling sorry for yourself in subtle, lyrical verses. Can I fall any lower?

I come to an abrupt stop on the road. *Oh gods.* I *have* fallen lower. I was feeling sorry for myself in haiku form. I fucking composed a fucking haiku. Who even am I? I squeeze my eyes shut, willing myself to cease existing this instant. But it doesn't work. I guess you can't actually die from shame.

And I've come to visit the reason behind my unfortunate poetic episodes. I shouldn't have come. This was a mistake.

As I turn to leave, I hear a low, urgent voice whispering my name even though there's no one close enough to whisper in my ear. I glance back, and a dark figure leaps over the outer wall of General Bak's estate, landing effortlessly on their feet.

Did I doubt for a moment who whispered my name? Did I need the silvery moonlight to know that it was Ethan walking toward me? *No.* I felt him in my soul before any of my senses could detect him.

"Sunny." He stops a few feet away from me, devouring me with his eyes.

I take a shuddering breath, my pulse fluttering in my throat. I remember the feel of his calloused hands on my body, both rough and reverent, and the heat of his mouth as he claimed mine. I remember the idyllic days we spent at my childhood home, pretending we were alone in the worlds . . . pretending there was hope for us.

I've missed him so much that it hurts to look at him. I want to run into his arms, but I stand exactly where I am and clench my hands into fists behind me, using the bite of my nails as an anchor. Because now I know we don't have a chance in hell of being together.

You saw him. Now leave.

Unclenching my hands, I lean a casual shoulder against the tree and pray that my face gives nothing of my yearning away.

"Ethan," I drawl, as cool as a cowgirl. *Leave before you make everything worse.*

"What are you doing here?" he asks with a catch in his voice.

He looks even taller dressed in an emerald silk dopo and a gat. The rich, vibrant green of his long robe gives his face a luminous glow even under the shadow of his black, wide-brimmed hat. He is so beautiful. I wonder if his skin would taste fizzy like champagne against my tongue.

"What? Me?" My shoulder slips from the tree, and I stumble before righting myself. "I'm . . . out for a jog?"

His lips curve into a crooked grin. *Cocky bastard.* I should kiss that arrogant smile right off him. Maybe nibble on his bottom lip for good measure. *Right.* What I should do is get the hell away from his effervescent skin and yummy bottom lip.

"Well, it was nice running into you." I give him a dorky little wave because I apparently haven't humiliated myself enough.

I take off in a sprint, but I gasp and lurch to a stop when his arms wrap around my waist from behind. I forgot Ethan was so fast.

"Stay. Please." He presses me flush against his front and buries his face in the crook of my neck. "Just for a minute. Just like this."

Just for a minute. I lean back into his warmth and close my eyes. I breathe in the crisp, woodsy scent of him and place my hands over his. He threads our fingers together and tightens his arms around me like he never wants to let go. We hold still, synchronizing our breaths, and let the moment wash over us. If only time could stop . . . *Just like this.*

"You know my spirit eyes?" I whisper, knowing time stops for no one. I have so much to tell him, so much I want to hear, but time is something we will never have. "I thought it was a Shingae thing, but it turns out it's a Yeoiju thing."

"It is?" His lips brush against the sensitive skin at my neck.

"Mm-hmm." I shiver. "Apparently, no one else can do it, which means I'm extra special."

"Of course you are." His rumbling laughter vibrates low in my stomach.

"Fuck you." I smile, feeling safe for the first time since returning to the Kingdom of Sky.

"Gods, I missed you," he rasps, his whole body wrapping tighter around me.

"Whatever." *I missed you too. I missed you so much.* "You could've come see me anytime."

Don't invite him. You're trying to make him believe you don't care.

"What excuse would an emissary from the Kingdom of Mountains have to see a suhoshin cadet?" Bitter frustration threads his words.

I step out of the circle of his arms, and he lets me. I immediately miss his warmth, but I face him with a carefully neutral expression. It belatedly sinks in that the rich green of his dopo is not a color often worn in the Kingdom of Sky. Ethan is dressed for his role as an emissary of the Kingdom of Mountains, a special guest of General Bak.

"Off the top of my head?" I quip even as concern tightens my chest. He looks thinner. "You can ask for a tour of the training grounds."

"I'll keep that in mind," he says with forced levity.

But it's no use. I've reminded him of our stark reality, and his face hardens into a distant, ravaged mask. It's the tortured face of a stranger—the face of the Prince of Mountains, who lost everyone he loved to the greed and ambitions of his father. When he stares down at his hands, I know he sees blood on them.

Not for the first time, I want to kidnap Ethan and take him far, far away from his bloody legacy. But the moment he wielded the legendary golden axe and silver axe, gifts bestowed by the Spirit of Mountains, he vowed to the Shingae that he would accept his destiny—the destiny to become the King Foretold and kill the bearer of the Yeoiju.

Distance. I step back. I need to keep my distance.

"Do you ever wonder how I ended up in LA with you and Ben?" I blurt out.

Maybe it would've been better for everyone if we'd never met. Ben might still be alive if Daeseong hadn't come looking for me. Then Ethan could have navigated his new reality with his older brother by his side. All I can do is break his heart now so he will hurt a little less when he kills me.

Ethan gives me a long considering look. "No."

"No?" I gape at him. "You think everything is a convenient coincidence? We somehow came to live in the same city at the same time . . . just because?"

"I don't have to wonder *how* because I know *why* you ended up with us." His gaze doesn't waver. "It's because you and I are meant to be together."

"Stop being a cheeseball," I quip even as my heart trips in my chest. "I can't believe you said that with a straight face."

"I'm not being cheesy." A grin tugs at his lips, but his voice rings with absolute certainty. "You and I are tied by the threads of fate. I feel it in my bones."

Could he be right? Is our love destined by the heavens? Are we part of some divine plan? But what kind of sick, twisted deity plans for a person to kill the one they're destined to love for eternity? *Fuck it.* Suddenly, I don't care about the how or why of anything. I don't want to care. If everything is destined, what's the point of caring?

"In your bones? You should have that checked out. It might be arthritis." I force myself to joke even though I want to cry. "Other than arthritis, any new developments on your front?"

Ethan sighs and drags a hand down his face. "General Bak wants me to *bide my time.*"

Bide his time until war ravages the Kingdom of Mountains? Until more death and blood stain his hands? *Oh Ethan.* A war will tear his kind soul to shreds. There has to be another way. Why can't the general see that?

"So you've basically been sitting on your ass all this time?" I roll my eyes, hoping to get a smile out of him. "Wow. You must be getting really good at twiddling your thumbs."

"Shut up," he says with a lopsided grin and flicks my earlobe with his finger.

"Ow." I shove his hand away, tucking my chin into my chest to hide my smile.

"When I'm not busy twiddling my thumbs"—Ethan ducks his head to catch my eyes—"Jihun and I are figuring out a way to bring the King of Mountains to justice *before* General Bak wages his war."

"Oh thank gods." I sag with relief. I have no idea if that's even possible, but I'm glad they're trying. We have to stop the king *and* the war. For Ethan's sake. For everyone's sake. "Any luck?"

"Nothing concrete, but we have a spy in the Shinsi Palace, where the king resides." He lowers his voice even though there is no one else around. "Her latest message said the tyrant was ill."

"Ill?" I try to remember the last time I was sick, and I can't. I'm like the Shinbiin. I don't get sick. "How can he be ill? Maybe she meant he was hurt . . . *Can* he be hurt? Or is he invincible like you?"

"We don't know the details yet." His brows furrow. "We'll find out more soon. But if the king really is sick, then we might have a fighting chance of overpowering him."

My stomach drops. I've been so preoccupied with the Yeoiju and Daeseong that I didn't fully grasp what lies ahead for Ethan. Maybe I deliberately looked the other way because it hurt to think about him at all. Worrying about him and his future, so soon after Heaven Lake, would have wrecked me, but there is no avoiding it now.

To fulfill his destiny of becoming the King Foretold without an all-out war, Ethan has to defeat the King of Mountains face to face and overthrow him from the throne. *How?* With his magic unbound, Ethan is more powerful than I could ever have imagined. But until he masters his powers, he has no chance of defeating his father. How will he be ready before General Bak wages war against the Kingdom of Mountains?

I'm not going to burden him with my worries. I have to trust he has this since I can't both push him away *and* be there for him. My heart clenches. That's the hardest part—not being able to comfort him and lend him my strength.

"Okay. Keep me posted," I say brusquely, but the next words slip past my lips before I can stop them. "And don't do anything stupid without me."

"But I *can* do stupid things with you?" He presses his hand on the small of my back and leads me to the nearby tree. Then he tugs me down next to him, and we sit with our backs against the trunk. "How's your cadet training going?"

"Let's just say I miss my shitty job at the casino." I let him turn the subject away from his murderous father. "But this dobok is a step up from that tiny sparkly dress I used to wear."

"I don't know . . ." His gaze lingers on my body. "I kind of liked that dress."

"Perv," I tease, hoping the night hides my blush.

"Hey, that's not fair." His wounded expression is fairly convincing. "It's not my fault you look fetching in everything."

"Did you seriously use the word *fetching*?" I crinkle my nose at him even as I blush harder.

"What? Not a fan?" Ethan shrugs his broad shoulders. "I thought it more polite than *hot as fuck*."

"We've never been polite to each other." I shift in my seat, heat spreading through my body. "I see no point in starting now."

"Agreed." He laughs softly, and my heart mimics a baby bird attempting to take flight. "And how's your . . . other training coming along?"

"Other than my magic gi goggles?" My shoulders droop. "Absolutely nothing. But Minju thinks my connection to the Yeoiju is growing stronger. Whatever that means."

"Give yourself some grace." He nudges his knee against my calf. Where we sit side by side on the ground, his legs stretch on way longer than my puny ones. "Not everyone can claim to have magic gi goggles."

"Actually, *no one* can," I mutter morosely. "Extra special, remember?"

"How can I forget?" Ethan tugs my head onto his shoulder. "You'll figure it out. You always do."

I want to lean on him and let him tell me everything will be okay. But what good has that ever done?

"I better get going." I hop to my feet before I change my mind and swat dirt off my ass, but I don't step away.

Turn around, Sunny. Leave.

"I'll walk you back." Ethan scrambles up next to me.

"Why would a fancy emissary escort a humble cadet back to the barracks?" I cock my eyebrow, even though I would give anything to spend more time with him. "Besides, how do you know I'm not moon shifting back?"

"I doubt they have bowls of water outside the barracks to make sneaking in and out easier for the cadets." A muscle jumps in his jaw. "But if I'm wrong and you can moon shift back, I won't be able to accompany you."

"Why not?" I frown at his obvious frustration.

"Grand—" He curses under his breath. "General Bak is adamant that I don't use my magic."

"What?" I breathe. Ethan's magic is much too powerful to leave untrained. He needs to master his powers for his safety, as well as the safety of others. And . . . *oh gods* . . . if he can't master his magic, we have no hope of stopping the King of Mountains without a war. "Why the fuck not?"

"He's worried my magic trace will reveal that I come from two life sources," Ethan says with a heavy sigh.

41

How can anyone discern Ethan's two life sources if I'm the only one with gi goggles? The traces left behind by beings of the Shingae are more like fingerprints than DNA samples. They allow you to identify a person, not analyze their genetic makeup. Something doesn't seem right.

But I nod as though I'm convinced. "He doesn't want your cover blown."

"Yeah," Ethan mutters.

I let my gaze trace the lines of his features. I can't imagine what he must be going through. If he can't defeat his father—if he can't stop the war—Ethan will blame himself for every life lost. He must be drowning in helpless anger and frustration. But his relationship with his grandfather is so new, so precious, even I wouldn't want him to endanger that by opposing the general outright.

"Hey." I tap the tip of my shoe against the tip of his. "Did you know you were a miracle?"

"A miracle?" He side-eyes me.

"Yup," I chirp in an awkward attempt to cheer him up. "Apparently, it's basically impossible for beings of two different life sources to have a child together."

"Ah that." He shrugs with a bittersweet smile. "*Basically* impossible isn't the same as impossible."

"Wait." My brows draw together as I come to a belated realization. Shinbiins from different kingdoms are forbidden from marrying each other. "How did your parents . . ."

"My father trapped my mother into marriage." Ethan grits his teeth. "And no one dared to stop the King of Mountains."

I clap a hand over my eyes. "Why can't I say the right thing for once?"

"I love everything you say." He tugs down my hand, the corners of his eyes crinkling. "I would give anything to spend a day with you, listening to the things that come out of your mouth."

"You're such an idiot." I give him a tremulous smile, and his gaze drops to my lips. The heat and yearning in his eyes make my breath hitch in my chest. Before I do something very foolish, I squint up at the sky. "It'll be dawn in a few hours. Wh . . . what are you doing up so late anyway?"

"Shit." He cringes. "I promised Draco I'd stop by tonight, but I wanted to make sure everyone was asleep before I left."

"Why? Have you not told General Bak about our lovable dragon shifter?" I cock my head to the side. "Don't you trust your grandfather?"

"I trust him with my life," Ethan answers without hesitation. "But I'm not taking any chances with yours."

"Mine?" I draw back in surprise.

"No one outside our core group can know about the Yeoiju. You're already in danger from the Jaenanpa in the Mortal Realm." He shakes his head wearily. "If someone here finds out, it'll only be a matter of time before every power-hungry shinbiin in the Realm of Four Kingdoms will be after you too. I can't risk that happening."

"And we can't explain Draco's presence without explaining that we need to meld their dragon scales with the sacred ashes in order to forge the sword of light," I murmur, thinking out loud. Then we would have to explain why the Seonangshin entrusted me with the sacred ashes—why I have to be the one to defeat Daeseong. "You're right. We can't risk more people finding out about the Yeoiju. Not until I figure out how to wield its powers without killing myself."

"Exactly." Ethan's lips press into a grim line. "Even the Council of the Suhoshin doesn't know the full extent of our mission against the dark mudang."

"But shouldn't they know that Daeseong plans to unleash the Amheuk from its prison beyond the abyss?" I glimpsed into the dark mudang's tortured mind at Heaven Lake. I saw what he intended to do. "Darkness will devour the worlds if he succeeds."

"The council can't help us. No one can." The moonlight casts harsh shadows across his somber face. "*We* have to defeat Daeseong."

I struggle to swallow, fear rearing its head again. "He escaped from Heaven Lake."

"I know." Ethan squeezes my arm. "But he went into hiding again. It means we still have time."

"Sure." I fist my hands to stop them from shaking. "We just have to unlock the mysteries of the Yeoiju and figure out how to forge the sword of light before the dark mudang gets bored playing hide-and-seek."

"That about sums it up." Ethan lightly chucks my chin. "No pressure, right?"

My laugh turns into a sob. "I hate this."

"I know." He pulls me into his arms and plants a kiss on the top of my head. "But in all fairness, you hate everything."

"Dingus." What happened to keeping my distance? I bring my hands up to his chest to push him away, but I . . . don't.

"Aww, my favorite term of endearment." He chuckles, holding me closer.

Despite my best intentions, I melt against him with a helpless sigh. And just like that, the air around us grows taut with electric tension. Slowly, his hands smooth across my back, then run down my sides, his thumbs grazing the curve of my breasts. My breath hitches as fire spreads across my skin. But when his hand dips under my shirt and his fingers dig into the soft flesh of my waist, I come to my senses and stumble back from him.

"You know I was kidding about you asking for a tour, right?" I make a face, going into damage control mode. "I'll be busy with my training, and you'll be busy twiddling your thumbs. We don't have time for distractions."

"Don't worry." His smile holds both devastation and understanding. "I won't bother you."

"Cool." Gods, I hate myself. "I'll see you around."

This time, Ethan doesn't stop me when I run off into the night.

CHAPTER FIVE

"Will you stop wiggling?" Hailey laughs.

"I'm not wiggling," I say through gritted teeth, contorting my torso in an attempt to stop wiggling.

"Oh my gods." She chortles harder. "You're ticklish, aren't you?"

"Don't be absurd." I am ticklish as hell. "Why is Minju making you draw all this shit on me anyway?"

"How would I know? She never tells me anything. Minju is *so* secretive about your lessons. She just said in a really serious voice that I had to memorize all these symbols and paint them on your back." Hailey puts a firm hand on my bare shoulder to hold me still. "But I have a theory. I think these symbols are arcane words of power. Depending on what they mean—I obviously can't read them—they can either amplify or suppress your powers. Or do something else entirely."

"Wow. That is *so* illuminating," I deadpan.

"Don't be a jerk," Hailey admonishes mildly. "This is high, *high* magic. It's way above my pay grade. Besides, Minju will explain everything to you tonight."

The suhoshin cadets get one measly day off a month, and I'm spending it shirtless in Jihun's study, getting weird-ass symbols painted on my back with cold ink and a brush made for torture. I twist my torso in slow motion, trying not to squeak or giggle. I will *not* giggle. I make a guttural, clicking noise in the back of my throat instead. Well, that's new.

"If you don't stop squirming, I'm going to have to redo this whole damn thing." Hailey sounds dead serious.

"I'm not squirming." My voice rises to a high-pitched yelp. "Get on with it."

"I don't know who is worse. Draco or Jaeseok," Jihun mutters, sliding open the door to his study. "They don't have a speck of common sen—"

Hailey stops the torture for one blessed second, and I glance toward the door. Jihun stands frozen with one foot in the study and the other raised midstep, just outside the door. He could be mistaken for a statue if not for his eyes, which roam over me.

I look down at myself. It's not like I'm indecent. I'm holding my black tank top against my naked chest. And I'm facing the side wall, so all Jihun can see is the outer curve of my left boob and some of my back. I roll my eyes hard enough to see the top of my skull. *Guys.* These shinbiin males are no different from the men in the Mortal Realm. Their dicks are like idiot switches. When you turn them on, their brains shut down.

"Captain, do you mind closing the door?" Hailey says drily. "Some of us are half-naked in here."

With an odd choking noise, Jihun spins away from us and slides the door shut. A red flush creeps up the back of his neck above his fitted gray T-shirt, which accentuates his broad shoulders and narrow waist. My eyes drop to his dark jeans, but I snatch my gaze away before I notice how well they fit. Who's being an idiot now? I shouldn't be too hard on myself, though. The seraphim are renowned for their beauty. It's hard not to notice his otherworldly good looks.

Hang on. He's wearing mortal clothes. He either picked out his outfit on a whim—I snort at the preposterous thought of Jihun having a whim, much less acting on it—or he plans to go to the Mortal Realm on official Suhoshin business. I consider badgering him to take me with him—I haven't been back since Las Vegas—but I quickly dismiss the idea. I don't have the bandwidth to endure the Gray Void.

But panic grips me by the throat as a different thought occurs to me. Is Jihun going to the Mortal Realm to track down Daeseong? Maybe the Suhoshin have already found the dark mudang. My heart pounds against my rib cage and echoes in my ears. *Gods.* I can't do this. I'm not ready.

Then in my mind's eye, I see Ethan standing under the silvery moon, determination in every line of his beloved face. *We have to defeat Daeseong.* I fill my lungs on a slow inhale. I can do this. Even if I'm scared, I can protect Ethan and my friends. Even if I can't master the powers of the Yeoiju, I *will* protect them.

"What are you . . . ," Jihun sputters, still facing the sliding doors, and I jerk out of my grim thoughts. "Why is she . . ."

"Half-naked?" Hailey finishes his question for him, then answers, "Minju gave us homework. This was the securest place to do it."

"She can . . ." Jihun clears his throat. "Sunny, you can use your old quarters at the Sunset Pavilion anytime you wish."

"Good to know," I croak huskily, touched by his generosity, but I quickly arrange my face in a grumpy frown. "Anyway, we have to finish what we started here. I'm not putting on my tank top before the ink dries. I'll bash this table into little toothpicks if I have to do this all over again."

"I'm with Sunny on this one." Hailey groans. "We've been at this for almost an hour. I do not want to start over. My hand is cramping up."

"Jihun?" I begin in an attempt to be both brave, to face my fears about Daeseong, and cowardly, to stall the tickle torture. "Are you going to the Mortal Realm today?"

He whips his head around in surprise, then turns back toward the door just as fast. "Why do you ask?"

That's the shiftiest answer I've ever gotten from him. "Unlike Hailey and Jaeseok, you don't wear mortal clothes for fun when we're in this realm. Also, why are you stalling?"

"Minju asked us not to distract you until we have concrete news." Jihun sighs.

My hands clench the tank top I'm holding against my chest, but I keep my voice nonchalant. "About Daeseong's whereabouts?"

"Yes." He doesn't elaborate.

I'm getting tired of his evasion, and I refuse to talk to his back a moment longer. "Will you please turn around?"

"I'm comfortable as I am," he says stiffly.

"For the love of gods." I look up at the ceiling, praying for patience. "Do you or do you not know where Daeseong is?"

"I do not." Then he finally relents and says, "But I am going to the Mortal Realm to follow a potential lead."

What am I going to do if Jihun finds the dark mudang today? I take a shuddering breath. Whatever these symbols are on my back, they better fucking work. I need the power of the Yeoiju.

"It'll probably be another dead end," Hailey reassures me, giving my shoulder a squeeze. "We've had several leads sputter out already."

I reach over and pat her hand in silent thanks. But there is no denying that I'm running out of time. Instead of worrying about things beyond my control, I need to focus on what I can do.

"Come on, Hailey." I grit my teeth and steel myself. "Let's get on with this."

When she resumes her drawing, I squeak high and loud. I forgot how cold and tickly the brush was in my brief reprieve. And Jihun twists around in alarm, his longsword materializing in his hands.

"Easy, Captain," Hailey says in a singsong voice. "There's no danger. Sunny is just ticklish. Isn't she adorable?"

"I'm going to kill you," I whisper scream at her, embarrassment flooding my cheeks. Jihun withdraws his sword, his lips quirking in amusement. I narrow my eyes at him, and he wisely presses his lips into a flat line.

Then I remember I have to kill him as well for asking Captain Seo to train me one on one. On the not-entirely-horrible side, the private training sessions have been honing my skills to a lethal sharpness. Maybe I'll let Jihun live another day. Besides, I get why he did it. He wanted to prepare me for my death match with Daeseong. Why is my life like this?

"I'm a jeoseungsaja, remember?" Hailey teases. "Making death threats to a grim reaper is a bit precious, don't you think?"

"Then I'll settle for hurting you real bad," I grumble affectionately.

But she *should* be scared of death threats. She has the power to escort the dead to the other side, but that doesn't mean she can't end up there herself. Grim reapers aren't any more immortal than your run-of-the-mill shinbiin. They heal fast, but they can be killed.

"Will you be much longer?" Jihun takes a seat at the end of the conference table, as far away from us as possible. Then he angles his chair slightly so he's not looking straight at us.

"That depends on Wiggly here. I'll never finish if she won't stay still." When I inadvertently whimper, Hailey relents. "I just have two more symbols to paint. It'll only be a few more minutes."

I exhale in relief but immediately cringe and arch my back away from the cold tip of her brush. She growls, her fingers digging into my shoulder.

"Sorry. I'll be still," I say meekly. "Just finish already."

"I think Sunny can use some distraction." Hailey swirls the brush against my back.

Is she fucking with me? What arcane symbol requires *swirling*? I'm tempted to use my tank top as a bit, but I don't want to flash Jihun. I settle for sinking my teeth into my bottom lip till tears spring to my eyes.

"Why were you so worked up about Draco and Jaeseok earlier?" Hailey continues.

"You can ask them yourself." Jihun wipes a hand down his face. "They'll be here soon . . . *Shit*."

The suhoshin captain shoots up to his feet and rushes out of the study, closing the doors firmly behind him. I give Hailey a bewildered glance over my shoulder. She has a hand clapped over her mouth, and the one holding the brush wobbles precariously.

"Hey, careful with that." I lean away from her so she doesn't smudge ink all over my newly illustrated back. "What is up with Jihun?"

"I think he went out to guard the door." Hailey snorts. "It might actually be a good idea. Jaeseok will probably pull up a chair to watch if he walks in on us."

"And Draco will be traumatized." I grimace. "Do you know how many times they told me that I'm *really old*? To my face?"

"What? They're seventeen," Hailey protests with real indignation. Even though I don't want friends, I'm going to have to keep this one. "You only look a year older than them."

"They said my eyes look ancient," I say glumly.

"What do they know?" She pats my shoulder. "They're a teenager."

But for a teenager, Draco seems wise beyond their years. Maybe dragon spirits take after Yongwang, the god of Water, who is the wisest of all the gods. Or maybe they grew up in a hurry when they lost their parents much too soon. They said they were thirteen when their dad died, and even younger when their mom passed away.

I sniff away the sudden sting in my nose. I'm glad the kid isn't alone anymore, even though they're a pain in the ass.

Commotion erupts outside the sliding doors, but I can't make out a single word. I'm impressed at how well the latticed doors mute the noise, considering they're made of thick paper and wooden slats. The door slides open an inch, and a sliver of Jihun's face appears in the crack.

"Are you finished?" Jihun growls, a tuft of cerulean hair popping up and down behind him.

"Finished with what?" Draco manages to sound both curious and sullen. "Why can't we go in?"

"I'm done drawing the symbols, but she can't cover up until the ink dries," Hailey reports.

"What do you mean, she can't cover up?" One sexy, long-lashed eye squeezes past the sliver of Jihun's face. "Does that mean she's *uncovered* right now?"

"Do *not* test my patience," Jihun snarls with enough menace for both the sexy eye and the blue hair to disappear from view. "Sunny, turn your back toward the door."

I comply without hesitation, too tired from my tickle torture to question him. Then a warm breeze sweeps across my back. I shiver despite the warmth, a confused blush rising to my cheeks. Jihun is only manipulating the air to dry my back. It's not like he's actually touching me, or blowing air on my bare skin through his lips. Even so, the wind at my back feels strangely intimate.

"Okay. It feels dry," I say abruptly and pull on my tank top. "You can unleash Thing One and Thing Two."

"I better not be Thing Two." Jaeseok wags a finger at me as he steps into the study, with Draco skulking in behind him.

"But you're okay with being Thing One?" Hailey side-eyes the dokkaebi.

"What can I say? I like being number one." With an incorrigible grin, he drapes himself onto a chair across from us, oozing sex appeal.

He looks like a rakish pirate in his white linen shirt and tight black jeans. While Hailey doesn't blink an eyelash at his seductive display— she spends enough time with the goblin to be immune to him—I let myself enjoy the view for a moment. I see no point in fighting it.

With Ethan, I feel like I'll spontaneously combust if I look at him for more than a second. But with Jaeseok, who is hopelessly in love with Minju, the flirty exchange feels harmless and fun.

"Why don't you tell them what you've been up to, Lieutenant Cha?" Jihun arches his brow, reclaiming the seat he'd vacated. "It'll help them make an informed decision about whether you're indeed number one . . . in wreaking havoc in our lives."

"Sure thing, Captain Song. I'm happy to share about our breakthrough." Jaeseok ignores Jihun's scoff of outrage. "You know how we haven't been able to get the forge hot enough to meld the dragon scale and the sacred ashes together?"

"Of course I know," Hailey groans. "Even your dokkaebi fire isn't hot enough."

"Wait." I glance between Draco and Jaeseok. "What are you using to test the temperature?"

"My dragon scales and the sacred ashes," Draco says from their seat next to me, the unspoken *duh* made explicit by their expression.

"You're using the actual sacred ashes?" I shout in alarm. The poor kid flinches away from me, their teenage apathy slipping for a moment. *Shit.* I immediately wrangle in my panic and modulate my voice. "You *cannot* waste the sacred ashes on failed experiments."

I had to relive my mother's death to obtain the sacred ashes. Samshin Halmeom, a manifestation of the Seonangshin, sacrificed a part of her arm for me . . . She burned her forearm, the root of an ancient cypress tree, into ashes. She is like my own grandmother, and I had to watch . . .

"Sunny." From my other side, Hailey places a gentle hand over mine. "Minju dug up every last bit of information she could on the Gwangdo, but there is no instruction manual on how to forge another one. Jaeseok and Draco can't figure out how to make the sword of light without using the actual material."

I blow out a shaky breath. I know they're doing what needs to be done. I get that. But I'm still worried we won't have enough left to forge the sword of light. Samshin Halmeom entrusted me with the sacred ashes. We have to treat them with respect.

"I promise we won't waste a speck of it," the dragon spirit says with rare gravity.

As I offer them a solemn nod, I realize I'm not worried about disrespecting the Seonangshin or wasting the sacred ashes. At least, that's not all of it. I'm more worried about not being able to forge the sword of light, making the Yeoiju our only hope. I'm terrified that *I* will become our only hope.

I'm so sick of letting people down—I can barely come to terms with *having* people to let down—but I have to face the very real possibility that the Yeoiju might be a lost cause. *I* . . . might be a lost cause. With the dark mudang already stirring, I don't have months to master the Yeoiju's powers. I have weeks, maybe days. I'm not giving up, not by a long shot . . . but we *need* the sword of light.

"If I may continue." Jaeseok raises his brows at me, and I give him a weary nod. "This morning I—"

Draco clears their throat loudly, back to their cocky teenage self.

"That is, *Draco* and I had a brilliant realization." Jaeseok pauses dramatically. "I have two words for you. *Dragon. Fire.*"

Hailey and I share a wide-eyed glance. He's not overselling it. That *is* brilliant.

"I can't believe we didn't think of it before." Draco breaks the awed silence. "Dragon fire is the only thing that can melt dragon scales. It's *so* obvious."

"How about what happened afterwards, Draco?" A muscle jumps in Jihun's jaw. "Was that *obvious*?"

"What happened afterwards?" Hailey asks warily.

"Well, we had to test our theory." Jaeseok shrugs sheepishly.

"Of course." I drum my fingers on the conference table. "Go on."

"So Draco took their dragon form . . ." Jaeseok pauses when Jihun groans and drops his head into his hands.

I feel Jihun's pain. Considering we *secretly* snuck a dragon spirit into the Kingdom of Sky, Draco taking their dragon form is . . . problematic. The Kingdom of Sky is filled with angelic beings with *wings*. Even in the confines of a walled courtyard in a heavily guarded estate, an enormous serpentine dragon with glowing blue scales would be hard to miss for someone with a bird's-eye view.

"Look, I know how it sounds." Jaeseok holds out his hands. "But there was no other way. We can't make dragon fire without a dragon."

Jihun raises his head to glare at the dokkaebi. "You two could have waited for the cover of night."

"Huh." Draco huffs as though the thought never occurred to them. "But that wouldn't have changed what happened afterwards."

"Once again." I'm afraid to ask, but I might as well rip off the BAND-AID. "What happened afterwards?"

"You want the good news?" Jaeseok hedges. "Dragon fire is hotter than any fire we've ever—"

"No more good news," Hailey cuts him off. "What's the bad news?"

"The bad news is . . ." Jaeseok cringes. "We accidentally burned down the forge."

"It took all of us a fortnight to build that forge," she cries.

"I should be grateful I checked in on them when I did," Jihun says with a resigned sigh. "Otherwise, they might have burned down my entire estate."

"It's not all bad. I might go so far as to say that there's more good news," Jaeseok continues with renewed pep. "The glamour held even against dragon fire. It stayed invisible until the forge burned into literally nothing."

When Hailey narrows her eyes at him, the dokkaebi tucks his chin into his chest and wisely ceases delivering good news. I bury my face in my hands as a heavy silence descends on the room. No matter how bad things have seemed, I've soldiered on out of pure bullheadedness, but this is too much even for me. We don't have time to start over. Not now. Does this mean it's all down to me? *Gods, no.*

"But the *real* good news is," Draco says with a sly smirk, "we did it. We melded the dragon scales and the sacred ashes into one."

"What?" I lurch forward.

"Behold." Jaeseok withdraws something shimmering and pearlescent from his pocket and holds it out on his palm. "The needle of light. Or the tiny sword of light. I'm flexible on its official name, but here it is."

Hailey, Jihun, and I scramble to our feet and gather around Jaeseok, who is all smiles again. I stare at the slender needle gleaming with white light. *Oh thank gods.* The force of my relief sends a wave of dizziness through me, and I sink down onto the nearest chair.

"It's beautiful." Hailey presses her fingers to her lips.

"Any reason you didn't start off with this?" Jihun pinches the bridge of his nose.

"Where's the fun in that?" Jaeseok shimmies his shoulders, presumably to express how much fun he's having with his way.

"For fuck's sake," I hiss under my breath. I'm ecstatic that our hope for the sword of light lives on, but I was ready to curl up and die in a dark corner a minute ago. *How's that for fun?*

Rather than shoving the sexy dokkaebi off his chair, I discreetly bang my fist on the conference table. *More of a tap, really.* But everyone jumps back as the table shatters into a thousand tiny splinters. It's like I dropped a bomb on it, not bopped it with my fist.

"What . . . How . . ." Coherent speech is beyond me.

"Now we know what those symbols do," Hailey whispers.

I glance over my shoulder as though I can look down my own back. Of course, I can't see a damned thing since I'm not a giraffe. But I don't need to see the arcane words of power to know they are bad news.

CHAPTER SIX

When I return to Jihun's study that night, the office chairs form a loose oval around the empty space where the conference table used to be. Someone had cleaned up the pile of rubble from the floor but left the chairs in place. Minju sits perched on her usual seat, reading a fragile-looking scroll.

"If the words of power help with today's lesson, we need to get them permanently tattooed on your back," she says without looking up from her reading.

I spent my entire off day building a new forge with Hailey, Draco, and Jaeseok. No natural material is strong enough to withstand dragon fire, so we had to use magic to fortify every stone. Needless to say, we didn't get far on the build. And I couldn't stay and eat dinner with the others because I didn't want to be late for this lesson.

"*I'll* decide what I do with *my* body," I say pointedly.

I take a deep breath. Minju means no harm—it's just the way her brain works—but I'm dusty, hungry, and tired of being treated like a container for the Yeoiju. Plus, I'm on edge because I haven't seen Jihun since this morning, when he left to follow a lead on Daeseong's whereabouts.

What if he found the dark mudang? I clamp down on my rising panic. No, he would've told us right away if he'd found the madman. I don't even know if Jihun is back from the Mortal Realm.

"I assumed you'd want to avoid getting repainted after every bath, because Hailey told me you're ticklish." Minju blinks owlishly at me. "However, if you enjoy being tickled with a wet brush for upwards of an hour, then I apologize for my assumption."

"I don't enjoy . . ." I choke and sputter, flabbergasted enough to forget Daeseong for the moment. *That* is where her mind went? A tickle fetish? Not bodily autonomy?

"Perhaps you can consider other options of tickling?" the historian continues, tapping her finger on her chin. "How about applying a duster to the bottom of your feet? Or a feather under your chin? Give it some thought. We don't have to decide anything until we know the runes work."

"Work how?" I sigh with affectionate exasperation and sink into a chair across from the endearingly clueless historian. "Does shattering the conference table into tiny splinters count as them *working*?"

"Hmm." She purses her lips. "I liked that table. We should get another one."

"Minju." I rub a hand down my face. On days like this, a simple, straight answer would be nice. "What. Are. The runes. *For?*"

"The words of power make your body stronger," she explains, finally zeroing in on the issue. "You might be afraid of summoning the Yeoiju because you believe you're too fragile to contain its power. I can think of no other explanation as to why you've failed every single attempt to manifest the light of the Yeoiju."

"*Failed* is a strong word." I don't much like *every single* either. "I feel like I managed a little spark here and there . . ."

"No." Minju cocks her head like a confused puppy. "You failed every single—"

"Will you stop saying that?" I can do without any more reminders of my inadequacies. "For the record, I am not afraid. And I don't think I'm *fragile*. I'm a gumiho. I'm already strong enough, even in my human form."

"That may very well be true, but your *subconscious* is holding you back." Minju pulls her lips to one side. "I believe it has to do with the unresolved trauma of your near-death experience at Heaven Lake."

I flinch. "But I didn't die."

"You almost did," Minju counters.

I didn't die. I disappeared. I became light until there was no me.

"But I didn't." I give my head a sharp shake. "I came back."

"Exactly." She nods. "You *almost* died, and you had to fight to come back. Hence, the trauma. You're afraid of experiencing that again. You might also be afraid of not being able to come back this time."

"Do you want a nickel for your psychoanalysis, Lucy?" I pout and cross my arms like a petulant child. But when Minju makes a face that tells me she does *not* get the *Peanuts* reference, I straighten in my chair with my mouth gaping. This is tragic. Everyone needs Charlie Brown to help them through a rainy day. "Never mind. You're wrong, though. I'm not afraid of the Yeoiju. But I *am* worried that I won't be able to master its powers in time. I don't know. Maybe I'm not cut out for this."

"You hold the Yeoiju," Minju says with an amused smile. "You are the only one *cut out for this.*"

"Then why can't I wield the damn thing?" I plow my fingers through my hair. "We're running out of time."

"Your powers have already started to evolve. You can see life forces with your bare eyes." She reaches for my hand and grips it tight. "When you're not held back by your fears, you are already drawing from the powers of the Yeoiju. You are . . . limitless."

"I . . . I don't know. I just . . . I'm really relieved we're close to forging the sword of light." A touch of pleading creeps into my voice. "We might not even need the Yeoiju. I can just stab Daeseong with the sword—because I'm definitely cut out for stabbing things—then we can go on with our lives."

Minju releases my hand and draws a knife from the folds of her hanbok. I jump to my feet and scramble to put my chair between us. I forgot the historian is also cut out for stabbing things. Namely, me.

"Sunny, come here." It doesn't help that she beckons me with her sharp knife. "I want to show you something."

She tugs my chair close to her and pats the seat. I inch forward and warily lower myself onto it. She takes my hand and places it on top of her thigh. "Open your hand."

I look down to find my hand clenched into a tight fist on her lap. I slowly unfurl it, watching the historian with narrow-eyed suspicion.

"I'm going to stab you in the hand." Minju grabs my wrist when I try to jerk away. I'm strong enough to break free, but I take a deep breath and relax. "I'm going to *try*, but I won't succeed."

"Why? Because you're going to change your mind midswing and stab me in the heart instead? Like last time?" Sarcasm is my friend, especially when I'm nervous.

"Remember you have your hand on my thigh. If I stab through you, I'll stab myself." Minju ignores my jab. "We're in this together. Do you trust me?"

"I guess." I squirm in my seat, but I do. "I trust you."

The blade moves so fast that all I see is a flash of metal before Minju slams it down on top of my hand. I don't even cringe because I already know. The knife didn't so much as nick my hand.

"Ouch," I say out of principle. She *did* try to stick a knife in me. Again.

And it does kind of hurt. I peer down at the small bruise blossoming in the middle of my hand where the point of the knife hit my skin. The magic armor the runes cast over me seems to work like a bulletproof vest. I feel the impact of the blow even if I don't bleed from it. Even so, it's extraordinary.

"Do you feel invincible?" Minju asks with a teasing smile.

"A little." I go for a careless shrug.

Strength surges through me, and the small part of me that shrank away from the Yeoiju peeks out from its hiding place with curiosity and excitement. I don't necessarily feel invincible, but I feel a little braver and a lot hopeful. I wonder if this is how Ethan felt when he came into his powers. Then again, he's always been brave, even without his magic. He was far from invincible when he put himself between me and danger time and time again.

"Are you still scared of wielding the Yeoiju?" The historian sheaths her knife, getting back to business.

"For the last time, I am *not* scared." And maybe I *can* do this. I can be brave like Ethan. *For* Ethan.

"Then take a seated position on the floor." Minju claps twice in rapid succession, like an obnoxious PE teacher who says things like *Drop and give me twenty.* "And close your eyes."

I know the drill. I settle on my ass and slow my breathing, inhaling and exhaling through my nose. I quiet my mind and look inward. Well, it's more like listening intently than looking. When you close your eyes, your consciousness is a vast darkness. You can't really *see* anything. But if you listen hard enough, thoughts, images, and emotions take form and solidify, taming the wilderness of your mind.

And I listen for the light within me. At first, I only hear the rush of my blood. I concentrate harder, my brows drawing together, until I hear a gentle hum, a soft chime, resonating deep inside me. My frown clears away as I recognize the sound.

It's my Yeoiju calling me. And this time, I don't shy away from it. I float toward it, weightless and fearless, a sense of calm stealing over me.

There it is.

The light glows serenely, chasing away the darkness of my consciousness. It isn't turbulent, wild, and insatiable like I feared. It's powerful but utterly at peace. I blow out a careful, shaky breath. In my mind, I cup the light in my hands, and my body mimics the movement. Warmth gathers in my palms and travels up my arms.

Minju gasps, and I open my eyes. White light, as small as a candle flame, floats in the cradle of my hands. My lips tip up in a smile of wonder. It's . . . beautiful. The light pulses in rhythm with my pounding heart, and the flame grows with every heartbeat.

Something tugs at my chest. It's a question. *Yes,* I answer. My gi flows into the white light. It flows and flows. A shiver spreads from the base of my spine until my entire body quakes with it. My fingers grow numb, like they've fallen asleep, then my toes.

"No," Minju screams.

I'm thrown into the air and land on my back with an *oof.* I lie unmoving as sensation creeps back into my body. When I finally blink open my eyes, I find a hole about the size of a basketball in the ceiling. Stars glint like gems in the inky sky. *Yup.* Jihun is going to kill me. What a waste of poetic genius.

"What happened?" Minju helps me sit up.

"I . . . I don't know," I rasp past my parched throat, then I point at the hole in the roof. "Just to confirm, did I do that?"

"Yes, when you threw the flame into the air." Minju dabs at my damp forehead with the ink-stained sleeve of her jeogori.

"Huh." I feel woozy. I don't remember chucking the flame, but I remember something else. "Why did you scream?"

"You turned really pale, then started convulsing." Minju's voice breaks. I take the hand still wiping my forehead and squeeze it gently. "I . . . I'm sorry I pushed you so far, Sunny."

"But it worked." Everything is hazy. I can barely remember what happened after I manifested the white light. *I manifested the white light.* "I finally did it."

"Yes, you did." She nods thoughtfully. "Your tickle fetish aside, you might've been right about not getting the runes tattooed on your back. I didn't think you would succeed on your first attempt."

"Thank you?" I don't bother telling her I don't have a tickle fetish.

"To answer your earlier question . . ." she continues, brushing aside my sarcasm.

"What earlier question?" I interrupt.

"You asked me what the runes were *for*, but I only told you what they *do*. The arcane words of power made your body stronger, but I used them to restore your self-confidence. They were *for* helping you get past your psychological barrier."

"I don't have a psychological barrier," I mutter.

"Not anymore," Minju says in all seriousness. "That's why you no longer need the runes."

"Good riddance." Helpful or not, I still have a bad feeling about them. "What do they even say?"

"I still don't understand what happened after you conjured the flame, though." She doesn't answer my question, her mind already five steps ahead. "Maybe you kept it alight for too long. Next time, we have to do this methodically and increase the time in five second increments. Like everything else, you need to train to become stronger."

Minju draws a bound booklet out of her hanbok and waves her hand to summon a brush and ink. Then she writes furiously in the book, not even noticing the ink splattering everywhere. What can she have to write so much about? I manifested the light, then I blew a hole through the ceiling. The end. But the hole is a good sign, right? Even the small orb of light was powerful enough to do some damage.

"What else do you carry in that hanbok of yours?" I ask to distract myself from my growing restlessness. I'm impatient to move on to the next steps. Maybe I can try summoning the light again, without breaking anything this time. But I know Minju won't be able to focus on anything until she finishes her notes. "And *where* for that matter? It doesn't even have pockets."

"Necessities," she murmurs absently. "And I had pockets sewn in."

"That's what I'm talking about." I raise my hand for a high five, but she doesn't look up from her notebook. I lower my hand after giving myself a sad high five. "Hey, do you happen to have a mirror in there?"

Minju rummages around her hanbok and hands me a silver handheld mirror. I take it with a surprised laugh. "This mirror is a *necessity*?"

"I have to . . ." She shoots me a sheepish glance. "Sometimes . . . people show up unexpectedly, and I take a quick look to make sure I don't have ink on my nose. Or anywhere else on my face."

"*People?* Anyone in particular?" I say with a sly smile. "And does he happen to be a sexy dokkaebi?"

"All the runes mean the same thing," Minju blurts. "Strength."

"What?" I squint at her.

"You wanted to know what the runes on your back say." So she *was* listening. "In my research, I found stories of legendary warriors who were as strong as a hundred soldiers and had skin like armor."

"Like my magic armor." And the amplified strength also explains the shattered conference table. Curiosity gets the best of me. "Can I look at my back?"

Minju pushes to her feet and walks toward the back wall, and I follow her. She sweeps her hand down the wall, and it turns into a shimmering reflective surface.

"Is there a spell you don't know?" I whistle. "I'm impressed."

"You can use the hand mirror to look." She tucks her chin shyly.

I lift the bottom of my tank top, baring a swath of my lower back, and angle the small mirror in front of me. "Whoa."

The arcane words of power might actually make cool tattoos. They look like a blend of ancient Sanskrit and traditional Chinese characters, the strokes sweeping and powerful. I pull the back of my tank top up higher, reveling in each new symbol. Then I go deathly still as a scream climbs up my throat. My hand holding the small mirror shakes hard enough to distort the reflection of my back. But it's there. I can see it.

My past and present blur together.

I'm in the study, but I'm also on the mountainside surrounded by an angry mob. When Daeseong draws the bujeok from his sleeve, it looks like a harmless strip of paper. But as he chants a string of words, the talisman rises above his hand and floats midair, stiff as a sheet of metal.

I can't read anything on the bujeok, but one elegant rune stands out to me because of its beautiful symmetry. Fear and confusion coalesce inside me as the identical rune on my back turns bloodred.

The past remains layered over the present like a transparent film. I know what happens next. My mother dies. My heart rips down the middle, and tears stream down my cheeks. Daeseong should have died. Not my mother. The rune flares on my back, and rage burns through me. The dark mudang opens his mouth, but the curse slips past my own lips in a jagged whisper.

"Sa."

The mirrored wall blows out behind me, and I'm jolted back to the present, the past clearing from my vision. The roof creaks above me, seconds away from collapsing. Minju stands in the middle of the study, her eyes wide with horror.

I reach her in a streak of white and leap out through the latticed window. I carefully set her down on the ground, releasing the back of her jeogori from my mouth. Minju turns around and stares at me unblinkingly.

My nine tails drift to the ground, and I hunch in on myself. She has never seen my gumiho. Is she afraid of me? Or is she more afraid of what I've just done? What *have* I done? I don't understand.

"Sunny." She throws her arms around my neck and buries her face in my white fur. "Are you okay? What happened?"

"Are *you* okay?" I ask her telepathically.

"I'm fine, thanks to you." She steps back and runs a hand down my snout. "Now tell me what happened."

"I don't know." I step back from her touch, returning to my human form, and wrap my arms around my stomach. I glance over my shoulder at the study and shiver when I find a pile of rubble. "I recognized one of the runes. It brought back some bad memories, and . . . I don't know."

"No." Minju staggers, her hand on her forehead. "I'm so sorry. I didn't mean for it to . . . I nullified the alternate meanings and offensive powers. You shouldn't have been able to—"

"Sunny." Jihun runs toward me with his hand outstretched.

But I'm swept into another pair of arms before he can reach me. The fear and adrenaline jangling through my veins quiet when I breathe in Ethan's scent. I cling to the solid feel of him, even though I know I shouldn't.

"Are you hurt?" He slides his hands down my arms and spans them around my waist before stepping a few inches away. Then he scans me from head to toe, his eyes frantic with worry. "What happened?"

"It's all my fault," Minju chokes out.

Ethan's fingers dig into my waist as his face ices over with rage, and he turns toward the historian. "Explain yourself."

Minju gasps and pales at the unmistakable ring of authority in Ethan's voice. When he's like this, even I feel cowed by him, my instincts telling me to bend to his will. But my instincts can go to hell on this one.

"It's *not* her fault." I glower at him. "I'm the one who blew—"

"No, Sunny. Thank you, but no." Minju takes a shuddering breath and straightens her shoulders. "Your Highness, it is definitely my fault. I know what happened."

"Oh my gods." Hailey, Jaeseok, and Draco run toward us. They must've been working on the forge again because their clothes and hair are ashen from fresh dust. But I probably caused the pallor in their faces by blowing up the study.

"Is everyone okay?" Draco asks with a break in their voice.

I turn my head toward them so fast I might've given myself whiplash. They're terrified. *Poor kid.* They've experienced so much loss already. I can tell from their expression that they're expecting the worst.

"Not a scratch on us, kid." I cough to clear the emotions clogging my throat, and I quickly turn my sympathy into steely resolve. I can't let Draco lose anyone else. I won't. Whatever I did tonight, I'll do it again to destroy Daeseong. "I can't say the same for the study, though."

Draco's shoulders rise and fall with relief, then their face scrunches back to its moody scowl. "No fucking way. I never would've guessed the study was damaged if you hadn't pointed it out."

I narrow my eyes at their bratty sarcasm. "Well, now you know."

Commotion rumbles in the distance as bobbing torches appear in the night. Jihun glances toward the cluster of flames, then swiftly at Ethan. I frown, my eyes jumping between the two of them. What's Ethan doing here anyway? He obviously wasn't visiting Draco, who came from the other end of the wing.

Were he and Jihun strategizing on how to take down the King of Mountains? Did they receive more intel from their spy? I hope Ethan keeps his promise and doesn't do anything stupid without me—like go after his father on his own.

Neither of us have mastered our magic, but together, we might be able to do some damage. And if we can't stop the King of Mountains without killing him, I won't let Ethan be the one to do it. No child should have to kill their own father, even an evil, murderous one.

Then my gaze shoots to Jihun. He's *back*. I search his face as though I can decipher whether or not he found Daeseong from his expression. But he's already moving toward the commotion.

"The collapse must have roused the staff from their sleep." He flares his wings, and my hair flutters across my cheeks. "I'll have them turn back."

When Jihun flies off, Hailey looks from Minju to me. "What *happened* here?"

"I kind of blew up the study." I cringe. "But I have no idea how."

"I'll explain when the captain gets back," the historian says in a subdued voice, glancing toward the retreating torchlights.

"I'm back." Jihun lands on the ground beside me and stands close at my side. The back of his hand brushes against mine and stays there.

I sneak a peek at him from under my lashes, but his gaze is focused on the historian. He must be seeking reassurance that I'm okay in his own stoic way. I nudge his hand with the back of mine, our knuckles brushing. *I'm sorry for making you worry.*

For some reason, I glance at Ethan on my other side and start when my eyes clash with his. He looks at Jihun, then slowly down at our barely touching hands. When he raises his head, his face is a cold, inscrutable mask. *What the hell?* Does he think . . . that Jihun and I . . .

"Please proceed," Ethan says to Minju before I can tell him it's not what he thinks.

My heart lurches when I realize I nearly gave myself away. Thank gods he spoke before I could run my big mouth. I'm not supposed to care what he thinks. It's getting harder and harder to hide my true feelings from him. Maybe it'll be for the best if Ethan misunderstands my friendship with Jihun. Even so, I pull away from the seonnam and clasp my hands in front of me.

Minju tugs on my arm and urges me to turn my back on everyone. I let her position me however she likes since I'm as curious as the others about what happened. She carefully sweeps my hair over one shoulder so my upper back is visible above my tank top. I know some of the runes branch onto my shoulder blades.

"These runes on Sunny's back are arcane words of power." The historian's voice trembles. "They originate from . . . That is . . . they are a form of—"

"It's dark magic," Draco growls and takes their dragon form in a blaze of blue fire. "That female used dark magic on Sunny."

CHAPTER SEVEN

The entire eastern wing of Jihun's estate is reserved for his private use. Its perimeters are heavily warded, and no one is granted access without his express approval. The forge, Draco's hideout, the study—or where the study used to be—and Jihun's personal quarters are all within the eastern wing.

Ethan and Jihun must've been in Jihun's quarters when they heard the crash. That's how they got to the study so fast. I still need to find out why Ethan came to see Jihun at this time of night. But I'll have to wait.

Pandemonium broke out at the mention of *dark magic*, and everyone is shouting over one another. I'm just here thinking random thoughts, thanks to my Olympic-level avoidance skills. Because, if what Draco said is true, I don't think I can handle it.

My attention snaps back to the present when the very air around Ethan quakes with the promise of violence. *Oh gods.* He's losing his shit and losing control of his powers along with it. This is one of many reasons why General Bak is a shortsighted fool for barring Ethan from using his magic. How can he control his immense power without practice?

I'll deal with my own panic once I calm Ethan down. Besides, I'm sure Minju has a perfectly sane explanation for why she used dark magic on me. I school my features into a picture of serenity. *"Ethan."*

He turns to me with silver-and-green fire churning in his eyes, and my stomach drops as my nervous gaze skips around the courtyard. It's not just his eyes. The entire area is drenched with the silver-and-green gi pulsing off him in towering waves. On the one hand, even untrained, he might be able to defeat the King of Mountains with power this immense. On the other hand, he might destroy all of us tonight if I can't help him rein in his magic. So I swallow my fear and face him again.

"I'm okay, Ethan. *I am fine.*" I cup his face in my hands, holding his fiery gaze. His irises flicker between brown and silver green. "She was *not* trying to hurt me. I promise. And I bet she has a good explanation for what she did. Right, Minju? Now would be a good time to share that explanation."

When she doesn't respond, I swivel my head to glare at her, but my jaw drops instead. Jaeseok stands in front of Minju with his arms stretched wide, facing off with a very big, very angry dragon.

"Come on, Draco." Jaeseok flashes his winningest smile. "You don't even like Sunny."

The dragon keens with pure fury, and everyone grabs their head at the piercing sound. I don't have the balls to hush Draco in their current state . . . and size. I glance at Ethan and sigh with relief. He's reeling back his magic with slow, deep breaths. I let my palms linger on his cheeks for a second longer before I drop my arms to my sides.

"I'm *kidding.*" Jaeseok's smile turns laser sharp, and twin balls of fire ignite in his hands, burning as red as his eyes. "But back off, Draco. I won't let you hurt Minju, and I don't want to hurt you."

The threat rings crystal clear in the air. He doesn't want to hurt them, but he *will* to protect Minju. *Shit.* I don't pause to think. I leap between the dragon and the dokkaebi on all fours, my nine tails flaring. And Hailey runs to my side, stretching a stream of water between her hands like saltwater taffy.

"Hey." I speak into Draco's mind. "We're all on the same side, kid."

"Dark magic is more terrible than you can imagine, Sunny. I've seen what those runes can do. The Jaenanpa used them to . . . They hurt my dad before . . ." Draco is a human kid again, tears streaming down their face. I shift back and pull them into my arms, even though they're a foot taller than me.

"Shh. It's okay. I'm okay." I run my hand down their soft cerulean hair. "No one's going to hurt me. And I won't let anyone hurt you."

"Minju," Jihun says in a solemn voice. "Please explain yourself."

"Sunny has been . . . struggling." Minju comes out from behind Jaeseok, who wraps a protective arm around her shoulders. "I wanted to help her, but nothing seemed to work. She was too afraid . . ."

I sigh heavily in protest but don't interrupt her. With one last pat on their back, I drop my arms from Draco and turn to face the historian. Ethan steps close behind me and cups my shoulders with his big hands. I don't shrug him off because I *have* been afraid—maybe I still am—and I can use his comfort. And although he has his magic under control, he might need to touch me to reassure himself, as much as I need his touch.

"I began researching amplifying spells, but I realized the problem wasn't her lack of power. It was its *abundance*. She did not feel strong enough to wield the might of the Yeoiju. I changed directions with my research to find something that would restore her confidence, something that would make her feel invincible." Minju begins pacing, and tenderness steals over Jaeseok's face as he watches. "That's when I discovered the words of power. The runes were the solution I was looking for, but an imperfect one, because they can cause great harm if used offensively. They are forbidden for a reason."

"They are forbidden?" Jihun pinches the bridge of his nose. He does that a lot, but I can't say I blame him.

"Yes of course." The historian nods earnestly. "How can they not be? They are much too dangerous."

"Yet you used them on Sunny." Ethan sounds more perplexed than angry as he steps forward to stand next to me. I miss the weight of his hands on my shoulders, so I shuffle a tiny bit closer to him.

His gi has receded from the courtyard and shimmers around him in a vibrant rush of silver and green—the colors so pure and rich that I want to reach out and touch them. I want to touch *him*.

With a choked breath, I force myself to look away. It drains me to hold back my longing—to hide my love—when my very blood flows toward him like the rushing river. But I will swim upstream until I'm beaten and broken if it means I can protect him from more heartache.

For now, I'll hoard this moment so I can swim a little longer before I shatter. I shift even closer to him and let his warmth skitter across my skin. I breathe in his scent and soak up his strength.

"*I* didn't use them on Sunny. I had them painted on her back so *she* could use them." Minju resumes pacing, gesturing with her hands. "Of course, I cast a spell on the ink to nullify the runes' offensive powers."

"Of course." Hailey laughs in exasperation. "But did it ever occur to you that Sunny and I might've wanted to know that we were playing with dark magic?"

"A rune itself isn't dark magic, per se, until you actuate the word of power by saying it out loud." Minju's eyes flit toward me when I gasp, but she finishes her explanation. "I only nullified their offensive powers in an abundance of caution, but the runes should have been perfectly safe for our uses. The pronunciations for those words were destroyed ages ago."

"Not all of them. Draco witnessed the Jaenanpa actuate the runes, so those magic thieves know how to pronounce them somehow. And . . . I recognized one of the symbols on my back." I step away from Ethan because I need to lock down my emotions to get through the next part. "It was the one Daeseong used to . . . to kill my mother. Seeing the rune jarred my memory, and I remembered what the dark mudang said to actuate the word of power. I must've repeated it without thinking. He said—"

"Don't say it, Sunny." Minju throws out her hand. "The runes . . . they're still on your back."

Then everything hits me at once—grief, rage, and horror.

I used the word of power that killed my mother. I felt its dark magic flare through me. I want to scream. I feel dirty. I don't want that cursed symbol on me. I want to peel the skin off my back. But a desperate part of me wants to cling on to the power . . .

I snap out of my spiral when Hailey grasps my hands and gently pulls them away from my face before I can claw my fingers down my cheeks. I can only stare at her helplessly. I don't know what to do.

"Jihun, we're going to borrow your bedroom," Hailey says in a no-nonsense tone. Ethan and Jihun both step toward me, but she shakes her head once. "*Alone*, Captain. That goes for you as well, Your Highness. She needs space."

"Yes, of course." Ethan halts, clenching his fists.

Jihun gives her a curt nod. "Go."

Hailey tucks me into her side and leads me away from the ruined study. I unseeingly put one foot in front of another, keeping my mind quiet and still. Everything will be fine once I wash the runes off my back.

"We're here," Hailey says in front of an unfamiliar hanok, just around the corner from the study.

Once we're inside, she guides me down a hallway and slides open a double door, revealing Jihun's bedroom. I blink away my stupor and focus on my curiosity. Being nosy is worlds better than spiraling over the arcane runes on my back.

An enormous bed framed in rich mahogany takes up a chunk of the sizable room, and a desk and chair in the same hue stand against a side wall. The modern furnishing contrasts sharply with the latticed hanji doors and windows, but the overall effect is quite pleasant.

The bed looks tantalizingly comfortable, in direct contrast to the hard floor I call *my* bed. When I first came to the Kingdom of Sky, I asked Jihun if he had a bed, and he deflected by teasing me for my interest in his sleeping arrangements. I glom on to the prickly familiarity of annoyance. Anything to put some distance between myself and my near meltdown. Even now, it doesn't feel that far off.

"Fucking Jihun," I mutter grumpily.

"*There* you are." Hailey laughs and lightly ruffles my hair. I'm too wrecked to duck away from her hand. I might even lean into her touch a little. I guess I don't mind her affectionate teasing that much, especially when she says, "Now let's wash all that ink off."

She opens an inner door to reveal a modern bathroom and a glass-walled shower big enough for a soccer team. My eyes pop as my jaw drops. He has a *rain* showerhead. First, it bears repeating, *Fucking Jihun.* Second, I want.

"Wait." I flatten my hands against the glass and peer inside the shower. "Is that *shampoo?* I've been washing my hair with orchid oil, and he had shampoo all along? Did you know about this?"

"I had a hunch. His hair can't glisten like that without proper care." Hailey shrugs. "Do you need help in here? If not, I'll go find you some fresh clothes."

"I'm good." I bite my lip, feeling too awkward to say what's on the tip of my tongue. But as she turns to go, I blurt, "Thank you. I would've lost my shit in front of everyone if you hadn't spirited me away. So . . . thanks, Hailey."

"I got you." She winks and closes the bathroom door behind her.

And not a moment too soon because unwanted tears sting my nose and tighten my throat. I don't want to get used to this—to someone having my back. No matter how secure it makes me feel. I swipe my forearm across my eyes.

"For fuck's sake." I strip my clothes off with impatient jerks and turn the shower on to full blast.

When I step under the hot spray of water, I moan at the decadence of it. But I quickly sober as the water beneath my feet turns gray with ink. I stare at my toes, my hair a wet curtain around my face, and wait for the water to run clear. Then I grab a bar of soap and breathe in its clean citrus scent before I lather my hands and scrub my body until my skin is pink and tingly. I wash my hair—twice—with the fancy-smelling shampoo before I shut off the water.

I step out of the shower and wrap a fluffy towel around my body. Using a hand towel to wring the water out of my long hair, I patter over to the sink, then wipe away the condensation from the mirror. Then I stare at the pale, drawn face looking back at me.

"Cheer up, Sunny." I push the corners of my mouth up with my index fingers, then let them drop back down. "You'll be back at Roxy's Diner eating your rare steak and sunny-side up eggs before you know it."

I clamp my lips together, appalled that I've fallen so far as to give myself a pep talk in the bathroom mirror. I sigh and twist around to look at my back. Thankfully, it's still the same old back . . .

"No." The denial leaves my lips on a whoosh of breath.

I throw my hair over my shoulder and twist some more so I can see better. I scrub at the skin with the hand towel, but it's no use. One rune remains, dark and ominous, below my left shoulder blade. The word of power that killed my mother. I wet the towel and rub at the symbol until my skin stings. *Still there.* I sink to the floor, panting and shaking. What does this mean?

Unbidden, the pronunciation for the arcane word flickers in the far recesses of my mind, fainter than a passing thought, and I arch my back as heat scorches my skin. Hissing in pain, I struggle to my feet and look in the mirror again. The rune on my back . . . it's bloodred. It's actually *raw* like someone branded it onto my back with a smoldering iron. But as I watch in horror, the rune turns black again and the heat seeps out of my skin. What is happening?

When I hear the bedroom door slide open, I gasp in relief and rush out of the bathroom, too scared to be alone.

"Hailey, I'm so glad . . ." My words trail off when I see Jihun standing at the opposite end of the room. "Oh, sorry. I'm still . . . here. Hailey went to find me some clothes . . ."

"There's no need to apologize," he says in a husky rasp. "You can stay all night if you'd like. I . . . that is . . ."

His discomfort startles a laugh out of me. "Relax, Jihun. I know what you meant."

"Is that right?" His gaze, which had been roaming my towel-draped body, snaps up to my face. "Tell me. What *did* I mean?"

"You know . . ." It's my turn to feel awkward. "Nothing like . . . *that*."

"Hmm." Jihun stalks toward me, blazing heat flickering in his eyes. "And you know that how?"

"Be . . . because we . . . we're friends," I stammer and retreat until my back hits the wall.

He stops in front of me and leans a forearm against the wall, his face only inches from mine. I tip my head back to meet his gaze and immediately wish I hadn't. His pupils are blown wide, making his eyes nearly black, and my breath gets trapped in my chest. This . . . this isn't friendly teasing.

"Are you sure about that?" His deep, silky voice rumbles in the charged air between our bodies, and his head slowly dips until I can feel his breath skating across the bridge of my nose.

My eyelids flutter as though tempted to fall closed, but I will them to stay open. I should look away, but I . . . can't. My chest strains against the loose knot of the towel as I inhale, desperate for air. Jihun sweeps his thumb across my collarbone in a touch so light that I might've imagined it, but for the goose bumps spreading down my arms. A bewildered frown tugs my brows together.

"Sunny?" That thumb of his traces the line of my jaw, gentle but greedy. "Are you sure we're just . . . friends?"

"I . . ." He's breathtaking up close. I gape at his wide eyes and ridiculously long lashes, his dark brows and aristocratic nose, and his perfect lips. My pulse flutters at the base of my throat, my body responding to his proximity. *Gods.* He isn't trying to give me a hard time. He *wants* me. "Jihun, please don't—"

"Sorry I took so long. Someone took away the bowl of water in front of my room. Don't ask me why. So I obviously couldn't moon shift there and . . ." Hailey trails off. "Am I interrupting something?"

"No." I shake my head.

"Yes," Jihun growls at the same time, still leaning over me, and I can't breathe or look away.

Please don't fall for me. A strangled whimper escapes my lips as tears fill my eyes. Did I mislead him somehow? My awareness of him, my body's reaction to his beauty, is real—I see that now—but not intentional. Whatever attraction I feel for him is purely physical, something I can easily brush aside because our friendship means more to me.

I can't bear for Jihun to hurt because of me—I care about him too much. But my heart belongs to Ethan. I wish I could tell him not to fall for me because I love Ethan and always will. I wish I could give him something more concrete than *don't*. But I can't tell anyone. I have to hide my love deep inside me so Ethan never finds out. I know I'm choosing to protect Ethan over Jihun, and my heart breaks for all of us.

"Don't," I whisper helplessly. "Please."

Jihun closes his eyes for a long moment, then sighs. He straightens to his full height at what seems like glacial speed and takes a step back, then another. I exhale shakily and rush over to Hailey, grabbing the clothes out of her hands.

"Sorry. I was in a hurry and—" Hailey cringes.

"It's fine." I run into the bathroom and shut the door behind me. "Thank you."

I slide to the floor with my back against the wall, clutching Hailey's clothes against my chest. I bite down hard on my trembling lower lip and swipe an impatient hand across my leaky eyes. I'm blowing things way out of proportion. Jihun saw me standing in his bedroom, with nothing but a towel. His idiot switch got turned on, that's all. Any straight, red-blooded male would've reacted the same way. His heart had nothing to do with what happened. Besides, did anything happen? Nope, nothing actually happened.

With a firm nod and a sniff, I shake out the clothes Hailey handed me. I blink at them for two seconds, then slap a hand over my eyes. "You gotta be kidding me."

"Sorry," Hailey squeaks from the other side of the door.

"Come on." The dress is a fluttery silver slip, short enough to make my casino uniform look demure. "This can't be all of it."

"It's a mini dress on me, but it should hit midthigh for you."

"I'm not *that* short," I grumble, then push off the floor because a dry scrap of satin is better than a damp towel.

I shiver as I drop the towel onto the floor and slip the dress over my head. The soft satin feels annoyingly good against my skin, and the dress does in fact fall to midthigh for me—because I *am* that short. Well, I can retain some dignity at least. After a fortifying breath, I step out of the bathroom.

Hailey sits perched on the side of the bed, so I plunk down next to her, tugging on the hem of my dress. I glance at Jihun, who stands against the far wall with his arms crossed over his chest. His gaze travels the length of my body in a slow, heated perusal, but I quickly look away before our eyes meet because I'm chickenshit. I tug again on the scrap of fabric masquerading as a dress. After a pause, he strides over to his desk and turns the chair around before lowering himself onto it.

I'm exhausted, and I don't really want to know, but the tense silence is suffocating. "Did you find Daeseong?"

"Not yet." Jihun rakes his fingers through his shoulder-length hair, making it ripple like liquid silk. "It feels like we're being sent on a wild goose chase, but I know we're close. I can feel it."

"Oh," I say faintly.

We're almost out of time, but I focus on the *almost*. Today was a lot to handle, but we made progress with the Yeoiju *and* the sword of light. I intentionally don't think about the rune on my back. If we keep busting our asses, we might actually be ready to take down Daeseong by the time we find him. But I hope he stays hidden until then— especially since we have more immediate concerns like stopping a war from breaking out with the Kingdom of Mountains.

"Was Ethan here to discuss new intel from the Shinsi Palace?" I narrow my eyes into slits when Jihun smooths his face into a blank slate.

"I'll drop-kick you if you say 'This isn't my story to tell.' Ethan already told me you guys are planning to deal with the King of Mountains on your own to avoid an all-out war."

"You two have been talking?" A muscle shifts in his jaw.

"Yes." I throw my hands up. "Quit stalling."

"Our spy couldn't explain the king's illness, but she said he grows more paranoid and desperate with each passing day." Jihun's voice dips grimly. "He has been summoning physicians from all across the Kingdom of Mountains, but none of them have been able to heal him."

"That might be for the best, though," I murmur, thinking of Ethan's untamed powers. "The tyrant will be easier to defeat if he remains ill."

"Perhaps," Jihun says with a conflicted expression. "But the king blames the physicians for his illness. None of them have made it out alive from the palace."

"Dear gods," I rasp, and Hailey reaches for my hand. I give her what I hope is a reassuring smile, then glance toward the sliding doors. "Where is Ethan anyway?"

Even as I worry about how he's dealing with the new intel, my heart skips a beat, expecting him to walk in with a crooked smile.

"He had to return to General Bak's estate before the guards discover he's gone," Jihun says.

Disappointment washes over me, but it's for the best. The less Ethan and I see of each other, the better. For both our sakes. Who knows? I might get used to missing him. I honestly can't imagine getting used to this hollow ache in my chest, but it can't hurt this much forever.

"Wait. *Discover he's gone?*" My eyebrows shoot up as I belatedly register what Jihun said. "Why? Did his grandpa put a curfew on him?"

"A curfew? No way." Hailey giggles nervously. "What's going on, Captain?"

"The general is . . . protective of the prince." Jihun breathes a weary sigh. "Perhaps overly so."

"What does that even mean?" Unease tightens my scalp.

"The prince's quarters are heavily guarded. At all times," he says darkly. "And he's forbidden from leaving General Bak's estates without an escort."

"You can't be serious," I breathe, shaking my head. My heart twists as I understand the extent of Ethan's frustration, which I only glimpsed the other night. Gods, he must be suffocating.

"I mean . . . I guess that's understandable? It's no secret the general was devastated when the Queen of Mountains passed away." Hailey worries her bottom lip. "She was said to have died during childbirth, along with the baby, so General Bak thought he'd lost both his daughter and his grandson on the same day. But now that he has his grandson back . . . it kind of makes sense that the general feels overprotective of the prince."

"He didn't know his grandson was alive?" I glance between Jihun and Hailey. "The two of you, Jaeseok, and Minju all knew about Ethan. You were *waiting* for him, like 'the King Foretold will cometh,'" I chant, waving my hands by my face. "You talked about *long-awaited* plans to carry out when he returned to the Realm of Four Kingdoms. How could his own grandfather not have known that Ethan was alive?"

Jihun gives Hailey a significant look, and she hurries to check all the doors and windows. When she nods, he answers in a low voice, "Only a select few know about the prophecy of the King Foretold— those chosen by the Queen of Mountains before her death."

"What?" I rear back. "How?"

"To ensure her son's survival, the queen created a list of those who could be trusted with the prophecy. Only those on the list—those who understand the true extent of his destiny—were told that the prince lived. My great-uncle is not one of them." Jihun leans forward in his chair, planting his elbows on his thighs. "When we returned to the Kingdom of Sky, it seemed cruel not to reunite him with his grandson, but the general is still in the dark about the prophecy."

"It was *cruel* to let the general believe his grandson was dead for all these years. Why didn't the queen include her own father on the list?"

I'm so sick of all this cloak-and-dagger bullshit. General Bak is our one true ally in the Council of the Suhoshin, and Ethan trusts him with his life. "What the hell was her criteria?"

But if the general isn't trying to help Ethan fulfill his destiny, then why is he dead set on starting a war with the Kingdom of Mountains? I click my tongue. He obviously wants to see Ethan on the throne. And the old general probably didn't even consider other ways to put his grandson there since war is all he knows. I don't want to mistrust Ethan's only family just because he didn't make it onto the queen's list.

"We have no way of knowing her criteria," Jihun says with grim acceptance. "Trying to figure it out will only drive you mad."

"Are you serious?" My eyebrows shoot up. "The *not* knowing should be driving you mad."

"I know it's a lot of information to process." Hailey sits back down next to me. "But trust the captain on this one."

"What? No." It's just too much. Why does this fucking dumpster fire have to be Ethan's lot in life? I hate it for him. "Minju, Jaeseok, and the two of you are obviously on the list. What do you guys have in common? You're all shinbiins from the Kingdom of Sky and the Kingdom of Underworld—what humans consider heaven and hell."

"Sunny." My name is a quiet warning on his lips. "The queen's list has been in my keeping since my mother passed it on to me. There is no possibility we haven't considered."

"Or . . . maybe it depends on your affinity to the elements," I continue, ignoring him. "Between you, Hailey, and Jaeseok, you already have air, water, and fire. You're only missing earth and wood. But you said there are others, right? Who else is on the list?"

"You." Jihun glares at me, and Hailey gasps next to me. "*You* are on the list. So how do *you* fit in? Please enlighten me."

My mouth opens and closes several times before I manage a choked wheeze. "Fuck . . . me . . ."

CHAPTER EIGHT

It's been one of those days, which is basically every day since my private training started with Captain Seo. And my real day hasn't even begun yet. The captain is a morning person—because of course she is—so we train for two hours before dawn. That usually leaves me plenty of time to carry out my penalty before breakfast time.

She deems anything other than complete and immediate compliance—even when she's being patently unreasonable—as insubordination. Unsurprisingly, I am often "insubordinate" under her definition and get reprimanded in the form of tedious chores. My least favorite, cleaning the barracks floors, is doled out most often for obvious reasons. The esteemed captain can't stand me.

Today, I spoke "out of turn" because she sucker punched me in the eye. She claimed I was "unacceptably" distracted. I called bullshit. My attention *may* have been split—because why am I on the Queen of Mountains's list?—but I barely had a chance to step into the sparring circle before the captain's fist connected with my face.

I worry my bottom lip and stare morosely at the floor. Captain Seo definitely has it out for me. What did I even do? Then I click my tongue, impatient with myself. It doesn't matter. I don't need her approval.

With my right eye swollen shut, my depth perception is shot to hell. I keep missing the bucket by a mile. Cursing under my breath, I finally manage to dunk the rag into the murky water, washing off the grime. I curse some more as I wring it out to clean the rest of the barracks floors.

"Gods." I stretch my aching back. I actually feel one hundred and thirty-two.

With a weary groan, I put my head down and finish spit shining the floors. After a grueling hour, I get to my feet like a rusty Tin Man and catch a glimpse of early morning light out the window. If I were back in Las Vegas, I'd be getting off my night shift at the casino, looking forward to sleeping the day away. But that sublimely boring life is long gone.

At least I won't miss breakfast this morning. I sigh and head for the mess hall. When I smell the haejangguk in the hallway, I grin and pick up my pace. You have got to love a culture that has a dish literally called *hangover soup*.

Haejangguk is one of my favorite Korean foods, especially the way the cadet chef makes it. She seasons the rich bone broth with the umami saltiness of fermented soybean paste and fills it with dark, leafy vegetables. The good chef is also not stingy with the melt-in-your-mouth chunks of beef and seonji. I've seen other cadets turn their noses up at the congealed cow's blood, but I'm a fan of its mild, sweet taste and dense yet crumbly texture. Besides, nothing hastens the healing process like seonji.

I'm early enough that most of the tables are empty, but I head to my customary corner in the back and settle cross-legged on the floor. I imagine sitting smack in the middle of the mess hall and watching the sea of cadets part around me, scampering to the farthest table away from me. I huff a bitter laugh. *No thanks.* I want to eat my hangover soup in peace.

A kitchen attendant practically tosses a steaming bowl of haejangguk and white rice in front of me. Then she hurries away without a word, peeking over her shoulder like I might chase after her. When she steals another glance at me, I offer her a timid smile because I'm grateful for my hangover soup. Instead of smiling back, her eyes go wide with fear, and my throat tightens with hurt. No, I am *not* hurt, just irritated. I gave the female no reason to be afraid of me.

Since I'm a big, scary monster to her anyway, I turn my smile sharp and toothy. But when the attendant yelps and runs into the kitchen, I hunch in on myself, tucking my chin to my chest. I'm not the asshole here, but it sure feels like it.

I bury my nose to the table and shovel haejangguk into my mouth. I burn my tongue several times, but the seonji fixes it right up. Hungry cadets soon flood the mess hall, but my corner remains undisturbed. I should be used to it by now, and being a loner should be the least of my worries. I keep eating with grim determination, then I pound my chest to force the food down.

"Oh my gods." Hana plops down next to me, close enough that our knees bump under the table. The knot in my chest loosens a bit at the sight of her friendly face. "I feel like I never see you anymore, Sunny. You leave before I wake up and come back after I'm asleep. Where do you go every night?"

I grunt noncommittally as a trill of nerves skitters through me. It won't be long before my roommate suspects that not all my extracurricular activities involve chores and punishments from Captain Seo. I need to be more careful. I have to return to the barracks as soon as my lessons with Minju are over, instead of blowing up studies. I can't draw any more attention to me and my friends.

"Good morning, Hana," a different kitchen attendant says cheerfully, careful not to look my way. She sets out an overflowing bowl of haejangguk, rice, and myriad banchan in front of my roommate. I didn't even get a measly plate of kimchi. "Here, I brought you extra side dishes. You look thin, my dear. You should eat more."

"Thank you so much." Hana graciously accepts the extra attention with a sweet smile. But when the kitchen attendant bustles away, she pushes all the banchan toward me and proceeds to pick out the seonji from her soup and pile them into my bowl. "Talk about looking thin. You are literally skin and bones."

"Skin, bones, and *muscles*." I flex my biceps, but the dobok hides my guns from view. "I'm so cut, I don't even need a sword to make bad guys bleed."

"Mmm-hmm." To her credit, Hana tries to keep a straight face. "So . . . um . . . muscular."

"Save it." I spear a braised baby potato with my metal chopsticks and shove it into my mouth. Then I mumble my version of an apology for the cringey joke—"I'm in a crappy mood."

"Does it have anything to do with . . ." She points at her own unbruised right eye.

"What? This shiner?" I snort and nearly sniff a bit of potato into my nose. "Are you kidding? I love it. I'm thinking of keeping it forever."

"You *are* cranky." Hana gives me the side-eye.

I shrug my assent. "Where's your shadow?"

"Duna?" My roommate frowns, then covers it with a jerky shrug. "She said she had an errand to run."

I raise an eyebrow. "This early in the morning?"

"I guess she wanted to get it over with." Hana stirs her soup, not meeting my eyes.

I study her troubled expression with gnawing concern, but I don't press the issue. It isn't any of my business. I have enough problems of my own without borrowing others'. I resume inhaling my haejangguk, but I look up when a huge shadow looms over the table.

"Good morning, Hana." Haesan sits across from us with a rosy blush, his golden barbels swishing shyly. Then he gets a proper look at me and does a double take. "What happened to your face, Stormy?"

"Gee thanks." I narrow my one good eye at him and consider telling him that Stormy sounds like a stripper name just to watch him turn into a giant tomato. But the Realm of Four Kingdoms might not be renowned for their strip clubs like Las Vegas. Do I risk having to explain what a stripper is to the merman? Perhaps another day. "Good morning to you too."

"Is that from your session with Captain Seo?" He stares longingly at my black eye. "I wish I had private training with her. She's one of the most accomplished suhoshins in the Kingdom of Sky. Her combat skills are unmatched."

"Don't forget her charming personality," I mutter, stabbing another braised potato. "Or maybe she reserves her disdain just for me."

"I do get the sense she doesn't like you very much." Hana purses her lips in sympathy. "Did you do something to get on her bad side?"

"That's exactly it. I didn't *do* anything." I sound as wounded as I feel. *Shit.* To cover for my slip, I run my hands languorously down my torso and offer them my profile, chin tilted up. "She's clearly intimidated by this triple threat. Talent, brains, *and* beauty."

Haesan makes an exaggerated ick face, and Hana giggles into her hand. I dip my head to hide my grin and stuff more food in my face. Maybe I *should* give the merman an intro-to-strippers talk in front of my sweet roommate. I give up holding back my smile. Even when they're giving me a hard time, it's nice to have friends at my side.

By the time we finish breakfast and head out to the training yard, I can open my right eye again. Hana hands me a small mirror before roll call. All the swelling has gone down, with only a hint of yellow-and-green bruising left. I give thanks to the haejangguk, the breakfast of champions. I hand the mirror back to Hana and come to attention when Captain Seo strides into the courtyard, the junior instructors flanking her.

The captain scans the rows of cadets—there's close to a hundred of us—and says in a ringing voice, "Today, we put our sword skills to the test."

A giddy grin spreads across my face at my lucky break. It's the first one I've gotten in a long-ass time. I catch myself and smother the smile instantly, but Captain Seo's narrow-eyed glare already bores into me. The junior instructors notice her displeasure and scowl at me as well.

"*Some* of you may not know, since you joined the cadet training late," she drawls, "but we've spent every month since Lunar New Year learning and honing our sword techniques."

The Mean Girls titter behind me because I'm the only one who joined the training late. My nails dig into my palms as I fight the embarrassed flush rising to my cheeks. Who cares if I joined the cadet training a few months late? If you want to get technical, I'm more than a century late, since the other cadets are only twenty-four years old. But that means I've had a century longer to *learn and hone* my sword techniques than them. *Bring it on.*

I deliberately catch Captain Seo's gaze and cover a yawn with my hand. Her eyes flare with menace. Maybe I went too far, but I'm not going to second-guess myself. My instincts have kept me alive for this long, and my gut is telling me to hold my ground. There are too many eyes on me. I can't show any signs of weakness.

"Jo Danbi." Captain Seo's voice claps across the training yard like thunder.

Oh shit.

"Yes, Captain." Danbi comes to attention.

"You'll spar this round with Cho Mihwa." The captain tilts her chin toward me.

Shit shit shit.

The bloodthirsty smile that slashes across Jo Danbi's face makes me rethink my decision to follow my instincts. She is *the* Mean Girl—the Mean Girl that rules them all—and I've lived long enough to know a sadist when I see one. I've watched the female from the Kingdom of Mountains spar. Tall and rail thin, she moves like a whip cracking through the air. But more importantly, she fights with vicious intent— not only to win but also to humiliate her opponent, or to send them to the infirmary. Oftentimes, she accomplishes both with a ruthless glee that sends a chill down my spine.

The short sword I grab from the weapon rack feels awkward, the hilt too thick for my small hands. Blowing out a long breath, I step into one of the sparring circles with Jo Danbi. I give her a nod of acknowledgment, which she returns with an *I'm going to flay you alive* smirk.

I vaguely hear Captain Seo pairing off eighteen more cadets for this round. The remaining cadets linger by the sparring circles instead of heading to the other end of the training yard for their drills. The junior instructors drag their heels as well, only halfheartedly urging the spectating cadets to get a move on. Bile fills my mouth at their eagerness to see Jo Danbi spill my gumiho blood.

My only comfort comes from Haesan's solemn frown and Hana's round, worried eyes. I nod at them in reassurance. Then I extend one hand in front of me and raise my sword horizontally above my head, the sharp end pointing toward my opponent. Danbi lifts her longsword in a two-handed grip, widening her stance. She looks like she's about to chop down a tree.

"Begin," Captain Seo shouts.

The first minute passes in a blur as I block strike after strike. Jo Danbi is taller than me by a head, and her reach is longer, especially with her longsword. I can't get close enough to execute an attack of my own as she takes advantage of her greater reach with sweeping arcs of her sword. I need to get inside her swinging radius. She won't be able to do much with her bulky sword when I'm that close to her.

"Shit," I hiss when Danbi draws first blood with a slash on my upper arm.

"Sorry." She doesn't even try to sound sincere.

I bare my teeth and move in on her. I'm overthinking it. My body already knows what to do. I parry her strikes as I wait for an opening, but I can feel my next block all the way down my arms. Gods, she's strong. But so am I.

I slide on my knees as her sword swings inches above my head, and I jump to my feet at her side. She put too much power into her strike and can't stop midswing as I diagonally slash her unprotected torso from her armpit to belly button. I spin out of her reach as she clumsily swings her sword from side to side.

"Do you yield?" I ask somberly. As much as I dislike her, Jo Danbi isn't my enemy. I don't enjoy hurting her.

"No," she snarls even though she's bleeding too fast to continue.

My eyes shoot to Captain Seo, but she's busy demonstrating an intricate offensive strike to a pair of cadets who have just finished their round. Danbi's sword clatters to the ground. I turn toward her, sensing her move before I see her.

She rushes me with glazed, murderous eyes. Something's not right, but I hesitate because I don't want to make her injury worse. That second of indecision gives my opponent enough time to land her fist in my gut. Only it isn't her fist . . . but a wooden stake. She morphed her arm into wood.

"What . . ." I choke on my own blood, coughing red drops onto the ground. Jo Danbi broke the cardinal rule. She used magic during sparring. I stare down at my ruined stomach, her wooden stake still inside me.

She cheated. She cheated to *hurt* me. To *kill* me. When she flashes her nasty smile at me, a fiery heat burns across my back. Hatred, raw and acrid, roils inside me, and blinding rage drenches my consciousness. I forget everything but the hunger to make her bleed.

I grab her forearm with my hands and pull the wooden stake out of me, screaming in agony. Something like fear flashes through Danbi's eyes as she backs away from me. Blood gushes out from my stomach, but I no longer feel the pain.

I don't even feel my feet touch the ground as I approach her, an unfamiliar power gathering inside me. I raise my arms, and a shadow falls across the training yard. I ignore the panicked cries around me and focus on killing the cadet cowering on the ground, the sharp, bloody point of her wooden arm cradled in her other hand.

"Cadet Cho." Captain Seo's voice is urgent but gentle, and it breaks through the fog of my bloodlust. Somewhere deep inside, I'm still me, but my mind stutters like it's being flipped through the channels too quickly. "Stand down, Sunny. This isn't you."

My consciousness snaps back to me, and the scene around me comes into focus. Everyone looks shorter than me, as though I grew ten inches. But I didn't grow. I . . . I'm floating a foot in the air. I yelp and drop down to my feet, but I crumple into a pile of limbs because I'm too weak to stand.

The wound in my stomach hurts like a bitch. I moan and curl into a fetal position. *Gods.* What is happening to me? I feel a cool hand on my forehead. Then everything goes black.

EVERYTHING BURNS

Fire burns everywhere. Rivers run dry. Trees wither. The earth hardens and cracks. The very life forces of Mountains, Sky, Water, and Underworld feed the fire. Together they are infused with all the colors of light, and a blinding white gi—full and wild—is born.

A female stands in the midst of the fiery ruin with her arms spread wide. Her snow-white hair billows around her head as though she's floating in water. Her eyes are closed, her expression serene, as though she is soaking in the warmth of the winter sun.

Suddenly, she opens her eyes, and white fire burns in them. Her face hardens even as tears stream down her pale cheeks. She clenches her fists and screams, a piercing sound of sorrow and defeat.

Everything burns.

CHAPTER NINE

"Sunny." Someone brushes my hair away from my face. "You have to wake up."

I sit up with a gasp, which immediately turns into a moan. "Fuck."

"I told you to wake up, not sit up," Minju chides as she brings a cup to my lips. "Drink."

I take a few sips, then push the cup away. "No more. Wh . . . what happened?"

"You were injured." She helps me lie back down. "I was summoned to heal you."

My forehead crinkles as I try to remember. I was sparring with *the* Mean Girl, and I cut her. Nothing lethal, but enough to end the round. And . . .

"Oh gods." Everything rushes back to me. "Was anyone . . . Did I . . . hurt anyone?"

"No, you didn't hurt anyone." Minju pulls her knees up under her hanbok chima and rests her chin on them.

Someone changed me into a clean, bloodless dobok. I reach my hand under the shirt and gingerly feel my stomach. My skin where the fist-sized hole used to be is smooth. I peek under the covers. The area feels a bit tender to the touch, but there isn't even a scar. If left on its own, the wound would've taken days to heal unless I bled out first.

"Good work." I offer the historian a wan smile. Minju is impressively competent at healing spells. "With skills like this, I'm surprised you didn't become an uinyeo."

"I was advised against becoming a nurse. Something about inappropriate bedside manners," she mutters. "I still don't get it. Don't the patients *deserve* honesty? A dying person should know they're dying, right?"

I sputter a laugh, then wince, grabbing my stomach. It looks pretty on the outside, but it still feels like I did a thousand sit-ups on the inside. Jihun picks that exact moment to slide open the door to the room—I actually don't know where I am—and falls to his knees at my side.

"Gods, Sunny." He cups my cheek in a warm, calloused hand, his expression soft and unguarded with concern. "Are you all right?"

"I'm fine." I lean away from his hand and glower at him. "Why are you acting like I'm on my deathbed?"

"Cheyun told me what happened . . ." He runs his hand through his hair, and his silken strands stream down the sides of his face. "Your injury sounded . . . alarming."

"Well, *Cheyun* was exaggerating." I sit up to prove my point but regret it right away. The effort hurts me enough to make bile rise to my throat, and the room spins so fast I can't tell if I'm in Kansas or Oz.

And I must sway, because Jihun shifts to wrap his arm around my shoulders and offers me his chest to rest my head. My scoff sounds too much like a whimper. I don't want to burrow into his rock-hard chest, but my head falls against it regardless. On the upside, it feels like a lightly padded brick wall and is surprisingly comfortable.

"Will she be okay?" Jihun asks Minju.

"Her body heals fast," she hedges. "We don't need to worry about that part."

Is she implying there's a part we *do* need to worry about? I'm too woozy to ask, but luckily, Jihun has the same question. "What *do* we need to worry about?"

"Her bloodlust." Minju lowers her voice as though she's suddenly concerned about her bedside manners. "Captain Seo believes Sunny is too even keeled to lose her head like that, and . . . she sensed dark magic coming off of her."

The captain actually said something not insulting about me? I'm more shocked by that than the dark-magic part because I might already know the answer to that one. I haven't told Minju, or *anyone*, about the word of power branded on my back. I don't know if it was shame that held me back, or something else. I think a part of me didn't want anyone to take it from me.

But that can't be right. Why would I want to cling on to the dark magic that killed my mother? It doesn't matter. Whatever it was that held me back, I have to get over it. I can't risk hurting anyone.

I'm tired of not being able to trust myself. I'm done being afraid that my powers will harm people. I finally came to terms with being a gumiho. I came to terms with the Yeoiju being a power for good. I accepted that *I* can be good. I will not let a fucking *stain* on my back sentence me to a life of paranoia again. That's one part of my old life I definitely don't miss.

"I think I know . . ." I lift my head away from Jihun's chest and shake his arm off my shoulders. He drops it immediately but doesn't move away. *Fine.* I surreptitiously lean my shoulder against his arm to keep myself steady. "I think I know the source of my bloodlust."

Minju grabs my hand. "Tell us."

Biting down on my lip, I shift on the bedding and push my shirt off one shoulder. "It won't wash off."

"Is that the rune Daeseong used against your mother?" the historian asks haltingly. "The word of power you spoke out loud?"

"Are you asking if this is what I used to accidentally destroy the study?" I tug my shirt back into place, covering the rune. "Then yes. That's the one."

The room grows quiet. Minju glances at Jihun with something like panic in her eyes, and he wraps his arm around my shoulders again. I don't shake it off.

"So what do we need to do?" I clasp my hands in front of my bosom like anything is possible with a little gumption. "I bet you know some good cleansing spells, right? Should we chant one to scrub this little stain off?" When she doesn't say anything, I prattle, "Worse comes to worst, I'll go back to the Mortal Realm and get it lasered out like people do with drunk tattoos."

"You can't go through the Gray Void." Minju shakes her head as the blood drains from her face. "It will sense the dark magic in you and destroy you."

"Wh . . . what?" I rear back and nearly headbutt Jihun's face. "I have to go through the Gray Void to get to the Mortal Realm. It's the *only* way home. What do you mean I can't go through it?"

"The Gray Void exists to stop the Amheuk from reaching the Realm of Four Kingdoms." The historian sends Jihun another wide-eyed look, and he nods for her to continue. "It will detect and destroy any trace of dark magic that comes within its reach."

"Why are we talking in circles?" I throw my hands up. Then I double over, feeling the pain in my stomach all the way to the back of my teeth. I hiss out a long breath, holding still until the throbbing subsides. "Let's get this creepy rune off my back. I don't want it."

"I . . . I'm so sorry. I don't know how to remove it." Minju covers her face with her hands.

"What do you mean you don't know how?" Panic and . . . triumph clench my insides into a confused knot.

"I'm so sorry," she says, repeating the useless apology. "This is all my fault."

It is her fault, an insidious voice says in my head as heat spreads across my back. I clench my jaw to hold back the words. To hold back the rage. I twist the blanket in my hands and fight to slow down my breathing.

"There's no use assigning blame at this point." Jihun watches me with a troubled expression. "We need to focus on finding the solution."

"Yes." Minju sniffs loudly, then turns to me. "I'll make it right, Sunny. I'll find a way to erase the rune. I promise you."

"Soon?" I ask in a small voice, exhausted from keeping my dark anger in check. "I . . . I don't feel like myself."

A part of me wants this power—this broken and tortured magic, jarring in its wrongness. Something in me *craves* it. It makes me powerful, and I'm desperate to destroy Daeseong. If I cross this line, what does that make me? Then I remember the awful magic that has always been a part of me—the forbidden power I've buried so deep inside that I nearly forgot its existence. Have I been fooling myself all this time? *Can* I choose to be good?

"This darkness inside you . . ." The weight of Jihun's hand feels comforting on my back. "It isn't you, Sunny."

I meet his eyes but quickly look away. The sincerity in his gaze—his faith in me—is too much. Because I want it too much. I'm afraid to need it—to need friends who believe in me, even when I doubt myself. But I hesitantly take strength from Jihun and remind myself that I can control my hidden power. I can choose to never use it. There's that, at least. As for the word of power on my back, Minju will make it right. She promised.

"Whose room is this anyway?" I clear my throat and glance around the small bedroom.

"Mine." Captain Seo walks in without bothering to knock, which makes sense in light of what she just said. "The uinyeos at the infirmary are petty cowards . . . At any rate, I needed to find you somewhere private, and close to the training yard, to heal. My room was the obvious choice."

"Thank you, Captain." I force out the words even as they cling to my throat for dear life.

"I did my duty." She arches a perfectly shaped eyebrow.

I want to think she would've left me to bleed out if it wasn't for *her duty*, but that doesn't ring true somehow. So I arch my not-so-perfect brow and say, "Nevertheless."

"Of course, she can't stay here much longer." She addresses Jihun. "The cadets are . . . wary."

"But they aren't *wary* of Jo Danbi?" My voice rises with each word.

They're happy to rub elbows with that cheating, murderous piece of shit, but not me. Not the big, bad gumiho. What have I ever done to them? Except what happened in the training yard today. In my defense, I only went after Jo Danbi, and dark magic or not, she had it coming.

"Her conduct was unacceptable," Captain Seo says with a steely glint in her eyes. "As a consequence, she is no longer a cadet."

"She got off easy." Jihun seethes.

To my utter shock, Captain Seo nods in agreement. "Bloody politics."

"Politics?" I ask Jihun, because I get the sense Captain Seo doesn't want to talk to me unless it's strictly necessary.

"The relationship between the Kingdom of Sky and the Kingdom of Mountains, which has always been tenuous, became even more unstable after the death of the Queen of Mountains," he says. "The Council of the Suhoshin *strongly* advised that we do not discipline Jo Danbi to the extent that it would increase the tension between the kingdoms."

"Oh." I can't express a proper level of outrage as a wave of vertigo hits me and cold sweat breaks out on my forehead.

"You should lie down." Jihun wraps his arm around my waist to hold me steady as I mimic a tall, delicate willow swaying in the breeze.

"I'm fine." My head lolls onto his shoulder without my consent, and I squeeze my eyes shut against the tilting room.

"Minju, the comforter." He shifts onto his knees and sweeps me into his arms.

I'm too busy trying not to hurl to object to the manhandling. He carefully lays me down on the sleeping mat, and my head gradually stops spinning. I crack open an eye and see Captain Seo frowning down at Jihun, who kneels by my side with his body curved protectively over me.

"Why is she so weak?" he barks, his voice cracking on the last word. "Are you sure she is fully healed?"

"She needs rest, Captain," Minju says calmly. "And we should send for dinner. It'll help her get her strength back."

"Dinner?" I had breakfast right before I sparred with the Mean Girl. "How long was I out?"

"About twelve hours." Minju places her hand on my forehead. It feels so cool and soothing that my eyes drift closed on a sigh. "First, you need to eat, then you can sleep."

"Jihun," Captain Seo says. "Can I talk to you? Outside?"

I force my eyes open in time to see him glance up at Captain Seo, then frown down at me, hesitant to leave my side. I scowl at him because even the thought of rolling my eyes makes me dizzy. "Why are you sitting here? Go talk to her. Outside."

"Only if you're *sure* you don't need me," he teases, his lips quivering at the corners. For some reason, Captain Seo looks furious at this.

"Bye, bye now." I sink as much sarcasm into my words as possible, but it's not up to my usual standards.

I don't bother watching the suhoshin captains leave and close my eyes again. I drift in and out of sleep until Minju urges me to sit up.

"Here, have some dakjuk." She holds a spoon to my lips.

I try to grab the spoon from her, but I end up swiping at the air because I see two spoons laden with chicken porridge. It smells so good that I give up and open my mouth like a baby bird.

"Mmm." I swallow and open wide for another bite. "Yummy."

After a few more bites, I manage to eat the rest on my own, feeling strength return to my limbs. Then I drink from a small bowl, thinking it's tea, but it's savory.

"It's bone broth," Minju explains. "I want you to eat well and get plenty of rest for at least twenty-four hours. I doubt you can stay still for longer than that."

"What about our lesson?" I yawn.

"We can take one night off." Minju helps me lie back down and pulls the comforter up to my chin. "You're in no shape to wield the Yeoiju."

I'm too sleepy to argue. The next time my consciousness floats to the surface, I feel my hand engulfed in another. I blink my eyes open to a softly lit room. I'm not in Captain Seo's room anymore.

"Why are you awake?" Ethan brushes my hair off my forehead. "You need more rest."

"Where am I?" I rasp, my voice scratchy from sleep.

"You're at Jihun's estate." He pours tea into a small, handleless mug. "I think this is one of his guest quarters."

I rise to one elbow and drink the tea from the mug in his hand, guiding him with the tips of my fingers. When I struggle to sit up, he reaches out to help me, but I weakly shove him away. I manage to maneuver myself into a seated position, but I sway and droop in exhaustion. Still, I stay seated out of pure stubbornness.

I look blearily around the room and realize I'm in my old room at the Sunset Pavilion. Jihun must have brought me here. Grateful tears sting my nose, but I sniff away my sentimentality.

"Why are you here?" I harden my expression even as my heart thuds in my chest and my eyes roam his face.

"Is that even a question?" Ethan shakes his head and shifts to sit behind me, his legs outstretched on either side of me.

"What are you doing?" I yelp. He ignores my question and tugs me close until my back rests against his chest. I lurch forward, then promptly flop back against him in a wave of dizziness.

"Letting you use me as your backrest since you're too stubborn to lie down." He drops his chin on top of my head and wraps his arms loosely around my waist.

I don't push him away. It has nothing to do with how strong and warm he feels. I'm just too weak to move. *Liar.* I ignore the accusatory whisper in my head, but I stiffen my body and don't let myself melt against him.

"What time is it?" I peer at the hanji-covered window.

"Late." He absently sweeps his thumb back and forth on a bare slip of my stomach, and a shiver travels down my spine. "I'm sorry I didn't come sooner. No one told me you were hurt until they moved you here."

"I don't know why they told you at all." I clamp my hand over his to tug it off, but my fingers somehow get tangled with his. "There's nothing for you to do."

"If I'd known sooner, I would've tracked down the person who did this to you." Menace laces his voice. "But they sent her back to the Kingdom of Mountains."

"A good thing too." I look over my shoulder at him. "You can't take on everyone who hurts me."

"Watch me," he growls, his arms tightening around me.

"I can take care of myself," I say flatly, even as my heart knocks against my ribs. "You have your own problems to deal with."

"It's hard for me to see you hurt." He tugs me back to him before I can stop him. "I want to keep you safe, Sunny."

"I know," I whisper. I can't accept his love, but I won't insult him by pretending I don't know he loves me.

He draws a ragged breath and slips his hand under my shirt, spanning his fingers wide against my stomach. "Does it still hurt?"

"No." I shake my head, willing my body not to react to his touch. "I'm fine."

"I need to make sure," he pleads.

"Okay." I can't accept his love, but I won't let him hurt for me when I can make it go away. I can do that much.

Ethan drops his arms from my waist and widens his legs. I draw my knees up and turn around to face him, then raise my shirt past my smooth stomach. His gaze travels over me, not missing a single detail. I hold myself still and keep my expression even so he can see for himself that I really am okay.

After a long moment, he breathes a sigh of relief, his face lighting up with a tremulous smile. I lower my shirt and meet his eyes. Neither of us speak, and the silence stretches on. Now that I've reassured him, I should politely but firmly ask him to leave. But I can't bear to let him go.

"Minju took good care of me." My words come out in a nervous rush.

A flash of anger passes over his face, but he only says, "I hope she continues to do so."

"She will." I look away. He knows about the word of power and my bloodlust. I hate that I'm such a mess. "She promised to find a way to remove the rune."

"No matter what"—Ethan gently grasps my chin to turn my face to meet his gaze—"you will always be perfect to me in all your imperfections."

I bite the inside of my cheeks and look away from him, afraid my eyes will betray me. He tucks a strand of hair behind my ear, and the backs of his fingers brush my cheek. My pulse quickens with want, sharp and hot, and I have to fight to not reach for him. When he brushes his thumb across my bottom lip, I forget why I should stop him.

"Sunny." He savors my name on his tongue.

There is so much love in the single word that my heart swells. One word from him, and I feel cherished. I feel perfect beyond measure. I am a wonder so precious he can hardly believe I'm real. I am loved in a way I never dreamed possible.

I jerk away from his hand. *That* is why I have to stop him.

Because *he* is cherished. He is so precious that my heart feels like it will burst. *My perfect, wonderous Ethan.* I love him with every broken part of me, so I have to push him away. If fate would have him end my life, I could at least spare him from knowing I love him.

But it isn't enough that he believes I don't love him back. He has to believe that I don't *want* his love. He won't give up until I hurt him, and I have to make him give up. Because if he doesn't . . . I'll give in and ruin everything.

"I'd love to blow off some steam with a hot make-out session." I offer him a wicked smile and scrape my fingernails down his five o'clock shadow. I lean in until my lips are a breath away from his. "But I would hate for you to get the wrong idea."

He rears back as though I slapped him. I might've hurt him less if I had. I feel as though I've buried a dagger in my own heart. I harden my resolve even as my soul bleeds.

"Come on, Ethan." I click my tongue with feigned irritation, encasing myself in the cold, tough veneer I've hidden behind for a century. "Don't take it personally."

"I *know* you, Sunny," he rasps, fisting his hands on his lap until his knuckles turn white. "I don't know why you're doing this, but you would never be cruel to me without a reason."

"How am I being cruel?" I arch my brow, but nausea roils in my stomach. I am being cruel, and I hate myself for it. "I thought we already went over this. Like I told you in Vegas, I don't want any attachments to *anyone*—more so now that I'm a walking bull's-eye. Why is that so hard to understand?"

"And *I* told you in Vegas that I don't expect anything from you." The intensity of his gaze bores into me, but I force myself not to look away. "Just don't push me away."

"I'm not pushing you away." I shrug, then smile coyly at him, even though I'm screaming inside. My next words feel like jagged shards of glass as I push them past my tight throat. "All I'm saying is that I'm open to fooling around if you're willing to keep things purely physical."

Ethan turns to stone, all the warmth flickering out of his eyes. My chest constricts, and I can't breathe. It hurts so much. Still, I smirk at him with my head cocked to the side. My nails dig into my palm, breaking skin.

"We both know I'd be lying if I said I can do that." Ethan draws away from me and rises to his feet. "I can't take my beating heart out of my body, Sunny. If you ever decide you want me, you'll have to take all of me."

I hug my knees to my chest, gripping my arms tight to hide the shaking in my hands. *Please don't go.* Tears blur my vision as he turns toward the door, with his back braced against the pain *I* caused him. Maybe he hates me now. My breath comes in panicked pants. I can't do this.

"Ethan, I . . ." *I'm sorry. Stay with me.* But a sharp knock cuts off my plea.

"Come in," Ethan says in a deep, commanding voice.

"Your Highness." Jihun steps inside the room, then halts, catching sight of me. "Sunny, you're awake."

"What gave it away?" I drawl, both grateful for and furious at the interruption. "The fact that I'm sitting up? Or that my eyes are wide open?"

Jihun walks past a stiff-shouldered Ethan and crouches down by my side. "How are you feeling?"

"I'm fine." My bluster seeps out of me at his steady gaze. "A bit woozy and weak, but nothing some food and sleep won't fix."

"I hope I'm not interrupting anything." He glances up at Ethan, who watches us with an unreadable expression.

"No . . ." I say in a small voice. I look down at my hands, and Ethan's gaze heats the curve of my neck. "He was just leaving."

"That's good," Jihun mutters.

"How exactly is that good?" Ethan arches an arrogant brow at him.

"It's time for you to return to General Bak's estate, Your Highness." Jihun manages to sound deferential despite the challenge in the jut of his jaw. "I came to remind you that the guards will be changing shifts soon."

"Thank you for the reminder, Captain," Ethan says coolly, his narrowed eyes belying his words.

Jihun rises to his feet and bows his head. "Of course."

When Ethan turns toward the doors once more, I think he'll leave without a word to me. But he pauses with his hand on the door and murmurs, "Get well, Sunny."

I stare at his back until the door slides closed behind him. *It's for the best.* Too bad I don't believe it for a second. Doing the right thing shouldn't feel this apocalyptically wrong.

"I need to sleep." Numb and hollowed out, I lie down and turn away from Jihun. "Thanks for letting me stay at the Sunset Pavilion."

"I told you." If he's offended by my terseness, I don't hear it in his voice or feel it in the tender way he pulls the blanket over my shoulder. "You're always welcome here."

Jihun blows out the candle, plunging the room into darkness, and lets himself out with steps so light that I don't hear them fall. Then, I close my eyes against the darkness, feeling more alone than ever. *I'm so sorry, Ethan.*

I wouldn't have thought it possible, but I fall asleep before the first tears fall.

CHAPTER TEN

Everything hurts. *But what's new?*

With that lovely thought, I open my eyes to the muted morning light brightening my room at the Sunset Pavilion. Gods, I love this room. I love everything about it. The wooden armoire with the brass appliqués, the matching dresser, the low desk in front of the . . .

"Hello lover," I say to the silk embroidered room divider, my gaze roaming over the delicate details of the flowering branches and the birds perched on top. I'll figure out a way to smuggle it out of the Kingdom of Sky when I return to the Mortal Realm. I just have to make sure my hwando, my other prized possession, doesn't get jealous. I snort at the image of a frowny-faced short sword.

Shit.

I scramble up to sitting and frantically pat the floor around me until my hand wraps around the hilt of my hwando. I release a long breath, which immediately hitches again when I remember why I'm back at the Sunset Pavilion. I gingerly lay a hand on my stomach. It hurts much less than last night, only feeling slightly bruised.

"My lady." The door to my room slides open after a soft knock. "I hope you had a restful sleep."

"Miok?" My lips spread into a wide grin at the welcome sight of the handmaiden. She cared for me with such genuine warmth from the moment I set foot in the Kingdom of Sky—always kind and without judgment. "What are you doing here?"

"I have the honor of serving as your handmaiden again," she says with a gentle smile. My bottom lip trembles at her friendly face before I can check my emotions, and Miok's eyes widen. "My lady? What is the matter?"

"It's nothing." I dash away my tears with an impatient swipe of my hand. My argument with Ethan might have ruined me. *Stop being so wimpy, Sunny.* "I'm just salty that everyone at the Suhoshin headquarters hates me."

"What? Who hates you?" She pushes up the sleeves of her jeogori past her elbows. Even with a ferocious scowl, my handmaiden looks perfectly poised. "Please provide me with their names."

"What are you going to do, Miok?" I laugh, affection warming my chest. "Go beat them up for me?"

"If needs be," she says in a voice laced with steel. I definitely shouldn't give her any names.

Despite her refined manners, my handmaiden has backbone. I saw it during my first stay at the Sunset Pavilion when she put me in my place—a place of honor as Jihun's guest that I was too embarrassed to readily accept. She was unintimidated by my tough facade and made me feel deserving of care and respect.

"Thank you, Miok, but don't trouble yourself. They're not worth it." I sigh and glance around the room. "And I don't think I'll be needing much assistance from you today. My orders are to eat and rest all day."

As much as I love this room, I'm not looking forward to being confined to it all day. My hands and feet already feel wiggly with restlessness.

"And my orders are to prepare you for an outing." A mischievous light enters her eyes. "You don't need to eat and rest only in this room."

"An outing?" My brows pull together. "With who?"

"You will see, my lady." Miok demurely lowers her head, but I spy a smile at the corners of her mouth. "Please come with me. I have a bath prepared for you."

"I . . . I'll wash up on my own," I stutter, self-conscious about someone seeing the rune on my back. "I'm used to it. Cadets don't have attendants washing their backs."

"There won't be any attendants," my handmaiden says gently. "I'll assist you myself this morning, my lady. You have nothing to worry about."

Miok is as good as her word, discreetly averting her eyes as I chuck off my dobok and climb into the wooden tub. Even when she washes my back, she doesn't so much as gasp. Scrubbed squeaky clean and dressed in a simple white hanbok, I walk back to my room, with my handmaiden behind me.

I know the drill from my first stay at the Sunset Pavilion. I settle down on a satin floor cushion behind the low desk. Miok brushes my hair with a fine-tooth comb, then braids it down my back. When she lightly squeezes my shoulders, I turn in my seat and offer up my face.

She frowns slightly and stains the rose petals in darker shades of pink than usual. I peek at my reflection on the rectangular mirror on the desk and see the reason for her concern. I'm so pale my lips have a blue tint to them.

"I'm okay, Miok," I say in a soft voice. "All I need is a day to rest and eat. I heal even faster than your typical shinbiin."

"I know, my lady." She sniffs. "But allow me to make you appear fully healed already. It will help remind me that you will be well soon."

She picks up a cherry pink petal and brushes it against my cheeks, then uses the same petal on my lips. Then she dabs her ring finger in a vial of orchid oil and taps it along my bottom lip. When she presses her lips together and nods at me, I mimic her and smack my lips to even out the gloss.

"There." Miok sits back with a satisfied smile.

The subtle touch of color on my cheeks and lips somehow makes my skin creamy white and my hair jet black. The effect is striking, the sharp contrast making my features pop and my complexion glow. Is this what I would look like if I were born and raised in the Realm of

Four Kingdoms? To my embarrassment, I can't stop staring at my face in the mirror.

"You look the picture of health, not to mention exquisite." My handmaiden gives me a warm smile. "Now, it's time for you to get dressed. I have a feeling you will love this hanbok."

"I wouldn't be so sure." I side-eye her. She knows I'm not the biggest fan of hanboks, with its full, floor-length skirt and cropped, swoop-sleeved top. It's hard for a girl to throw down in that getup.

"The chima is the color of the moment before nightfall—orange, purple, and smokey blue." The handmaiden pauses impishly. "And the shirt is . . . midnight black."

I perk up immediately. "Well, why didn't you say so?"

"I was saving this for you to wear one evening during your first stay at the Sunset Pavilion, but you had . . . work to do." Miok rises to her feet and reaches down to help me. "I don't know when I'll have another chance to serve you, so you will have to wear the black jeogori in broad daylight."

"Miok . . . thank you." I clear my throat, standing up with her help. "And black is the perfect color for any time of day."

"Are you ready, my lady?" she asks, with her hand on the handle of the armoire. At my nod, she opens it with a flourish. Then she drapes the mile-long skirt over her arm, the fabric rippling to the floor like liquid dusk. "It's beautiful, is it not?"

"It's stunning," I whisper.

The color perfectly captures the last precious moment of daylight before darkness settles in. For some reason, my chest tightens as I gingerly brush my fingertips over the soft silk. Unlike the beauty of nightfall, the darkness that's coming can mask a stormy sky, or drown a cloudless day. Will I still be able to wield the Yeoiju with dark magic inside me?

Feeling out of sorts, I meekly allow Miok to help me into the first layer of undergarments—a chest band and darisokot, which is a rudimentary string bikini. But I shake my head in panic when she brings out the next two layers of undergarments.

"No, I can't today." It's been a while since I wore a proper hanbok, and I forgot there were six layers of undergarments . . . just on the bottom. "I'm not putting on shorts *and* pants beneath an underskirt *and* petticoat."

Miok purses her lips in disapproval. "But my lady . . ."

"I'm not fully recovered, remember?" I scramble for an excuse. "The extra weight will tire me."

My handmaiden narrows her eyes dubiously, but she capitulates with a sigh. She skips the shorts and pants—thank *gods*—and helps me into the underskirt. I don't push my luck, and I let her wrap the petticoat around me, then I docilely slip my arms into the undershirt.

"*Now* do I get to put the actual hanbok on?" I say with a huff.

Miok smiles as she dresses me in the beautiful hanbok, her hands gentle and careful on my body. After she ties the goreum into a single-looped bow at my chest, she leans back and admires her handiwork.

"You look so lovely, my lady." She presses her fingers to her lips, then briskly shakes her head. "Come see for yourself."

It isn't the first time I've worn a hanbok in the Kingdom of Sky, but I'm still startled by my reflection in the full-length mirror. The swirling colors of the skirt are beautiful, but the midnight black of the jeogori takes my breath away. I move this way and that, watching the silvery stars wink in and out of the shimmering fabric.

"I didn't know black could be . . . dazzling," I murmur.

In the Mortal Realm, I lived in the night, and wearing black helped me blend into the darkness—made me invisible, made me safe. But this black makes me . . . shine. I don't mind it so much because I choose to live in the light now. Being with my friends in the light makes me feel safer than being alone in the night. I don't want to be invisible. I want Ethan and my friends to see me.

My stomach drops. *No, not Ethan.* I can't let him see all of me. After last night, he probably doesn't want anything to do with me. My tears blur my reflection. *Good.* I can't stand the sight of myself anymore.

"Oh dear. I lost track of time." Miok flutters her hands. "We must hurry. He is waiting."

"He . . . who?" I ask, blinking away my tears, and follow her out the door. "Jihun?"

When I walk out to the semi-open main hall, I see a male in a slate gray dopo standing in the courtyard with his back to the pavilion. My heart contracts until I can't breathe. I don't need him to turn around to recognize him. I'll know Ethan anywhere. I resist the urge to dig the heel of my hand against my chest.

Thank gods.

I'm *relieved* he's here. What the fuck is wrong with me? It gutted me to hurt him last night, but I did it because I love him. How can I be glad he came back when it means I have to hurt him again? Have I always been this selfish?

Miok helps me down the stone steps—I need the help because my gaze is still glued to Ethan—and I slide my feet into the satin slippers she lays out for me. I inhale deeply through my nose, firming my resolve. I paid too big a price—we both did—to let him close that hard-won distance again.

Ethan turns at the soft rustling of our movements. I step out into the courtyard, forcing my face into an indifferent mask.

"What are you . . ." I trail off when his lips part on an indrawn breath.

His gaze sweeps over me, once then twice, and a deep flush rises to his cheeks. He closes his eyes and clenches his fists by his sides. My pulse flutters in my throat. Ethan has never seen me like this. He's seen me in a sparkly minidress, a pair of bloody jeans . . . I skip over the memories of him seeing me in various states of undress . . . and most recently a dobok. But never like this—dressed with loving care and attention to accentuate my femininity, my softness.

I roamed America on my own, resolutely alone, for over a century. For survival, I had to hide the soft parts of myself, especially in the early years. There were those who would've perceived my femininity as a weakness. They would've swooped in to take my possessions and violate my body. They would have tried. They *have* tried. But the hard, snarling part of me stopped them, and that was the only side I let the worlds see for as long as I can remember.

Being soft doesn't equate to being powerless. I know that now. It's just a different kind of power. The kind that could bend knees—not through fear and violence—but through trust and devotion. Strength that could heal and inspire.

I'm cold, hard, and vicious. I'm grumpy and sarcastic as hell. But I am also soft, lush, and beautiful. This is a part of me too. I should take care not to forget, even while I hide that part of myself from Ethan.

As I brace myself to meet his gaze again, I wrap my aloofness around me like armor. It feels tight and unnatural, but I'll adjust to it soon. I've done it for a hundred years. It'll come back to me.

When Ethan finally opens his eyes, strands of silver-and-green light streak through his pupils like shooting stars. *So beautiful.* My breath leaves me in a whoosh. This is going to be even harder than I thought.

He doesn't take his gaze off me as he approaches, but I don't let myself get self-conscious. I pull my shoulders back and lift my chin, carelessly accepting his blatant admiration. No one needs to know that my knees are knocking under my chima.

"Fuck," Ethan breathes. "I need to rethink your offer from last night."

A startled laugh tumbles out of me, but I cover it with an affronted scoff. "You said you couldn't keep things purely physical."

"I changed my mind." He swallows with effort. "I can definitely do that."

"Yeah right." I roll my eyes, even though I feel oddly triumphant inside. "You need to learn to lie better."

A sheepish grin quirks his lips. "It was worth a try."

"Am I supposed to be flattered?" I narrow my eyes at him.

"You should be." He leans close and whispers in my ear, "You had the *King Foretold* seriously consider becoming your boy toy."

"Whatever." I press my thighs together, the full skirt hiding the telltale movement. What he doesn't know is that *I* would never be able to keep things purely physical. If I let him inside me, I would love him with every inch of my body. Which is why *that* can never happen. "*You* should be *honored* I offered to make you my boy toy."

"I *am* honored." He gives me a roguish grin.

I sketch a mocking bow. "You're welcome."

Ethan chuckles softly and steps back, even as his eyes burn with desire. But my heart breaks for us because underneath the lust and humor, I see his devastation. He believes me. He believes that I don't love him. I avert my eyes and bury my ragged emotions even deeper inside me.

Then I remember with a start that we are not alone. *Shit.* I completely forgot about Miok. I'm afraid to look at her. Did she hear the "boy toy" part? My mouth pulls into a cringe as I turn toward her . . . but there's no one at my side. *Oh thank gods.* She must have silently faded away to give us privacy when Ethan looked at me like I was Venus rising out of the sea. I bite my lip. No matter what happens, I'm storing away that look for my long, lonely nights.

"What are you doing here?" I change the subject before I climb him like a tree and ruin everything.

"I'm here to take advantage of this rare opportunity . . ."

"Of me being weak and injured?" I lean into my sarcasm, my favorite coping mechanism.

Ethan sighs ponderously. "Of you having an off day."

"I get one off day a month." I'm being difficult for no reason, but I guess that's kind of the point.

"Which you used to blow up the study." He holds up a finger when I scoff indignantly. "An *actual* off day where you *have to* rest and relax."

111

I wrinkle my nose at him. "Is aggravating me your idea of rest and relaxation?"

"I'm here to take you on a picnic." He scratches the back of his head as a blush rises to his cheeks.

"A picnic?" I side-eye him, even though my heart flutters in my chest. A picnic with Ethan sounds like a dream . . . I *have* to shut him down. "Do I look like a person who enjoys sissy-ass picnics?"

Hurt flashes across his face, and my stomach twists with regret. But steely determination swiftly replaces his wounded expression, and my brows dip into a frown. What is he up to? Before I can ask him point blank, he plants a hand on my lower back and my brain short-circuits for a second.

"Yes, you do," he drawls smoothly and urges me toward the archway leading to the main entrance. "This way."

I dig my heels in and glare at him. "Ethan—"

"Just trust me. Okay?" He moves his hand in soothing circles on my back, and I twist away from his touch. He lowers his arm to his side, a shadow darkening his eyes, but he presses his lips into a stubborn line.

"You're not letting this go, are you?" I ask, wavering. Ethan can be even more stubborn than I am. I might be better off just going along with whatever he has in mind, then sending him on his way. "Fine. Let's get on with it."

He accepts my ungracious acquiescence with a wary nod, then leads me out of the courtyard to a stunning set of wooden palanquins. I can't help stepping up to them and tracing the intricate carvings of tigers and phoenixes with my fingers.

I drop my hand and clear my throat. "We're going in gamas?"

"Yes, for privacy." His tone sobers. "I don't want to draw unwanted attention."

"Do you have shadows on you?" I scan our vicinity with sharp eyes as his overprotective grandfather rushes back to my consciousness. "I thought you couldn't leave General Bak's estate on your own."

"I told the guards they don't want to find out what I'll do to them if they follow me. They wisely decided to stay behind." A muscle tics in his jaw. "The general is away on official business, so they can't run to report me to him."

"But won't they tell him once he comes back?" I wonder if Ethan's ever seen his grandfather angry. I have a feeling it won't be pretty.

"If they want to save their necks, it'll have to be our little secret. General Bak is *not* known for his leniency." Ethan shakes his head as though chasing away his dark mood. "We better get going."

Ignoring the hand he offers, I duck into the gama on my own and sit cross-legged on the floor. I glance around the tight, shadowy confines and frown. "Are you going to fit in yours?"

"You do know these are magic, right?" Ethan opens the two sliding windows on either side of me to let in the sunlight.

"I know they carry themselves . . ." My eyes grow wide, and I bounce a little on my ass, forgetting to act distant in my excitement. "Is yours bigger on the inside than it looks from the outside? Like the TARDIS?"

"Not that big, you nerd." He taps me on the nose so naturally that I barely remember to slap his hand away. "Just big enough for me to sit upright without hitting my head."

I'm impressed nonetheless, but I rearrange my features into bored impatience. "Where are we going anyway?"

"Don't you like surprises?" he teases. "Or are they too *sissy ass* for you?"

I look away from his smile, wrinkling my skirt in my fists. "I hope this little outing is worth the risk you're taking."

"Oh, it is." Ethan climbs into the palanquin next to mine and opens the window facing me. "You are worth every risk."

Before I can make a callous remark to hide my fluster, my palanquin lifts off the ground and lurches forward. I shoot out my hands to brace myself. "Whoa."

"Sit tight," Ethan says from the shadows. "We'll be there soon."

The gama settles into a gentle bob, and I slowly relax. I hug my legs to my chest and glance out the open window, resting my cheek on top of my knees. I can only see his arms and chest, but I stare at Ethan anyway.

No matter what happens, I'll always know he loved me, and I loved him back. To me, our love is a treasure to be cherished even if we can't be together. A single tear drops from the corner of my eye and seeps into my skirt. It wrecks me that he can't ever find out.

When another tear threatens to fall, I turn my face away from him. This is why I can't have nice things. I get a chance to look my fill of Ethan—his torso, at least—and I immediately become a weepy mess. I have to get myself together. He can't see me like this.

By the time our palanquins slow to a stop, I have myself under control. Even when Ethan opens the front panel with a boyish smile, I manage not to lose my vaguely irritated expression. When he offers me his hand, I take it this time because my stomach is still too sore for me to get out on my own. Or so I tell myself. As soon as I step out and straighten to a stand, he releases my hand.

"Now then." I fold my arms tightly over my chest to hold onto the lingering warmth of his hand. "Let's see what all the fuss is . . ."

I trail off as I take in the verdant garden surrounding a large rectangular lily pond, with an open pagoda on the water's edge. Four thick wooden beams hold up the pagoda's sloping tiled roof, elaborate enough to sit atop a luxurious hanok. And the garden is . . . green. I've never seen so much green in the Kingdom of Sky.

"My mother loved the mountains. The smell of earth, the vibrance of trees, the strength of nature . . . all of it," Ethan says quietly. "My grandfather didn't understand her connection to the mountains, but he loved his daughter more than anything, so he had this garden built for her."

"It's beautiful." I press a hand against my chest, soaking in the sight. "It does remind me of the mountains."

A tight knot inside me loosens. Unlike the usual jewel-toned gardens found in the Kingdom of Sky, this garden isn't manicured to perfection. Instead, the trees and foliage grow freely, flourishing in messy, verdant abundance as nature intended.

Las Vegas isn't exactly surrounded by green mountains, but I've never felt as severed from nature as I do in the Kingdom of Sky. I wonder if any of the Shinbiin from the other three kingdoms—beings of Mountains, Water, and Underworld—feel it too. Like there's a foot on the oxygen hose, pressing down with increasing pressure.

"This used to be my mother's favorite place in the Kingdom of Sky." His lips curve into a sad smile.

"I can see why," I whisper.

"Come on." He tugs me toward the pagoda with a light hold on my elbow. "Let's get you some breakfast."

We cross to the other side of the pond on a curved wooden bridge. As we near the pagoda, I take off in a sprint and skid to a halt at the steps. I look over my shoulder at Ethan, my eyes round with disbelief.

"What is that on the table?" My voice is an octave higher than usual.

"Has it been so long that you don't recognize your favorite meal from Roxy's Diner?" His grin practically dangles from his ears.

I climb the stairs and fall to my knees in front of the low table. "How?"

"I made a late-night trip to Vegas." Ethan sits across from me and waves his hand over my plate like he's removing an invisible lid. "Don't worry. I kept it warm for you."

I can't believe he went to the Mortal Realm, and endured a round trip through the Gray Void, for some stupid diner food. I know he did it all for me. This perfect, precious idiot would do anything for me. And it breaks my heart.

"Diner food is definitely not worth the risk." Other than the slight huskiness to my voice, I do a good job of hiding my emotions. Ethan, on the other hand, can't hide his flinch. I hate myself for hurting him, even though I do it to protect him. I sink all the anger I feel toward myself into the glare I send his way. "What if your grandfather finds out about what you've been up to? What if your *father* finds out that you're in the Kingdom of Sky?"

"This is a private garden, and my grandfather already knows I come here often." A muscle jumps in his jaw. "As for the King of Mountains, let him come for me."

"What the fuck, Ethan?" I don't have to feign my anger toward him this time. "Why are you being so reckless?"

"Reckless? It's a fucking picnic." Frustration flashes in his eyes, but I don't think it's toward me. "If I can't enjoy a simple picnic, how am I different from a prisoner?"

A silent beat passes between us, both of us breathing heavily from our argument. Every cell in my body tells me to comfort him, but that will only hurt him more in the long run. Ethan's life is already difficult enough. He doesn't need me to make it harder by giving him hope where none exists.

A frustrated scream builds in my chest, but I squash it ruthlessly. I don't comfort him, but I don't keep arguing with him either. Surely, we can eat some steak and eggs without making things worse for us.

Ethan drags a hand down his face and blows out a long breath. I meet his eyes and give him a careless shrug to signal a truce. He holds my gaze with something like despair. "You can't even be bothered to argue with me anymore?"

"The food's getting cold," I say callously, looking down at the table. I need a second to build up my armor again.

After a beat, he sighs. "We can't have that."

"You got the same thing?" I settle my bottom onto the floor cushion and point my chin at his plate. "Do you even like steak and sunny-side up eggs?"

"Of course I do." He slices off a good third of his steak and slides it onto my plate. "But you need it more than me."

"Stop trying to fatten me up," I grumble even though my heart melts at his gesture.

"Should I take it back?" He reaches out with his fork, and I curve my arms around my plate. He chuckles, and the warm sound dances down my spine. "And last but not the least . . ."

A thermos appears on the table, and I nearly gasp, my eyes bugging out. "Coffee?"

"Yeah." He rubs the back of his neck. "But I forgot the mugs."

"I got this." I wave my hand and summon two earthenware teacups from my room in the Sunset Pavilion. He's not the only one who picked up some practical magic. "If these tiny cups work for tea, they'll work for coffee."

"Good thinking." His expression turns suspiciously bland as he lifts the carafe. "I asked Rachel to add plenty of cream and sugar, just the way you like it."

This time I do gasp and slap my hand over the cup. I don't care if the hot coffee scalds my hand. "Don't you *dare* pour a drop of that atrocity in here."

"Relax." Ethan smiles at me with such affection that I almost smile back. "Rachel knows you drink your coffee black. She would've boxed my ear if I asked for cream and sugar in it."

"Asshole." I watch him pour the nectar of the gods into my cup. I take a reverent sip, then groan, "*Fuck me.* Now I can die happy."

"At least finish your steak before you die," he says drily.

I pretend to ignore him and drink more coffee, then I turn my attention to my steak and eggs. Is there *anything* as satisfying as popping the yolk on a sunny-side up egg? I slice a generous strip of steak and dip it into the yolk, my mouth salivating for the perfect bite.

"Mmm." For a moment, there is nothing but me and the meal I secretly feared I'd never have again. Then I pick a safe topic to discuss. "How is Rachel doing?"

"Running a tight ship as always." Ethan glances up from his dish. "She misses you."

"I do too," I admit quietly. "Where did you tell her I was?"

"That you enrolled in a specialty academy with a demanding schedule."

"Vague, yet true." I nod, impressed. "Good one."

"Thanks." Ethan raises his teacup in a playful toast, then takes a sip of his coffee. He immediately puts it down with a grimace.

I tuck my chin to hide my smile. He has a sweet tooth that I find adorable. I wish I could get him some sugar for his coffee, but I don't have free access to the kitchens at the cadet barracks. There's so little I can call my own in this realm. *In any realm for that matter.*

The melancholy thought sneaks up on me and rattles me, and the steak turns to dust in my mouth. I wish I could call Ethan mine. Even if there is no place in all the worlds for me, he could be my home, and that would be enough. Too bad even that much isn't possible.

THE SIGN

The King of Mountains flipped over the table laden with food and threw a porcelain bowl across the room. It shattered against the wall, and the jagged pieces rained down over the three cowering court ladies. But none of them moved, other than to tremble in fear, as they knelt with their foreheads pressed to the floor.

"You bitches expect me to eat this trash you served me?" he snarled. "You dare insult your king?"

"N . . . never, Your Majesty. We w . . . would never," the oldest of the gungnyeos stuttered without raising her head.

The king gripped her low bun and jerked her head up. "Now you contradict me?"

"Please, Your M . . . Majesty." She sobbed. "I beg your forgiveness."

The sheer terror in her eyes appeased the king for the briefest second, but his lust for suffering roared back to life when a younger court lady whimpered from the floor. He shoved away the old gungnyeo, who cried out as she fell atop the shattered porcelain bowl. The king salivated at the sight of her blood and picked up a sharp, pointed piece as he turned to the other gungnyeo.

He held her chin in a punishing grip and forced her to look at him. He saw her fear in the whites around her pupils and calmly pressed the tip of the broken porcelain into her exposed throat. When her eyes nearly rolled back, he laughed.

"It would be an honor for you to die at the hands of your king, would it not?" The king licked his lips as a crimson drop of blood rolled down the court lady's pale neck. "Would you like for me to take your pathetic, worthless life?"

He forgot that even animals fought for their lives when they were cornered. So when the young gungnyeo thrashed against him and the sharp porcelain slipped in his hand, he instinctively tightened his grip on his crude weapon. The king hissed, wincing in pain. Annoyed at the interruption to his playtime, he glanced down at his hand.

"No." With a beastly scream, he brought down the broken porcelain on the gungnyeo's throat and threw her twitching body aside. "Out. Get out of my sight. Now."

The two remaining court ladies each grabbed an arm of the dying female and scrambled out of the room, dragging her behind them. He was too distraught to take pleasure in the streak of blood left on the floor. His hand stayed clenched at his side for a long while. He had to be mistaken. It had to be that lowly gungnyeo's blood on him. Even so, he shook with dread as he opened his hand and stared down at his palm.

The King of Mountains wanted to unsee the sign—the sign that the Kingdom of Mountains had accepted his son as its true king—but the blood continued to well from a gash that should never have been.

CHAPTER ELEVEN

Ethan and I sit with our backs against the wooden railing of the pagoda and look out at the serene lily pond. The only thing saving me from a food coma is the pot of coffee I drank. Even so, my body feels heavy and relaxed, and I yawn into my hand.

"Are you tired?" Ethan shifts beside me. He clears the table away with a wave of his hand, and a neatly folded blanket appears in its place. "You should take a nap. I'll watch over you."

"What are you? My nanny?" I scowl but ruin the effect by yawning again. "I don't need a nap."

"Right." He reaches for the blanket and shakes it open, then he pats his thigh.

"What?" I ask crossly, even as my traitorous cheeks heat.

"At least lie down. You don't have to sleep. Just rest a little." He pats his thigh again. "I'll be your pillow."

"You'll be my pillow?" I know I'm just repeating what he said, but my brain is trying to shut down. I tug on my bottom lip with my teeth, then get a grip on my libido. "It'll be like laying my head on a brick block."

"I promise it'll be an upgrade from those wooden blocks they use as pillows here." His lips stretch into a lazy grin, and my pulse flutters. "Come here."

My center turns molten at his low command, but I give him a sardonic smile. "I'll pass."

"You keep pushing me away." Ethan stares out at the pond, his throat working, then he turns back to me. "I think I know why."

How? My heart lurches as my eyes skip around the garden. *How does Ethan know?* I have to fix this. *Oh gods.* My thoughts churn aimlessly in my head.

Stop it, Sunny.

I take a calming breath. The best lie is a half truth.

"We have a history, Ethan. I've known you since you were a teenager, and I've come to think of you as a friend," I say in an even tone. *You can do this.* "And I can tell you want something I can't give you. I care about you, but if you keep doing this, we can't even be friends."

"Then I'll take friendship." Ethan's shoulders sag on a shuddering exhale, and I'm both heartbroken and relieved. "And you don't have to feel responsible for my feelings. That's for me to worry about."

"Easier said than done," I whisper. I'm in love with him. I care more about his feelings than mine.

Suddenly, I'm dizzy with exhaustion. I slide down the wooden railing onto the floor and use my own scrawny arm as my pillow. After a forlorn sigh, Ethan covers me with the blanket—it smells like him—and carefully smooths it over my body.

I would purr if I were a cat. Even the fox in me wants to lean into his touch with a happy growl. But I hold myself stiff, and he removes his hands without lingering. Being friends is *so awesome.*

"Go to sleep, Sunny." He tucks a stray strand of hair behind my ear as though he can't help touching me. "You need to rest."

"I want to hear your story." I close my eyes.

"You do?" He sounds hesitant. "It's not a happy one."

"I want to hear your story," I repeat. Then I blink my eyes open and rush to add, "I'm tired of being in the dark about things that everyone else knows."

"M . . . my mother was kind and full of life. When my father forced her into marriage, she didn't give in to despair and tried to make the best of their life together. And she tried to see the good in my father, even though he stole her dream of becoming a mother.

"Then, despite the impossibility of beings from two different life sources having a child together, she conceived me." He swallows thickly. "You said I was a miracle, but I can't help thinking it would've been better if she never had me."

"No, don't ever think that." I shift to look up at him. "Your mother *never* would've thought that."

"I know. She was ecstatic when she found out she was pregnant with me." Ethan gets a faraway look in his eyes. "She thought she would finally have a child to love with all her heart. She thought she and the King of Mountains would be a real family at last. Happiness seemed within her grasp, but . . . she couldn't have been more wrong.

"When my mother foresaw my destiny and shared it with my father, he became obsessed with killing me. Becoming a *real family* was the furthest thing from his mind." His smile isn't a smile at all. "And you know the rest of my story."

"No, I don't." My hand twitches at my side, but I don't reach out for him. "No one does. Your story has only just begun."

"Has it? It doesn't feel like I'm living my own story, though." He brushes his knuckles down my cheek. I don't have the heart to pull away, but he catches himself and snatches his hand back. "I feel like a pawn in my grandfather's story. A story of war and vengeance."

"I know you don't want to risk ruining your relationship with your grandfather, but can't you talk to him?" How can General Bak not understand that a war against his own people would devastate his grandson? "You need to tell him you don't want more bloodshed."

"You think I haven't tried? He is dead set on starting a war. He won't even *consider* another way." Ethan straightens and looks out at the water. "He said that it's *my* duty to liberate the Kingdom of Mountains from the tyrant king, and an outright war is the only way. He told me it's what my mother would have wanted."

"That is *not* true, Ethan. You must know that." I dig my nails into my palms. *That manipulative old snake.* General Bak has been guilt-tripping his grandson this whole time. "Your grandfather has always wanted vengeance, hasn't he? You just provided him with a convenient excuse to exact it."

"I . . ." He wipes a hand over his face. "I don't know what to think."

"You *know* what your mother would've wanted. You know her truest self. She shared her memories with you." I sit up and face him. "She would never have wanted you to start a war. She wouldn't have wanted the people of the Kingdom of Mountains—*her* people—to suffer." I reach out to take his hand, then pat him awkwardly on his arm instead. "You're like your mother, you know. You're kind and full of life. War is not the answer."

"You're right," he says with a determined nod. "And we found a way to infiltrate—"

I'm knocked onto my back so fast and so hard that I bang my head on the wood floor of the pagoda. I have no idea what's happening because Ethan's huge body is sprawled over mine, shielding me from danger.

"Get off me." I push at his shoulders to zero effect. "What the hell's going on?"

"Stay down," he growls.

"You fucking have to *stop* using your body as my personal shield." My rant turns into a sharp yelp when he rolls both of us behind a pillar and bodily props me up against it. "I can take care of my—Ethan!"

His eyes widen as he stares down at the arrow shaft sticking out of his shoulder. I push him against the pillar, switching places with him, and peek my head out to scan the woods for enemies. But I draw back as an arrow whooshes a hair's breadth away from the tip of my nose. The assailant is an expert marksman. He is nowhere near the pagoda, but his aim is deadly.

"How are you hurt?" I crouch low in front of Ethan. I'm small enough that the pillar actually hides most of my body. "Shouldn't that thing have bounced off you?"

"I don't know." He rips the arrow out with a grunt, and his wound starts closing immediately. "It's nothing."

"Nothing?" If my voice rises any higher, dogs will come running. The word of power prickles on my back, but I can't let my bloodlust overtake my logic. Ethan needs me. I capture his face between my hands and peer into his eyes. "Do you have blurry vision? Are you having difficulty breathing? Does your mouth taste metallic?"

"The arrow wasn't poisoned." Ethan grasps my wrists and tugs my hands off his face. "I need you to stay here while I go check things out."

"That's precious." I laugh in his face despite the grim circumstances. "We don't have time to play around. I'll take left. You take right."

"Fine." He scowls but knows better than to argue with me. "Ready?"

"Go." I shoot out from behind the wooden pillar and jump over the pagoda's railing. With a muttered curse, Ethan takes off in the other direction.

I hike up my floor-length chima as I run and inelegantly unsheathe my hwando from my thigh strap. It's not as cool as summoning my weapon with a subtle flex of my hands, but I haven't mastered weapon summoning yet. I couldn't risk slashing my palms by calling my hwando blade-side down.

A flash of beige flits through the trees. *Shit.* Bunching up my skirt to one side, I chase the assailant. The trees are thinning—we're in a garden, not a forest—and we'll soon hit the streets. I can't endanger the civilians.

In a burst of speed, I catch up to the bad guy and grab him by the scruff of his shirt. He's dressed like a commoner, in a hanbok made of rough, unbleached fabric, but he has a quiver slung across his back and a bow in his grip. He's our marksman.

Using both of our momenta, I spin him away from the direction of the streets and slam his back into a tree. The male is so big that his shoulders almost span the width of the trunk, and I have to tilt my head way up to look into his eyes. But when I do, my face goes slack

with shock. His lips tremble as tears slide down his gaunt cheeks. He's
. . . afraid.

"It's okay." What am I saying? This bastard shot Ethan with an
arrow. But when his tears come faster, all my rage drains out of me. "I
won't hurt you."

"I'm s . . . sorry," he stutters, then his eyes widen when he sees
something behind me.

"Who sent you?" Ethan raises the golden axe and the silver axe,
ready to strike.

"Y . . . you . . ." The male stares at the axes and slowly shakes his
head. "How . . ."

"Ethan, he's scared." I release my hold on the male and take a step
back. "I don't think . . ."

"Sunny!" Ethan pushes me behind him as the assailant draws an
arrow from his quiver in a lightning-fast move.

But the male doesn't reach for his bow. He buries the arrowhead
deep into his own neck.

"No," I shout, my hand uselessly reaching out for the assailant.

Ethan catches the male as he slides down the tree and lowers him
to the ground. With my limbs wobbly from shock, I stumble over to
kneel next to them. I take a calming breath and focus my gaze on the
male. His green life force wavers weakly around him. He's . . . a being
of Mountains.

"I . . . didn't know. I would never . . . Not even for . . . ," the assailant
mutters, his head lolling listlessly. "My children . . . so hungry . . . Even
so . . . I would never . . ."

His children. A bleak picture takes shape in my mind. His
hanbok is clean but threadbare, neatly mended with patches over
well-worn parts. The bow lying next to him isn't elegant but sturdy
and well used, like the weapon of a hunter. The weapon of someone
poor but hardworking. Someone with a family. My chest constricts
painfully.

The male continues mumbling incoherently. I lower my head to hear him better, but his glazed eyes suddenly focus on Ethan. "Forgive me . . ."

I grip Ethan's forearm, and he covers my hand with his own.

"Were you sent to kill me?" Ethan's voice is kind even though his dopo is stained with blood from his wound. The male is distraught and only has moments left to live. If I didn't already love Ethan, this would've done the job.

"Y . . . you look just like her. I would never . . ." He whimpers. "I wouldn't have come if I'd known."

"It's okay. Your . . . prince will keep your family safe," I assure him, following my intuition.

Ethan shoots me a startled glance. He can't see the male's gi—his green life force. He doesn't realize he is easing one of his own people on to the next life.

"The gi of Mountains flows through him," I explain in a low whisper. The confusion lifts from Ethan's gaze, and he gives me a solemn nod.

"I *will* protect your family. They are my people, as are you," Ethan says with a break in his voice. "Will you tell us who sent you?"

"I didn't know . . ." he repeats, too far gone to help his prince. He wraps his hands around Ethan's and brings it to his chest, cradling it like a newborn. His eyes flit to the sky, endless tears seeping out from the corners. "Forgive me, my queen."

"Please tell us who . . ." I begin, hoping for some answers.

"Sunny, he's gone." Ethan frees his hand and closes the male's vacant eyes. The last of the male's tears roll down his temples as though he still seeks forgiveness even in death.

I take a shuddering breath, then push to a stand, gritting my teeth. "Your father."

"He knows I'm here." Ethan rises to his feet, vibrating with fury. "It's time he answers for his wrongs."

I shiver at his imposing presence, every inch the Prince of Mountains. But I don't long for my Ethan this time. *This* is the Ethan his people need. The people of the Kingdom of Mountains need his sorrow to fuel his strength—his rage to harden his determination—to free them from oppression. And when they're free, my Ethan can heal his people with his kindness, warmth, and generosity. Then and only then can he finally let go of his pain and sorrow and heal with his people.

But the determined jut of his jaw makes my stomach twist with worry. I open my mouth to remind him not to do anything stupid on his own, when a shadow passes above us. With a muttered curse, Ethan pushes me behind him and raises his axes. I roll my eyes and step around him, tightening my grip on my hwando.

Captain Seo lands in a rush of wind and falls to her knees in front of him. "Forgive me, my prince. I should have come sooner."

I clasp a shaky hand to my forehead. Seo Cheyun knows Ethan is the Prince of Mountains? Does that mean she's on the queen's list? I have no words. This day is doing its damnedest to give me a heart attack. It doesn't help that I'm weak and sore from the pursuit.

"Rise, Captain Seo. You couldn't have anticipated this," Ethan commands, lowering his axes. "Where is Captain Song? We have much to discuss."

I sense her hesitation as she gets to her feet, her eyes darting toward me. I know everyone is worried about me after the injury—and apprehensive about how the rune will affect me—but I refuse to be kept in the dark. I'm a part of this team, and I won't be left out, no matter how well intended their concern.

"Jihun is most likely in the Mortal Realm, following a lead on Daeseong." I cross my arms and dig in my heels, every line of my body mutinous.

"Captain Seo?" Ethan arches an implacable brow, and triumph surges through me. The captain might not trust me, or my ability to control the bloodlust, but Ethan does.

"Cadet Cho is correct, Your Highness." She acknowledges me with a tilt of her head. There is . . . trust behind that gesture. For me.

I check my bitterness, and the captain's solemn words in the training yard ring in my memory. *Stand down, Sunny. This isn't you.* She helped me break free from the bloodlust. Captain Seo isn't hesitating because she doesn't trust me. She might genuinely be concerned about me. I rub the heel of my hand against my chest, trying to ease the sudden tightness.

"We received intel on the dark mudang this morning," the captain continues. "One of the sentries located Daeseong's hideout. Captain Song and his lieutenants went to the Mortal Realm to confirm his location."

I have no desire to smile anymore. I might never want to smile again. I feel Ethan's worried gaze on me, but I can't look at him. I dig my nails into my palms. I need to stop freaking out every time someone mentions the dark mudang. But if the intel proves correct, then I'm out of time. I have to fight Daeseong, even if I'm not ready.

My fear awakens the rune on my back, and searing heat brands my skin. *It's not fair.* Why do *I* have to risk my neck to save the worlds? What have they ever done for me? I wrap my arms around my midriff and hold off the dark anger.

"Once they confirm his location, they plan to *observe* his movements to discern his plans," Captain Seo says meaningfully. "We won't move in until the sword of light is ready."

My head swivels toward her. Despite my tentative hope that the captain doesn't actually hate me, I'm shocked that she might be trying to reassure me. *Is* she? I have my answer when our eyes meet.

"We still have time." Her gaze doesn't waver from mine.

"Yes," I say numbly. Even if I can't wield the Yeoiju, I can defeat Daeseong with the sword of light. The burning on my back eases to a prickle, and I belatedly understand the captain's subtle emphasis. *We.* I won't be alone. My breath leaves me in a tremulous whoosh. I offer her a grateful nod. "And *we* will be ready when the time comes."

Ethan moves closer to my side—close enough to brush the back of his hand against mine. *Are you okay?* he asks with the soft touch. I nudge his index finger with mine. *I'm okay.* His expression doesn't change, but I feel his relief. *Good.* I step away and put some distance between us.

"Captain, have Minju analyze the body for magic traces," he orders with the confidence of someone who expects obedience. "He was sent from the Kingdom of Mountains, but someone granted him access into the Kingdom of Sky. I want to know who."

"Of course." Captain Seo glances uneasily at Ethan's bloodied robe. "But first, she should attend to your wounds, Your Highness."

"There's no need." He waves his hand dismissively. "I do, however, require a change of clothes before I return to General Bak's estate. No one must learn about the assassination attempt until we find the accomplice."

Of course there's an accomplice—a spy in the Kingdom of Sky. If we have a spy in the Kingdom of Mountains, why wouldn't they have one of their own here? I widen my stance for balance as dizziness weaves through me. Perhaps General Bak was right to keep Ethan's identity a secret.

"I'm sure they can find something for you at Jihun's estate." I glance at the dead hunter, sadness washing over me. "But how are we going to move the assassin's body unseen?"

Ethan looks across the garden. "We can put him in one of the palanquins."

"Since you can't be seen wearing that"—I huff a resigned sigh—"I guess I'll have to walk back."

"You will do no such thing," Captain Seo snaps. "You haven't recovered from your injuries. And from the state of your clothes, you obviously didn't hold back in apprehending the assailant."

"All I did was chase him down." My voice cracks, but I push through. "He didn't even put up a fight. He . . . he wasn't an assassin by choice. He was a hunter being used for his skills. I . . ."

"We'll discuss everything once Captain Song and the lieutenants return." Ethan squeezes my upper arm, and I let him because my knees feel alarmingly wobbly. "For now, let's get you back to the Sunset Pavilion. Captain Seo is right. You need to rest."

"How am I supposed to get back if I don't walk?" I obviously would rather not, but I have no other choice. If we want to keep the assassination attempt under wraps, we need to transport the body in my palanquin, and Ethan needs to take the other one. I arch an eyebrow at Captain Seo and half joke, "Will you fly me back to Jihun's place, Captain? You can carry me in your arms like I'm a damsel in distress."

"Yes," she deadpans, "because that would be *very* discreet."

"Good gods." My jaw drops. "Was that a joke?"

"Come on, Sunny." Ethan doesn't quite meet my eyes.

"Come . . . where?" I ask, suddenly leery.

"To my palanquin." He clears his throat. "We're going to have to share."

For some inexplicable reason, I turn desperately to the captain. She glances between me and Ethan, then offers me an apologetic shrug. I feel betrayed. I thought females were supposed to stick together and shit. But to be fair, what can the captain do?

"I know it won't be comfortable, but Jihun's estate isn't far from here." Ethan pitches his voice low. "You don't have to worry. I . . . I won't try anything with you. You're just not in any condition to walk."

After our talk in the pagoda, I'm not worried about Ethan, but I am very much worried about *me*.

Grow up, Sunny. You're making things unnecessarily awkward.

"It's fine," I mutter. "Don't worry about it."

Ethan scratches the side of his neck, and I look everywhere but at him.

"My prince." Captain Seo breaks the uncomfortable silence. "I will transport the body with utmost discretion."

"Thank you, Captain." Ethan nods at her. Then, with a hand hovering behind my back, he says, "Let's get you back to the Sunset Pavilion."

"I'm not going to keel over." I stomp away from his hand, only to have my knees promptly buckle. Ethan catches me and sweeps me into his arms as though I weigh nothing. And I squirm against his gentle hold, blushing to the roots of my hair. "I can walk to the gama."

"I know you can," he says without an ounce of sarcasm. "Just humor me. Okay?"

I can't even stand, much less walk, but he doesn't point out the obvious. How did I fall in love with the most decent and supportive male in all the worlds? *Just my luck.* I don't need more reminders that I don't deserve him, especially since I can't fucking have him.

"Okay." I'm much too tempted to burrow into his chest, so I hold my head awkwardly away from him.

His long legs eat up the distance in what feels like a blink. And too soon, he sets me down in front of the palanquin, holding me steady by my arms.

"Will you be okay to stand on your own?" He studies my face with tender concern, and my chest becomes a squishy mess. "I need to get in first."

To compensate for the blush staining my cheeks, I roll my eyes extra hard. "Just get in."

Ethan gives me one last worried glance before quickly ducking inside. After a moment, he reaches his hand out from the shadows. "Okay. Your turn."

I stare down at his hand, worrying my bottom lip. I can't see his face, but he sits cross-legged with his back pressed up against the wall. He made enough room for me . . . to sit on his lap. My heart takes off in a gallop. It would be much too easy to settle my ass on his legs and melt against his broad chest. The hard part would be pretending to be immune to the effect he has on me.

"Is everything okay?" Ethan leans out of the shadows to peer up at me, and I catch sight of the bloodstain on his dopo. I'm too upset by it to feel relieved at the perfect excuse to stay off his lap.

"You're hurt." How could I have forgotten? I can't believe I let him carry me. "I don't want to aggravate your wound."

"What wound?" He tugs down his shirt far enough to show me his shoulder.

I release a sigh of relief, my stomach unclenching. A small, puckered scar is the only evidence left of his injury. He heals even faster than I do. *Thank gods.* But . . . now what do I do?

With a frustrated growl, I duck my head inside and poke lightly at his injured shoulder. He blinks and glances down at my finger without so much as a wince. I back out of the palanquin in defeat and watch him put his clothes to rights.

He extends his hand once more, arching an eyebrow. I can do this. It takes less than thirty minutes to get to Jihun's estate. Surely, I can endure half an hour on Ethan's lap without making a fool of myself. Pressing my lips into a determined line, I take his hand and step into the palanquin.

"Sorry." I turn to face the door, unavoidably shoving my voluminous skirt in his face.

"You're good." Placing his hands lightly on my hips, he guides me down onto his lap. When he speaks next, I can feel his voice vibrating against my back. "Is this okay?"

"Uh yeah." I shiver. "It's cool."

It is in fact *not* cool. It's actually *very* warm in here. And it gets scorching hot when Ethan rests his palms on my thighs. I can't even yell at him to put them on his own thighs because my ass is currently occupying that real estate. In the tight confines of the palanquin, he doesn't have anywhere else to put his hands, unless I make him raise them in the air like I have a gun trained on him.

It's fine. I'm fine. Everything is fine. I sit with my back straight so I don't snuggle into him like he's my favorite recliner. *One minute down, twenty-nine more to go.*

"You can relax," he grits out, frustration threading his words.

"I *am* relaxed," I snap.

The gama levitates off the ground and begins moving forward with a subtle jerk—oh my gods, we hadn't even left yet—and I tip back into his chest. I squirm frantically to regain the one-inch space between our bodies.

"Stop," Ethan rasps, clamping his hands around my waist. "You need to stop moving, Sunny."

I freeze mid-wiggle because his gravelly voice sounds more pleading than commanding. Once I'm still, I notice his hard length pressing against my ass even through the layers of fabric between us. I squeeze my eyes shut, biting back a moan.

"Ignore . . . this." His breath comes in uneven pants, rustling the hair on the top of my head. "I just need a minute."

I don't respond—not to be an asshole—but because I can't speak. My heartbeat thunders in my chest, echoing in my throat and temples. I use every ounce of my willpower not to tip my ass up and grind my aching core against his thick, steely erection. Liquid heat seeps out of me, making me slick with desire.

My nails dig into his thighs as I fight for control, but I can't stop the choked whimper that escapes my lips. I was wrong. I *can't* endure thirty minutes on Ethan's lap without making a fool of myself. I can't even last five minutes before turning into a wet, writhing mess.

"Sunny? Do you need . . ." Ethan finishes his question with a slight tilt of his pelvis. I moan so loud that I have to clap a hand over my mouth. His hands flex around my waist, and he exhales a shaky breath. "Let me help you blow off some steam, like you asked last night. It'll be purely physical."

I can't. It wouldn't be fair to him.

"I don't expect anything from you. Just . . ." He pushes open my wraparound skirt with a rough snap, then pauses, giving me time to stop him. "Let me give you this much."

Fuck. I grow dizzy with anticipation, and our coarse breaths fill the small space of the palanquin. It'll be purely physical. He said so.

I don't stop him. And when he spreads apart my petticoat, I lift my ass, urging him to pull up my underskirt. He wraps one arm tightly around my waist and grabs a fistful of the undergarment with his free hand. I whimper when he pauses again.

"I need you to say the words," he growls in my ear. "Tell me to touch you."

"Just fucking do it." My voice comes back in a rush of desperation.

"Give me the words, sweetheart." He scrapes his teeth against the side of my neck.

"Touch me." I'm begging, and I don't care. "Ethan, touch me."

"Good girl." Ethan bunches my petticoat at my waist and slides his hand over my hip onto my thigh. He chuckles when I wiggle impatiently, but he obligingly dips his hand lower, brushing the inside of my thigh with his fingertips. "You feel like silk."

My head tips back against his shoulder at the featherlight touch. He licks the side of my neck with a long sweep of his tongue and blows softly on the strip of damp skin. The shock of cool air against my hot skin sends a shudder down my spine. I bite my lip when he cups me over the last layer of undergarment.

"You've soaked through this." He pushes aside the wet fabric. I'm too far gone to feel embarrassed.

I cry out when he slides two fingers down either side of my clit. With a dark chuckle, he circles his thumb over the swollen nub, and my eyes nearly roll back.

"You're so wet. Is this all for me?" When I don't answer right away, he draws a rough circle over me, and my body curves like a bow. "Is it, Sunny?"

"Yes." There's no point in denying it when his fingers are slick with my desire. "All for you."

"Gods," he groans.

He buries his face in my neck, kissing, biting, and licking his way down. With his thumb still drawing circles of fire under my skirt, he tugs open my top with his free hand and roughly cups my breast.

I moan, arching into his touch, and cover his hand with mine. He links our fingers, and together we squeeze and knead my breast, his palm rubbing against my aching tip, until my entire body writhes with pleasure.

"You need more, don't you?" His voice is as rough as gravel.

Yes. I thrust my hips against his thumb. With a grunt of approval, he glides a long finger down my folds and traces his fingertip over my entrance. I groan, deep and long. "Stop teasing and—"

Ethan thrusts his finger inside me, and I choke on the rest of my sentence. He draws his finger out and pushes in even harder. When he picks a brisk rhythm, pumping in and out of me, I lose my mind. I pivot my hips to take his finger in deeper and whimper in gratitude when he adds a second. I tip my hips off his legs and thrust against his hand, again and again, grateful he doesn't break easily. I throw one arm behind me and grab the back of his neck, seeking purchase. My head thrashes against his shoulder.

"Fuck, Sunny." He shoves his other hand under my skirts to put glorious pressure on my clit as I ride the hand penetrating me with three fingers. "Come for me."

At his command, I scream, loudly enough to wake the dead. Ethan claps a hand over my mouth—it smells like me—and eases me down from my orgasm with the other. I slump against him, gloriously spent, and bury my face against his neck. He brushes his lips against my temple and wraps his arms around my waist, hugging me to him. Still and quiet, we catch our breaths in the shadows of the gama.

"Ethan." My throat closes up. *What have I done?* I don't have it in me to pretend like this meant nothing. "I didn't mean for this—"

"I know." His breath ruffles my hair as he nuzzles his cheek against the top of my head. "I just wanted this for you. That's all. It changes nothing."

I nod wordlessly. He's right. Even when he worships my body with love and wonder. Even when I respond to his touch like I was made for him. It changes nothing. I will always love him more than anything, and I can never tell him.

The palanquin stops in front of the Sunset Pavilion minutes later. When Miok opens the door to the gama, I look every bit the noble maiden, without a hair out of place. But on the inside, I am bruised and battered, bleeding from the heart. Ethan lets me go with a soft squeeze of my hand, and I walk away without looking back. Because I am a lie, inside and out.

CHAPTER TWELVE

"Wake up, my lady." Miok gives my shoulder a firm shake. "You will be late to the meeting."

"What meeting?" I croak and yawn into my hand. "What time is it?"

"It's long past sunset." My handmaiden wraps an arm around my shoulders and helps me sit up on the sleeping mat.

"What day is it?" Sleep clings to my mind like cobwebs.

"I dressed you in that hanbok this morning," Miok says kindly.

I glance down at myself, and the memories of the day chase away the last traces of sleep. *Ethan surprising me with a picnic. Ethan getting shot in the shoulder. Ethan setting my body on fire. Ethan getting past my defenses despite my best intentions.*

When I got back to my room at the Sunset Pavilion, I crawled under the blanket without changing and let the oblivion of sleep claim my tired body and soul. I toy with the idea of going back to sleep. I might prefer oblivion over what I'm about to learn at the meeting.

"They are waiting, my lady," my handmaiden says, interrupting my skittish thoughts. "You don't have far to walk since the meeting will be held here tonight."

At Miok's gentle but firm urging, I reluctantly get off my ass and make my way to the meeting. But my jaw promptly hits the floor when I step out to the semi-open main hall. It faces a serene courtyard with a lily pond, surrounded by flowering shrubs in countless shades of pink. The sight never fails to steal my breath. Except tonight, I don't spare it even a passing glance because every ounce of my attention is snagged by Jihun, Hailey, and Jaeseok, who look like they walked off the cover of *Vogue*.

What in the name of . . .

Jaeseok looks ridiculously hot in a fitted white tux and a black dress shirt, sitting propped against a wall, with his wrist dangling off a bent knee. Hailey's fishtail gown must have been poured onto her because it clings to her every curve, and the fabric shifts and glimmers like molten gold as she restlessly paces the floor. As for Jihun, he carries off his classic black tux like tuxedos were invented with him in mind. He somehow manages to look dashing—yes, I just used the word *dashing*—even as he sits like an uptight suhoshin, cross-legged in front of a square table with his back impossibly straight.

"Why didn't anyone tell me there was a dress code for this meeting?" I mutter, frowning down at my wrinkled hanbok.

"Sunny," Hailey cries and envelops me in a lung-collapsing hug, squeezing a grunt out of me.

"Uh, hey." I awkwardly pat her waist because she has my arms pinned to my sides.

"They told me you were impaled with a wooden stake." She crushes me harder.

"I'm okay," I manage to wheeze in reassurance.

"It was more like a wooden pole," Minju says unhelpfully. I hadn't seen her sitting in a corner with her nose buried in a book. "Jo Danbi had girthy forearms."

"I'm going to *kill* her," Hailey snarls, while simultaneously nuzzling her cheek on top of my head like I'm a cuddly puppy.

"Get in line," Ethan drawls as he walks up the stone steps to the main hall, looking impossibly handsome in a pristine jade green dopo. After a fleeting but heated glance my way, he settles down across from Jihun at the table.

My body gets some wildly interesting ideas from that look—like summoning a palanquin *posthaste*—but I resolutely ignore them and untangle myself from Hailey's death grip.

"Were you able to leave your quarters without anyone's notice, Your Highness?" Jihun murmurs.

"Yes." Ethan gives him a curt nod. "But we don't have long before someone realizes I'm gone."

"Okay then. Now that everyone is here"—I wave my hand to encompass the three suhoshins—"can somebody tell me why . . ."

I'm interrupted by the flap of powerful wings as Captain Seo lands lightly in the courtyard. *"Now* everyone is here."

"Lucky us," I mutter with such wimpy sarcasm that I almost sound sincere. *Who even am I?*

I shoot Jihun a narrow-eyed glare for not telling me about Captain Seo. His shoulders shift in a barely perceptible shrug, but a hint of a grin plays around his lips. That traitor wanted me to be wary of her so she could keep me on my toes. It may, or may not, have made my training more effective, but it was a dick move regardless.

Before I can decide whether or not to break his perfect nose, Jihun looks at Seo Cheyun. "Were you followed?"

"That's why I'm late." Her lips twist in annoyance. "The Council of the Suhoshin is getting suspicious of our extracurricular activities. I had to shake one of their minions."

"It was only a matter of time before they caught on that there's more to our mission—especially General Bak," he says grimly. "Captain Seo, will you debrief us on the assassination attempt?"

"Cadet Cho has more insights to share than I do." Captain Seo tips her chin at me, then sits down to Jihun's right.

Is she publicly deferring to me? I turn to her with a questioning glance, and she gives me a nod of confirmation. She does want me to take this one. That doesn't jibe with the arrogant, implacable captain I've come to know and loathe.

Well, she hasn't been a *complete* asshole lately. She is arrogant and implacable, but she is also fair and loyal. I wouldn't go so far as to say I like her, but I might admit to a pinch of grudging admiration. I nod back at her and take a deep breath.

"By the looks of his clothes and weapon, the assailant was a hunter from the Kingdom of Mountains, not a trained assassin. He had deadly aim, but he didn't have deadly intent. I think that's the only reason Ethan got away with an arrow in his shoulder." I clench my fists to steady my voice. Even though the hunter hurt Ethan, he didn't deserve to die. "The male was already remorseful when I chased him down. But when he saw Ethan with the golden axe and the silver axe, he became downright distraught. He somehow recognized him as the Prince of Mountains."

"According to legend, the Spirit of Mountains gave the golden axe and the silver axe to a woodsman, worthy of ruling the Kingdom of Mountains," Minju explains. "The people of the Kingdom of Mountains believe that only the true heir of Mountains—someone with honor, integrity, and compassion—can bear the legendary axes."

I guess everyone in this realm, like in the Mortal Realm, grew up listening to "Golden Axe, Silver Axe." Except their version carries more significance than the quaint Korean folklore. No wonder the hunter became distraught.

"The assailant saw the axes and realized he'd been sent to kill the true heir of Mountains." I rub my pounding temple, wishing I could crawl under my bedding and sleep this whole nightmare away. "Before we could stop him, he s . . . stabbed an arrow into his own throat. As he bled out, he begged for forgiveness. He tried to explain that he wouldn't have come if he'd known who he was, even . . . even though his children were starving."

"That poor hunter. Someone took advantage of him because he and his family were destitute and hungry." Hailey's eyes spark with anger. "Only the worst kind of coward would do something like that."

Furious murmurs of agreement ripple across the room. My eyes seek out Ethan, because we know his father is that coward. His expression doesn't change, but his hand fists on top of the table. I want to rush over and hug him until the rigid lines of his back relax. But I'm held back by more reasons than I can count on one hand.

"You said the assailant was a hunter from the Kingdom of Mountains." Jihun brings the discussion back on track, and I belatedly realize my slipup. No one other than Minju and Ethan know about my magic gi goggles. "I understand you identified him as a hunter from his clothes and weapon, but how can you be sure he was from the Kingdom of Mountains?"

I raise my eyebrows at Minju. I don't mind sharing with the class, but she's more careful about revealing my powers than I am. She pinches her lips to the side, then nods, coming to a decision.

"Sunny can discern which life source we originate from." She drops the bomb so matter-of-factly that it feels anticlimactic.

"What?" Jaeseok sits forward so fast that he rebounds slightly. Maybe it wasn't anticlimactic for everyone. "How? And just to be sure, *what?*"

"I can see the colors of the life forces." I take the last seat at the table, across from Captain Seo, with Ethan and Jihun on either side of me. "The hunter's gi was green."

An awed sort of silence descends on the room. I welcome the distraction, even though it's over my weird, no-one-but-me powers. I just . . . Grief isn't an emotion I often allow myself to feel. But lately, it's as though the walls that protected my heart for over a century are cracking and crumbling. I feel *too* much, *too* often. I need a break from the emotions I don't want, like mourning the death of a hunter I didn't even know. I exhale slowly and force myself to relax.

"That's fire," a disembodied voice says in my head, scaring the shit out of me. "Can you see *my* gi? Is it the same color as my hair?"

"Draco?" I rise to my knees, scanning the dark courtyard for blue scales. I can't believe they are frolicking in the moonlight in their dragon form. "Come out this instant."

I cringe as soon as the words leave my mouth. *Eww.* I sound like a naggy parent. But the teenage dragon spirit emerges from the shadows of a bejeweled tree, with their hands stuffed in the pockets of their jeans. At least they had the sense to shift back to their human form.

"What are you doing here?" Jihun manages to convey cool displeasure without sounding naggy. I should work on that.

"I'm here to help." Draco climbs the stone steps and sits with one leg dangling off the raised floor. "I can contribute more than just my dragon scales."

"It's too dangerous," Jaeseok protests, earning a shocked glance from me.

I never suspected him of being the overprotective type. Then again, he did try to throw down with a dragon to protect Minju—except he is now trying to protect said dragon. Either way, I stand corrected. The dokkaebi is definitely the overprotective type.

"Don't forget that Draco fought at our side at Heaven Lake," Ethan says with quiet authority. "Haven't they earned their place in this meeting?"

Draco stretches his arm out and points at Ethan. "That's on god."

"Are they on the queen's list too?" I lean toward Jihun, and his entire body tenses. I give him a *what the hell* look.

"Yes." Jihun rubs his forehead as though he feels a headache coming on. "Everyone here is on her list."

"While we're on the subject"—I glance around the room—"what do we call *everyone*?"

"The suhoshins here have been sworn in as the prince's royal guards," Jihun suggests.

"His Royal Guards." I nod slowly. "That works."

"What about me?" Draco grumbles.

"Do you want to be an honorary royal guard?" I coo like those ladies who gush over cute babies at the checkout line. "Would you like a little sticker badge that says *Junior Royal Guard*?"

I snort when they flip me off, but they do have a point. Ethan and I aren't royal guards either, but we are very much a part of this team. And somewhere along the way, our endgame stopped being about protecting Ethan and became about protecting the worlds.

"The Sentinels. We stand watch against the eternal darkness," Minju says, her nose still buried in her book. The rest of us hum and nod.

I glance around the room and grin. "That works."

"Welcome to the Sentinels," Captain Seo says, addressing Draco. "I assume you heard everything we discussed so far."

"Bruh." The teenager gives her a hooded glare.

I'm not sure whether that means a *yes* or a *no*. The captain frowns like she doesn't know either. When our eyes meet, we shake our heads with baffled laughter. *Holy Twilight Zone.* Did we just *share* a moment? We hastily look away from each other, implicitly agreeing to pretend it never happened.

"If I may continue, Sunny confirmed that the hunter was from the Kingdom of Mountains." Jihun picks up where we left off. "Why would the King of Mountains send an untrained assassin to kill the prince?"

"The tyrant spread the lie that the queen died during childbirth along with the baby." I remember the hunter's last words. *Forgive me, my queen.* "But his people are still loyal to the queen. If they find out that her son is alive, they will rise up to put *their* prince on the throne."

"And that's the last thing the king wants," Ethan says darkly. "He must not trust anyone in his court, which is consistent with our spy's intel about his mounting paranoia. That must be why he blackmailed a poor civilian to do his dirty work."

"Once the king finds out the hunter failed, he will want someone else to finish the job." Captain Seo sits forward. "His spy in the Kingdom of Sky is bound to make a move soon, either to smuggle in another assassin from the Kingdom of Mountains or to recruit one from here."

"Do you really think they might try to recruit someone from the Kingdom of Sky?" Hailey asks. "Isn't that too risky?"

"They might be desperate enough to try, and there are poor, vulnerable people to manipulate in every kingdom." Captain Seo turns to Minju. "Did you find any foreign magic traces on the hunter's body?"

"Not enough to identify anyone," the historian says with a frustrated sigh.

"But we can narrow it down to people from the Kingdom of Mountains, right? There can't be that many of them here." Draco arches their brow with the supreme arrogance of youth. "I mean, who else would spy for the King of Mountains?"

"While that is likely the case, it's too early to rule anyone out." Jihun crosses his arms over his chest.

"Conversely, not everyone from the Kingdom of Mountains should be pegged as potential spies," I add. My roommate Hana and her twin Duna are from the Kingdom of Mountains. It wouldn't be fair to suspect them based solely on their birthplace. "With that said, I wouldn't think twice about putting the homicidal psychopath Jo Danbi at the top of the list."

"Wasn't she exiled a day *before* the assassination attempt?" Jaeseok cocks his head to the side.

"Maybe the hunter came through when they opened the portal to send her back to the Kingdom of Mountains." Hailey shrugs. "He would've only had to stay hidden for a day."

"Jo Danbi knew she would be exiled for what she did." Captain Seo drums her fingers on the table. "She could have alerted the King of Mountains to send the assassin right away."

Jihun hums. "That is a possibility."

"Is the portal guarded?" I ask, trying to fill in the missing pieces.

"Yes, at all times. Every kingdom has two portal keepers on alternating shifts." Jihun's eyebrows dip into a frown. "The keepers of the Kingdom of Sky are formidable warriors with powerful magic. No one can get past them unless they allow it."

"I spoke with both of our portal keepers this afternoon." Captain Seo shakes her head. "Neither of them had anything unusual to report."

"Then how did the hunter come into the Kingdom of Sky?" I don't want to question anyone's loyalty, but something is not adding up. "Are the portal keepers . . . trustworthy?"

"Keeper Bae has been a faithful servant of the Kingdom of Sky for over two hundred years," Captain Seo says with an edge in her voice. "And while Keeper Choe is relatively new, he comes highly vetted."

"It was an honest question." I hold out my palms. "You know, Occam's razor and all that."

"Uh." Draco raises their hand. "Is that the one that says the simplest answer is most often correct?"

I confirm with a nod, but Captain Seo's scowl deepens. "Betrayal is hardly a *simple* answer."

Jihun intervenes. "Whatever the case may be, we *will* find the answers. In the meantime, either Captain Seo or I will be at your side at all times, Your Highness."

"I'm not *completely* helpless," Ethan says drily. "I can protect myself, especially since I have better control of my powers now. Didn't you say you were pleased with my progress? Or was that flattery?"

He's been training with Jihun? *Thank gods.* I'm so relieved that I can't even be mad that neither of them told me. Ethan will be formidable once he masters his magic. He *will* be powerful enough to stop the King of Mountains when the time comes.

"You are becoming proficient at magic—faster than I could have hoped—but that arrow pierced you." Jihun's lips press into a grim line. "You aren't invincible against their weapons. We cannot risk your safety."

"My findings on the trace magic were inconclusive, but I had better results analyzing the hunter's arrows." Minju finally looks up from her book and rises to her feet. "I know how the arrow pierced the prince."

"How?" Ethan leans forward.

"The arrowhead has traces of properties similar to the sacred ashes." Minju paces the floor, gathering her thoughts. "When Dangun, the truest manifestation of the god of Mountains, abandoned the Realm of Four Kingdoms, he left behind a tombstone in the highest peaks of the divine mountain, Shinsan. No one knew what the tombstone signified, but the people of the Kingdom of Mountains understood that it was sacred."

"Wait." My brows furrow. "What?"

According to Korean folklore, Hwanung, the god of earth, came to rule the human world with the blessings of his father Hwanin, the god of the heavens. One day, a bear prayed to Hwanung, entreating him to turn her into a human, and the god of earth heard her prayers. The bear became a beautiful woman, and Hwanung fell in love with her. They married and had a son named Dangun, who went on to establish Gojoseon, the ancient kingdom that evolved into Korea.

The takeaway from that folklore is that Dangun was the son of a god and had excellent pedigree—it was human bullshit made up to deify and legitimize him as the first king of Gojoseon.

Besides, be it ancient history, folklore, or an amalgam of the two, the man is long dead by all accounts, if he ever existed in the first place. *Wasn't he?*

I shake my head. It doesn't matter. Dangun can go on my ever-growing list of *Things Sunny Doesn't Know* for now. I have no time for distractions.

"Never mind. Just . . . how is the arrowhead similar to the sacred ashes?" I nudge the historian back on track.

"The tombstone." Minju doesn't add *obviously*, but her frown says it for her.

"The tombstone?" I frown back at her, thoroughly confused. "What about the tombstone?"

"Dangun is the god of Mountains. The tombstone he left behind likely holds magical properties similar to the sacred ashes Samshin Halmeom entrusted to you." Minju reclaims her seat on the floor. "In his desperation to remain on the throne, the King of Mountains must have desecrated the tombstone to create weapons from it. Weapons strong enough to kill the prince."

"He is going through so much trouble to assassinate his own son." Ethan scoffs bitterly. "I should apologize for being so difficult to kill."

I sit on my hands to stop myself from reaching for him. My heart constricts painfully. It's not fair that I can't even offer him this small comfort.

"How do we keep Ethan safe from those weapons?" I croak.

"Uh." Draco flicks their blue bangs out of their eyes. "Me?"

"You?" I stare at them, blinking slowly, and they shake their head as though I'm a bigger idiot than they'd thought.

"I meant what I said. I have more to offer than my dragon scales," Draco continues in comprehensible English. "*But* for this particular problem, my scales are obviously the best solution."

"Your dragon scales are meant to protect *you*, Draco. Every scale I take from you will make you that much more vulnerable." Ethan levels a steely gaze at the teenager. "I can't risk your safety to protect myself. You've sacrificed enough."

I glance between Draco and Ethan. I don't want either of them to be vulnerable. Ethan is the one with the assassins after him, but I can't bear the thought of exposing the kid to even the slightest danger.

"Let me make this simple for you. You have two options." Draco starts counting off on their fingers. "One: Take a few of my scales. I won't be mad if you wear them under your shirt, even though they're too pretty to hide. Two: Paint arcane words of power on your back to make yourself invincible. Fair warning, though. I might have to kick your ass if you choose option two. So maybe that means you only have one option to keep yourself safe."

The hard set of Ethan's jaw softens as he looks at the kid. "I'll take option one. Thank you, Draco."

I open my mouth to protest but close it without saying anything. I have to respect Draco's decision. I don't like this one bit, but I'm also proud of them. They're such a good kid.

"Bet." Draco grins as the rest of the room release their breaths in relief. "I'm glad I don't have to kick your ass."

Jaeseok stretches his arm out and lightly smacks the back of Draco's head. "Show some respect, little dragon."

"What?" Draco grumbles. "Ethan is the prince of a kingdom I'd never heard of, in a realm I didn't even know *existed* until a few weeks ago. I would rather fawn over Prince Michel of Rouleme."

"Who?" Hailey crinkles her nose.

"Exactly." The teenager laughs. "You should look him up, though. Prince Michel is hella hot."

"And *our* prince isn't?" Minju blurts, then promptly turns into a tomato. Jaeseok's expression turns sullen, while the rest of us chuckle.

"Don't be sad." Draco pats the dokkaebi's shin with a *so sad* pout. "You have aura."

Jaeseok shakes their hand off with an affectionate scowl. "Brat."

"If you're all finished, why don't we move on? I know it's not an easy topic, but we need to address the elephant in the room." Ethan squeezes my hand, but I snatch it out of his grasp. He means to lend me strength, but I much prefer avoidance.

A heavy silence falls as my eyes jump between Jihun, Hailey, and Jaeseok in their red-carpet attires. My avoidance mechanism helped me block out the whole thing for a blessed half an hour. I can't ignore where they went today anymore, but I still give it my best shot.

"There's a dragon and a fox," I quip, "but I don't see any elephants."

But when Jihun's solemn gaze falls on me, I give him a stiff nod, even as every muscle in my body tenses to reject what he's about to say. I close my eyes and force myself to breathe.

"We found Daeseong."

CHAPTER THIRTEEN

"Can you repeat that?" I croak. "I wasn't listening."

The old instinct to run rams against my skull, trying to break free. I shove my hand through my hair, digging my fingers into my scalp. I can't run. I have to stop Daeseong. I have to *fight*. But I'm not ready. The rune on my back burns, feeding on my fear and panic, and I'm tempted to give in to the bloodlust just to stop being afraid.

"Where is the dark mudang?" Ethan places a heavy hand on my bouncing knee. He thinks I'm strong enough to handle this. He doesn't want me to be kept in the dark about Daeseong. I appreciate the gesture of respect, but he cannot be more wrong.

I am not strong enough. For any of this.

"Los Angeles." Hailey waves a weary hand at her haute couture attire. "We infiltrated a fundraising gala held by the Jaenanpa, ostensibly to raise money for the preservation of Korean American cultural heritage."

The blood drains from my face, down my arms, to the tips of my cold fingers until I feel sapped of life. The dark mudang alone is terrifying. But Daeseong allied with the Jaenanpa is so much worse. I'm hardly breathing. My heart rate slows to a bare minimum, like my body is pretending to be dead.

"What were they actually doing?" Captain Seo asks.

"Promising rich, bored humans a taste of real magic." Jaeseok grunts in disgust, then pulls out a cell phone from his pocket. "Daeseong headlined the dinner show, and I taped his finale."

The Jaenanpa is made up of corrupt, bloodthirsty shamans. They torture and kill beings of the Shingae to usurp their magic. The upper echelon of the faction brainwashes their minions into a frothing frenzy by convincing them they're fighting for equality between the human world and the Shingae. There is nothing more dangerous than a mob of psychopaths who believe their atrocities are justified.

"We don't get cell service in this realm, but hopefully, magic and technology will play nice enough for me to show you this video." Everyone gathers around the table as Jaeseok coaxes his cell phone to play back the video. "The humans wanted a taste of true desolation, so Daeseong drenched the ballroom in darkness for them. If I could just get this damn thing to work . . ."

The dokkaebi succeeds after five tries, and even then, the footage freezes every other second and the audio is half static. It's a small miracle that the cell phone is working at all in a realm with this much magic.

I glance at Draco, who sits alone at the edge of the raised floor. They don't talk about it much, but they've said enough for us to know that the Jaenanpa killed their father. The magic thieves kill their prey in the most gruesome, horrific ways possible. They believe suffering makes the magic stronger. If Draco witnessed even a glimpse of what they did to their father . . .

I flinch when the humans in the recording gasp in horrified delight, and a tremor starts deep in my chest. I squeeze my eyes shut, trying to get my mind and body under control.

Draco must want vengeance. I don't blame them, but I can't let them get blood on their hands. I can't . . . My teeth clack together as the shivering spreads to my limbs. I think I'm going into shock.

The dark shamans are as evil as they come, but they're still human. The kid doesn't understand that taking even a single life will alter them forever—and not for the better. Draco . . . The edges of my vision go black, but I fight to stay alert.

"They make me sick to my stomach," Jaeseok growls, putting away his phone.

"Why did Daeseong join forces with the Jaenanpa?" Draco snarls, their gorgeous young face set in stone. "He doesn't need their help."

"Maybe he does." Jihun's voice sounds far away, even though he's sitting right next to me. "He might need their help to continue his mission for the Amheuk because he hasn't fully recovered from his standoff with Sunny. She nearly destroyed him at Heaven Lake."

"Do we know his next move?" Ethan asks, then glances over at me. His eyes widen in alarm, and he gives my thigh a reassuring squeeze. Or is he seeking reassurance? Either way, I barely feel his touch.

"Not yet," Hailey says, "but we're watching him closely."

"We'll keep everyone updated," Jaeseok adds.

"Thank you, Lieutenant." With an arm around my waist, Ethan tugs me to a stand with him. My legs are practically useless, and I sag against him.

"What's wrong with her?" Jihun leaps to his feet. "Sunny—"

"My lord." Jihun's man of business bows from his waist, standing at the bottom of the steps to the main hall. "General Bak will arrive at his estate shortly."

"Shit." Ethan shifts me in his arms and ducks his head to meet my eyes. "Sunny, I can't tell you everything will be okay, but we'll face whatever lies ahead *together*. You will not be alone. I swear to you."

I try to nod, but I'm trembling too hard. I hold his gaze, wanting him to know I believe him.

"You must hurry, Your Highness." Jihun gently extracts me from Ethan's arms.

"Take care of her, Captain," Ethan says flatly, dropping his hands from my body. Then with a tender smile, he tucks a strand of hair behind my ear. "I'll see you soon, Sunny."

I make a soft, whimpering noise when he walks off into the night. With Ethan gone, my fear threatens to drown me. At least the word of power stopped burning across my back. Or maybe I just can't feel it anymore because my body is shutting down.

"She's in shock." Minju lightly presses her fingers against the base of my throat. "I can barely feel her pulse."

"Her hands feel like ice." Hailey clasps both my hands in hers.

"We need to get her to her room." Captain Seo's concerned expression hardens when Jihun picks me up in his arms. "You, Captain Song, have much to do. Minju, Hailey, and I can take care of Sunny. Remember your duty to the prince comes first."

"And the prince bid me to take care of her," he responds in an implacable voice, then turns to Jaeseok. "Lieutenant Cha, I need you to work with Draco on the protective armor for the prince. I trust you don't need a reminder of the urgency."

"No, Captain. We're on it," Jaeseok says with rare solemnity, then drapes an arm across Draco's shoulders. "Come on, kid."

"Wait." The teenager shrugs off the dokkaebi's arm and peers closely at my face. "Sunny? You're going to be okay, right?"

I don't know how I manage to speak through my chattering teeth, but I whisper, "Yes."

"G . . . good. That's good." Draco's voice breaks. "You better not be lying."

"Take care, Sunny." Jaeseok lightly ruffles the top of my head and leads the kid away from the Sunset Pavilion.

"Minju, please examine the hunter's body again." Jihun shifts me in his arms, drawing me closer. I shiver and burrow into him. "I know you're thorough, but there might be clues to the spy's identity you missed the first time around. It might be something unexpected."

"Of course, Captain." Minju lays a cool hand on my forehead. "It's okay to be scared, but you're the strongest person I know, Sunny."

"Lieutenant Gim." Jihun moves toward the sliding doors to the inner hallway. "I need you to—"

"I got it, Captain," Hailey assures him. "Go. She needs to lie down and get warm."

"You'll pull through this, Cadet Cho." Captain Seo's no-nonsense voice fades as Jihun carries me back to my room with long, urgent strides.

Miok is there, waiting to open the door for us. She turns down the covers, and he lowers me onto my bedding.

"We need to raise her legs," he says in a lost voice I've never heard him use before.

"She will be all right." Miok places a rolled-up blanket under my legs before tucking the duvet tightly around me. "So will you. Courage, my lord."

"She's our only hope against Daeseong, and she's . . . afraid." He takes a shuddering breath. *Oh Jihun.* "It's too great a burden for one person to bear, Bomo."

Miok was Jihun's nursemaid? No wonder he trusts her. She helped raise him.

"But you cannot bear it for her." Miok's voice is warm and steady. "You have your own burden."

Burden? He does have a lot of responsibility on his shoulders.

"The prince, Sunny . . . and everyone on the queen's list," he says haltingly. "Why does it have to be us?"

"We will know in time, my lord." Miok kneels near my head and pours something into a small teacup. "This is honey tea. It will help warm her up."

"Here, let me." Jihun raises me partway up, with my head cradled against his chest, and takes the tea from Miok. "Drink, Sunny."

I sip obediently, and the warm liquid chases away a bit of the cold. I take another sip. The honey tastes fragrant, like chrysanthemums. Suddenly desperate for air, I suck in a heaving breath and immediately start coughing up my lungs.

"Easy there," Jihun croons, rubbing my back and holding me tighter against him.

"I will leave you then," Miok says quietly and gets to her feet. "Please let me know if you need anything."

"Thank you, Bomo," he murmurs.

"Of course, my lord." She slips out of the room, closing the door behind her.

"C . . . cold," I stutter. "So . . . cold."

"I know. It's the shock." Jihun lowers me onto the sleeping mat again and wraps the comforter around me. "You'll warm up soon."

But I'm shaking so hard that my limbs convulse wildly. With a muttered curse, he stretches out on top of the bedding and hauls me flush against him, clamping his arm and leg over me. Even through the thick blanket, the heat of his body seeps into mine, and the steady beat of his heart soothes my frayed nerves. He holds me tight until the violent shivers ease into faint tremors, and my mind clears and quiets.

Daeseong is back. I breathe through my nose until my heart rate slows, becoming strong and steady. The demented megalomaniac is back—and he's booking party appearances. Welcome to my tragicomedy life. Fittingly, I want to laugh and cry all at once. *Fuck this.* My hands curl into fists as strength returns to my body. There's nothing I can do but destroy Daeseong, because the alternative isn't an option.

I lick my dry lips and taste salt on my tongue—salt and something distinctly male. As the shock finally recedes, I realize my face is buried against Jihun's neck, with my mouth pressed against his throat. I feel his Adam's apple work as he swallows. Somewhere between shaking like a leaf and settling into calmness, I must have plastered myself against him.

"I . . . I'm okay now," I squeak as I try to scramble away from him.

"Hush." His growly voice skitters over my body. "Let me hold you while I have an excuse."

"Jihun . . ." I protest weakly, but I quiet in his arms.

"Just this once," he whispers.

I nod against his neck, a single tear slipping out of the corner of my eye. I knew, didn't I? Deep down, I must have known Jihun had feelings for me. But I refused to see that it was more than basic attraction and harmless flirtation for him. And I . . . didn't dissuade him. Not enough.

From the beginning, I wanted to lean on him. His steadfast strength always made me feel grounded and secure, and I couldn't bear to lose that. I was so afraid of losing his friendship that I ignored his lingering touches and tender glances. But friendship goes both ways. If I really am his friend, then I can't let him throw his heart away on me.

With a long, shaky sigh, he presses his forehead against mine. "Sunny, I—"

"Don't," I say sharply and lean back to look into his eyes. "*Please* don't say anything you can't unsay."

"Why?" Pain bleeds into the single word. "I'll take even a fraction of your heart, Sunny. All I want is a chance to keep you safe. A chance to make you happy."

"Jihun, you deserve someone who can offer you their whole heart." Tears stream down my cheeks. "I care about you too much to see you sell yourself short."

"Love isn't a transaction." He chuckles softly. "I don't care if I sell myself short. You can rip me off all you like."

"B . . . but you can't keep me safe," I blurt, pulling at straws. Maybe I can dissuade him from giving me his heart by appealing to his sense of honor. "Your loyalty lies with Ethan. He comes first for you. If both he and I were in danger, you would have to save your prince, not me. How can I be h . . . happy, knowing I'll always come second?"

"Yes, I would save the prince." He grasps my chin and lifts my eyes to meet his. "Then I would *die* with you."

A small part of me wavers. I'm tired and scared, and he's so strong and true. And if I choose him, Ethan will never know that I love him . . . I stop, appalled at myself. How can I even *consider* using Jihun to protect Ethan? This is precisely why I can't accept his generous heart. I love Ethan with everything in me. I have nothing to offer Jihun when he deserves *everything*.

"Stop." A broken sob escapes me, and my face crumples. "Don't make me break your heart. Please."

"Don't tell me what to do." With a heart-wrenching smile, he wipes away my tears with the pad of his thumb. "I will do as I see fit with *my* heart."

"You're such an asshole." I take a shuddering breath, my tears falling faster. "Contrary to what you think, you're not always right. Just this once, can't you choose to protect *yourself*? Gods damn it, Jihun. *Please.*"

He leans down to place a soft kiss on my cheek. "Good night, Sunny."

"Do not *good night* me." I raise my head to sob and blubber some sense into him, but he's already gone. I flop back onto my bedding, throwing an arm over my red, puffy eyes. "Fucking Jihun."

I ache and long for Ethan like I'm missing a vital organ. My heart breaks for Jihun, who remains loyal and generous, even when I don't deserve it. I'm terrified I won't be able to defeat Daeseong. And I'm afraid what that would mean for all of us. Yet . . . I've never felt so whole in my life.

I must have a heretofore-unknown masochistic streak. Or having people to miss, to hurt for, and to worry about makes my life mean more. It makes *me* more alive. Rather than denying that I care deeply about these people—because I'm afraid to lose them—maybe I should make it my all-consuming purpose to keep them.

THE BEAR AND THE TIGER

Long ago, in the days of old, a lonely bear loved a beautiful tiger. The tiger liked the bear well enough, but he liked very much how desperately she loved him.

The bear would have done anything to build a life with the tiger. But he wanted to be with a tiger, lithe and graceful like him, not a hulking, cumbersome bear. Still, the tiger enjoyed being adored by the bear, so he would tell her, "If only we were the same."

The bear prayed every night that she and the tiger could become the same so that they could be together. Hwanung, the god of earth, appeared before the bear and the tiger, moved by her devotion.

"You wish to become human?" the god of earth asked.

"More than anything, my lord," the bear answered without hesitation.

The tiger stayed silent. He did not object to becoming human. He would be strong and handsome either way. Perhaps, the bear would become beautiful enough as a human to be worthy of him.

"Go dwell in a lightless cave for one hundred days, not a day less, eating only garlic and mugwort," Hwanung commanded. "Endure this trial, then I shall make you human."

"Thank you, my lord." The bear bowed low, determined to succeed for the sake of her love.

Although the tiger was horrified at the prospect of such hardship, he did not want to appear weak, so he bowed to the god of earth as well.

Together, the bear and the tiger entered the dark cave to begin their trial. As days stretched into weeks, the tiger could not hide his cruel and selfish nature. He claimed he could not stand another day of eating garlic and demanded the bear give him her allotment of mugwort. The next day, when the bear gathered only garlic for herself so the tiger could have all the mugwort, he roared with anger and said he wanted all the garlic, not the mugwort.

The bear endured his bad temper in silence. She believed this wasn't really him. He was suffering. But on the twenty-first day, the tiger dragged her toward the cave's entrance, ignoring her pleas to let her go.

"We're done here," he snarled. "This foolishness stops now."

"No. Please." Confused and afraid, the bear dug her heels in, and the tiger had no choice but to release her because she was stronger than him. "We cannot leave this cave until the hundred days are over. It is our only chance of being together."

"We do not need to become human to be together," the tiger purred. "Of course, I will mate with a tiger as beautiful as me, but I will allow you to serve me at my side. That should be good enough for you."

The bear stumbled back. "How could you mate with another if you love me?"

"Love you?" The tiger laughed cruelly. "You should be honored I tolerate you."

Deeming the conversation over, the tiger stalked toward the entrance, then looked over his shoulder. "Well? Aren't you coming?"

"No." She would be a fool no longer. "I am not leaving with you."

"You ugly, useless beast," he roared. "You will regret this. You are nothing without me. You will see."

The bear swallowed her tears and gathered the broken pieces of her heart to her chest. Hwanung had heeded her prayer and had given her a chance to become human. The tiger disappointed her, but she would not disappoint the god of earth. She would not throw away the god's kindness.

The first few days after the tiger's betrayal felt endless . . . hopeless. But in the days that followed, the bear came to understand her love for the tiger was born of loneliness. And she had been afraid of being alone because she did not think she was good enough. She had thought she needed the love of another to make her whole.

In the dark solitude of the cave, the bear saw that she was brave. That she was strong. That she was enough. At peace with herself, the days passed with calm swiftness, the hundred days no longer insurmountable.

Even before Hwanung appeared to her after one hundred days—even before the god of earth turned her into a human as promised—the bear already knew she was a new person. Someone brave and strong. And when she walked out of the cave on her human legs, she was still her. Someone complete and whole.

The woman named herself Ungnyeo and prepared to flourish.

CHAPTER FOURTEEN

The next morning, I'm up early and waiting in the courtyard of the Sunset Pavilion for my private cadet training—private until the bigots at the Suhoshin headquarters calm the fuck down about the "scary" gumiho.

Captain Seo strides into the courtyard and gives me a curt nod in greeting. I cringe with shame because I'm relieved she showed up instead of Jihun. Cowardly or not, I'm not ready to face the stubborn male after last night. I wouldn't know whether to punch him or tackle hug him. Who am I kidding? I'm definitely leaning toward punching his pretty face. *Then* I'll hug him and blubber all over him. *Shit.* I'm a hot mess.

"You need to hone your defensive skills," the captain says in her uppity British accent. She doesn't bother asking if I'm feeling better, and I prefer it that way. I don't need reminders of Jo Danbi and my bout of levitation.

I need to focus on becoming one formidable badass. I used to think I already was one, even without my gumiho, but Captain Seo showed me that I have a long way to go—especially since I can't rely on my gumiho when I face Daeseong. I need opposable thumbs to wield the sword of light.

The dark mudang is back. We know his exact location. The only reason we're still in a holding position—and not taking advantage of Daeseong's weakened state—is because I'm not ready yet. I can't wield the Yeoiju with any amount of control, but I'm not giving up. I'll use every day I have left to master its powers. In the meantime, though, I need to be prepared to vanquish the dark mudang with the sword of light.

Captain Seo is dressed in a gray dobok that distinguishes the suhoshin instructors from the cadets, but she isn't wearing the long outer vest belted over it. She obviously sacrificed fashion in favor of mobility. My stomach dips. She even tied a black headband across her forehead to keep the sweat out of her eyes. *Gulp.* The captain isn't messing around today.

"Ready?" She has her hands clasped behind her back, with her legs about shoulder width apart. It is *the* most arrogant fighting stance I have ever seen. But instead of annoyance, an odd feeling bubbles up in my chest—admiration.

"I was born ready . . ." My lips tug down in a mortified grimace. *Did I really say that out loud?* I've lived for one hundred and thirty-two years, but the '80s seem to have made an indelible mark on me. I raise my fists and angle my body. I can't unsay what I said, so I lean into it. "Ready to *rumble.*"

The captain strikes even before she finishes rolling her eyes. She shoves my right shoulder back, which opens up my torso, and I glance down reflexively in irritation. No one likes being shoved in the shoulder. Then I double over when she buries her fist in my stomach—thank gods my injury is completely healed—and I see stars when her knee connects with my face.

"For fuck's sake," I groan with a hand on my nose. I wiggle it to make sure it's not broken.

"What did you do wrong?" She's not even out of breath.

"I made my upper body vulnerable *and* took my eyes off my opponent," I grit out.

"And?"

"And what?" I throw my hands up.

"And you were too slow," she says evenly. "At the very least, you should've been able to avoid being kneed in the face."

"The blow to my stomach took the wind out of me." My pride hurts more than anything. "I wasn't prepared for you to plant your extraordinarily knobby knee in my nose. It's like having one giant brass knuckle plowed into my face."

"*That* is your biggest problem." She punctuates her sentence by poking at the air in front of her. "You don't anticipate your opponent's next moves."

"Are you saying I should learn how to *read minds*?" I channel Draco's teenage scorn.

"I'm *saying* that you have a decent brain. Use it." A flush spreads across her cheeks and the bridge of her nose. I've never seen the captain this close to losing her temper. It's actually a refreshing change from her icy aloofness. "I've seen you let your mind recede and have your body take over during sparring matches. I'm not denying that you're a skilled fighter. But if you rely solely on your speed and technique, it makes you reactive, and you'll end up dancing to your opponent's tune. You need to *think*. Be three steps ahead of your opponent, consider multiple scenarios and outcomes, and never be caught unawares."

"Like I said, mind reading." I understand what she's saying, but I can't resist the urge to nudge her over the edge.

"No, *not* mind reading." To my disappointment, she takes a calming breath. "Think of it more like choreography. You determine the flow of the fight from your very first move."

"What if my opponent"—I flick a hand toward her—"makes the first move?"

"The same rules apply. Defend yourself in a way that will let you set up your next attack three moves down. Be patient. Take back control."

"Okay," I concede with a shit-eating grin. "Why didn't you say so in the first place?"

A vein pulses in her forehead before she kicks out at me. And I'm ready. I block her kick with my forearms and crouch to sweep her other leg out from under her before she gets both feet back on the ground.

Captain Seo breaks her fall by rolling into it, then lightly jumps to her feet. I think she'll be pissed, but a corner of her lips curls into a smirk. "Not bad, Cadet Cho. That head of yours is more than a decoration, after all."

My middle finger twitches, but I don't push my luck. She's the head instructor of the suhoshin cadets, and whether I like it or not, I am a cadet. And like it or not, the captain deserves my respect.

"The whole thinking thing . . ." I trail off, then try again. "I used to plan, strategize, and *re*plan every minuscule aspect of my life. I couldn't let anything take me by surprise and risk being found by the Shingae. But when everything blew up in my face, I . . . stopped thinking.

"The last few months, all I've done is *react* to one thing after another. I forgot to *think* because I was too busy panicking. I flailed around, trying to deal with everything, but it only got harder and harder to stay afloat.

"Just because I'm done running doesn't mean I can't choose *how* I face my problems," I say quietly. "It's time I stop to think again. Plan, strategize, and replan. I need to take back control of my *own* fucking life."

"I didn't think this lesson would be this easy," Captain Seo murmurs.

"All I needed was a refresher." I grin at her, feeling lighter than I have in months. Nothing has changed—except me. My problems are still there, but I won't be taking wild swings in the dark anymore. "So what's next?"

"I'm not sure." The captain purses her lips in a bemused expression. "I didn't plan any other lessons for today."

"What do you say we work on sword fighting? As you know, the last sword practice was cut short due to . . . unfortunate circumstances. I don't want my technique to get rusty in case I need to wield the sword of light—as a backup plan if the Yeoiju decides not to cooperate." I tap a finger to my temple. "Thinking ahead, you see."

"Thinking ahead? Or chickening out?" She arches an eyebrow. "Still intimidated by the Yeoiju, are you?"

"Fuck you." Respect only goes so far. I won't let her call me a chicken, whether or not it's true.

Her only reaction is to raise her eyebrow a millimeter higher. "Do you know how long the sword of light is? How heavy it is?"

"No," I grumble. "Have you forgotten? There is no sword of light. Jaeseok and Draco are close, but they haven't forged it yet."

"You raise a good point." Captain Seo nods slowly, crossing her arms over her chest.

"Yes, I do." I nod as well. "But just to make sure I know *you're* thinking what *I'm* thinking, maybe you should tell me what that point is."

The captain's reserve falters as laughter spurts out of her. "Like you said, the sword of light hasn't been forged yet, which means you can still ask them to make it to the same specifications as your hwando."

"You're *right*." Wielding my short sword is second nature to me. If they can forge the sword of light to match my hwando, then that will be a game changer. I have very few advantages against Daeseong. I'm grabbing this one with both hands. "I *did* raise a good point."

"Very well then." Captain Seo summons her twin swords with a flick of her wrists. "Shall we *rumble*?"

"You're hilarious." Without giving myself a chance to hesitate, I summon my hwando from my room and sigh in relief when the hilt pushes against my palm. And this time, I launch the first attack.

I don't win every spar, but I win enough to satisfy us both.

"Let's take a break," Captain Seo pants, untying the band around her head and wiping her face with it.

"Oh thank gods," I say in a heartfelt groan, not bothering to act tough. We spent the last two hours proving to each other that we are both *scary* tough.

It feels great to stretch out in the shade of Sunset Pavilion's main hall, my feet dangling off the side of the raised floor. Captain Seo is decidedly less starchy than before, but not enough to splay out next to me. Instead, she sits with her back against one wall, with her legs stretched out in front of her.

We both sigh after gulping down ice-cold sikhae, a sweet fermented rice punch, that Miok brought out for us. I'm ridiculously happy when the empty bowl immediately fills again. I have the bowl halfway to my mouth when Jaeseok rushes into the courtyard and heads straight toward us.

"Just the dokkaebi I was looking for." I smile, remembering I need to tell him about forging the sword of light to match my hwando. "Do you—"

He cuts me off in a strained voice. "There has been another assassination attempt."

I jump down from the main hall, my heart pounding in my throat, and rush toward Jaeseok. Heat radiates from the rune on my back, and I barely stop myself from shaking him by the shoulders. "Is Ethan okay? Where is he? Tell me."

Captain Seo takes a firm grip on my arm and maneuvers me out of the dokkaebi's face. "Let's give him a little room, shall we?"

"The prince will be okay." Jaeseok rubs a hand down his face. "He took a dagger to his back, but it didn't hit any major organs. And he started healing as soon as they pulled out the dagger."

"How the hell did this happen?" I roar, fiery bloodlust wrapping around me. "Weren't you and Draco supposed to make him a protective vest?"

"They haven't had much time," the captain says steadily. "Sunny, remember your lesson. *Think.* Don't let the word of power control you."

I take a shuddering breath and draw my mind away from the pulsating heat of the rune. Jaeseok and Draco have had less than twelve hours to work on the vest. More importantly, Ethan is okay. We have time to figure everything else out. That means I need to calm the fuck down.

"Jihun was guarding the prince because the vest wasn't ready." Jaeseok sounds exhausted. He must've stayed up all night, working on the protective armor. "If he wasn't there, it would've been a lot worse."

"Sorry, Jaeseok." A shiver runs through me as the heat dissipates from my back. "Where is Ethan now?"

"General Bak made a big stink over it, but Jihun thought it best to bring him here." He shrugs. "I mean, the assassin got to the prince at the general's estate. It makes sense for us to move him where we can guard him better."

"Did they catch the assassin?" I ask over my shoulder, already walking toward the east wing. It's the securest place on the estate.

"Yeah, they caught him." Jaeseok hisses a frustrated sigh, matching his stride to mine. "But this one unfortunately killed himself as well."

"Come on," the captain says from my other side. "Captain Song will have more information."

We find Ethan and Jihun in the newly rebuilt study. Ethan is wearing his hanbok with the jeogori open at the front. I see the white cloth bandage wrapped around his chest and nearly lose my shit again. *Think, Sunny.* He's sitting up, and his coloring doesn't look too bad.

"What? You haven't healed yet?" I quirk an eyebrow at him to hide my relief.

"Nearly." Ethan waves a dismissive hand at the bandage. "I just didn't want to get blood on another shirt. It probably stopped bleeding already."

"Don't get cocky now." I sit down next to him at the conference table. "You were sloppy enough to get hurt in the first place."

"An assassin threw a dagger *at my back*," Ethan protests. "I don't have a rearview mirror mounted on my forehead."

"Not *a* dagger." Jihun holds up three fingers from across the table, and I belatedly notice the bandage around his biceps. "He threw three daggers at you."

Ethan glares at him. "You're not helping."

"So you *flung* yourself in front of the other two daggers?" I squawk at Jihun, then turn to Ethan. "Did he fling himself in front of the other two daggers?"

"Yes." Ethan sighs. "He leapt into their trajectory, swinging his sword to block them. But the daggers were already too close, and one sliced him in the arm."

"Now *that* is sloppy." I glare at Jihun, both grateful that he protected Ethan and pissed that he got himself hurt.

"The assassin was fast," Jihun mumbles sheepishly, then a shadow crosses his face. "Gods, he was just a kid."

"A . . . kid?" Captain Seo looks stricken.

"Yes, even younger than Draco," he says, anger sparking in his eyes. "The Suhoshin have a file on him. He's a street urchin turned pickpocket. The kid had the fastest hands in the Kingdom of Sky. We're lucky his aim wasn't as good."

"That poor kid," Ethan whispers. "He looked so scared."

"He takes care of his grandmother, who isn't doing well, and his younger sister." Jihun's hand fists on the table. "The Suhoshin tried to help him, but he was too proud to accept our help. We should have tried harder."

"The King of Mountains and his underlings are recruiting desperate commoners—poor folks who need to provide for their families." I grit my teeth, fighting my anger and grief. This problem needs cold logic, not bloodlust. "But why the suicides?"

"I don't know." Ethan wipes a hand down his mouth, his fingers digging into the sides of his face. "The kid . . . he said he didn't want to die, but before I could tell him he didn't have to . . . he swallowed something, some kind of lethal poison. He was gone too quickly for us to even try to help him."

Ethan is hurting. Ben died in his arms before he could do anything to save him. I have to stop myself from reaching out for him, tightening every muscle in my body.

"The king must be threatening these people with their families. They have to either succeed or die. If they come back alive, the king will make their families suffer," Captain Seo says with clipped anger. "They are forcing the assassins to kill themselves so we won't be able to question them."

"But they made some mistakes this time around." I cross my arms over my chest. "The assassin was recruited in the Kingdom of Sky, which confirms the spy is nearby. And I presume the daggers had the same trace elements as the arrowhead?"

Jihun nods. "Minju is analyzing the daggers to be sure, but there's no other explanation for how the dagger pierced the prince."

"And whatever poison the kid . . ." My voice breaks, and I dig my fingers into my upper arms. "The poison must have left traces in his body. If we find the source of that poison, it might lead us to the spy."

"And *there's* the person who can get to the bottom of that." Jaeseok tilts his chin toward the sliding doors as Minju and Hailey rush into the study.

The historian bows distractedly at Ethan before taking a seat at the table, with Hailey at her side. She blinks owlishly as all heads turn toward her. "What?"

"We would like to hear what you found out," Ethan answers patiently. Even a few weeks ago the Prince of Mountains would've demanded the information, but my Ethan's warmth and kindness seem to have smoothed the ragged peaks of the prince's pain and anger. "About the daggers and the poison."

"Of course." Minju straightens in her seat. "As expected, I found traces of what we presume is Dangun's tombstone in the daggers. But my findings on the poison are not as straightforward."

"How so?" Jihun rests his forearms on the table. "Is it a common poison that anyone can acquire?"

"No." Minju shakes her head. "The opposite. It is only used for a singular purpose, and it is almost impossible to acquire."

Jaeseok purses his lips. "What kind of poison only has one specific purpose?"

"Sayak," the historian says.

"Sayak?" I draw back in shock. "You mean the poisonous elixir used during the Joseon Dynasty? The Kingdom of Sky still has capital punishment?"

"Unfortunately, yes. It's the only kingdom in the realm that hasn't repealed the antiquated law. The old guard apparently make progress virtually impossible in the Kingdom of Sky." Hailey continues more gently at my horrified expression. "For what it's worth, the elixir is prepared with an analgesic and sedatives in addition to the lethal poison, so it's supposed to be quick and painless."

"Well, the assassin only took the lethal-poison part of the sayak, so it was quick but not painless," Minju corrects, earning a death glare from Hailey.

"Was it arsenic?" I ask, the arcane rune pulsing on my back.

"No, that's what the humans used. It takes something stronger to kill the Shinbiin." Minju taps her chin with a finger, clueless that my bloodlust is dangerously close to surfacing. "It's the root of a rare plant even deadlier than doksacho. Only the royal physicians know where to harvest it and how to process it."

"Sunny, I know this is upsetting, but the Kingdom of Sky isn't utterly hopeless." Hailey sends me a worried glance. "There haven't been any executions for over a hundred years."

"Exactly." Minju slams her palms down on the table, and Jaeseok jumps. "Even a royal physician wouldn't have ready access to the poison because it's been so long since sayak was used. Any poison from a hundred years ago would have lost its potency. And processing the poisonous root is a long and arduous process. It can't easily be hidden, especially if you're a royal physician residing in the Celestial Palace."

"But if anyone could have gotten their hands on the poison, it *is* the royal physicians," Captain Seo murmurs.

"It doesn't make sense, though." Jihun rubs his temples. "Why would the spy use a poison that might expose them?"

"It's guaranteed to kill and kill fast." Minju confirms my suspicion.

"The spy wanted to make sure the boy died before he could talk. They're becoming reckless because they're afraid of being discovered." I exhale slowly, fighting my fury, and force myself to think. "Besides, the spy might not be a royal physician at all . . ."

"Just someone close to one," Ethan says, finishing my thought. "Their connection to the physician must be tenuous enough for them to risk using that poison."

"Even so, they might try to tie up loose ends—" Captain Seo gasps and pushes to her feet. "They're going to kill the royal physician who provided the poison. We need to find them before it's too late. Lieutenants?"

Hailey and Jaeseok are right behind her as the captain heads out of the study. I'm torn between chasing after them and staying close to Ethan.

"He'll be safe here," Jihun assures me.

"Are you sure about that?" I ask archly. His eyes narrow into intimidating slits, and I cock an eyebrow at him in challenge. "Both of you are bleeding."

"She has a point." Ethan grins wryly at Jihun and turns to me. "We'll be extra careful. We wouldn't want to risk your wrath."

"No, you wouldn't." I glare at both of them to show I'm dead serious. "Look out for each other."

I run out of the study and catch up with the suhoshins heading for the Celestial Palace. I tighten the belt around my dobok and put both males firmly out of my mind.

It's time to kick some spy ass.

CHAPTER FIFTEEN

I've said it once, and I'll say it again. The Celestial Palace is creepy. Something about the life force shimmering inside it feels *off*. And now that I know about my unique affinity for perceiving gi, it's not as easy to wave it aside as paranoia. Even my gold-medalist avoidance muscles aren't up for the task.

"Where are we going?" I catch up to Jaeseok, who trails a few steps behind Captain Seo and Hailey.

"The royal apothecary," he says. "I doubt we'll find our physician conveniently hanging out at the apothecary, but there are plenty of lower-ranking personnel who might point us in the right direction."

My stomach drops when we arrive at the apothecary to find it surrounded by a horde of palace guards. Captain Seo holds out a glowing white emblem to the guards at the entrance, and they immediately come to attention.

"Have you come to investigate the murder, Captain?" one of the guards asks. "I wasn't aware the Suhoshin had been notified."

"Of course they have. A murder in the Celestial Palace is a serious matter," Captain Seo says smoothly, without outright lying. The Suhoshin had to have been notified of the palace murder, even though the captain didn't come in response to it. She arches her eyebrow with enough disdain to make the guard pale. "Do you plan on letting me through to do my job?"

"My apologies, Captain." He and the other palace guard hurriedly step aside, and Captain Seo and the rest of us march in as though we own the place.

I can't get over the opulence of the palace grounds. The hanok buildings in the apothecary stand under sloping tiled roofs and arching eaves that glow like the liquid gold of dawn. Even the wooden lattices of the doors and windows are stained in every shade of the sky.

We pass a large courtyard, where various apothecary personnel huddle nervously in corners while others sit in the main hall, staring blankly into space. Then we walk into the regal pavilion housing the main apothecary. The medicinal herbs hanging off the rafters, their musky scent infusing the air, send a wave of nostalgia through me. My mother was a gifted healer, and much of my childhood revolved around gathering and drying herbs.

Several officers stand questioning a weeping group of uinyeos in apron overcoats and rectangular fabric headwear. But what catches my attention is the body on the ground in a shadowy corner of the apothecary. She is—was—also a nurse like the ones being interviewed. She looks so young and small. I kneel down next to the body, and a scowling officer heads toward me. But he halts and comes to attention when Captain Seo raises her identification emblem.

"Did you sweep the area?" she demands.

"Yes, Captain," the officer answers crisply.

"Finish interviewing the witnesses in the courtyard," Captain Seo orders. "My team and I need privacy to conduct our investigation."

I don't hear the rest of the conversation as my ears start ringing. The uinyeo was poisoned by . . . She still holds an intact jumeokbap in her fist, with one bite taken out of it. The rice ball has crumbled pieces of roasted seaweed in it, and—I lean down to sniff it—it's seasoned with toasted sesame oil.

Dread runs down my spine. I'm overreacting. Jumeokbap is a popular on-the-go meal and snack. Just because Hana brought me rice balls once doesn't mean she has anything to do with this murder. But my face goes numb with shock when I see the edge of a sage green fabric peeking out of the uinyeo's apron pocket. I slowly tug the handkerchief free and run my fingers over the embroidery in the corner. *Lilacs.* Hana's favorite flower.

"No," I breathe. "It can't be her."

"What is it?" Captain Seo asks, crouching down next to me.

"The handkerchief . . ." I pull myself together and say quietly, "My roommate, Shim Hana, uses the same one."

She takes the handkerchief from my limp hand and peers at the lilacs. "Does she have this embroidery on hers as well?"

"Yes, lilacs," I croak. "It's her favorite flower."

"Such intricate embroidery on a handkerchief is not at all common." Captain Seo hands the handkerchief back with a concerned glance at me. "Are you close to Cadet Shim?"

I shrug stiffly. As a general rule, I don't let many people get close to me. But I can't deny that Hana, my sweet, guileless roommate, and Haesan, the marshmallow masquerading as a mountainous merman, have gotten under my skin. *Damn it all to hell.* They're my friends. Hana is my friend.

How can she be the spy? Even with her handkerchief in my hand, I can't believe that my roommate is capable of blackmailing a kid with his family to . . . to force him to end his own life. And I can't believe that Hana would kill an innocent uinyeo to cover her tracks. It'd be easier to believe that the sun rises in the west.

Hailey leans down to squeeze my shoulder. I don't have the heart to shake her hand off. I actually have to fight the urge to cover her hand with my own and take the comfort she offers. In the end, I compromise by giving her hand a swift pat, then shoving it off my shoulder.

"The cadets should be at the training courtyard, right?" Jaeseok asks quietly.

"Right." Captain Seo rises to her feet. "But they'll break for lunch soon."

"We better find Hana before those gluttons clog up the hallway, stampeding to the mess hall," I mutter as I stand, pocketing Hana's handkerchief.

I head for the doors without meeting anyone's eyes and keep walking even though the rest of my group stops to speak with the officers waiting in the courtyard. The suhoshins know the way to their headquarters and cadet training yard. And I need a moment to myself.

The evidence points straight at Hana, but my instincts scream against it. Am I letting sentimentality get the best of me? Am I getting *soft*? Through my confusion and frustration, cold fear snakes up the back of my head. This is exactly why I don't let people get close. I can't let my roommate off the hook because it hurts to think about her betrayal. I can't let our friendship—if it's even real—cloud my judgment.

I use my preternatural speed to get to the Suhoshin headquarters ahead of my companions, but I slow down at the entrance in case going superfast counts as using magic. I can't afford to openly break the no-magic rule and risk Jihun being punished in my stead. So I settle for speed walking to the cadet training yard.

I crack open the back door to the courtyard and search for Hana, but she isn't there. I can't even find her twin sister, Duna, to ask about her whereabouts. With a frown tugging at my brows, I head inside the cadet barracks. She has to be here somewhere. I hurry down the hallway and turn the corner, but I skid to a halt and double back, then plaster myself against the wall. My heart pounding in my chest, I peek around the corner.

"Don't—" Hana stretches her hand toward the other end of the hall, but I only catch the barest glimpse of a retreating shadow. She shifts as though to follow the shadow—maybe a would-be assassin she tried recruiting—but I step out from behind my corner.

"Hana, stop." I hold out my hands. "I need to talk to you."

"Hi, Sunny," she says distractedly, glancing down the opposite end of the hallway. "Now isn't a good time. Can we chat later?"

"No." I take a careful step toward her, and she takes a skittish step back. *Damn it.* I don't want her to bolt. "Hana, it has to be now."

"But—" Hana's eyes widen when Captain Seo, Hailey, and Jaeseok round the corner.

"Cadet Shim, we have some questions . . ." the captain begins in her least threatening tone, but it's enough to send Hana running down the hallway.

"Hana, stop." I chase after her, with the suhoshins close behind me. "I won't let anyone hurt you."

I realize I mean it. Hana can't be the killer. I know this in my gut. She's involved somehow, but I'm going to protect her—as soon as she stops running. But she kicks out a latticed window and leaps through it.

"For *fuck's* sake." I groan. "That's it."

I don't hold back. I jump headfirst through the window, roll onto my feet, and chase after Hana in a burst of exhilarating speed. Captain Seo will just have to vouch for me so Jihun isn't punished. It is a justifiable infraction due to extenuating circumstances. I watched a lot of *Law & Order.* Either way, I have to catch Hana before she lands herself in more trouble.

"Will you *stop* running?" I pursue my roommate past the cadet barracks and across the training yard. The other cadets have cleared out. Must be lunchtime.

Hana clears the walls enclosing the courtyard in a running leap. I launch myself into the air to follow her and barely make it over, my toes nicking the top of the wall. *Damn tiny human body.* Captain Seo and Hailey take to the air to continue their pursuit, and Jaeseok vaults over the wall, planting his hands at the top, then gracefully swinging his legs over.

"She's heading for the Donggul," I shout at him over my shoulder.

"Why the hell would she go there?" The dokkaebi makes a face even as he runs flat out to keep up with me.

I don't bother answering his rhetorical question and focus on closing the distance between Hana and me. She runs straight for the shadowy hanok and spins around to face us with her back to the entrance. Jaeseok skids to a stop beside me, and Captain Seo and Hailey land on my other side.

"What . . . what do you want?" Hana is shaking hard enough for her teeth to chatter.

"Why did you run?" the captain asks instead of answering, but my roommate's eyes stay glued to mine.

"An uinyeo was killed at the royal apothecary today." I falter. "It looks like she was poisoned. She . . . she died with a half-eaten jumeokbap in her hand."

"All this because I brought you some rice balls once?" Hana scoffs, but her bravado seems forced. "That's really stretching it. Don't you think, Sunny?"

"Hana." I withdraw her handkerchief from the sleeve of my dobok and hold it out so the lilac embroidery faces her. "The jumeokbap was wrapped in this."

"No." My roommate gasps and turns a shade paler. "No, that can't be."

"I know you didn't do this." I take a step toward her. She turns her face away from me, scrunching her eyes shut. My heart cracks a little. "I know you, Shim Hana. You're not a killer. I just need to talk to you. You can help us find the real killer and stop them before they hurt more people. They're cruel and ruthless. They blackmailed a child into taking his own life."

Her eyes snap open, her expression slack with shock. "No . . ."

"Hana, it's okay." I take another step toward her.

"Stop," she screams. "Don't come any closer. Or I'll . . . or . . . I'll release the monster in here."

"No," the suhoshins shout in unison.

"Monster?" I gape at Hailey, Jaeseok, and Captain Seo. "What monster?"

"Speaking of it—even *thinking* of it—will summon it," Hailey says faintly. "Please, Hana. You need to calm down."

But my roommate laughs with more than a hint of hysteria, tears streaming down her face.

"Gods damn it, Hana." My stomach clenches with dread.

"I'm the killer," she whispers, no longer laughing. "I killed that uinyeo."

"You're lying." I shake my head. "Why are you doing this?"

"I am the spy from the Kingdom of Mountains." Her voice turns eerily calm.

"No," I spit vehemently. "You are *not* the spy."

"Sunny." Jaeseok wraps his hand around my wrist, holding me back from storming up to Hana. "Let her speak."

"I se . . . seduced Keeper Choe to open the portal between the Kingdom of Mountains a . . . and the Kingdom of Sky," Hana says haltingly.

"No." This time my voice is nothing more than air. Only the spy could know that.

"I befriended that lonely uinyeo and used her." Her face is oddly without affect, as though her mind is somewhere else. "I tricked her into making the sayak for me. I told her one of the guards raped me."

Hailey gasps at my side, and my knees nearly give out. Jaeseok steadies me with an arm around my shoulders.

"We need you to come with us, Cadet Shim," Captain Seo says. "We need to confirm what you've told us before we come to our own conclusions."

"I am the spy. Why won't you believe me?" Hana screeches, her calm shattering. "I did it all. *I* am the spy."

"Okay. I'll believe you for now." I nod at Jaeseok, and he drops his hand from my shoulder. I take small, measured steps toward Hana. "Since you're the spy, you have to go with the suhoshins. It's only fair, right? Now, come away from that door."

"No, I don't think I'll go anywhere with the suhoshins," she says in a childlike voice. "They found me out, and that's the end of the story."

"It's not the end of the story." I swallow past the lump in my throat. "It isn't, Hana."

"I'm so sorry, Sunny." Her smile is achingly sad. "You're a good person. Don't forget that."

"You're s . . . so full of shit," I stutter, freaked out by her sad smile and sweet words. "But you can try to . . . to convince me."

"Promise me you won't be sad. This isn't your fault." One tear, then another slide down Hana's round cheeks. "You're always so hard on yourself. Give yourself the same grace that you give others. Okay?"

"I don't know what you're saying—"

"Goodbye, Sunny." Hana pulls something out of her sleeve and stuffs it into her mouth.

"What is that? Spit it out. Gods damn it, Hana. *Spit it out.*" I'm at her side in a blink, shaking her by the shoulders. But Hana's eyes roll back in her head, and she crumples in my arms. "No, no, no. Open your eyes, Hana."

I lower her to the ground, but I keep her in my arms. To my relief, her eyes flutter open and focus on me. She smiles, the corners of her eyes crinkling. "I'm so happy I got to be your friend."

"Me too. I don't have many, so—" My voice gets caught in my throat, then my tears rain down on my friend's face . . . even on her open, unseeing eyes. "So I need you to stay my friend for a long, long time."

"Sunny." Hailey rubs my back. My whole body shakes to hold back my sobs. "It's okay to cry."

Jaeseok pats the top of my head with a heavy sigh. "I'm sorry."

"We need to take her back to the headquarters so Minju can confirm the cause of death," Captain Seo says evenly. "Based on the speed the poison took effect, it must be sayak, but we need to make sure regardless."

For some reason, her practical words give me the most comfort, and the flow of tears slows to a trickle. But I can't make myself let go of Hana. I slide her eyes closed with my hand. She still feels warm. Tears cloud my vision again, so I look away from her face and down at her lifeless body. I notice the sage green handkerchief in her fist for the first time. I tug it free from her hand and stare down at the embroidery. I suck in a sharp breath and bring the handkerchief closer to make sure I'm seeing it right.

"Please take good care of her," I tell Captain Seo, laying Hana on the ground. "She was a good female."

"Where are you going?" Hailey asks as I get to my feet.

I grip the handkerchief tightly against my chest. "I have some business to take care of."

"But Sunny . . ." Jaeseok trails off as I walk away.

The flowers embroidered on this handkerchief aren't lilacs. They're *lilies*. Duna's favorite flower.

THE LEGEND OF UNGNYEO

While Hwanung had granted the bear her wish to become human, who she became had been entirely up to her. Her serene beauty, her sharp intellect, and her quiet strength had all come from within her. And the woman she became brought the god to his knees.

Hwanung had been born the son of Hwanin, the god of the heavens, but he could not turn his gaze away from earth. The humans, so fragile yet so full of hope, had enchanted him, and he had longed to guide and protect them. So Hwanin, knowing his son would never be happy in the heavens, had granted Hwanung permission to rule earth and its people.

He had descended to Mount Baekdu onto the Sacred Tree of Life, Shindansu, to establish the divine city of Shinsi. Hwanung, the god of earth, ruled the humans with wisdom and compassion, never forgetting the trust his father, Hwanin, had bestowed on him.

But when Hwanung set his eyes on Ungnyeo, he understood his true purpose. The god of earth took the form of a man so that he could be with the woman he loved. All he had to do was convince her to spend a lifetime with him.

"Be my wife," he said.

"I am not worthy, my lord," Ungnyeo demurred.

"It is I who is unworthy, but I will do anything to deserve you," he vowed. "Let me earn your love and trust."

"On the peak of Mount Baekdu, there are wild and beautiful flowers called *the cloud*." She lowered her eyes. "If you bring me a cloud blossom every day for one hundred days, you will have my love and trust."

Every day, Hwanung climbed Mount Baekdu. Every day, his frail human body threatened to give out. But every day without fail, he brought his beloved a cloud blossom. Giving up was not an option, for he could not imagine life without Ungnyeo. On the one hundredth day, Hwanung crawled the last of the way toward her.

"Ungnyeo, I cannot accept your love and trust, because I will not live to see the sunset." He held out the cloud blossom with a trembling hand and collapsed to the ground. "I cannot take your heart with me to the next life, my love. Hold on to your heart, and give it to someone who is worthy of you."

"Once I foolishly believed myself to be in love with another, but that was not love. I know what true love feels like now. From this moment on, my heart will beat for no one but you, my lord." Ungnyeo fell to her knees, tears flowing down her perfect cheeks, and she collected her tears into a bowl filled with the cloud blossoms he had given her. "When the time comes, I will follow you on to the next life, but that time is not today. Drink, my lord, so that I may be your wife."

Hwanung sipped the cloud blossoms steeped in Ungnyeo's tears and felt life return to his veins. The god of earth rose to his feet with his bride.

"Ours is a love destined by the heavens," he said, cradling her hands. "I will love you until my dying breath."

"And I will love you in this life and the next," she vowed.

In a union of earth and the heavens, Ungnyeo and Hwanung became wife and husband. Their love remained true, and they were blessed with the birth of their son, Dangun.

Dangun became the first king of Korea and ruled for nearly two thousand years until he ascended to Shinsi as the god of Mountains.

CHAPTER SIXTEEN

I shift into my gumiho form just outside the Suhoshin headquarters and run into the streets. The seonnams and seonnyeos shriek and clutch their chests as they scramble out of my way, their exquisite, glowing faces twisted into caricatures of terror. But I'm too busy to give a fuck.

I need to find Shim Duna. If I were a spy from the Kingdom of Mountains, where would I run when the shit hits the fan? To the portal to the Kingdom of Mountains, of course. I speed up and become a white blur in the streets, which seems to calm the seraphim's fragile sensibilities. *An unidentifiable white blur is fine. But a nine-tailed fox spirit? Heavens forbid, she might give us cooties.* Damn bigots.

When I reach the busy main street, I slow down to take a sweeping glance around me. The merchants sell their wares in stalls on either side of the wide street. The nobles strolling by stop to peruse the tempting array of colorful silk, baubles, and trinkets. The commoners walk swiftly with purpose, heading for their favorite produce stalls to buy what they need rather than what they want.

The females already finished with their shopping hurry home, with round, low-rimmed baskets filled with fresh vegetables on their heads. But those vegetables go flying in the air with shrill screams from their bearers as this new batch of shinbiins, commoners and nobles alike, notice the nine-tailed fox standing in the middle of the street. *Shit.* Where the hell is the portal? A shadow falls over me, and I glance up at the sky.

"Follow me," Captain Seo says and flies off.

"Thank fucking gods," I say into her mind as I take off running. "I almost caused a stampede."

The captain is too high up to answer me, but she doesn't have to say it. *What did we learn about thinking before acting, Cadet Cho?* My gumiho can't make the *yeah, whatever* face, so I settle for an annoyed huff.

Even in the air, Captain Seo can't keep up with my gumiho, and I slow down to keep pace. *Faster. We need to go faster.* Shim Duna might get away if we don't hurry, but I don't know where I'm going, so I meekly follow the captain into a small forest.

Captain Seo lands behind a stand of trees and presses up against the wide trunk of the nearest one. When I skid to a stop beside her and shift back to my human form, she turns to me with a finger on her lips. I nod and back close into the tree. Then I steal a quick glance around the trunk, only one eye peeping out.

Duna stands beneath an open pagoda, holding the hands of a handsome seonnam wearing a shimmering silver robe, with silky black hair that falls halfway down his back. Honestly, he's even prettier than Duna.

"Who is he?" I whisper to Captain Seo.

"Keeper Choe," she says, keeping her eyes trained on the couple. "And that's Shim Duna, right? I've never seen her smile that sweetly to anyone."

"That's because she's pretending to be her twin sister. Hana tried to take the fall for her sister, saying *she* seduced Keeper Choe to open the portal, but it had been Duna all along." I grit my teeth. "Duna framed her own sister to save her neck, and Hana *still* died to protect that lying bitch. Leave Shim Duna to me."

Captain Seo holds my gaze for a second, then nods curtly. "I'm going to have my hands full with Keeper Choe. The portal keepers are formidable warriors."

"I have a feeling you can take him." I give her a wry smile. Before she can respond, I step around the tree and charge toward the pagoda, bellowing at the top of my lungs, "Shim Duna. Your ass is mine."

"Hell and damnation," Captain Seo curses as she rounds the tree and sprints alongside me. "*Think*, Sunny. Don't forget to *think*."

Keeper Choe throws off Duna's hands and leaps over the railing of the pagoda. With another curse, Captain Seo changes course to pursue the pretty keeper. I close in on the pagoda, and Duna backs into one of the pillars with a hand pressed to her chest. I climb up the steps and stop in the middle of the platform. I don't dare get any closer, because I might choke the life out of her before I get my answers.

"Hana is dead," I say bluntly, aiming to rattle her. Even though she framed and betrayed her twin sister, Duna must have some feelings left for poor Hana.

She goes deathly still, all the blood leeching out of her face. "You killed her?"

"Me?" My laugh is cold and jagged. "No, *you* killed her. Even though you betrayed her, Hana confessed to being the spy to protect you, then she took the sayak in your handkerchief. She gave her life for you."

"No." Duna shakes her head and begins sobbing into her palm. Just as the sharpest edge of my anger dulls with sympathy, she drops her hand, and an ugly, hateful smile twists her face, even as tears continue to streak down her cheeks. "Hana was a *stupid* bitch. She tried so hard to be sweet and likable, always showing me up. Now look, she's making me look bad even in death."

Shock leaves me speechless for a heartbeat, then a low growl rumbles in my chest, heat flaring from the rune. "Hana didn't need to make you look bad. That's one thing you do well on your own."

"Shut up, shut up, shut up," Duna shrieks, her eyes bulging. "You didn't know her like I did. Hana thought the world revolved around her and monopolized everyone's attention. She even fooled our parents into loving her more than me. She tricked *everyone* into loving her more."

"Hana always put up a kind and caring front, never losing her smile. What a fucking phony." Spittle gathers at the corners of her lips, but she doesn't seem to notice. "She made me *sick*."

My stomach roils with nausea. Shim Duna isn't sullen and reclusive. She's insane. She is literally foaming at the mouth.

"Hana took *everything* from me. I wanted to become a suhoshin for as long as I can remember, but *she* was chosen instead. It wasn't fair. I'm stronger and smarter than her. It should've been me. But she wouldn't even let me have the one thing I wanted more than anything. She couldn't stand the thought of *me* being the special one for once.

"I bet she was surprised when I got selected as a second cadet from our family. You see, the King of Mountains saw something special in me. He asked me to be his spy while I trained as a cadet in the Kingdom of Sky. I, of course, accepted.

"But Hana kept hounding me about how I became a cadet when only one member of the family could be chosen. I told her the king granted my petition to be chosen as a second cadet, but she didn't buy it. I was telling the truth, though. I just left out the part that the king added a condition for granting my petition."

"So the 'something special' he saw in you was your desperation?" I drawl.

"Hana thought you were hilarious. I have to agree with her on that one. *Desperation*. How funny." Duna laughs with unhinged delight. "But no. The king saw my loyalty and determination. His Majesty saw that I would do *anything* for him, even help kill his unworthy son."

The word of power burns across my back, and I take a step toward her, my nails and incisors elongating. But by sheer force of will, I stop myself from advancing any farther. Thankfully, Duna doesn't notice that I'm *this* close to ripping her throat out.

Good. I need to keep her talking—the more tea she spills, the better. She must've been dying to boast about her importance to someone. Narcissism is the downfall of all villains, it seems.

"How did the King of Mountains know that his son was in the Kingdom of Sky?" I rasp past my tight throat.

"His Majesty didn't know at first. He merely wanted me to keep a close eye on the high officials of the Kingdom of Sky. The king is as meticulous as he is wise." Duna sighs, her face shining with maniacal worship. "But a few days ago, a powerful friend of his informed him that his worthless son lives and is hiding in the Kingdom of Sky."

A *powerful friend*? What powerful friend?

"Why does the king want his son dead?" I demand, focusing on Duna again.

Is staying on the throne really that important to the King of Mountains? More so than his family? I still can't wrap my head around it. I would give anything to have my mother back. *Anything.* How could a father be willing to kill his son for power?

"Because the deceitful prince is stealing the king's magic for himself," Duna hisses.

I cringe at her vehemence. What does she mean, stealing the king's magic?

"His Majesty didn't explain that to me, of course. I need no explanation to do his bidding. But I saw the scar on his palm myself," she brags in a conspiratorial whisper, preening at her own cleverness. "The King of Mountains has the power of invincibility. A *cut* should be impossible. It can only mean that the ungrateful prince is stealing that power for himself, leaving the king vulnerable. I would want to kill anyone who steals something so vital to me too."

The King of Mountains has the power of invincibility. Does Ethan's invincibility mean the Kingdom of Mountains already accepts him as its true king? It's too much to process right now. But the takeaway I *can* process is that his father is vulnerable. He *bleeds.* Could that be the mysterious illness that our spy meant?

"Like I said, I'm smart. Even the king can't keep secrets from me." She giggles, then scowls the next second, her mood as volatile as a tempest. "A son who lacks filial piety is worse than an animal. The traitor must be stopped. I was so close to finishing my mission, but my stupid sister ruined everything, as usual.

"She didn't stop being suspicious of me even after we came to the Kingdom of Sky. The conniving bitch kept an eye on me. Today, she found the sayak in my room and confronted me. She started nitpicking about where I was this night or that morning. She went on and on about how I was risking my chance to become a suhoshin by breaking the rules.

"Hana didn't have a clue that I was already much more important than a suhoshin. I was the king's own spy. I couldn't stand her lording it over me when she was nothing compared to me, so I told her everything. I finally put her in her place. I mean, what was she going to do?"

"You weren't worried about her turning you in, were you?" The bloodlust pounds under my skin. I don't know if I can control the rune for much longer. "You masqueraded as Hana when you did your dirty work. You always planned on framing your sister."

"I told you I was the smart one." Duna smirked.

"The only reason I'm not going to kill you . . . yet . . . is because Hana was my friend, and she fucking *died* to protect you," I snarl. "How could you not realize how lucky you were to have someone who loved you unconditionally? Someone who loved you enough to die for you?"

"The only thing she loved was her perfect little self." The entire left side of Duna's body twitches, like she's fighting an internal battle. "She wanted to die a martyr. It had *nothing* to do with me."

Shim Duna was loved, but she's too twisted and bitter to see it. She never allowed her sister's love to envelop her, making her safe and content. It is so tragic. She did it all to herself, but I can't help but pity her.

"You're coming with me," I say in a tired voice. We need to put her away and focus on our next steps. If what she said is true, the King of Mountains might be preparing to welcome the Amheuk into the Realm of Four Kingdoms.

"Come with you?" She cackles. "You're not very smart, either, are you?"

I narrow my eyes at her. "I don't want to hurt you."

"Don't worry." She pouts with feigned sympathy. "You won't get the chance."

She throws a handful of dirt over her shoulder, and a piercing green light spills out from the pillar behind her. What the hell? I step toward her even as I shield my eyes with my hand. Then the light is gone . . . and so is Duna.

CHAPTER SEVENTEEN

I spin around the empty pagoda, blinking away the halo left behind by the beam of light. I rush to the railing and scan the woods on the off chance that Shim Duna is hiding behind a thick shrub. No such luck. She's really gone. I can't believe I let her get away. The word of power flares on my back.

"Fuck my life." I slam my fist against the pillar that swallowed Duna, the wood splintering from the impact. I inhale slowly through my nose to suppress the bloodlust.

"That's what he said." Captain Seo pushes Keeper Choe toward the pagoda. He stumbles precariously, his arms trapped at his sides by invisible binds. It takes me a second to realize the captain meant what she said literally.

The keeper's long hair is a disheveled mess, and his robe is slashed and torn, with blood staining the silver fabric. He's a far cry from the fairy-tale seonnam who stood beneath the pagoda moments ago. And his sullen frown makes me wonder why I ever thought he was pretty.

"Did you grant Shim Duna passage to the Kingdom of Mountains, Keeper Choe?" Captain Seo demands, surmising the situation. Other than a faint bruise along her jawline, she looks no worse for wear. She gives the keeper another shove in the back. "That's twice you've broken your cardinal duty."

"Duna?" The corners of his mouth turn down in distaste, causing the split in his lip to reopen, and he hisses in pain. "What has she got to do with any of this?"

"Oh, that's right. He thought he was helping Hana all along." I stomp down the steps of the pagoda. "I hate to break it to you, buddy. But you've been dallying with the evil twin."

"I didn't give you permission to speak to me, gumiho." Even defeated and bound, he sweeps a repulsed gaze up and down my body.

"How *dare* you speak to her that way?" The captain's voice is soft and terrifying.

"It's okay. I know his type." I step into his personal space and say to his face, "You're just a privileged, entitled male, who is outraged at having to answer for your actions. It's called *consequence*, asshole."

"Do you know who my father is?" he says shrilly.

"Nope." I shake my head. "And I don't care to find out. All that matters is that you helped Shim Duna, a murderer and a spy, escape to the Kingdom of Mountains."

"Why do you keep saying Duna? Why would I help that surly bitch?" he yells, panic entering his voice. "I helped *Hana* because I'm in love with her. She would never harm anyone."

"Well, Duna—the one you've been opening the portal for—framed Hana for being a spy from the Kingdom of Mountains. Hana is *dead* because of her." I almost feel sorry for the keeper when his face crumples. "If you really loved Hana—if you really *knew* her—you never would've confused Duna for her."

"Oh gods. Hana is . . . dead?" Keeper Choe pales, finally grasping the gravity of the situation. "What have I done?"

"I'll tell you exactly what you've done on our walk to the Suhoshin headquarters." Captain Seo tugs on the invisible binds, and the keeper stumbles after her.

I walk next to the captain, wiping a weary hand down my face. We can deal with Shim Duna later. I won't let her get away with framing

Hana, but we have bigger problems on our hands. I have to get to Ethan and Jihun as soon as possible.

I become my gumiho, and ignoring Keeper Choe's high-pitched scream, I speak telepathically to the captain. "Shim Duna revealed something during her unhinged monologue. A few days ago, a 'powerful friend' informed the king that Ethan was in the Kingdom of Sky. That explains why the assassination attempts started when they did."

Captain Seo shoots a questioning gaze my way. She can't speak freely with the keeper blubbering on her other side.

"But . . . something else happened a few days ago." I nod when her eyes widen. "Daeseong came out of hiding. The timeline fits too well for it to be a coincidence. And if the dark mudang is indeed the 'powerful friend,' then it means the King of Mountains has aligned himself with the Amheuk."

"That fool," the captain growls. "What are you going to do?"

"We need to stop the King of Mountains before he puts the entire realm in peril. I hope Ethan and Jihun already have a plan in the works to infiltrate the Shinsi Palace."

"In case I don't see you before you leave"—Captain Seo smiles wryly—"good luck, Sunny. Don't forget to think."

With an amused huff and a quick nod, I leave the captain with her captive and sprint toward Jihun's estate. More like *spirit toward it*. I don't want to deal with the screaming shinbiins in the streets, so I run fast enough to be a white blur to them. They seemed to tolerate that better last time.

I'm miles away from Jihun's estate when I spot a shimmering silver-and-green dome over the eastern wing. Ethan's magic. Are they under attack? I have to get to them. Wind rushes in my ears as I pick up even more speed, and I reach the main gate in two heartbeats. I don't bother knocking. I leap over the high walls and run lightly across the tiled roof, jumping from structure to structure.

I drop to the ground in my human form right outside of the eastern wing—next to Jihun, who stands with his hands clasped behind his back. He doesn't even start at my abrupt appearance. The male has nerves of steel.

"What the hell is going on?" I wheeze, out of breath and sweaty.

"The prince is training. The only real solution to the assassination attempts is to stop the King of Mountains." His gaze takes in my pink cheeks and heaving chest. "What hap—"

"That's *training*?" I point toward the dome, forgetting that Jihun can't see it. "He put a protective dome over the entire eastern wing."

"You can see that?" His eyebrows rise close to his hairline. "That will take some getting used to. At any rate, I didn't realize that's what he had done. I assumed he'd widened his parameters since I got pushed all the way out here, but I had no way of knowing exactly how much his shield encompassed. Did you say the shield is shaped like a dome?"

"Yeah, it's a silver-and-green dome." I reach toward it. "It's beautiful."

"Don't touch . . . ," Jihun says, but it's too late. I've already laid my hand against it. It beats like a heart against my palm. "Are you . . . touching it?"

"Yes," I whisper, my eyes wide with wonder.

I press harder, testing its resistance, but there isn't any. My hand sinks through. The shield of gi is as thick as my forearm and slightly hotter than comfortable. But the air my hand touches on the other side is cooler than the dome. It's warm, familiar—my heart clenches—and so fucking dear. I *feel* Ethan.

"What's happening?" Jihun gingerly stretches one finger toward the dome, invisible to him. I gasp when he's thrown back more than a yard before he catches himself by digging his longsword into the ground. The barest tip of his finger had touched the shield. "Sunny?"

"I don't . . . know." I blink when the dome suddenly disappears. "It's gone. The shield is down."

Jihun runs into the eastern wing, and I follow close. We skid to a stop in front of the study to find Ethan bent over at the waist, with his hands planted on his thighs. His entire back is contracting and expanding as he fights to get air into his lungs.

"Ethan." I rush to his side. "Are you okay?"

He holds out a wobbly thumbs-up even though he can't lift his head yet.

"You might have overextended your powers, too soon after your injury," Jihun says, concern drawing his brows together. "We should conclude your training for today."

Ethan manages to tilt his head up and rasp, "I'm okay."

"Like hell you are." I throw his arm over my shoulders and bodily lift him upright. Then I drag him to the main hall and gently lower him onto the raised floor, propping his back against the wall.

"Sunny, I'm fine." This time he manages to sound more convincing, his breathing quickly evening out. "Tell us what happened."

I flop down next to Ethan, and Jihun climbs up the steps to sit across from us. I can't speak right away as everything that happened rushes back to me. My sinuses burn, and I taste salt at the back of my throat. Hana is dead. She was my friend. I watched her die a senseless death, then let the real spy get away.

"Take your time." Ethan wraps his arm around me and pulls me close to his side.

I bury my face against his neck to hide my tears, and I let myself stay there for a fleeting second, no longer. I pull away and clear my throat. "There is no time."

I take a shuddering breath and relay everything that happened at the royal apothecary and the Suhoshin headquarters in a detached, clinical voice. I can't let my emotions surface. If I do, I might awaken the word of power with the guilt and grief roiling inside me. I don't have time to wrestle with my bloodlust.

"I'm so sorry." Ethan squeezes my hand, but I snatch it away, afraid of breaking down.

"Shim Duna seduced Keeper Choe, pretending to be Hana. She used him to open the portal for the hunter. And she used him to escape to the Kingdom of Mountains today." I bang the back of my head against the wall. "We caught up with her at the portal, but I had no idea how it worked. I don't know how *anything* works in this fucking realm. She opened the portal right in front of me and went through it before I could even figure out what was happening."

When I throw my head back toward the wall again, Ethan's hand takes the brunt of the impact. I glower at him, but the tender concern in his eyes threatens to undo me. I hastily turn my head, only to meet Jihun's understanding gaze.

"Fuck." I strike my fist against the floor.

"This isn't your fault, Sunny," Ethan says.

"In what universe is this not my fault?" Anger, especially at myself, seems like a safe emotion to lean into. "I should have apprehended her instead of being distracted by her villainous monologue. Such a rookie mistake. There has never been a gullible gumiho in the history of the Shingae. Until me."

I stack my arms on top of my drawn-up knees and drop my forehead against them. Ethan smooths his hand down the back of my head, and despite the shitty circumstances, I want to purr. The thought gives me enough rancor to lift my head and straighten my back.

"But there's no time to dwell on Shim Duna." I cross my legs and plant my hands on my thighs. "We need to leave for the Kingdom of Mountains tonight."

"The Kingdom of Mountains?" Jihun arches a brow. "Tonight?"

"Yes and yes." I glance between Ethan and Jihun. "Please tell me you two came up with a feasible plan to infiltrate the Shinsi Palace."

"We're working on it," Ethan mutters. "It's not as easy as you make it sound."

"How hard can it be?" I say drolly. "Tell me what you have so far."

"Before I tell you anything, I have one question." He levels me with a steely gaze. "What do you mean *we* need to leave for the Kingdom of Mountains? Who's this *we*?"

"Don't be precious." I roll my eyes at him. "You can't talk me out of coming with you, so let's not waste time arguing."

"You *cannot* risk your life—" Ethan tries anyway.

"You're our only hope against—" Jihun has the same idea.

"Shut up. Both of you. We literally have *no* time to waste." I glare at them. "Daeseong was telling the truth at Heaven Lake. The King of Mountains has aligned with the Amheuk."

"No," Ethan rasps.

"How do you know this?" Jihun looks grim but not surprised.

"Shim Duna said a 'powerful friend' told the King of Mountains that Ethan was hiding in the Kingdom of Sky." I wave my hand impatiently. "Long story short, everything lines up. Daeseong has to be the king's 'powerful friend.' The assassination attempts started as soon as the dark mudang came out of hiding."

"If Daeseong and the king are on friendly terms," Ethan says, "it doesn't bode well for the rest of us."

"The king must have bartered for the information on the prince." Jihun shakes his head. "Who knows what the dark mudang asked for in exchange."

"Whatever it is, we have to stop the king from fulfilling that bargain before it's too late." I struggle to swallow. We are well and truly out of time. And we don't even have the sword of light yet. I clench my fists as panic flutters in my throat. "We don't have a moment to waste."

"Gods, this is sooner than I'd hoped." Ethan wipes a hand down his face, then barks a harsh laugh. "But when has the Amheuk ever waited for our convenience?"

I'm not the only one who must soon face an impossible foe. I can't begin to imagine the conflict Ethan feels at having to overthrow his father from the throne. He might have increased his odds of defeating the tyrant with his training, but I'm afraid his kind heart will make him falter.

"You are ready to face the King of Mountains, my prince." Jihun nods solemnly at him.

"Ethan." I grip his forearm. "Shim Duna said something else important. Invincibility is a power the Kingdom of Mountains bestows on its chosen king. I think your father lost that power when you gained it. He can bleed. *That* is his illness."

"Even if that's true, the King of Mountains still has immeasurable powers." A conflicted frown settles over Ethan's face. "Even if he *can* bleed, I don't know if *I* can make him bleed."

"*You* have immeasurable power," Jihun reminds him. "Just moments ago, you enclosed the entire eastern wing in a dome of gi. You've mastered your magic."

"The magic we know of," Ethan corrects him. "There are powers I haven't even discovered yet. I know in my gut that I have more."

"We'll cross that bridge when we get there. For now, remember that you have more than enough magic to defeat the tyrant king. Do not second-guess yourself. I have every faith in you, my prince." Jihun claps Ethan on the shoulder, then rises to his feet. "I'll make preparations for tonight."

"Will you be able to reach our spy in time?" Ethan asks, standing up as well.

"I can only hope." Jihun offers him a ghost of a smile. "We have everything in place. We're just moving things a little ahead of schedule."

So they *do* have a plan. I sag with relief. *Thank gods.* I can get the details later. For now, I'm just glad we aren't winging the whole damn thing. With a good plan, we might even not die. But I shouldn't get ahead of myself.

"Thank you." Ethan returns his smile. "I truly appreciate your guidance, Captain."

"I gave Ben my word—" Jihun's eyes widen with something as close to panic as I've ever seen from him.

"Ben?" I jump to my feet and close in on him. "Benjamin Lee?"

"Did you know my brother?" Ethan stumbles back a step.

"I'm sorry." Jihun holds up a hand. "Now isn't the time—"

"Like hell it isn't," I growl. "We're about to leave on a suicide mission. There might not *be* a better time."

"Very well." Jihun pauses to glance at our faces, worry marking twin grooves between his brows. "Benjamin Lee was . . . my bonded brother."

Ethan's breath stutters next to me, and I demand, "What does that mean?"

"It means that we were bound together by a blood oath, the most powerful kind of spell in existence." Jihun's eyes stay on Ethan. "Ben and I shared a bond that allowed us to speak to each other through our minds, even from two different realms. We exchanged knowledge freely, sometimes unconsciously.

"And we were able to sense each other's emotions in a rudimentary way, where bursts of simple but intense emotions passed involuntarily through our connection. In many ways, we lived our own lives but lived through each other as well."

While I try to wrap my head around all this, Ethan drops to his knees. I gasp and crouch down next to him. "Hey, are you okay?"

He shakes his head once, then looks up at Jihun with grief-drenched eyes. "Where were you when Ben died?"

"I was . . ." Jihun struggles to swallow. "I was with him."

The implications of everything he said finally hit home, and I fall limply to my ass. He must have sensed that Ben was in danger. He must have figured out what was happening . . . what Ben intended to do. He was with Ben the entire time . . . until he felt their bond break . . . until he reached out and felt nothing. *Oh Jihun.* I glance up at his stoic, beautiful face, and hot tears fill my eyes.

"Why didn't you stop him?" Ethan roars. "Why did you let him die for me?"

"Because it was *his* duty. He was your royal guard." Jihun goes as still and taut as a statue, then cracks. "Even so—even though I knew it was his sworn duty—I begged him not to do it. I begged him to find another way, but there *was* no other way."

"I know that." Ethan's voice breaks. "I *know*, but I wish . . . I miss him so much."

"I do too. Before he died, he asked me to take his place as your royal guard, and I accepted. Ben moved on to the next life knowing he served you well—knowing I would serve you next. He was at peace. I felt it." Jihun gets down on one knee in front of Ethan and cups the back of his neck, bringing their heads close together. "I gave Ben my word that I will always stand by your side. Ethan, I will serve you as my prince, but I will love you as my brother. I swear it on my life."

Ethan leans in the rest of the way and presses his forehead against Jihun's as silent tears stream down their faces. I cry too, my heart breaking for them.

So much loss. So much sorrow. All because of Daeseong.

CHAPTER EIGHTEEN

The pagoda in the woods looks much more sinister in the dark. And so does the scowl on Keeper Bae's unlined face. *Cool.* This is more my scene. Much better than the love-shack vibes Shim Duna and Keeper Choe were giving it earlier today.

Then again, I'm not sure I like the tension coiling around the Sentinels. Jihun went full suhoshin captain on them and ordered them to stay behind—that was the only way he could get them to agree—and they're understandably furious.

It's a big ask. They're good people who care about Ethan, Jihun, and me, and we're making them stand on the sidelines, riddled with helpless worry. I don't envy them. But someone has to keep an eye on Daeseong in case—in the *likelihood*—our mission goes awry.

Besides, our spy can only get three of us inside the Shinsi Palace. She already took a big risk to add me to the plan. The *original* plan had only included Ethan and Jihun. I still can't believe those two boy scouts were planning to infiltrate the palace by themselves—even after I told Ethan not to do anything stupid without me. But I can't say I'm surprised. I know he and Jihun will try to convince me to stay behind till the last second. I would laugh if I wasn't nauseous with nerves.

"I don't like this." I've never seen Hailey's face so cold and set before. "What if it's a trap? What if the dark mudang *wants* you to go get yourself killed in the Kingdom of Mountains?"

"That's a good argument for *not* taking you guys with us," I point out, even as I reach out to squeeze her hand. "You're basically saying, 'Why should only the three of you get to die? We want to die too!'"

"Besides, Daeseong doesn't want Sunny to die in the Kingdom of Mountains. He needs her alive." Minju distractedly rubs at an ink stain on the sleeve of her jeogori. "She and the Yeoiju are intertwined. No one can take it from her if she's dead, because the Yeoiju will be extinguished without her. The dark mudang can only take it from her while she's alive."

I'm relieved Minju doesn't proceed to explain that once the dark mudang takes the Yeoiju from me, *then* I'll die because of the whole *intertwined* business. But I'm not completely sold on the idea. I mean, if we're intrinsically connected, why is it so hard for me to harness its powers?

"How alive?" Draco growls. "She doesn't have to be alive and *well*. That psychopath might keep her alive by a thread to force her to give it up."

"Daeseong isn't in the Kingdom of Mountains, kid," I say. My heart hurts that they care about me. *Damn it.* Now I have to worry about them being sad if I die. "And you guys have to stay here and forge the sword of light. Once we stop the King of Mountains, the dark mudang is next."

"Don't worry. We're nearly finished. And we'll make sure Daeseong stays nice and snug in Los Angeles until Gwangdo 2.0 is ready." Jaeseok's eyes are shadowed with concern, but he rallies with a wide, sexy grin. "But you can just blast him with the Yeoiju and end him in the blink of an eye. You won't even need to draw the sword of light. Make your oppa proud and do the little choreo from 'APT.' when you obliterate him."

"Like hell you're my oppa. I'm *decades* older than you. Call me noona, child." I offer the dokkaebi what I hope is a cocky *oh I'll end that SOB, all right* smile. "With that said, I'll try my best to do the choreo. I've played that drinking game often enough."

Unfortunately, Minju and I haven't been able to continue my training in the midst of the recent shitstorm. The only thing I've managed to do with the Yeoiju is summon a tiny ball of light on my palm. The sword of light might be our best shot at destroying Daeseong.

But even the lone cypress didn't believe the sacred ashes would be enough to stop the dark mudang. *Nothing might be enough to forestall the coming of the Amheuk.* No matter how much I want to deny it, I need the Yeoiju. Only, it feels even farther from reach with the word of power etched on my back. How can I call forth the light when I have to fight the rune's dark magic every time the wind blows wrong?

"Cadet Cho, you will do well to remember your lessons. Captain Song and the prince will need your help apprehending the tyrant king." Captain Seo pauses with a wry arch of her brow when Ethan makes a choked sound of protest. The stubborn male does not want to accept that I'm coming with them, even though we are literally standing at the foot of the portal. "Even if they don't realize it yet."

Jihun jogs lightly down the steps of the pagoda and joins the rest of us, gathered a few paces away. Keeper Bae stands in the middle of the covered platform, muttering darkly into a mound of earth cupped in his palms. From the looks of it, he doesn't have anything nice to say. I feel bad for the dirt.

"It took some convincing without official papers, but he'll let us through the portal," Jihun says grimly.

"What did you tell him?" Ethan asks.

"The same thing the council will hear tomorrow morning." Jihun somehow manages to look grimmer. "I'm investigating the infiltration of a spy from the Kingdom of Mountains with the assistance of Cadet Cho. The matter is under the Suhoshin's jurisdiction because of the death of Shim Hana. And due to the diplomatic implications, we're also escorting the emissary back to the Kingdom of Mountains."

"General Bak won't stay convinced for long." Ethan crosses his arms, matching Jihun's frown. "But I played the obedient grandson long enough for him not to immediately suspect that I am going against his wishes. Hopefully, by the time my grandfather figures out our true objective, it'll be too late for him to stop us."

"Once we have the king in our custody, even General Bak will have no grounds to start his war." Jihun holds his gaze, and Ethan nods solemnly. "We will not fail, my prince."

"Great pep talk, guys. I'm really fired up to go save the Kingdom of Mountains. For real." I clap my hands not entirely facetiously. I'm going into this mission with the two males I trust most in the worlds. If anyone can succeed, it's the three of us. "But can I talk to you for a second, Jihun?"

"Now?" He side-eyes me suspiciously, then glances at Ethan, who is speaking quietly with Draco.

"Come on." I motion to the other side of the pagoda and walk over with him. "Ethan is still unsure of his powers, and I can't blame him. We don't know what's going to happen when he uses his powers in battle for the first time. A battle against his own father."

"I have a feeling you're bringing up this obvious but unavoidable issue for a reason." Jihun arches an arrogant brow at me.

"We can help stack the odds against the king." I match his arrogant brow and raise him a cocky grin. "As luck would have it, I'm the daughter of a talented healer, so I'm actually qualified for my cover as a physician's assistant. Since the tyrant's skin is as pierceable as the rest of us, thanks to his 'illness,' I can administer acupuncture to temporarily paralyze both his body and his magic. The paralysis will only hold for a few minutes tops, but it'll give Ethan enough time to confine him under a dome."

Jihun's eyes widen. "That might actually work. If we work fast, we might be able to transport the king to a secure prison without even alerting his royal guards."

"Captain Song, the token is ready," Keeper Bae calls out.

"We'll discuss the details tonight." Jihun squeezes my arm and turns back toward the pagoda.

"The travelers may approach the portal." The grumpy keeper glowers at the rest of the Sentinels. "No one else sets foot on the pagoda."

"That's one salty dude," Draco observes with a hint of admiration. "He reminds me of my favorite science teacher from middle school."

"I thought you were homeschooled." Hailey purses her lips.

"I've had a few stints at different schools in the US." They kick a small divot in the ground with their toes. "I even stayed at a boarding school in the UK for a couple of months."

"Did you name yourself Draco at the boarding school because those Brits couldn't pronounce Boknam?" Jaeseok deadpans.

Draco's growl sounds unnervingly *dragon*. The crotchety keeper might perish with outrage if they shift into their dragon form without official papers.

"Whoa." I put a hand on their shoulder. "He's just messing with you, kid."

"Sorry, Draco." Jaeseok's shoulders droop when Minju gives him a disapproving look. "I joke around when things get intense."

Hailey snorts. "You always joke around."

"Because things are *always* intense with you lot." Jaeseok pouts. "A dokkaebi has to cope, doesn't he?"

"It's calm." Draco runs their fingers through their cerulean hair. "I'm just touchy because I don't like Ethan and Sunny leaving without their armor and sword of light, especially when I can't be there to protect them."

"It's not your job to protect us," I say softly, patting their back. "It's our job to protect you. You better get used to it. Because once this is all over, you're going to finish enjoying your childhood."

"I'm not a child," they grumble.

"Fine. Your teenage-hood then." I laugh wistfully. "Maybe we'll go back to the States for you to finish high school, then we can send you off to college."

Draco crinkles their nose but doesn't immediately balk at the idea. Maybe I'll join them and try my hand at college, or go for a job a little more rewarding than selling cigars at a crappy casino. But for now, I'll settle for not dying.

"Ready?" Ethan leans close, and a shiver runs through me. My visceral reaction to him is a damn nuisance. "Or you can stay here and find out what Daeseong is planning on his end."

"Nice try." I shake my head at him. "But you have another think coming if you seriously believe I'll ever let you out of my sight again."

Ethan sucks in a sharp breath as his eyes bore into mine, and I freeze. *Shit.* Am I found out? Did I reveal too much of my heart? I try to turn my head, but he catches my chin between his fingers. My pulse flutters in my throat.

"Say that again," he rasps.

"S . . . say what? We agreed to stick together. Re . . . remember?" I stutter before the words I can't voice spill out of me. *I love you, I love you, I love you.* "Until w . . . we stop Daeseong."

"I remember." He lets go of my chin but holds my gaze. "I remember everything."

Images of cozy meals and laughter in an enchanted house, of long conversations beneath the blue sky, of his hands and lips on my naked body . . . flicker through my mind. But that was before. Before we found out his true identity. Before we learned about the prophecy. Everything was different then, and there is no going back.

"I *said*," Keeper Bae booms, "the travelers may approach the portal."

"That's my cue." I spin away from Ethan and stomp toward the pagoda. Without turning around, I wave over my shoulder at my friends. I hate goodbyes, especially when this could really be goodbye. "Laters."

"Rude," Draco grumbles. My sinuses burn at the hurt and worry in their voice. "I'm not saying goodbye to your back."

Then they tackle me from behind in a crushing hug and storm off before I can say a single word. I'm not sure I would've been able to with my tears so close to the surface.

"Be careful, Sunny," Hailey shouts, and my throat works to swallow. This is why I hate goodbyes.

Ethan and Jihun take time to say proper goodbyes to the Sentinels. It must be nice to be emotionally well adjusted. I stomp up the stairs and stop in front of the keeper. He glares at me.

"Do we have a problem?" I glare right back at him.

"Problem?" Keeper Bae's frown shifts from surly to confused. "Why would we have a problem? Stop talking nonsense and hold out your hand."

I meekly do as I'm told because I'm oddly touched by his confusion. He doesn't care that I'm a gumiho. Without ceremony, he pours some of the dirt from his hands onto my palm. My skin tingles under the soft mound of earth, and I peer at it, holding it up to my eyes. Ethan and Jihun come quietly to my sides and hold out their hands without being asked. The keeper fills their palms as well.

"This is for your passage to the Kingdom of Mountains tonight." Keeper Bae then hangs loose necklaces with small pouches of dirt around our necks. "And these are for your passage back. Do *not* lose them. I have no way of opening the portal on that end from over here."

"Understood." Jihun nods. "And this will take us to the portal at the lake?"

"That's what you asked for, isn't it?" the keeper mutters irritably. "That portal has been closed off for decades, but I did my part to get you there."

"Thank you, Keeper Bae." Then Jihun turns to Ethan and me. "I'll go through first and make sure nothing's amiss. Give me five minutes before you follow."

"What if the King of Mountains has an army waiting for us?" I scoff in disbelief. "Will five minutes be enough for you to dispose of them all?"

"You're right." The corners of his mouth twitch with amusement. "Give me ten minutes."

"We'll all go through together," Ethan says with wry affection. "Sunny, hold this for me."

He adds his dirt to my mound before I can ask him why. Then he dusts off his hands and sweeps me up in his arms.

"What the hell are you doing?" I yelp in surprise but manage to fist my hand around the dirt.

"You'll see. Throw the dirt against the pillar when I say now," he says with a crooked grin, then turns to Jihun. "Captain, whenever you're ready."

His unreadable gaze travels from me to Ethan, then he nods curtly.

"Against which—" I begin.

"Now," Ethan shouts.

"For fuck's sake." I throw my handful of dirt against the pillar nearest us, and Jihun does the same.

Before I can demand to be put down, I'm blinded by a beam of green light. The same light that Shim Duna escaped through. I get it now. The light is the opening to the portal, and the mound of earth is the token to the Kingdom of Mountains. But I don't have much time to be awed because as soon as Ethan steps through the light, we're free-falling toward a mirrorlike lake surrounded by emerald green mountains.

I scream and wrap my arms around his neck. I can't be sure, between the air whooshing in my ears and my shrill scream, but I'm pretty sure he chuckles before he slows our descent.

"I got you, Sunny," he murmurs in my ear, letting his lips brush its sensitive shell. The asshole is definitely laughing at me.

"I don't understand how you can fly," I grumble. "You're not a suhoshin."

"I'm half-seonnam, remember?" He pulls me tighter against him as he lands next to the lake.

"Lucky you." I shove at his chest but stop when he stares at the lake, his expression turning bleak. "Ethan, what's wrong?"

"Do you know the Korean folklore about the seonnyeo and the woodsman?" His voice is barely above a whisper.

"The one where the woodsman finds a seonnyeo bathing in the lake?" I lay a hand on his cheek, wanting to reach him through his pain, but his gaze remains trained on the water. "He hides her clothes to stop her from flying away so she will have to marry him."

In the old story, the woodsman saves a magical deer, who grants him one wish. The woodsman wishes to marry, so the deer tells him how to make an angel from the heavens his wife. The woodsman must steal the seonnyeo's celestial dress while she bathes in the lake so that she won't be able to fly away. Then he must hide her clothes from her until they have three children.

The woodsman does exactly as he's told to claim a beautiful seonnyeo as his wife. But when their second child is born, the angel begs him to return her dress. Ignoring the deer's warning, the woodsman gives his wife her clothes because he loves her dearly. And as soon as she has her celestial dress back, the seonnyeo flies away into the heavens, holding a child in each arm. The woodsman understands too late that the deer told him to wait until they have three children, because she could carry only two in her arms.

I never liked how the humans made the woodsman a lovesick victim and the seonnyeo a conniving, unfaithful female. That bastard forced her to marry him—forced her to bear his children. Is it any wonder she escaped from her captor the moment she got the chance?

"The humans got it all wrong, you know." A muscle tics in Ethan's jaw. "There was never a foolish, lovesick woodsman—only a cruel, greedy one. And the seonnyeo never got to fly away with her children."

"Oh Ethan . . ." I whisper.

The royal line in the Kingdom of Mountains are descendants of the first woodsman, the most powerful being of Mountains. His father was the woodsman who forced the seonnyeo into marrying him, and his mother was the angel from the heavens—a noble maiden bathing in the lake, seen naked by a powerful male. It doesn't take much imagination to see how he blackmailed her with her *virtue*. How he forced her to accept his hand to avoid bringing shame upon herself and her family.

Women in the Joseon Dynasty were taught that their virtue was worth more than their lives. When a girl turned fourteen, she was given a small silver dagger to keep on her body at all times. If a man raped her, she was taught to kill the rapist first, then end her own life. That was what the silver dagger was for—to dispose of her unpure, worthless self.

Purity culture has been fucking women over, be they human or shinbiin, for as long as men took it upon themselves to determine a woman's worth. Not only in Korea but also everywhere in the worlds. Not only in the Mortal Realm but also in the Realm of Four Kingdoms. To this day, they use our bodies to objectify us or shame us, depending on what suits their needs.

"I'm so sorry," I whisper. "But your mother did not stay a helpless victim. She captured the hearts of her people and gave them hope. She opposed and outsmarted a tyrant king. Because of her strength and courage, the prophecy of the King Foretold will be fulfilled. *You* will be her legacy."

"Thank you." He gently sets me down on my feet and presses his forehead against mine. I step back and look away from him as Jihun approaches.

"My prince." His jaw clenches as he holds my eyes for a second too long, then he scans the surroundings. "We need to get out of the open and find cover for the night."

"Of course, Captain." With a faint smile, Ethan cocks his head at me. "Do your thing, Sunny."

"Since you *asked* so nicely," I snark but turn my gaze toward the wooded mountains. I see the lay of the land in a single glance, the familiar gi of Mountains a balm on my weary soul. "There's a cave nearby, hidden by the trees. We can camp there for the night."

"I still cannot wrap my head around that." Jihun's lips quirk into a wonderous grin. "Please lead the way."

I roll my eyes at him, but it feels gratifying to be good at something for once. I'm actually proud of my magic gi goggles. My steps feel light as I lead them toward the cave.

"Your eyes are still brown." Ethan falls into step beside me, studying my face. "So you don't have to open your spirit eyes to see everything anymore?"

"Not exactly everything." I purse my lips. "I can perceive the gi of living things, including trees, mountains, bodies of water . . ."

"Don't forget caves," Ethan adds with a teasing smile. I'm so relieved he's back to himself that I beam back at him like a dork.

"Yes, anything created by nature. In *that* sense, my spirit eyes still work the same way." I wipe the dorky smile off my face with some effort. "But the more accurate way to describe this . . . evolution of my power is that my spirit eyes are always open." I steal a glance at Jihun, who walks quietly on my other side, listening to every word. "With a bit of focus, I can see the gi around me with my physical eyes. I don't even have to dip heavily into my magic."

As we trek toward the cave, we run through our plan for tomorrow and bring Ethan up to speed on my proposal to use acupuncture to temporarily paralyze the king.

"That sounds dangerous," he immediately objects.

"And trying to overpower him with brute magic force *doesn't?*" I gape at him. "What part of infiltrating the palace *isn't* dangerous?"

"But you have to get close to him," he insists. "What if he catches on and—"

"You make it sound like you and Jihun won't be right there beside me." I throw my hands up. "You also seem to have forgotten that I can take care of myself."

"I agree with Sunny," Jihun says, stepping in. "It's a risk worth taking, Your Highness."

I beam at him and mouth, *Thank you.*

Ethan narrows his eyes—and I tense myself to argue more—but he releases a sharp sigh. "Okay. That's two to one. I concede."

"Hooray for democracy. Thanks for not pulling rank on us, Your Highness," I say with a cheeky bow of my head. "Also, everything will be all right."

We walk in silence for a while, each of us lost in our thoughts. I breathe in deep, inhaling the scent of the vibrant trees around us. A sense of peace descends on me, which is odd since we're on a deadly mission. But maybe . . . everything will really be all right.

"It feels different here. *I* feel different here," Ethan murmurs as we hike through the woods. "I can't see the gi of Mountains, but I can feel it against my skin, like I'm absorbing it through my pores."

"Huh. I wonder if you look different." I focus on Ethan and promptly stumble. Jihun catches me by the arm, and I lean on him, my knees weak with shock. "Gods, Ethan. You're on fire."

His eyes round with surprise, and he glances down at his hands as though curious to see the fire for himself. But he isn't alarmed, like he knows the life force of Mountains won't hurt him. The gi surrounds him, not in a soft glow, but in pulsating green flames. And the fire isn't swallowing him but *filling* him. If I had doubts about Ethan being the Prince of Mountains, this would have convinced me twice over.

Above us, the sky shifts and the night deepens into an impossible black. The oppressive darkness siphons the light from around us, but the gi of Mountains only burns brighter around Ethan, as though it wants to light up the worlds. I'm mesmerized by its beauty, power, and vitality.

Without looking away, I pat Jihun somewhere in the vicinity of his shoulder, signaling for him to release my arm. I take a step closer to Ethan and extend my hand toward him, half expecting to snatch it away from the heat. But the fire is warm against the tips of my fingers. I gingerly sink my hand into the fire and watch the flames swirl around it. I laugh softly, twisting my hand this way and that, and I feel the contented hum of my Yeoiju in my chest.

But when the green fire snakes up my arm, I snatch my hand away and stumble back, bumping into the wall of Jihun's chest. He wraps his hands around my upper arms in a firm, steadying grip.

"Are you okay?" he asks in a voice laced with concern.

"I'm fine." I glance over my shoulder to smile wanly at him. "Nothing bad, just . . . surprising."

"My prince?" Jihun steps into Ethan's line of sight, and his eyes focus as he comes back from where his thoughts had wandered. "Are you well?"

"I . . ." Ethan chuckles dazedly. "I actually feel great."

"We should hurry, though." I look up into the dark sky. The stars are blinking out, and clouds as black as smoke swirl around the moon, snapping at its edges. "Looks like the Kingdom of Mountains takes their nighttime seriously. When midnight hits, we won't be able to see our own hands in front of our faces."

We pick up our pace and head deeper into the woods. I glance down at my palm, remembering the green life force wrapping around it like climbing vines. My pulse quickens in a frantic crescendo, and I shove my hand behind my back. When my heart rate returns to normal, I think logically about what happened. The gi of Mountains recognizes Ethan as the true heir of the Kingdom of Mountains—the King Foretold. I get that part. But . . . what does it want with me?

"Is this where the cave is?" Jihun asks as we approach an alcove in the woods.

"Uh . . . yeah." I focus on the present and scan our surroundings. "Over there. The entrance is behind those trees."

The cave will house the three of us comfortably and keep us from freezing in the night. And the ceiling is high enough for Ethan and Jihun to stand upright without bumping their heads, which is a plus. I don't want either of them concussed before we infiltrate the Shinsi Palace.

I open my mouth to volunteer for the first watch, but Ethan beats me to it.

"Fine," I say ungraciously, crinkling my nose at him. He needs the rest more than me. Being back in the Kingdom of Mountains must be a lot for him to process. And if the acupuncture stunt goes south, he'll be the one facing the tyrant. "You better wake me up for the second watch."

Jihun remains quiet, not volunteering for the third watch, which means he plans on staying up all night. I'm both grateful for his strength and support as well as annoyed. I wish he would get some rest too.

I drop my bojagi of supplies next to the back wall and lie down on the dirt ground, using the bundle as a pillow. I'm exhausted, and my eyes slide closed even as Ethan and Jihun murmur softly to each other, preparing to take their watch. I think I feel a warm robe being gently draped over me, but I'm too far gone to be sure.

YOU LOVE HER

The night in the Kingdom of Mountains is different from in the Kingdom of Sky. It's black, heavy . . . suffocating. The darkness in the Kingdom of Sky merely shrouds what is there. But the darkness here seems ravenous to swallow all that is there. I shudder as goose bumps spread down my arms.

My eyes instinctively seek out Sunny. She's sleeping near the mouth of the cave, huddled beneath my outer robe. In the faint moonlight, she looks so small and delicate. She would kick my ass if I ever called her *delicate*. I tuck my chin to hide my adoring smile.

"You must be cold," Jihun says, misunderstanding my shiver. "But we cannot risk building a fire. Forgive me, my prince."

"Forgive you? Why?" I smirk at him. "Is the chilly night your doing? Can you control the weather?"

A corner of his mouth slants up for a split second before it flattens. That counts as a smile where Jihun is concerned. I huff a silent laugh and glance up at the sky. We still have hours until dawn. I'm taking first watch, but my obstinate royal guard refuses to sleep. We sit in companionable silence for a while, keeping an eye on the dark woods beyond.

I break the silence. "How did you and Ben become bonded brothers?"

Jihun is quiet for so long I don't think he's going to answer.

"My mother, Ben's mother, and the Queen of Mountains grew up together. They were inseparable as girls, and their friendship only strengthened as they reached adulthood." He draws his knees up and rests his forearms on them. "When the queen married the King of Mountains, Ben's mother accompanied her as her lady-in-waiting."

"I knew that Mom—Ben's mom—was the queen's friend, but I only got glimpses of the queen's childhood memories, so I didn't know . . ." I say haltingly. I feel Jihun's solemn gaze on me, but he continues after a moment.

"My mother was devastated to lose her friends, but it broke her heart that Ben and I had to be separated. We were born within days of each other and refused to be apart from the start." Another barely there smile touches Jihun's lips. "My mother said I cried inconsolably all day until she took me to visit Ben. As soon as she laid me down next to him, I stopped crying. Ben was the same. The two mothers only found peace—and sleep—when we were together."

"So there was already a strong bond between you two." I can't help feeling a little envious of Jihun. But I had Ben by my side for twenty-four years. I shouldn't be greedy.

"A blood oath cannot create a bond that does not exist. It merely strengthens what is already there." Jihun absently traces his left palm—the soft, rounded part below his thumb—with his right index finger. "On our first birthday—our dol—an auspicious birthday second only to our twenty-fourth birthday, our mothers performed the blood oath on us.

"Performing such a powerful spell on mere infants was not without danger, but they couldn't wait much longer. The queen had to leave for the Kingdom of Mountains for her wedding, and the King of Mountains was not a patient male. In the end, our mothers had to trust that the bond Ben and I already shared was strong enough to protect us from harm."

"And did it?" I realize I've fisted my hands, so I deliberately unclench them. "Did the bond protect you and Ben?"

"Yes." He glances at me, then looks away. "The blood oath bound us without harming us. And since then, Ben was always with me even though we were apart."

"As you were with him." I draw small circles in the dirt, the feel of the earth soothing my grief. "Thank you for being with him. I'm glad he didn't have to die alone."

"I . . . feel like a part of me died with him. Ben had always been a part of me." Jihun's head droops as he blows a weary sigh. "Now I'm missing half of myself."

"I'm sorry," I whisper. "I hope you find someone who makes you feel whole again."

His gaze flits to Sunny for the briefest moment, and my stomach drops. I suspected he had feelings for her, but I didn't know it ran that deep. Jealousy wars with hope inside me.

"You love her." I don't phrase it as a question.

"She won't have me." Jihun's laugh is laced with an all-too-familiar heartbreak.

"That's one way of admitting it." I glance at my royal guard with a wry smile.

"You love her too," he says, staring into the woods.

"To her great annoyance." I chuckle under my breath, even though my heart twists painfully in my chest. "She won't have me either."

"That's one way of admitting it." Jihun arches an eyebrow at me.

I shrug. "I haven't made a secret of it."

Sunny stopped lashing out at me after the picnic—I'm glad because I know it hurt her as much as it hurt me—but it still feels like there's an ocean between us. She cares about me as more than a friend. I can feel it. But she's built an invisible wall between us that I can't seem to breach. If I push harder, she might withdraw completely, and I won't be able to bear that. Maybe it's for the best . . .

"I want you to protect her." I break the silence with desperation in my voice.

"My duty is to protect you." Jihun's jaw clenches.

"There is . . . another prophecy. The prophecy of the end of days," I confess in a wavering voice. "The Queen of Mountains didn't share it with anyone, but I discovered it through her memory."

"Wh . . . what is this prophecy?" my royal guard asks haltingly. "Did the queen truly foresee . . . the end of days?"

"I'm not sure. I think . . . the prophecy is about Sunny and me." I clasp my head between my hands. "My mother believed that it is my destiny—the destiny of the King Foretold—to kill the one who possesses the Yeoiju."

"I don't . . ." Jihun rears back, his face slack with shock. "My prince, I don't understand. Why would the queen . . . Sunny is on her list. It makes no sense."

"I keep having these dreams," I whisper, fisting my hands in my hair. "There is a female, encased in white fire. She is burning down the world around her. I . . ."

"Those are dreams, Your Highness. Only dreams."

"Please don't let me hurt Sunny." I jerk my head up and clutch at Jihun's arm. "I need you to stop me. Kill me, if you have to. Please."

"I can never stand against you . . . even if you must kill her." Grim determination hardens his features. "But I won't let her go alone. I will die with her."

"I envy you, Captain. I can't be with her even in death." I take a shuddering breath and strive for calm, but it feels more like resignation. "I can't take my own life. All the sacrifices my mother, my adoptive parents, and Ben made to protect me . . . I can't let their deaths be in vain. Not by my own hand."

"They believed you were greater than their sacrifice," my royal guard says. "All of us, who know of the prophecy of the King Foretold, believe that in the depth of our souls."

"I won't let them down." I meet Jihun's eyes. "I won't let you down."

And I won't give up on my love. I will find a way to change the prophecy. I won't have to be with Sunny in death because she will live.

I will be with her in life. I will love her till the end of days.

CHAPTER NINETEEN

My eyes snap open on a gasp, but I immediately make myself go deathly still. I scan the cave without moving a muscle, then again with the slightest shift of my head, but Ethan and Jihun are nowhere to be seen. The good news is there are no bad guys here to kill me either.

I let my head fall back onto my makeshift pillow and rub the heel of my hand against the ache in my chest. I drifted in and out of a strange dream that left me feeling heartbroken. I try to remember the dream, but it floats further away from me the harder I try. All I know is that I wasn't *in* the dream but it was *about* me.

At any rate, I feel well rested and alert. I rise to my elbows and look outside the cave. The lightless night is receding, and the faintest hint of indigo and orange peeks through the trees. Well, the answer is obvious. Those stubborn fools didn't wake me up for my watch and let me sleep through the night.

With a frustrated growl, I grab Ethan's outer robe in my fist to fling it off me, not giving a damn about wrinkling the fine silk, but I falter. With another quick glance out the mouth of the cave, I bring the robe to my nose and inhale deeply, and my eyes slide shut as the scent of the green forest and the musk of earth assail my senses.

"Ugh." I throw the robe off and kick it away for good measure. *Gods.* I'm *smelling* his clothes now? That's pathetic, not to mention creepy.

Muttering under my breath like a crotchety old man, I stomp outside the cave. Ethan and Jihun sit on opposite sides of a single tree, leaning against the trunk. They're both chuckling, and I slow my steps, not wanting to intrude. I'm glad they found another brother in each other. I wish Ben could see this. He would be so happy for them. I swallow a fist-sized lump in my throat.

"Sorry to break up the bromantic moment." I try not to sound like I mean it. "Which one of you assholes had the brilliant idea of not waking me up for my watch?"

As if they planned it, Ethan and Jihun point at each other and chorus, "He did."

"You're chickenshit. Both of you." I turn my head to hide my smile. "But you weren't doing any of us a favor. What good are you if you're tired and sluggish?"

"Not to worry." Ethan smirks, getting to his feet. "Adrenaline is our friend."

Jihun's cough sounds suspiciously like a snort, but his face is perfectly serious when he gets to his feet. "I need to change before I go into town to procure the palanquins."

My face catches fire, thinking of the last time I was in a palanquin, and my brain short-circuits. "Guh . . ."

A roguish smile spreads across Ethan's face, and his half-hooded eyes sweep the length of my body. Before I can pounce on the cocky bastard—to kiss him or kick his ass, who the hell knows—he turns toward Jihun.

"Of course, Captain." He nods at him. "We'll be ready to leave when you return."

Jihun bows his head stiffly, then spins on his heels and makes a beeline for the cave. I bite my bottom lip. I don't like hurting him, especially when Ethan and I can't be together anyway. I start when I feel the soft pad of Ethan's thumb on my lip as he tugs it free from my teeth. His eyes are solemn, and he drops his hand as soon as I stop worrying my lip raw.

"I can't help it," he says quietly.

"You can't help what?" I glare at him. My reaction to his touch mixed with my concern for Jihun has me conflicted and testy.

"Teasing you." He takes a shuddering breath. "Lov—"

"Don't," I snap. "I can't. Not now."

Pain slashes across his face, and my chest clenches, but I meant what I said. We're about to infiltrate the Shinsi Palace to apprehend the King of Mountains. We're basically walking into certain death. And I'm not . . . strong enough. If he tells me he loves me—if he tells me he wants to be with me—I'm not strong enough to refuse him. Not this time.

"You're right. I'm sorry." He glances away. "Just friends."

Jihun comes out of the cave in a rough commoner's hanbok, his hair knotted at the top of his head, with a strip of plain cloth tied around his forehead. Yet he is so beautiful, it kind of hurts to look at him. I use his return to move away from Ethan.

"I don't buy it." I tap my lips with a finger as I circle Jihun. "That won't do at all. Sit."

I gather some leaves, fallen from the trees, and crouch down in front of Jihun. I wave my hand over the leaves and turn them into various shades of a bruise. I learned some everyday magic from Miok to do my own makeup, when the occasion called for it. *Every occasion when Ethan was there.*

"Shut up," I mutter.

Jihun's eyebrows hike up. "Pardon?"

"Not you." I sigh. "Just sit still."

I pick up the blue-green leaf and brush it beneath his eyes to give him dark circles. I bite the inside of my cheeks to hold back my smile. He looks like he hasn't slept in a month. Then I pluck a shadowy brown leaf from my lineup and contour his face to make him look thin and haggard. I sit back and critique my handiwork. The seonnam remains much too handsome for his own good, but he looks gaunt and exhausted like the hunter assassin did.

My stomach clenches. The poor always suffer the most under an oppressive ruler. But the king will pay for what he did to the hunter. He will face the consequences of carelessly discounting the well-being of commoners to satisfy his hunger for power and wealth. The tyrant will pay for *all* the lives he's ruined. *Today.*

"That'll have to do," I tell Jihun as I push up to my feet. "Now you have a *chance* of passing as a commoner in the Kingdom of Mountains."

"Thank you, Sunny." Jihun stands and turns toward Ethan. "I won't be long, Your Highness."

Without further ado, the seonnam does a sharp about-face and marches away, his broad shoulders perfectly squared and his spine ramrod straight. I palm my forehead and groan. We're so dead.

"Can you at least slouch a little? If you walk into town like that, you might as well stamp *suhoshin in disguise* on your forehead," I shout after him. "Why can't you go as yourself, again?"

"Because I can't implicate the Order of the Suhoshin in this mission." The suhoshin captain looks back at me with a glower. "And before you ask *again*, I can't go as a noble because nobles do not procure their own palanquins. I have no choice but to disguise myself as an ordinary commoner."

"But you are so bad at being *ordinary*," I protest.

"Enough. I'm leaving," he barks but lowers his shoulders by a quarter inch and loosens his gait a smidgen.

"Maybe he could pass for a commoner with exceptional posture?" I rub my temples. When we lose sight of Jihun in the woods, I shoot Ethan an annoyed glance. "Who infiltrates a royal palace in broad daylight anyway?"

"It's easier to hide in plain sight," he says, "especially since our goal is to get to the jimil, the king's inner chambers. We have a better chance of going unnoticed during the day."

"Yeah, because you two are *so* unnoticeable." I roll my eyes. "You'll blend *right* in."

"You're one to talk." He scoffs.

"What's that supposed to mean?" I squint at him.

"What . . ." He draws back and side-eyes me. "You do know how beautiful you are, don't you?"

"Gods, Ethan." My cheeks burn, which makes me more embarrassed because he can tell I'm embarrassed. "I'm downright *homely* compared to the seonnyeos."

"H . . . homely?" His face goes slack with disbelief, and gods damn it, I'm flattered. He really thinks I'm beautiful.

"Never mind." I wave my hands in front of my face. "It doesn't matter if I'm a five or a ten. I just want to focus on not dying today. Okay? Okay."

"I won't let that happen." He steps close and captures my chin between his fingers. "I'll end anyone who dares lay a hand on you."

I can only gape at him as a shaky exhale escapes past my lips. I don't want to like it, but his protective side makes my insides melt. My knees wobble like Jell-O, and I press my hands against his chest to steady myself. His breath hitches, and a thousand butterflies take flight in my stomach.

"I said *don't*," I whisper.

"Don't what?" His lips barely move.

"Love me." I don't know if I'm answering him or asking him. All I know is that we might both die today.

"If friendship is all you can offer, then I'll take it gladly." He takes a shuddering breath. "But don't ask me to stop loving you, because it's not possible."

Oh gods. He still loves me. My blood pounds in my ears. Even after all the cruel things I've said to him—I squeeze my eyes shut—he still loves me. My chest tightens painfully, but my lips quiver as though they want to spread into a smile. *He loves me.*

Holding his eyes, I slowly rise to my toes. Ethan releases my chin and brushes his hands over the curves of my hips, so lightly they're barely there. Yet, I feel his touch spark against my skin like licks of fire.

222

I angle my head to the side, but I can't reach him, not even on the tips of my toes.

Ethan stares down at me without moving a muscle. Does he not want to kiss me? What am I doing? I should back away. But his pupils are blown wide, his gaze hot and black, and I am starving to taste him. I didn't realize they were out, but my claws dig into the firm flesh of his chest—*impatient, insistent.* The only reason I'm not drawing blood is because this is Ethan. My powerful, beautiful Ethan.

"What do you want, Sunny?" His voice is a rough growl, and his fingers flex against my hips. I sink my teeth into my bottom lip. "Give me the words."

"I want you." I can't give him the words in my heart, but maybe we can have this moment. "I want you, Ethan."

His lips crush against mine with the force of waves breaking against a rocky cliff, and my heels hit the ground from the impact. He dips his head lower to cling to my lips, and I tangle my arms around his neck and push back onto my toes. The kiss isn't elegant. Our teeth clack against each other's, and our tongues slip in and out of our mouths. Zero finesse, all desperation.

But all I can think is . . . *at last.*

With a muttered curse, Ethan picks me up, his fingers digging into the backs of my thighs, and I wrap my legs around his waist, pressing my torso against his. I moan when the sensitive tips of my breasts crush against his chest, and I rock my wet core against him, the ache already unbearable.

"Gods, Sunny." Ethan pulls my legs tighter around him to give me the friction I seek, and I hump his six-pack like a rodeo queen.

"More." I bite his bottom lip with my elongated incisors, making him hiss against my mouth.

He hitches me up higher and moves us without once taking his lips off mine. My back hits a tree with enough force to knock a grunt out of me, and Ethan rears his head back with wide eyes, an apology tripping off his tongue.

"Shut up." I fist my hand in his hair and tug his head back down. He groans into my mouth, his apology forgotten.

I protest when he loosens my legs from his waist. But all is forgiven when he shifts our bodies by a couple of inches and pivots his hips, pushing his hard length against the juncture of my thighs. My head tips back, and Ethan drags his mouth down the side of my neck, grinding against me, harder and faster. I squirm and jerk against him, needing to get closer.

"I need . . ." I whimper, clinging to his shoulders.

The delicious friction stops, and I squawk in outrage. But Ethan chuckles darkly and dips his hand into the waist of my loose dobok pants. I hold my breath in anticipation, then cry out when he runs his thumb down my seam.

"Gods, you're so fucking wet." He buries his face where my neck and shoulder meet. I suck his earlobe into my mouth and bite down hard. He jerks against me and groans deep in his chest. "Impatient, aren't you?"

My retort dies in my throat when Ethan slides a finger deep inside me, and my eyes roll back as he works it in and out of my hot core. I clench around his finger and swivel my hips, but with my legs wrapped loosely around him, I can't find purchase.

"I got you," he rasps and adds another finger inside me, his mouth devouring mine.

He pumps his hands until I thrash my head against the tree. He crooks his fingers, and a sharp, delicious ache gathers low in my stomach. He presses and presses against that magic spot, and shocks of pleasure travel down my stomach to the pulsating pinpoint at my center. I moan and whimper, digging my nails into his biceps.

"You're going to come for me," he rasps against my mouth, circling his thumb around my swollen clit. The ache at my core grows exquisitely agonizing, and a scream gathers in my throat. He pumps his fingers against the bundle of nerves inside me and presses his thumb down hard on my clit. "Now, Sunny."

I obey his command. With a hoarse scream, I shatter into a thousand pieces, stars bursting behind my eyes. My pleasure borders on pain, but I'm not ready for it to stop. Knowing exactly what I need, Ethan prolongs the sweet torture with soft sweeps of his thumb until I flop limply against him.

"There's my good girl." He drops a tender kiss on my temple, and I know that he's about to set me down on the ground. He thinks all I wanted was physical release. Of course he does. That's what I wanted him to believe.

But now . . .

"Ethan, I want you to . . ." I tighten my legs around his waist in desperation. What am I doing? I . . . I can't let him go. "I want you inside me."

"Sunny—"

"I won't get pregnant," I blurt gauchely, too frantic to feel embarrassed. "All the cadets have to drink an elixir every day. They can't risk someone participating in the trials getting pregnant. Ethan, please."

"If I make love to you . . ." He pushes my back more firmly against the tree and pinches my chin between his fingers so I can't look away. "If we make love, know that I'll be giving you *all* of myself—heart, body, and soul. Don't ask me to pretend it means anything less. Don't make me lie."

As impossible as it seems, I fall more in love with him. He offered me his everything but asked for nothing in return. Love shines in his eyes, ardent and heartbreaking, and I can only manage a jerky nod. I want all of him, no matter how selfish that makes me. I want him to have all of me. I can't give him the words, but at least *I'll* know I've given him my everything. I just hope my wordless nod is enough for him.

His mouth captures mine in a hot, hungry kiss. *Thank gods.* He stalks toward the cave as he sweeps his tongue inside my mouth, plunging it in and out, foreshadowing what we're about to do. Nerves stutter in my chest even as my body alights with desire.

I'm scared. Not only about the intimacy of having him inside me but also about how vulnerable it'll make me feel. But I *want* to share that intimacy and vulnerability with Ethan more than anything. I want to feel close to him. I want to show him all of me—which is the most terrifying part of all.

"Put me down," I say when Ethan carries me into the cave.

He immediately sets me down on my feet, uncertainty flashing across his face. "We don't have to do . . ."

I tug on the belt of his black dobok and untie it with surprisingly steady hands. Then I push apart his shirt, baring his chest and stomach. My mouth waters at the sight of him. I smooth my hands across his chest, then over his shoulders, sliding his shirt off his back and down his arms.

I reach for the drawstring of his pants and glance at Ethan from beneath my lashes. He stands as immobile as a statue, but I see the frantic fluttering of his pulse at the base of his throat. Holding his gaze, I slide his pants and undergarment past his narrow hips and down his legs until I'm kneeling at his feet. I tap him lightly on the calf, and he meekly lifts one foot, then the other out of his pants.

I slowly stand, letting the fabric of my dobok brush against his bare skin. He shivers, clenching his fists. I take one step back, then another, and sweep my eyes over his naked body.

"Beautiful," I murmur softly. His eyes darken, but he stays silent and still, relinquishing all control to me.

I study every sculpted muscle, every dip and shadow, but my eyes skitter away from his hard length. I focus my gaze on his face and reach for my belt. Oddly, my hands shake more as I work to loosen it. Once the knot is free, I let the belt fall to the ground, and before I lose my nerve, I shrug out of my shirt and let that drop as well.

Ethan struggles to swallow as he follows my every movement, and I grow bolder at the feral light in his eyes. I quickly untie the drawstring of my pants, and taking a deep breath, I push everything down to my ankles and kick it away. I doubt I did that last part with any semblance of grace, but his breath stutters as I straighten to my full height.

He takes himself in his hand as his eyes roam over the small globes of my breasts and the dark triangle between my legs. He groans as he pumps his fist once, then twice, and I watch fascinated. This time I don't look away. I remember how he felt in my hands, hot, hard, and silken. I want to touch him again. I take a step toward him.

"Wait." Ethan holds up both hands.

I falter, confused and worried. "Am I . . . doing something wrong?"

"No. Gods, no. I just need a minute." He rakes his fingers through his hair. "If I touch you right now—if *you* touch *me*—it'll be fast and hard, but I want to take my time with you. I want to make this good for you."

"I . . . I want it to be good for you too." My voice is small. "But I might be bad at it."

"You might be . . . what?" Ethan looks so incredulous that some of my anxiety melts away. "That's not possible."

"I don't . . ." I clear my throat. "I've never done this before."

I see the change in him right away. He doesn't look any less ravenous, and his . . . Well, he's still *obviously* very aroused. But an aching tenderness steals into his eyes, making something unknot in my chest.

"There's no chance in hell you can be bad at this." Ethan closes the distance between us and cups my cheek with one hand, sweeping a strand of hair out of my eyes with the other. "You'll be fucking spectacular."

"You don't know that," I say with an embarrassed laugh.

"I do know." He takes my hand and wraps it around his rock-hard erection. "See what you do to me? All you have to do is *look* at me to undo me. This is already the best sex I've ever had, and we're only getting started."

I beam at him, relief coursing through me. Relief and . . . desire. Gods, I love the feel of him. I tighten my fist around him, and he groans as though he's in pain. I slide my hand up and down his length.

"Easy." He grabs my wrist and holds me still. "We're going to take this nice and easy."

"That sounds boring." I tug on my wrist, but he doesn't let go. So I shrug and wrap my other hand around him.

"Unhand me, woman." He presses his forehead against mine with a chuckle. But when he leans back, his expression is tender and worshipful. "Let me make you feel good."

This time, I don't fight it when he draws my hands away. He rewards me with a toe-curling kiss, then sweeps me off my feet. Then he gently sets me down on top of the robe I flung away this morning, the silk soft and cool against my bare back. He covers my body with his, bearing most of his weight on his forearms.

Then he drops featherlight kisses on my eyelids, across my cheekbones, then finally the corners of my lips. When I try to deepen the kiss, he dips his head and slides down my body, trailing kisses on my neck, my collarbone, then my breasts.

My nipples pebble when his lips draw tantalizingly close to them. When he finally sucks one into his mouth, hard enough for his cheeks to cave, liquid warmth gushes from my core. After showering equal attention on my other breast, he moves lower, planting open-mouthed kisses down my stomach. I squirm, impatient to have him inside me.

"Shhh." His breath tickles the inside of my thigh. "I want to taste you. Let me?"

When he raises half-hooded eyes to me, I manage a fitful nod. He slips his hands down my legs and wraps his hands around my calves, pushing them up until my knees are bent and my feet are flat on the ground. When he settles his head between my legs, I give in to the temptation and open wide for him. With a dark, delicious laugh, he rewards me with a long sweeping lick from my entrance to my clit. I cry out as my hips shoot off the ground.

"Stay still," he whispers, pushing me back down. He pulls me open with his thumbs, and I swerve my hips. "Don't move."

Then he proceeds to lick me so thoroughly that I feel like an ice cream cone melting in the summer heat. He doesn't miss a drop, swirling his tongue to savor me. He scrapes his teeth lightly over my clit, and I turn into a quivering mess. But I want to please him, so I hold myself as still as I can. When he sucks me into his mouth, I can't help but whimper, long and plaintively.

"Ethan, please." I don't care if I'm begging because I'm dying a little. "Please."

"Since you asked so nicely." He buries a finger inside me and groans. "You're soaking wet."

"All for you. Only for you." My head thrashes from side to side.

Ethan surges up, and suddenly his lips are on mine, my taste still clinging to his tongue. I bury my hands in his hair and kiss him back like my life depends on it. And maybe it does. I wrap my legs around his waist, pulling him closer. But he holds himself back, then slides the head of his cock between my slick folds, and I buck against him with a carnal moan. I'm too far gone to be self-conscious.

"Gods, look at you." He rises up on his arms and stares down my body. "You're made to be worshipped."

"Ethan." I run my hands over the straining muscles of his shoulders and skate them up the sides of his neck until I'm cupping his face. "I want you inside me. Please."

"I don't want to hurt you," he says in a broken rasp. "Tell me if it's too much."

"Don't worry." I raise my head to kiss him sweetly. "I won't break."

Holding my eyes, he positions himself at my entrance, then pushes in, inch by inch, rocking his hips slowly. A muscle jumps in his jaw and a shaky breath hisses past his teeth as he fights for control. He fills and stretches me, and I want more. I want all of him. I wrap my legs around his hips and yank him toward me as I arch my back off the ground. Caught off guard, Ethan plunges into me to the hilt and groans at the same time a sharp gasp escapes from me.

"Fuck." He nearly pulls all the way out, but I stop him with my legs. His eyes are frantic as they jump over my face. "Did I hurt you? Are you okay?"

"Hush." I'm winded from the flash of pain but also by the surprising feel of him *inside* me. I breathe, letting my body quiet and adjust. Beneath it all, desire pulses in me and instinct takes over. I wrap my legs tighter around his hips and clench my muscles around him. His eyelashes flutter against his cheeks. "Ethan, I want you."

"Are you sure?" He brushes my hair off my forehead with a trembling hand, and I nod.

He blows out a breath and pushes back in so slowly that I want to scream. But when he's all the way inside—when I feel him deeper than I could've imagined, his girth stretching me—I appreciate the care he took. We stare at each other, taking each other in, and match the tempo of our breathing. I've never been connected to anyone this way before, and tears prickle my eyes. *I'm his.* The desolate loneliness in the darkest corner of my heart dissipates. *At last.*

"You okay?" he asks tenderly.

"Yes." I experimentally pivot my hips, and he jerks inside me. "Oh."

"Oh?" A wry smile quirks his lips. "Is that a good *oh?*"

"It's a very good *oh.*" I swerve my hips again. "Are you going to start moving, or do you expect me to do all the work?"

With a sound between a groan and a laugh, Ethan finally moves, and I want to shout *Hallelujah.* His tempo is excruciatingly slow and measured, but that feverish ache builds in my stomach again, shooting down to my core. I drag my nails down his back and sink my fingers into his ass. His rhythm falters with a moan, and he pounds into me as though he can't stop himself. I feel a thrill of triumph, laced with power, run through me. I did that to him.

I've always been an intuitive creature. I should trust my instincts. I lift my head and suck gently on his shoulder, loving the salty taste of his skin, then I sink my teeth in. A guttural growl rumbles through him, and his hips jerk helplessly against me, thrusting deeper and faster.

"Ethan," I breathe into his ear. I can't help nibbling on his lobe before continuing, "Let go. Take me like you want to."

"I . . ." A vein pulses in his forehead. "I want to make you feel good."

"I feel good. So good." I swivel my hips in a circle, and his lips pull back from his teeth. "But you can make me feel better. Take me harder. Faster."

"Gods, Sunny." Ethan groans as his control shatters.

He lifts my arms above my head and pins them against the ground with one hand. Then he plants his other hand next to my shoulder and raises his torso until his back arches. And he *moves*.

Ethan slams into me, withdraws to the tip, then slams into me again. I scream, the sound catching in my throat every time he drives into me. My staccato cries bounce off the walls of the cave in an erotic echo, and I'm beyond turned on. I scream louder, and he pumps in and out harder and faster. His pace is relentless, but he shows no signs of tiring.

"Oh my gods." I strain against his hold on my wrists, my body writhing. The ache expands and rises until the pressure concentrates into my center. "Oh my *gods*."

He releases my wrists, and I immediately cling on to his shoulders. Sweat beads on his forehead and slides down the sides of his face, dripping off his nose and down his chin like tears. *I'm* close to tears, my pleasure as sharp as pain. Just when I think I can't take it anymore, he inserts his hand between our slick, rocking bodies, and unerringly presses his thumb against my clit.

"Ethan," I cry, splintering into a thousand pieces.

His rhythm breaks down at last. Planting his hand on the ground, he pounds into me, drawing out my cries. The muscles in his neck cord and strain, and I clench around him again and again. With a final thrust that pushes me up the dirt ground, he shouts his release, his body going taut. Then his arms give out, and he collapses on top of me.

His weight makes it difficult for me to breathe, but I decide breathing is not essential. Ethan on top of me, pressing into me. Ethan heavy inside me, connected to me. Those things are essential. They're what I need to live.

My heart stops as I finally see the truth. I need *Ethan* to live. He is essential to my very existence. By refusing his love—by denying my love—I've been suffocating the life out of myself. Have I prevented him from truly living as well?

How could I have been so foolish? Why did I hide my love from him, worried about a prophecy—worried about a future—we may never live to see? One of us might die today. Both of us might die. Am I willing to risk him dying without knowing that I love him? That I love him more than anything . . . more than life itself? A choked sob escapes past my lips.

"Shit." Ethan jerks his head up, his eyes still half-hooded. But when his gaze focuses enough to see me beneath him, he damn near throws his body off mine, collapsing on the ground beside me. "I'm sorry. I was crushing you."

I shake my head, tears pouring out the corners of my eyes. I want to tell him that I love being crushed by him. That I already miss the feel of him inside me. That I love him with all my battered heart. I want to tell him I can't believe he loves me back. It feels like the most wonderful miracle, and I'm afraid it's all a dream. Another sob tears out of me.

"Oh gods. Are you okay? What's wrong?" He raises himself on his forearm and reaches out a hand to wipe away my tears. "What can I do? Sunny, please don't cry."

"Ethan . . ." I sob.

"Yes, baby. What is it?" His voice breaks. "Tell me what to do."

"I love you." Then I wail, falling apart and not caring. "I love you so much."

Ethan's lips part on a rush of breath, and his face becomes a blank mask, so completely devoid of expression that he looks lifeless. He slowly backs away and rises to his feet. I sit up and tug his outer robe free from under me to hold it against my breasts. I heave sharp, stuttering breaths, trying to stem the tide of tears.

He picks up his discarded pants and pulls them on, one leg at a time. I watch his quiet and careful movements, not knowing what to think. No, I don't *let* myself think. I hold myself still and wait. He straightens to his full height, but his eyes are unfocused, and he stares at the wall of the cave like he's confused why there are no answers written on it. When he stays that way for endless minutes, I can't hold my fear at bay any longer.

"Ethan?" I sound small and scared, like a lost child.

His eyelids flutter, then he glances down at me. At first, I'm not sure he even recognizes me, then he sucks in a gasping breath like he's surfacing from an airless place. When his eyes finally focus on me, it takes all my strength not to look away from the intensity of his gaze. I see relief and fear, joy and sorrow, greed and reverence. Above all, I see love, pure and endless.

"Thank the fucking gods." His voice breaks. "But if you love me . . . Why, Sunny?"

"Because the prophecy says—" I begin.

"I will *never* hurt you," he interjects.

"I know you don't *want* to hurt me." I clutch the robe tighter against my chest and take a halting breath. "But we don't know what lies ahead."

Ethan's lips press into a hard, straight line.

"If you have to kill me . . ." I hold up a hand when he opens his mouth to protest. "If you have to kill me, I thought it would hurt you less if you didn't know I loved you too."

"If I kill you"—crouching down in front of me, he takes his robe from my hands and wraps it tenderly around me—"there would be no *me* left to hurt."

"Ethan." I gasp, my eyes widening with horror. "D . . . don't you dare . . ."

"I won't forsake all those who sacrificed their lives for me," he says grimly. "But don't you see? I would be dead inside. Without you, there is no me."

What can I say to that? I understand too well what he means. It would be the same for me. I'm done trying to figure out how to make him hurt less. If the prophecy comes true, nothing can do that. I can only offer him the truth *now*, before our destiny catches up with us.

"I love you." I hold his gaze and whisper, "Now and forever. From this life to the next."

Fresh tears slide down my cheeks, and he jumps into action. He sits cross-legged on the ground and pulls me onto his lap. Tucking my head under his chin, he rocks us back and forth without saying a word.

His calm strength seeps into me, and my tears finally quiet. But I let him hold me awhile longer because I know he needs it as much as I do. This is our moment—the moment we became *us*. We are whole and complete, together at last. Nothing has ever been more *right* than us.

Is this what it feels like to accept your destiny? It's like all the puzzle pieces are falling into place, smooth and easy. None of it is forced. Everything fits perfectly. And I see the whole picture with crystal clarity. I tilt my head to meet his eyes and cup his beloved face.

"I love you, Ethan."

"I love you, Sunny."

No matter what happens, I am his, and he is mine. It is a fundamental truth, written in stone. Our love is eternal. Nothing can ever change that.

CHAPTER TWENTY

When I step outside the cave, the sky is still blue, the trees are still tall, and the ground still lies beneath my feet. But *everything* has changed in the span of hours. Ethan is mine, and I am his. I laugh and strut around in my hanbok, but I stop with a wince. I'm sore in an odd but not unpleasant way, which makes me grin harder. Pleasant or not, it seems I'm in no condition for smug strutting. Because of *sex.*

I might've dissolved into obnoxious giggles if Jihun hadn't walked out of the woods at that exact moment. But all thoughts of laughter evaporate when I don't see the gamas at his side. I pick up my voluminous skirt and run toward him.

"What happened?" I grab his sleeve. "You couldn't get the gamas?"

"Have some faith." His lips quirk as he gently loosens my grip. My stomach drops when he hangs on to my hand a second too long. *Gods, I don't want to hurt him.* "I glamoured them and hid them in the woods. They would be too conspicuous out in the alcove."

I slip my hand from his and smooth nonexistent wrinkles out of my apron overcoat. Unlike those worn by the palace uinyeos or even those at the Suhoshin headquarters, my hanbok is coarse and worn, with faint stains on the apron even after a good wash.

"Are you sure I'll be allowed into the palace in such shabby clothes?" I squint up at him. We discussed the overall plan, weaving in my modifications, but I still have lingering questions.

"You're supposed to be the assistant of a renowned but eccentric physician. Someone who refused to become a royal physician many times over." Jihun gives me a once-over and nods in approval. "He and his assistant only serve the poor, so they wouldn't have anything other than threadbare clothes to wear. Even when answering the king's summons."

"That makes sense. Also, I get that the physician needs to take a palanquin because he's blind"—I cock my head to the side—"but how do we justify his assistant taking one?"

"According to our palace spy, the king doesn't want word of his ailment to spread. So he ordered the province inspector to bring the physician and his assistant to him in secret," Jihun explains. "It's actually a stroke of luck for us. Even if you dampen your magic, a fellow being of Mountains might recognize the gumiho in you. That would give us away even before we made it to the Shinsi Palace."

"Okay." I shrug. "As long as we have a legitimate excuse for it."

"But I still don't like the idea of the prince escorting us as the province inspector." Jihun crosses his arms over his chest. "He'd be safer in the palanquin as the blind physician."

"I hate to break it to you, but you're starting to glow under your disguise. No amount of disguise or glamour can hide that you're a seonnam for long. You're dealing with fellow shinbiins, not skeptical humans who refuse to believe in magic." I arch my eyebrow. "But Ethan is half a being of Mountains. As long as he locks down the Sky in him, he'll pass muster better than you."

He grunts noncommittally. Gods, he's stubborn. I grin affectionately at him, but my smile slides off my face when I remember . . . I shut my eyes for a moment, searching for strength. I have to tell him about me and Ethan. He deserves to know.

"Jihun, I—"

"My prince." He looks past me and bows his head. "The gamas are waiting in the woods."

I glance over my shoulder at Ethan. Even wearing a jade dopo that has seen better days and with the shadow of his gat obscuring his eyes, he is handsome enough to make my knees weak. I blush even before I can fight it. He holds Jihun's gaze over my head, but the corners of his lips quiver as though he's fighting a smile. I blush harder.

Ethan clears his throat and asks, "Are we still good to go?"

"Yes," Jihun confirms. "Our spy will ensure our safe passage to the king's inner chambers once we get to the palace. But we must hurry."

"Of course. Here, Captain." Ethan hands him a modest overcoat befitting an impoverished physician. "I cleaned up our camp enough to pass casual inspection, so we can leave as soon as you're ready."

"Thank you." Jihun accepts the dopo with both hands and swiftly shrugs into it. It's a little tight around his shoulders and chest, but it'll have to do. Considering the time crunch we were under, he did an amazing job of gathering the appropriate disguises for all of us. "This way."

Ethan and I follow him into the woods, and with a short wave of his hand, Jihun unveils the gamas a few yards away. They aren't as beautiful as the ones from his estate, but they're more than sufficient for our needs. Ethan opens the door to the first palanquin and motions for me to get in.

With a sudden lurch of fear, I catch his eyes. The next time I step out of the gama, we might have to fight for our lives. He only just became mine. I'm not ready to lose him. "A . . . are you sure you know the way to the palace?"

"My mother's memories are clear," he says simply, but his eyes shine with understanding. He runs the back of his hand down my cheek. "Don't worry, Sunny."

"Have some faith," Jihun says, echoing his prior words from my other side. "I won't let any harm come to you or the prince."

I give him a tremulous smile. "I guess you're *okay* at what you do."

Jihun pretends to glower at me, but he can't hide the tenderness in his expression, and I want to hug the stupid, beautiful seonnam. But with a solemn nod at Ethan, he steps inside his palanquin, saving me from the embarrassing display of affection. Then I immediately stand on my tiptoes and plant a kiss on Ethan's lips—it's like I can't stop myself from these effusive emotional spectacles—and dive inside my gama before I start climbing him.

"I love you," Ethan mouths, then says out loud, "I'll see you soon."

I nod like a possessed Bobblehead and hold his eyes as the door closes, ducking my head to look at his face a second longer. I lay the tips of my fingers on the closed wooden door and whisper the words I couldn't say without falling apart, "You are my everything."

The palanquin levitates off the ground and moves forward with the slightest jerk. My lower lip trembles dangerously, and I bite down on it without mercy. I blow out a long breath and rest my palms on my knees. This is not the time for tears. This is the time to be brave and strong. No more avoidance. These males on either side of me, and my friends back in the Kingdom of Mountains, are precious to me. I cannot fail them. I *will* not.

I hold my palm out, remembering the flickering white light I summoned in the study. With everything that's happened, that night feels like a lifetime ago, but it has only been a few days. I should be able to do it again, right? *Easy peasy.* With a self-deprecating snort, I call to the light of the Yeoiju—carelessly, jokingly—and fall back in shock when a white flame ignites in the center of my palm.

"Sunny," Ethan whispers urgently. "Are you okay? What's going on?"

"Everything is o . . . okay." I close my eyes and count to five. *We need to do this methodically. In five-second increments.* Remembering Minju's advice, I fist my hand and extinguish the flame.

"You don't sound—"

"I'm fine." I crack the window open and peer up at Ethan. "I must've rocked the palanquin, checking on my hwando."

He doesn't need the added worry of my unsupervised Yeoiju practice. I didn't *really* mean to summon the light anyway. The element of surprise is the only thing going for us in this mission. If I'd known I could actually do it, I wouldn't have risked exposing us by accidentally blowing the roof off this palanquin.

But how did I *do* that? It was so easy, so effortless. I gingerly finger the word of power on my back, over my hanbok. I don't sense even a prickle of heat—the rune is completely dormant—so it isn't that. But *I* feel awake. I feel . . . *unleashed.*

Did surrendering to my love free me somehow, like a mountainous boulder rolling off my soul? Was I so focused on hiding my love from Ethan, holding everything in so tight, that I suffocated my own powers? Can it be true? Did my desperation to protect Ethan constrain my magic like the stone of tears had bound his powers?

I'm sorely tempted to summon the light again, but I restrain myself. *Later.* I'll see if it's just as easy to call on the Yeoiju's magic. I'll see if loving Ethan with all of me—if being braver than I've ever been—has somehow made me more powerful. *Later.*

I sigh, suddenly restless. I don't know how far we've come, or how far we have left to go. The anticipation is killing me. If we're going to die, I want to get on with it. Better yet, I want us to capture the King of Mountains and have him *peacefully* abdicate his throne to Ethan. But I have a feeling that is not how this is going to play out.

I drum my fingers against my knees, willing the time to pass more quickly. I can't even stare out at the passing scenery as I would on a long drive in the Mortal Realm. The wooden walls of the palanquin seem to close in on me, and I shut my eyes against the unexpected bout of claustrophobia. All I can do is breathe and wait.

Harsh whispers jerk me awake, and I lift my ass halfway off the palanquin floor. I fight the impulse to throw the window open to see what's happening. Instead, I calm my pounding heart and listen.

"You're late," a female snaps, sounding more afraid than angry. "We must hurry. I have been appeasing him, telling him the roads are muddy from the rain. But he will soon catch on that something is amiss."

"My deepest apologies." Ethan's voice is pitched low but sincere. "I know the risk you're taking by helping us. No matter what happens, we won't let any harm come to you."

"No one can keep any of us safe." The female scoffs, then softens her tone. "The king grows more paranoid by the day. He would have killed me, and the younger court ladies under my supervision, for one reason or another. I am risking no more than a handful of days with this betrayal."

"A risk nonetheless," Ethan insists. "I thank you for your courage."

"Come with me," she says gruffly.

My gama jostles as it picks up pace, and I shoot my hand out to steady myself against the side wall. I take deep breaths to halt the light tremors quaking through me. When breathing exercises fail, I wrap my hand around the hilt of my hwando, protruding from under my skirt. My shoulders immediately drop away from my ears, and I sigh in relief. My sword is like a warm, cozy security blanket, except it's pointy, sharp, and deadly.

"We're here," Ethan warns in a rough whisper a second before my palanquin settles on the ground.

I step out of the palanquin with my eyes lowered demurely, to stay in character as the physician's assistant. But I needn't have bothered. There is no one around, except us. Our spy brought us to the back entrance of a grand hanok, which stands at the center of a vast, walled courtyard.

I peek at the pale, drawn face of our spy, who casts a furtive glance around our surroundings. Her hanbok chima is the color of rich soil and her grass green jeogori has a dangui, an elongated front panel that hangs past her navel. My eyes widen in surprise as I realize she's a high-ranking court lady.

No pond, shrubs, or trees surround the opulent hanok with its crimson latticed windows and its arching, jade-tiled roof. Anyone approaching the structure would be seen from yards away from every side. Now I understand why sneaking in at night wasn't an option.

Ethan and Jihun flank me as we face the court lady. She pins us with her sharp gaze and gets straight to business.

"The king only steps outside his jimil to attend the morning assembly in the royal audience hall with his officials, then he remains in his chambers for the rest of the day. He has terminated all audience with visiting officials and scholars since his . . . illness." The court lady nods at us with grim determination. "My assistant gungnyeo is doing her best to keep the royal guards occupied, but they will return before long. You must follow me."

We climb the stone steps and remove our shoes before entering the king's quarters. The inner hallways are dim, as though even the sun is afraid to approach the volatile tyrant, and the silence feels ominous, like it isn't an absence of sound but a suffocation of it.

Playing the part of the blind physician, Jihun places his hand on my arm and moves with deliberate hesitance, lightly shuffling his feet. I take care to match my steps to his. Ethan's strides are sure footed as he walks ahead of us with the court lady. He must be familiar with the layout, thanks to his mother's memories.

Ethan has only spoken of the King of Mountains in anger, but a part of him must feel the pull of blood. No matter what the male has done, he is still his father. Jihun and I will find a way to kill the powerful king, if it comes to that. We agreed not to let that burden fall on Ethan. Even together, we are not strong enough to defeat the tyrant, but I'm willing to die trying. Or better yet, I'll take the motherfucker with me.

Whenever I see other gungnyeos coming down the hallway, I lower my eyes even as my adrenaline spikes. But every court lady we pass bows to our spy with deference, marking her as the most senior court lady, the jimil sanggung. She must have dedicated her entire life to obtain that position. Things must be worse than we thought if she is willing to risk her life's work to help us take down the king.

The sanggung comes to a stop in front of a room with wide latticed double doors, with two court ladies kneeling on opposite ends of the doors. When one of the court ladies glances up, our spy gives her a sharp shake of her head, and the young gungnyeo quickly shifts her eyes back to her lap.

"Your Majesty," the jimil sanggung intones. "The inspector has arrived with the physician."

There is a terse murmur inside the king's chambers, and a high-pitched male voice calls out, "You may enter."

The two gungnyeos slide open the double doors, keeping their heads bent. The jimil sanggung bows deep from her waist, and we mimic her from three steps behind. I whisper what's happening to Jihun—cueing him on when to bow and when to straighten—as though he really can't see. The sanggung walks into the chambers with featherlight steps, her hands clasped lightly over her navel, and we follow her inside.

The King of Mountains sits behind a low wooden desk, with a shaking hand fisted on top of it. Despite the haggard lines of his face and the dark circles beneath his eyes, he is undoubtedly handsome in a bold, rugged way. I see Ethan in the strong lines of the king's jaw and the dark arches of his eyebrows. But the cruel twist of the tyrant's lips and the madness in his eyes shatters the illusion of any likeness between Ethan and his father.

Even in his private chambers, the king wears a forest green silk robe with large circular embroideries on each shoulder. I only catch a glimpse before I lower my eyes, but the gold threads seem to depict a roaring bear, rearing up on its hind legs. *A bear?* I'm tempted to glance up again, but Jihun tightens his grip on my arm in caution.

"But *look* at him, Your Majesty." The shrill complaint comes from the male standing near the king's side in a voluminous robe the color of dry bark. He must be the king's eunuch. "He is no better than a peasant. A blind physician? Who has heard of such a thing?"

"Silence," the king hisses, his voice cold and sharp as a scalpel. The eunuch immediately scuttles back, dipping his head low like a turtle hiding inside its shell. "Inspector, I hope for your sake that you brought me the right physician."

"Thank you for your benevolent consideration, Your Majesty." Ethan bows obsequiously, but a muscle tics in his jaw. I feel his magic jerk against the surface. I bend my elbow until it brushes against his arm. *Please Ethan.* "Your humble servant has indeed brought Your Majesty the right physician."

"Leave us," the king says with a dismissive wave. I'm not sure who he's ordering to leave.

"Yes, Your Majesty." The jimil sanggung backs away toward the doors.

The eunuch comes out of his shell to whine loudly, "But Your Majesty—"

"Utter another word"—the king sounds almost bored as he glances at his fingernails—"and I will have your tongue for supper, sliced and grilled."

Pressing his lips tightly together, the eunuch scrambles out of the room with one last resentful glare at Ethan and Jihun. He doesn't condescend to give me, a lowly female, even a dirty look. I am so devastated by the slight. How ever will I recover?

So I guess the tyrant wanted the sanggung and his eunuch out . . .

"Wait." The king doesn't raise his voice, but every one of us freezes in place. I don't dare breathe, and I focus on keeping my magic locked down. Has the king found us out? Did something give us away? "Jang Sanggung, show the inspector out. I have no more need of him."

Ethan and Jihun stiffen on either side of me, and it takes all my willpower to keep my eyes trained to the floor. If the king is as paranoid as our spy said, he wouldn't miss a single out-of-place glance.

"This lowly one is honored to have stayed in your presence for this long. Thank you for your boundless forbearance, Your Majesty,"

Ethan says smoothly, his arm brushing against my elbow in a wisp of reassurance. "Your humble servant will take your leave now."

This isn't a disaster. Jihun and I can handle the first part of the plan without Ethan. I'll administer acupuncture on the king and paralyze him before he suspects anything. If the paralysis part goes awry . . . it might be better for Ethan not to be here.

Jang Sanggung and Ethan back out of the king's chambers, bowing from their waists the entire time. I don't dare glance behind me, but I hear the sanggung quietly urge the court ladies to close the doors. I feel Ethan's gaze on me until they slide shut.

"Do you know why you have been summoned, physician?" The tyrant arches an eyebrow at Jihun, who keeps his eyes unfocused.

"This lowly one has not been told the specifics of Your Majesty's condition," Jihun answers in a weedy, intimidated voice.

"I thought someone of your renown can take one look at me . . ." The king cackles, slapping his hand on his desk. "Pardon my . . . slip. You obviously cannot see me."

"No, Your Majesty." Jihun dips his head. "I beg your pardon, Your Majesty."

"You will have to do much more than beg my pardon if your blindness inconveniences me any further," the king roars in a sudden change of mood. "Why are you not examining me? You dare waste the king's time?"

Bowing our heads repeatedly, I help Jihun stumble over to the king, and we kneel in front of his low desk. The king's eyes focus on my face with narrowed intensity, and I duck my head as though I'm terrified, while suppressing my magic even deeper inside me. *Just a little bit longer.*

"Your Majesty." Jihun extends shaking hands across the desk. "May this lowly one examine your pulse?"

"If you value your life, do not keep your filthy fingers on my wrist for one second longer than necessary," the king snaps but offers his wrist to Jihun, exposing a long thin scar on his palm.

I nearly whimper with relief. Our plan would never work if Shim Duna's deranged rant about the king's scar had been a lie. If the king still had the power of invincibility, my acupuncture needles wouldn't so much as prick his skin.

But cold sweat beads on my forehead as I realize a flaw to our plan. Every subject in the Kingdom of Mountains must know that their kings have the power of invincibility. The physician and his assistant are not supposed to know that the tyrant's skin can be pierced. If we offer him acupuncture, he will suspect us right away.

"This l . . . lowly one would not d . . . dare," Jihun stutters in feigned fear as he places the tips of his fingers on the king's pulse point. I try to catch his eyes, but he has his head angled away from me.

"Tell me, physician," the king drawls, even though there's desperation in his eyes. "What is it that ails me?"

The king already knows he isn't ill. He knows his power of invincibility is gone, but he doesn't want to accept it. So he will kill Jihun and me—or rather the physician and his assistant—for being unable to cure him, just to have someone to blame and punish for his loss. The tyrant is killing his own subjects to vent his fear and frustration. He is as cruel as he is cowardly.

My hands fist beneath my apron. I can't let him get away with it. I have to figure out a way to paralyze him without raising his suspicions. I won't give up without trying. For Ethan. For the people of the Kingdom of Mountains.

"Your life force is weary, Your Majesty. You have given too much of yourself to the service of your people," Jihun says in a simpering tone. He and I decided beforehand to tell the king that his gi needs strengthening. That generic yet popular diagnosis had always appeased the hypochondriacs in my old village. "We are humbled and grateful for your sacrifice, but this lowly one implores you to think of your health."

The king harrumphs, even though he is obviously pleased by the flattery.

"My assistant—" Jihun continues, and I burst into tears, clapping a hand over my mouth to quiet my sobs.

"If only His Majesty weren't as powerful as the gods . . ." I stop to take a shuddering breath, risking the barest flicker of a gaze toward Jihun. "If only he could receive acupuncture like the rest of us . . ."

"Silence, you insolent girl." Jihun plays along with my act, a slight tilt of his head the only indication of his surprise. I hope he understands why I'm doing this. "You dare speak in the presence of the king?"

"Let the girl speak." A greedy kind of hope flashes in the king's eyes.

"This lowly girl has restored the life force of many commoners through acupuncture, Your Majesty." I dip my head and speak in a trembling voice. "I feel as though the heavens are collapsing at the thought that you, whose life is worth a million of ours, cannot receive the ministrations which may heal your gi."

"You dare presume to understand my powers?" the king blusters. "I should have your head."

"Please forgive the foolish girl, Your Majesty." Jihun bows with his forehead pressed against the floor.

I bow down as well, holding my breath. I took a gamble, hoping to tap into the king's desperation. I prepare for the tyrant to call for his royal guards to execute us on the spot, but I pray that he takes the bait.

"I can withdraw my invincibility at will," the king lies smoothly, and my body goes limp with relief. "If the girl is as good as she claims, I will permit her to administer acupuncture on me."

It worked. Thank gods.

"Gratitude fills this lowly one to the brim," Jihun intones, raising his head at last. "This uinyeo has been gifted with the most sensitive fingertips of her generation. The gods must have bestowed such a talent on this common girl so that she may be of use to you. It would be her greatest honor to administer acupuncture on you, Your Majesty."

"She would normally lose her lowborn hands if she touched the king's body." The tyrant wants to believe Jihun. He wants to believe that I can restore his magic. "But, perhaps, I will let her keep them if she can cure me."

"Your generosity and mercy know no bounds, Your Majesty," Jihun says. "Might this lowly one dare ask the king to lie down on his sleeping mat?"

Arching a condescending brow at Jihun, the king walks over to the sleeping alcove, then lies down on his mat. He sighs ponderously and closes his eyes, as though he cannot bear to look at our peasant faces any longer. "I presume you will ask to bare my chest. Do as you must."

"You are as wise as you are merciful." Jihun kneels near the king's head with my unnecessary guidance, and I kneel directly in front of the king's torso. "May she proceed?"

"The faster this ordeal is over with, the better." The King of Mountains smirks, as though he is impressed by his own munificence.

We *have* him. I carefully draw apart his robe and shirt, my blood pounding in my ears. I withdraw an acupuncture box from my sleeve and open it to reveal a row of silver needles. We're so close.

Please let this work.

Exhaling quietly, I press the first needle into the pressure point on the side of his neck. *Just three more.* My hand trembles lightly as I insert the next needle below his right clavicle, then another one over his heart. My breath quickens. Once I place a needle in the last pressure point, the king will be paralyzed.

Just one more.

I poise my needle over his solar plexus and fight to steady my hand. I can't miss the pressure point. I lower the needle, but before the tip can pierce his skin, the king's hand shoots out and grabs my wrist in a punishing grip. I only have time to gasp before his other hand is pressing a sharp knife against my throat. Jihun lurches forward, and I feel the rush of wind as his wings burst open.

"Steady, seonnam," the king croons. "I don't want to slit her pretty throat . . . yet. Unless you leave me no choice."

Jihun freezes, even as his lips pull back in a snarl. "Let her go."

"I wasn't entirely certain what she meant to do until she embedded the third needle over my heart. Why would you want to paralyze me, little girl?" The king presses the tip of his knife into my skin, and warm blood trickles down my throat. A look of surprises ripples across his face as he gingerly sniffs at my cut. "A *gumiho*? I am both intrigued and disgusted. Whatever do you want with me, beast?"

The king licks his lips and twists the knife against my throat, drawing more blood without pushing it in any deeper. He smiles when I hiss. *Fuck.* I hate that I gave him the satisfaction. I have to stop him. I don't want Ethan to kill his father. But I can't get out of the king's grasp before he opens up my carotid artery. I'll be dead in fifteen seconds.

"Leave her alo—" Jihun's roar is drowned out when the doors to the king's chambers rip off their hinges and crash into the room.

"Sunny," Ethan shouts as he runs toward me.

"Ethan, don't . . ." The knife presses deeper into my throat, cutting off my words.

"Stop where you are," the king shrieks, fear and confusion in his eyes. "Or she will be dead before you reach her."

Ethan jerks to a stop, his face contorted in fury. Then he raises his arm from across the room and holds his palm out toward his father. "I will end you."

From the corner of my eye, I glimpse the king raising his own hand, and I lunge to stop him. The next second, a fiery burst of energy skims over my head and rams into the tyrant's chest. I stay ducked low to the ground as the king is thrown into the air and slammed against the back wall. He grunts as he drops to the floor with a thud, his knife rolling out of his limp grasp.

I clap my hand against my neck to stanch the flow of blood. The king had the wherewithal to slice the side of my throat as he was thrown back. The cut isn't deep, but it's not a papercut either. Jihun's nostrils flare with rage when he sees blood seeping through my fingers. He closes the short distance between us and wraps his arm around my shoulders.

I glare at him to tell him to keep his mouth shut. If Ethan sees that I'm hurt, he is likely to lose his shit even more. Fortunately, he still stands halfway across the room, distracted by the sight of his father lying on the floor.

The King of Mountains struggles to his knees and stares at his son, tears flooding his eyes. Ethan comes to stand over Jihun and me, but his gaze stays glued to his father. I look at Jihun, and he nods. The king's tears look genuine, but we can't let our guards down.

"You look like her," the king whispers before his face crumples on a sob. "My s . . . son."

Ethan's eyes soften for a split second before the Prince of Mountains takes command. "Do not speak of my mother, tyrant."

"I loved her." He means it. The king believes that he loved the Queen of Mountains.

"Why do I find it hard to believe that the male who *murdered* my mother loved her?" Ethan snarls but walks up to his father as though drawn to him despite himself.

"Son." The king holds out a trembling hand. "Please . . ."

"'Please' what?" Ethan grabs the king by his lapels and raises him to his feet. Then he shoves him in the chest, sending him stumbling back against the wall. And his confusion, fury, and desperation distill into a single word. *"What?"*

"Please don't make me"—the king's face morphs into an ugly mask of hate as he lunges for Ethan—"*kill you.*"

Shock makes me slow to react, and I see the glint of metal too late. The bastard made a show of groveling on the floor to retrieve his knife. And suddenly, I know with chilling certainty that the king's blade is forged with Dangun's tombstone—a knife capable of killing his son.

Jihun and I rush toward Ethan, but Jang Sanggung somehow reaches him before us and throws herself in front of the king's knife. She gasps as the blade sinks into her stomach.

"No." Ethan catches her before she falls to her knees and lowers her to the ground. "Please no."

"You stupid bitch," the king screeches, backing away from them. "Guards. Come protect your king, you worthless bastards."

"Enough." Ethan doesn't raise his voice, but it booms through the chambers and smothers the king's shrill outburst. With one arm holding the wounded sanggung against him, he aims his palm toward his father and blasts a jet of tightly coiled magic from his hand.

Ethan caught him unawares earlier, but the king is prepared for him this time. He only stumbles back two steps before he regains his footing and pushes out both palms to counter the attack. Ethan grunts as the force of the king's magic shoves his shoulder back, but he manages to keep his arm outstretched.

Gritting his teeth, Ethan sends another pulse of magic out of his palm. The king staggers but holds his ground. The open flaps of his shirt whip around him, drawing my eyes to his torso. The needles I placed in him still protrude from his chest and the side of his neck. I spin toward the doorless entrance as the king's royal guards rush into the chambers with their swords drawn.

"Stand down, guards." Jihun steps in front of them and summons his longsword. "You have no reason to die tonight."

But the royal guards seem to have a death wish and rush the formidable suhoshin with a battle cry. With a resigned sigh, Jihun blocks and parries their strikes with unhurried swings of his sword, making no offensive moves of his own.

Ethan's shoulders are squared again, but his extended arm is trembling under the strain of battle. The king grits his teeth to hold himself steady, but he won't be able to last much longer either. Even so, Ethan can't win this battle with Jang Sanggung in one arm.

My hand is slick with my blood, but the wound has already stopped bleeding. I hastily wipe my palm and fingers on my apron and reach for my acupuncture box. Jihun still holds off the royal guards without attacking them, but his movements are sharper, more focused, as they advance on him. Trusting he has the situation under control, I withdraw a needle and grip it tightly between my thumb and index finger.

I focus my eyes on the magic pulsating between the King of Mountains and Ethan. Their life forces extend forward and outward, creating a long cylindrical stream of power between them. The green of the king's gi and the silver-green swirl of Ethan's gi clash evenly at the middle, where fiery bursts of magic erupt like crashing waves.

I definitely do *not* want to find out what happens if I so much as brush against such powerful magic. But my stomach lurches when the king launches a surge of power at his son and Ethan's silver-and-green gi loses half the ground.

I have to get the last needle into the king's solar plexus and paralyze him.

The king will see me coming. It can't be helped. I just have to be fast—so fast that the king won't get a chance to react and aim one of his hands at me. But if he does, then that would divert some of his power toward me and Ethan can overtake him. It's basically a win-win situation, except the second win will cost me my life. Ethan will live, though.

I shift into a runner's crouch, wishing I could take my gumiho form. I'm so much faster in that body. Too bad I need opposable thumbs for acupuncture. There's no time to overthink it. *Sorry, Captain Seo. I have to act, not think.*

And I take off toward the King of Mountains.

CHAPTER TWENTY-ONE

The chambers blur around me as I rush toward the King of Mountains. I'm stunned at my speed—my human body is moving as fast as my gumiho—but I'll take it and gladly. I can think about the why later. I near the king in a heartbeat and drop into a baseball slide, barely avoiding the stream of power. I pop up between his outstretched arms just as the king's startled gaze meets mine.

"Freeze." I stick the needle into his solar plexus, and the king does exactly as he's told. He freezes with his arms extended in front of him, wearing a look of gaping shock, and his magic shuts off all at once.

I spin around to face Ethan, the king's immobile arms bracketing my head, and my eyes widen in horror. Captain Seo was right. I should have thought this through. Since I paralyzed the king and severed his magic, Ethan's stream of power has nowhere to go . . . except straight at me. A scream lodges in my throat as I raise my hands to shield my face.

"Sunny," Ethan shouts.

I hear a deafening crash, and I'm tackled to the ground from my side and smothered under a large, hard body. I can hardly breathe, which is excellent news, because it means I'm not dead. *What about Ethan?* I flail under the big oaf, trying to get him off me.

"Are you all right?" Jihun lifts his torso a few inches, allowing me to suck in a heaving breath.

"Get off me," I wheeze, then flinch when I notice the debris crashing down on us. Jihun grunts, but none of the rubble hits my face, and I realize he has his wings spread over us. My voice softens. "I need to make sure Ethan is okay."

"He's safe," Jihun reassures me through clenched teeth, straining against the falling rubble. "I saw him throw his shield up."

"I still want you to get off me." I push against the wall of his chest. "You're getting hurt, you idiot."

Only when the dust settles around us does the stubborn ass push himself off me. I slap his hand away when he tries to help me up, and I push to my feet on my own. I immediately spin Jihun around to check his back for injuries.

"Gods damn it. Your fucking wings are invisible," I growl. "I can't see if you're hurt or not."

"I'm fine." Jihun gently pushes my hand off his arm and turns back toward me. His face is pale, and I scan his body with worried eyes. "Go check on the prince."

I gasp and spin around until I find Ethan, sitting inside a dustless circle with the jimil sanggung in his arms. I squeeze Jihun's hand in thanks and run over to them.

"Ethan." I kneel next to him, and he reaches out to cradle my cheek in his hand. I lean into his touch, cupping my hand over his. "Are you okay?"

"I'm fine." But he doesn't sound too happy about it. "I'm sorry I couldn't stop my magic in time. I could've hurt you."

"Ethan, look at me. You *didn't* hurt me." I glance up at the open sky, then at the wreckage around us. He must've thrown his hand up toward the ceiling to avoid hitting me. "But you did a number on the king's chambers."

"I apologize for the interruption." Jihun comes to stand in front of us, twisting his wrist to summon the sword he dropped when he threw himself over me. "But we aren't quite finished with our mission."

"Shit," I mutter as I jump to my feet, unsheathing my hwando from under my skirt.

The royal guards had formed a shield of bodies around their paralyzed king and suffered the brunt of the injuries. Bleeding from their heads, shoulders, and backs, the guards struggle to regroup, limping toward us with their weapons raised in shaking arms. But they're shinbiins. They'll heal soon, and we'll be outnumbered, ten to three. Worse yet, the king might soon free himself from his paralysis and add his might to their numbers.

"My prince," Jang Sanggung says in a ragged whisper. Ethan and I exchange a surprised glance. She must have overheard his brief exchange with his father. "Please help me stand."

"You shouldn't move." Ethan shakes his head. "We need to find a physician to care for your wound."

"Please." The sanggung grips his hand. "I beg of you, Your Highness."

"Very well." Ethan helps her up with an arm around her back, concern drawing his eyebrows together. She presses a bloody hand to her stomach and straightens to her full height, leaning heavily on him.

"Royal guards, we no longer need to serve the tyrant king." Even in pain, Jang Sanggung's voice rings with conviction. "You see before you the Prince of Mountains. The queen's son has returned to claim his rightful throne."

A confused murmur ripples through the royal guards, and a male who stands a head above the others steps forward. "Jang Sanggung, how can you be sure of this?"

"The king himself called him *my son*." She laughs softly even as she winces in pain. "And look at him, Captain Ha. He is her spitting image. I should have seen it immediately."

The captain swallows and pivots slightly to face Ethan with his whole body. After a searching gaze, he rasps, "Are . . . are you the son of our queen?"

"Yes," Ethan says solemnly, then he catches my eyes and raises his brows at me. Understanding his unspoken request, I rush to take the sanggung from his arms and support her weight with my body.

"Do not be alarmed." Ethan stretches a placating hand toward the captain and the royal guards. "I will not raise these against you."

Then with the barest flex of his wrists, Ethan summons the golden axe and the silver axe in his hands. With a collective gasp, the royal guards stumble back, eyes wide with fear and reverence. But after a shocked second, they fall to their knees and press their foreheads against the floor.

"Your Majesty," they intone as one.

"I am not your king yet." It is Ethan's turn to rear back in shock. "I summoned the axes to show you that I am who Jang Sanggung says I am. I have come to . . . *reason* with the King of Mountains. I am here to convince him to abdicate without resorting to bloodshed. The people of this kingdom have suffered enough."

The royal guards remain silent on the floor, and Jang Sanggung smiles at Ethan. "You must give them permission to rise, Your Majesty."

"I'm not . . . Never mind for now." He shoots her a flustered glance, then says, "Guards, you may rise."

"I thought you were our prince, but you have shown us that you are our king." The sanggung's lips tremble as tears well in her eyes. "You possess the golden axe and the silver axe. It matters not who sits on the throne. The Kingdom of Mountains has chosen you as its king."

"Your Majesty," the royal guards chorus once more, with their fists over their hearts, bowing their heads low.

"Jesus Christ," Ethan mutters under his breath.

"Relax, dingus. They're only swearing their undying fealty to you," I say with a teasing smile. Relief runs through me when he chuckles incredulously. "What's the big deal?"

He's understandably overwhelmed. Even though this has been his end goal since he broke the stone of tears, it's a whole other story to have it actually happen. Ethan is the King of Mountains. A shaky exhale flutters past my lips. *Holy fuck.* He is the ruler of this kingdom. *I* need a moment to process it. I can't begin to imagine what's going through his head right now. It feels hopelessly inadequate, but I squeeze his hand to lend him my strength. I'm gratified when he squeezes back.

"We should secure your father before he breaks free of the paralysis," Jihun reminds Ethan in a low voice.

"Yes, of course." Ethan draws his shoulders back and faces the captain of the royal guards. "Captain Ha, secure the tyrant. The paralysis will not hold for much longer."

"Yes, Your Majesty." After a bow, he turns to the guards. "What are you waiting for? Restrain him with the net."

The royal guards launch a shimmering silver net—similar to the one thrown at me when I first arrived at the Kingdom of Sky—over the paralyzed king. I breathe a sigh of relief. Even my gumiho couldn't break free of that net.

"Is there a prison capable of holding my father?" Ethan asks the captain of the royal guards.

"He built a dungeon to imprison powerful shinbiins who refused to submit to his will." A look of distaste crosses Captain Ha's face. "The deepest cell in there should be strong enough to secure him."

"May I offer you my assistance, Captain?" Jihun sheathes his sword at his back.

"I might consider it if I knew who you were." The captain takes a measuring look.

"My name is Song Jihun, captain of the Order of the Suhoshin." Jihun tilts his head in a wry bow.

Recognition flares in Captain Ha's eyes. "Your reputation precedes you, Captain Song. I would be honored to have your assistance."

"It would be *my*—" Jihun's response is cut short when Jang Sanggung moans as her legs give out.

With a grunt, I stop her from falling and gingerly lower her to the ground. I look imploringly at the captain of the royal guards. "We need a physician. The bleeding won't stop. Please, we need to help her."

Captain Ha meets and holds the sanggung's eyes, then gives her a slow nod before turning to me. "My lady, no physician can help her now. The former king's knife was forged with the sacred tombstone of Dangun. No ordinary shinbiin can recover from it."

"Why?" Ethan kneels next to Jang Sanggung. "If you knew this, why did you put yourself in harm's way?"

"We all loved your mother. She was good and kind. But in the end, we could do nothing to save her from the tyrant." Her hand flutters at her side, and Ethan cradles it between his own. "I could not stand by and watch her son die too. Not when I could save you."

Ethan looks away, his throat working.

"Please do not be sad, Your Majesty. I am honored to exchange my life for yours. You are needed here." Blood sputters from her mouth as a cough racks her body. "The queen sent you to the Kingdom of Mountains because we desperately need a good and kind ruler."

"Thank you, Jang Sanggung," I choke out, squeezing her free hand. Her fingers feel as cold as ice. She doesn't have long. "You don't know me, but you saved someone precious to me today. I can't ever thank you enough for that."

"You are very welcome, my lady," she says kindly before grimacing in pain. "You are someone precious to him too. I can tell by the way he looks at you."

"I guess he likes me okay." I half laugh, half sob. "And don't worry. You were right about him. He is good and kind like the queen. Please be at peace knowing that the people of this kingdom will be safe under his care."

"I am at peace. At long last." Jang Sanggung's eyes focus on the blue sky past the hole in the roof. Then she faces me again and smiles with sweet innocence. "You came back. I've been waiting for so long. Can we go to the harvest festival now?"

"I'm not . . ." I look helplessly at Ethan. She's hallucinating about someone she obviously misses and cares about. After a brief hesitation,

I decide to help ease her passing. "Y . . . yes, we'll go to the harvest festival. As soon as you get better. I promise."

"I am so happy you are back, dear friend." She coughs until her body convulses. When the coughs finally subside, she grips Ethan's hand with both of hers. "I must leave you now, Your Majesty."

"Jang Sanggung, I will not let your sacrifice be in vain," Ethan says in a rough rasp. "I will serve the people of the Kingdom of Mountains with honor, integrity, and compassion. I swear to you."

"Ethan." I hold back a sob and rub my hand down his arm. "She's gone."

He nods, taking a shuddering breath, then passes a gentle hand over Jang Sanggung's unseeing eyes to close them for the final time.

"You are so moved by the loss of a worthless life," the old king murmurs as he nonchalantly plucks out my acupuncture needles from his torso. "I cannot decide if it is touching . . . or nauseating. Your mother was a pathetic bleeding heart like you."

The royal guards flanking him stumble back in alarm, even though he's restrained under the silvery net. The tyrant can't break free. Still, goose bumps spread down my arms at the sound of his chilling voice.

Ethan moves so fast that I barely stop him from reaching through the net and wrapping a hand around his father's throat. He strains against my hold, and I tighten my arms around his waist.

"I will *kill* you," he snarls.

"Well, that did not take long." His father smirks and continues in an insufferably snide tone, "So much for *reasoning* with me to *avoid* bloodshed. You are much too eager to spill my blood."

"He's baiting you," Jihun warns. "He wants you to breach the net because he can't touch you otherwise."

"This isn't you, Ethan," I whisper, pressing myself against his back. "He isn't worth it. Think of your people."

Little by little, the tension seeps out of his body. After a deep breath, he lightly pats my hand. "You can let go now, Sunny."

When I drop my arms from his waist, he tugs me close to his side and laces his fingers through mine. Then he nods at Jihun and Captain Ha. "Captains, secure him in the dungeon. Let no one approach him. I will deal with him when I'm ready."

"You won't last a day on the throne," the tyrant seethes even as he's dragged away. "My generals will remain loyal to me. They will come for you."

"Jihun, does that net come with a matching muzzle?" I mutter.

"*I* will come for you, boy. And your pretty pet will be the first thing I kill. *Slowly.* I will enjoy watching you suffer—"

Before Ethan can lunge for him again, Jihun aims his palm at the old king, abruptly cutting off his words. The tyrant grabs his throat with both hands, his eyes bulging. Growling through gritted teeth, Jihun closes his fist, gagging him with invisible binds.

"Gods, he's powerful," Jihun pants. "But that should keep him quiet until we lock him up."

"I'll take that." I glance at Ethan's shuttered face before turning back to Jihun. "Thank you, and be careful. I wouldn't let my guard down around him if I were you."

"I appreciate your concern." Jihun arches a cocky brow at me, humor twinkling in his eyes. "But like you said, I'm *okay* at what I do."

I give Jihun the middle finger, the vise around my heart relaxing at this hint of normalcy. But I cringe when Captain Ha frowns in confusion at his side. I quickly morph my hand into a friendly wave, but the captain's frown grows even more confused. Wait, do shinbiins wave at each other?

"Please lead the way, Captain Ha." Jihun saves me from further awkwardness, but his lips twitch in amusement.

"Of course." The captain turns to the royal guards. "You two, take Jang Sanggung to her assistant court lady so she can prepare her body for a proper burial. The rest of you, guard the king with your life."

"Yes, Captain," they answer as one.

The king's chambers grow quiet. The remaining guards form a wide half circle around Ethan and me and turn their backs to give us privacy. I bring Ethan to a semi-intact corner of the chambers, away from the blood staining the floor, and tug on his hand until he sits down next to me.

Miraculously, I spot an unbroken teapot on a low table. Shifting on my ass, I reach for the pot and pour some fragrant tea on my apron. I pick up one of Ethan's hands and wipe the blood from it, then I clean his other hand. He believes his hands will always be covered with the blood of those who sacrificed their lives for him. He doesn't need literal blood on them.

I wipe my own hands clean, then pull the apron over my head and throw it to the side. Without a word, I climb onto his lap and nestle against him, wrapping my arms around his neck. He gathers me close and presses his cheek against mine. A sigh tumbles out of him, like he's been holding his breath. I drop one hand from around his neck and press it against his chest. I close my eyes as I feel the reassuring thump of his heart against my palm.

"We're here. We're alive," I whisper against the warm skin at his neck. "We get one more chance to hold each other. I'm counting today as a win."

"Gods, I love you." His arms tighten around me. "I don't know what I did to deserve you, but I'm never letting you go."

"My best guess is that you've lived a life of debauchery." I quip, even though I am swooning inside like a total dork. "I'm your penance for all your sins."

He chuckles, and his breath ruffles my hair. I shiver against him with a quick indrawn breath, and his laughter fades. He shifts under me, his fingers flexing against my waist. I'm tempted to kiss him even if the guards perish from embarrassment, and I have a feeling Ethan wouldn't mind. But even *I* know making out in front of his royal guards isn't the best way to kick off his reign as the King of Mountains.

"Has anyone told you how adorable you are?" He bites his lower lip.

"No." My eyes drop to his mouth, and I barely hold back a whimper. "No one would dare utter such blasphemy unless they have a death wish."

"Quit talking about death." He grins crookedly. "I thought we're counting today as a win."

"Shut up." I can't help smiling back at him. "But I love you and all that."

"Oh thank gods," Hailey says. "You finally put the prince out of his misery."

"Ahh!" I let out an unholy scream and nearly climb up Ethan's torso. Somewhere in the back of my mind, I must be wondering what the hell Hailey is doing in the Kingdom of Mountains. But my animal instinct is out front and foremost, telling me to run for my life.

I don't know how I recognize her as Hailey because she is *the* most terrifying thing I've ever seen. She is floating into the king's chambers as if on a cloud of dry ice, her eyes glowing bloodred. Her face is as white as snow, while her hair whips around her like a dark shadow. She looks creepy as fuck.

"It was hard watching you two hurt for so long." Wisps of icy fog spill from her mouth as she speaks, and the royal guards shake like leaves even as they hold their ground.

"Wh . . . what are you doing here?" I sputter. "And what the fuck, Hailey? Why do you look like that?"

"Look like what? Oh, oops." She changes back to herself before I can blink. "That was just my grim reaper thing. I couldn't think of a faster way to get past all the security."

"Oh gods." I drag my fingertips down my face. "I feel like I need to claw my eyeballs out."

"Hey, you're starting to hurt my feelings." Hailey pouts. "My jeoseungsaja doesn't look that bad."

"I beg to differ," Ethan rasps. "Your jeoseungsaja is terrifying."

I scramble to my feet and run toward Hailey. Now that she's back to her beautiful self, my friend is a sight for sore eyes. But the royal guards spread their arms out and block me. "My lady, it isn't safe."

"It's okay. She's a friend," I tell them, but they cast uncertain glances toward their king.

"Let her through," Ethan says. "Lieutenant Gim is a suhoshin, and a friend."

"What are you doing here?" I ask again, tugging her into my arms as soon as they let her through. Apparently, I'm a hugger now.

After squeezing me tight, Hailey pulls away and looks over my shoulder at Ethan. "You two might want to sit down for this."

CHAPTER
TWENTY-TWO

Ethan and I watch Hailey drink tea straight from the pot as we sit huddled in the corner of the king's chambers. I'm both impatient for and dreading this news we needed to *sit down* to hear. The pot must be enchanted because she's been drinking from it for a good minute, and the tea keeps coming.

"Conjuring all that icy fog really dehydrates me." She stops drinking at last and wipes her mouth on her sleeve.

"Stop stalling, Hailey." I stare enviously at her black turtleneck and jeans. Modern clothes in black. I sigh. "We're sitting down. Tell us the bad news."

"Who says it's bad . . ." She trails off when I narrow my eyes at her, and she drops her head. She looks so small and vulnerable that I feel terrible for rushing her. But she squares her shoulders and meets my gaze, then Ethan's. "Daeseong is stirring."

"It was a matter of time," I say stoically, even though I want to hurl. Ethan squeezes my hand, and I squeeze back hard enough to crush any other male. "How exactly is he *stirring*? Is he doing more dinner shows for the Jaenanpa?"

"When he first returned to the Mortal Realm, he moved stealthily . . . strategically. So much so that we still don't know the full extent of his activities before Heaven Lake." Hailey shakes her head slowly. "But something . . . changed. Since he surfaced at the Jaenanpa's fundraising gala, he's been giving us an education on what mayhem truly means."

"How?" Ethan asks with a dark frown. "Wasn't the gala only a few nights ago?"

"In just a few short days, the Jaenanpa attempted to kidnap hundreds of humans across the Mortal Realm. We managed to stop most of them, but they got away with a few." Hailey wipes a weary hand down her face. "But since yesterday, they succeeded in kidnapping close to a thousand people. We stopped hundreds of attempts, but we can't keep up with them. Every Jaenanpa follower seems to have come out of hiding. There are too many of them for us to track."

"That makes no sense. The Jaenanpa works in the shadows, never revealing their true numbers. That's how they've been flying under the radar from both the Suhoshin and the human authorities." My brows furrow in frustration. "Why would they risk exposure now?"

"Daeseong must be driving them." Hailey's lips press into a grim line. "I don't know what he has on them, or what he promised them, but these fanatics are not going for subtle. It's like they don't expect there to be a tomorrow . . ."

"Oh gods," I whisper, Hailey's words triggering the memory of what I saw in the dark mudang's mind at Heaven Lake. I remember the Amheuk's yawning hunger and Daeseong's terrified exhilaration of doing his master's bidding. "They're helping the dark mudang usher in the Amheuk to the Mortal Realm. That's why they're unafraid of the consequences of their actions. They *know* there won't be a future for humankind."

Hailey gasps, and I seek out Ethan, my stomach lurching with dread. He meets my eyes and reaches out to squeeze my hand. My fear fades gradually to be replaced by determination. We will stop Daeseong.

"I don't know very much about the Jaenanpa, but aren't they comprised of corrupt mudangs?" He thinks out loud. "They're human. Don't they realize the Amheuk will destroy them as well?"

"That must be the carrot Daeseong is dangling in front of them." My fist clenches on my lap. "He's promising them power and immortality, leaving out the part that they'll be mindless shadow monsters."

"But why are they kidnapping all those humans?" Ethan asks. I look at him with a sad shake of my head, and his eyes grow wide with alarm.

Daeseong was resurrected from the dead through an unthinkable blood sacrifice. When his followers grew to five thousand people with the birth of a baby, they synchronized a bloody ritual. All five thousand of them, including the newborn, took their final breath at the exact same moment and brought the dark mudang back to life as a creature of the Amheuk.

I turn to Hailey. "Have the Sentinels discovered where the Jaenanpa is keeping them?"

"Not yet, and that brings me to what I'm doing here," she says. "The Jaenanpa's activities are becoming more and more frenzied. It's obvious they're nearing some kind of D-Day. We need to find the kidnapped humans before it's too late. I was hoping you have the King of Mountains locked up somewhere and we can grill him about where his friend Daeseong is hiding out."

"What?" My stomach drops like deadweight. "I thought the dark mudang was in LA."

"He was, but we lost him." Hailey hisses out an angry breath. "We tried to track him down, but he's a slippery son of a bitch. He pops up all over the world but rarely stays in one place long enough for us to pin him down."

"Can't we squeeze one of the Jaenanpa's mudangs?" I say, already getting a bad feeling about interrogating the tyrant.

"Even the highest echelon of the Jaenanpa have no idea where Daeseong is, or what he's doing." Hailey shakes her head. "They just execute his orders without question. What's worse, the dark mudang doesn't tell them what to do until the last minute, adding to the chaos of the Jaenanpa's activities. There is no logical pattern to their behavior, so we can't study it to track him down."

"You think the tyrant knows where Daeseong is?" Ethan grimaces as though talking about his father has a bitter aftertaste.

"It's probably a long shot. Yet it's the only shot we have—pinning down Daeseong is the only way to stop this." Hailey bows her head apologetically. "I know this is the last thing you need, Your Highness."

I want to bury my face in my hands and curl into a tight, impenetrable ball, but I rub Ethan's arm instead. I don't want him confronting his father already. The poor guy needs a breather, for gods' sakes.

"You don't have to come with us," I say softly.

"You're not going anywhere near him without me." Ethan stands, pulling me up with him. "He'll try to hurt you to get to me."

I can only nod. I hate that the sick motherfucker still has the power to hurt Ethan after everything he has taken from him.

"I'm so sorry to add to your burden, my prince." Hailey looks miserable as she rises to her feet. "You, too, Sunny."

"You have nothing to be sorry for," Ethan says with warm sincerity. "Your journey here couldn't have been easy. I'm grateful you came to find us."

"Yeah." I give her shoulder a little shove. "It's not your fault. We have to work as a team to stop Daeseong. I thought that was the deal."

"Oh, Sunny." Tears flood Hailey's eyes, and I immediately regret the mushy things I said. When she tackle hugs me, I heave a put-upon sigh but surreptitiously wrap my arms around her.

"Ugh," I grumble out of principle. Before I get too comfortable in the embrace of my friend, I squirm and complain, "Get off me, you clingy grim reaper."

Ethan grins knowingly at me, and I bare my teeth at him to make sure he doesn't think I've gone soft. He chuckles under his breath, then turns to the nearest royal guard. "I need an escort to the dungeon."

"I know the way, Your Majesty." A royal guard at the other end of the half circle marches up to us. "It will be my honor to escort you."

Hailey spins to me with her mouth hanging open. I pat her back and explain, "It all happened so quickly, but yeah, Ethan is the King of Mountains."

Ethan groans and presses his fingers against his eyelids. "Let's focus on the task at hand. We need to find Daeseong before it's too late."

Fortunately, the palanquins stand where we left them, and Hailey and I each take one. Her modern clothes are too noticeable, and I am still a gumiho. We can't risk being noticed as we travel outside of the king's personal quarters. Ironically, the new King of Mountains is the least conspicuous of the three of us, so he walks ahead of the palanquins with the royal guard.

The palace grounds are quiet, so I crack open a side window and peek outside. Various court personnel go about their business and pay us no heed. With the king's jimil so secluded from the rest of the palace, no one seems to have heard the roof explode or the rest of the mayhem. I sigh with relief.

But word will soon spread that the tyrant has been imprisoned by his son. I hope the old king was bluffing about the generals who are loyal to him. Either way, we should be prepared for an uprising from the loyalists.

Ethan needs to start recruiting allies with the help of Captain Ha. Not only does the captain of the royal guards seem competent and trustworthy, but he should also have a good understanding of the court politics in the Kingdom of Mountains. I know Ethan will never let me handle his father alone, but he doesn't have much time to prepare.

The royal guard escorts us to the dungeon without delay. Hailey and I step out of the gamas and join Ethan at the front entrance. The hanok, located on the outskirts of the palace, looks like any number of buildings we passed on our way here. Other than its secluded location, nothing indicates that a dungeon lies within.

Ethan gives the heavy wooden doors a tug, but it's barricaded from the inside. Jihun and Captain Ha must be with the tyrant, somewhere deep, dark, and far away from the entrance. I doubt they'll be able to hear me, but I pound a fist on the door anyway. I yelp when the heavy doors immediately swing open, nearly knocking Ethan and me to the ground.

"I didn't expect you so soon, Your Majesty." Captain Ha draws back in surprise, seeing us right outside the dungeon.

"Neither did I," Ethan says darkly. "We have come to speak with the prisoner."

"Hailey?" Jihun steps out from behind the captain. "What are you doing here?"

She approaches him and speaks in a low voice. "The kidnappings are spreading like wildfire. Since yesterday, the Jaenanpa managed to kidnap close to a thousand humans. Captain Seo sent me here to get some answers from the former king. Daeseong is preparing to make his move, and we need to find him before it's too late."

"Captain Ha, I will stay here with the king and his guests." Jihun's expression is even grimmer than usual. "Please proceed with what we discussed."

The captain nods once at Jihun, then bows deeply to Ethan. He cocks his head at the royal guard who escorted us to the dungeon, and the guard bows to his king as well. Then the two of them walk away without delay, whispering in urgent tones.

"Will the captain help us recruit allies?" Ethan asks Jihun.

"Yes, we have come up with a preliminary plan." He bends his head close to Ethan's. "He will first approach the generals and nobles who have openly opposed the tyrant. Their wealth and power have diminished due to their stance, but they are the least likely to expose us. If they choose to join us, then they can help us identify those who not-so-openly oppose the old king and recruit them to our side. We need to be discreet to have more time to gather our allies."

"I agree. Thank you, Captain." Ethan claps him on his shoulder. "Now let's go have a chat with my father, shall we?"

Jihun scans the vicinity before stepping aside to let us through the door. Inside the so-called dungeon, a long corridor stretches out ahead of us. I squint my eyes, but I can't see very far even with the afternoon light streaming in from behind us. Then Jihun heaves the doors shut and bars them with a heavy wooden plank, plunging us into pitch black.

Hailey throws up a sphere of light, but I still don't see the end of the corridor. There's something unnaturally dense and stagnant about the dark. I slip my hand into Ethan's, and he laces his fingers through mine.

Jihun grabs a torch off a nearby wall, and a flame bursts to life at his murmured spell. Suddenly, the long corridor is nowhere to be found, and a stairwell that curves both up and down stands a few yards away.

"Gods, my mind can't take much more of this realm." I've never seen magic like this. I can see past glamour. The darkness that shrouded the dungeon wasn't that. I press a palm against my forehead, then side-eye Jihun. "Where did you learn how to do that?"

"Captain Ha taught me the spell to disperse the dark." He is annoyingly matter of fact, but annoying and matter of fact are his factory settings. "Let me take you to the prisoner."

Ethan, Hailey, and I follow Jihun down the stairs, which wind around and around until I feel like a hamster caught in an exercise wheel. Just as I'm about to suggest blowing a hole through the winding staircase to escape the hellish wheel, we reach the bottom, which opens up into a circular stone hall with eight wooden doors around it.

"Where is he?" Ethan's voice is ragged with anger and conflict, but his face is set with determination. "Which one is his cell?"

Jihun hesitates for second. "The dungeon is designed to hide the location of the prisoner."

"So you don't know which door he's behind?" Hailey asks. "What happens if you open the wrong door?"

"Something very unique and unpleasant awaits you at every wrong door." Jihun sighs and pinches the bridge of his nose. "I have to perform a spell to find the right door."

"Go on then." I blink at him. "What's up with the long preamble?"

Jihun scowls back, but a flush crawls up his neck. "It's a . . . movement spell."

Hailey slaps a hand over her mouth and nose, but her snort manages to escape, and Ethan's lips twitch, chasing away the shadows on his face. I glance back and forth at the three of them, then stare up at the ceiling, praying for patience.

"I'm not even going to ask what that is." I flap a hand at Jihun. "Just get on with it, will you?"

"I only watched Captain Ha do it once," he mumbles. "If I get a single detail wrong, it'll be disastrous . . ."

"Quit stalling, Captain." Hailey gives up trying to hold back her laugh. "You have a photographic memory. You know exactly how to perform the spell."

Ever the proper one, Jihun doesn't actually give his lieutenant the bird, but his narrowed eyes unequivocally imply it. He walks to the middle of the circular hall and draws his longsword from the sheath on his back. With a measured exhale, he lowers the sword to his waist with both hands on the hilt, the blade straight up, then he twists the sword until the edges form one thin line in front of him.

He sweeps one leg in a smooth arc, drawing a semicircle on the floor with his foot, and raises the sword horizontally above his head. Swinging and thrusting his sword, he executes some familiar offensive stances. Then his movement picks up speed and becomes a lethal dance of slashing blade and taut, balanced body. I wouldn't admit this at gunpoint, but I love yoga. And the fluid, graceful movements of Jihun's sword and body remind me of a masterful vinyasa flow.

But the spell's similarities to yoga end when every surface of his body begins to glow and his movement quickens until he is a blur of spinning sword and body. It is a stunning sight to behold. Then, the silver light emanating from him concentrates into his sword and travels up the blade until only the tip shines with blinding brightness. In a single lightning-fast move, he raises one knee in front of him and sweeps his arms open, one toward the ceiling and the sword arm toward the ground. When the glowing tip of his blade hits the floor, a line of fire ignites from his sword to one of the eight doors.

I am seriously tempted to clap until my palms sting. I feel as though I just watched the greatest performance of my life. But Jihun's sword arm trembles violently, and his chest heaves as he fights to breathe. The movement spell took a lot out of him, and my giddy excitement fades.

"He's in there," Jihun rasps as he withdraws his sword.

Ethan nods his thanks to him and walks over to the tyrant's cell with Hailey. I linger at Jihun's side and wait for him to catch his breath.

"You okay there?" I try not to sound as worried as I feel.

"I'm fine." He smirks when I gape at him in disbelief. "It's descry magic. Revealing something enchanted to stay hidden takes some work. I'll be fine in a minute."

"If you say so." I shrug offhandedly but stay close by his side as we make our way to join the others. When I'm certain Jihun isn't going to keel over, I go stand next to Ethan. "Do you think the tyrant will talk?"

"Oh, I'm sure he'll talk." Ethan narrows his eyes. "I just don't know if we can believe anything that comes out of his mouth."

"Can we do a dance to make him tell the truth?" I ask, mostly kidding. Jihun deigns to cock a brow at me.

"If I know one, are you willing to give it a go?" Ethan lets his gaze roam my body. I blush like an idiot, and his smile is both knowing and sad. I suddenly want to kick myself for withholding my love for so long. I have so much more to give, but we might be out of time.

"If Jaeseok were here, he'd already be dancing, regardless of spells." Hailey's sigh sounds forlorn. I miss that ridiculous dokkaebi too. "But I don't think there are any spells, movement or otherwise, that can compel a person to tell the truth."

We're all stalling, but I don't mind. I'll hoard as many seconds of normalcy with Ethan and my friends as I can. I know it's what will sustain me for all that is about to come. I haven't forgotten what I learned at Heaven Lake, even if my old loner habits are hard to break. Love and friendship don't make me weak. They are the very source of my powers. And I will do anything to protect the people I love.

Anything?

The bloodlust of the word of power is preferable to the power I hide deep inside me. The power I vowed never to use. The power that is the source of the disgust and fear that hound gumihos. *Beast. Monster. Abomination.* The moment I wield it, I become deserving of those very slurs.

"I'll talk to him alone," Ethan declares with grim determination. "He might enjoy having an audience a little too much."

"No, I'm coming with you." Maybe I won't have to wield that horrible power. It will be my last resort. "You'll need my help to manipulate him. Bullies are volatile narcissists at the core. He might let something slip if we toy with his overinflated ego."

"I hate that you're right." Ethan frowns. "You can come, but you have to stay close to me."

"And I hate being told what to do," I say archly.

A muscle shifts in his clenched jaw. "I'm *asking.*"

"Then I'll take it under consideration," I shoot back.

"The clock is ticking." Hailey interrupts our battle of wills. "The captain and I'll stand watch out here."

"Don't you have to unlock the door or something?" I ask Jihun.

"After all that, I should hope not," he says drolly. "The motion spell *was* the key. It should already be unlocked."

"I might have a plan," I tell Ethan as an idea comes to mind. "There's no time to explain, but we have to hide what we're really after for as long as we can. We can't give him any leverage. We have to trick him into volunteering information about his alliance with Daeseong."

He doesn't hesitate. "I'll follow your lead."

Ethan pulls open the heavy wooden door, and we step inside together. A small torch on the side wall provides the only light, so we pause to let our eyes adjust to the darkness. The tyrant sits cross-legged on the floor, deep inside the dimly lit cell. Even with a wooden cangue around his neck, the long end extending to the ground, he manages to look down his nose at us.

I release the breath I'd been holding when I spot the silvery pins securing the two halves of the cangue together. Like the net that held him earlier, the cangue binds the former king's magic as well as his body. I step farther into the cell, but Ethan wraps his hand around my wrist and half shields me with his body. I almost click my tongue in impatience, but the aggravating little smirk playing around the tyrant's mouth stops me. I'd be giving the bastard ammunition.

"Come to see me so soon?" He raises his eyebrows in pleased surprise, chillingly convincing. "Did you miss me, son? And look, you even brought your pet."

I give Ethan's hand a warning squeeze. *Don't let him bait you,* I say into his mind. His gaze shoots toward me at the same time I freeze in shock. How did I do that in my human form? *I don't know how I'm doing it,* I yelp. Telepathically. Because apparently, I can do that now. The tyrant's eyes skip back and forth between us. *We'll figure it out later.*

"We have come as a courtesy to the king father." I tilt my head in a half bow. "As you would understand, the throne cannot remain empty for long, so the coronation must proceed without delay."

"Must I listen to the animal prattle on about nonsense?" the prisoner snaps and bares his teeth at Ethan. "You will have to *kill me* to take my throne."

Don't, Ethan, I warn. *He's baiting you.*

"We will have to bind your magic, of course, but the king will be honored to have you attend the ceremony to signal peace and solidarity to the people of the Kingdom of Mountains." I continue as though the male hasn't spoken. "Are there any guests of honor that you would like to invite?"

The tyrant's laughter grows from a quiet chuckle to an unhinged cackle, then abruptly stops altogether. I've faced many horrors in my life, but nothing has turned my blood to ice like the madman in front of me.

"I will not relinquish the throne, boy." His eyes narrow into hateful slits, but his voice is cool and silky like the skin of a venomous snake. "Especially if you intend to muddy our bloodline with this filthy beast."

"*No one* speaks about her that way." Ethan growls, and a stream of magic pulses out of his palm, slamming his father against the wall and holding him aloft. The cangue jerks around the male's neck, making him cough and gag. "If you so much as look at her wrong, I will make you *wish* you were dead."

Come back to me, Ethan. This isn't you.

"He deserved that," I say out loud, pushing Ethan's arm down to his side. The tyrant falls to the ground, the wooden slats scraping against the rough prison wall. Flattery didn't work, so I attack his fragile ego. "But don't waste your energy on the pathetic fool. He's not worth it. Look at him."

I watch my taunt hit home, triumph flaring in my chest. The male scrambles to his knees, holding the unwieldy cangue aloft. His bulging eyes bounce off the walls of the cell as anger and denial twist his face. I can do this. I can make him talk without resorting to my sick power.

"It's true what Shim Duna said about him. He doesn't have the power of invincibility anymore. Even his own spy knew he was weak." But the old king is far from harmless. Even locked away in a dungeon, the tyrant will find a way to make sure Duna dies for revealing his secret and wounding his ego. I just signed her death warrant, and all I feel is grim satisfaction—especially since the next insult will tip him over the edge. "He's in no position to threaten anyone. The Kingdom of Mountains already rejected him as its king."

"Even if you usurp the throne, your reign will never be secure as long as I live," he rasps, desperation bleeding into his words.

"Are you *trying* to convince me to kill you?" Ethan arches a mocking brow, his anger back under control.

"N . . . no." The tyrant clambers across the hard ground on his knees. "You will die if you kill me. She will die too. *Everyone* will die."

Piercing horror slices through my skull. *Daeseong,* I think to Ethan. My fingers dig into his arm, and he steps closer, pressing the sides of our bodies together.

"Save the dramatics for someone who cares." Ethan scoffs, masking his shock with arrogance. "Will you cooperate in my coronation? Or will you rot away down here? Perhaps, you prefer a quick death."

"Everyone will die. Everyone will die without me," the prisoner mutters, with the whites of his eyes showing. "The Amheuk will swallow this realm whole. Only I can stop him."

"What are you going on about?" Ethan tsks impatiently, crossing his arms over his chest. "Stop who?"

The old king's expression suddenly turns sly. "Wouldn't you like to know?"

"Are you really *so* important that only you can stand between the Amheuk and this realm?" I jeer, delivering another blow to his ego. "I'm not surprised you suffer from delusions of grandeur. You've never even seen the golden axe and the silver axe, have you? You've never worn the true crown of the Kingdom of Mountains. The Amheuk wouldn't lower itself to bargain with an impostor."

I'm going by a hunch here. Ethan holds the golden axe and the silver axe, the true crown of the Kingdom of Mountains. The prophecy proclaimed him the King Foretold. The tyrant wouldn't be so obsessed with holding on to power if he didn't think his claim to the throne was tenuous. Perhaps the throne had never been rightfully his.

"What do you know about the crown of the Kingdom of Mountains?" His derision is underlined with uncertainty. "The golden axe and the silver axe are a children's fairy tale. *I* am the King of Mountains. Whatever crown *I* wear is the rightful crown."

"Why would the true King of Mountains join forces with the Amheuk?" He never said he had joined forces with the darkness, but my gamble pays off when the tyrant flinches. *Gotcha.* "That's what you've done, isn't it?"

He cackles that eerie laugh and says in a singsong voice again, "Wouldn't you like to know?"

"Explain yourself," Ethan commands with implacable authority, "if you value your pitiful life."

The old king sits cross-legged on the floor once more, his regal air at odds with the madness that possessed him just a moment ago. "Get out."

"What?" Ethan frowns, taken aback.

"Get. Out." The tyrant turns cold eyes on his son. "I will speak to the gumiho alone."

Ethan barks out a harsh laugh. "Like hell you will."

"It's okay." I place my hand on his arm, eyeing the prisoner. The old king tilts his head and smiles benignly at me. Bile rises to my throat. "I'll talk to him alone."

"You will—" Ethan begins in a low growling voice.

Ethan, don't. We have to stop Daeseong, I plead in his mind. *Trust me. I can get him to talk.*

"Give me five minutes," I say lightly, holding his gaze. *Please, Ethan.* I see it in his eyes. He's going to give in, because he can't say no to me. Because he loves me. Because he trusts me.

I love you more than life. Even telepathically, my words tremble with raw longing and vulnerability. His face remains impassive, but his eyes burn with love, desperate and beautiful. His hand clenches and unclenches at his side like he's holding himself back from hauling me into his arms. *I'll see you in five minutes, Ethan.*

"Fine, five minutes." He glares at his father with lethal warning, then he turns to me and whispers, "See you soon, Sunny."

I watch him walk out of the cell. Ethan will never know that I can make his father talk—that I can take away his free will. But I will do anything and everything else to find out Daeseong's whereabouts before I resort to that despicable power. Because Ethan deserves the best version of me. Not a monster.

BEWITCHED

The mother dragged the child to the corner of the villager's courtyard. The villager eyed them warily, holding her own crying daughter against her.

"Give them to me," the mother said in a low, icy voice.

The child started, never having seen the mother so angry before. Even so, she tightened her hand around the five smooth stones and hid her fist behind her back. "Mine."

"No, not yours." The mother snatched the child's wrist from behind her with frightening speed and strength. She turned her small fist, palm side up, and shook it sharply. "You stole the gonggi from your friend."

"Mihwa did not steal," the child wailed in outrage. "Yeongja gave them to me. It's mine."

The mother closed her eyes and breathed deeply through her nose. She gentled her grip on the child's wrist but did not let go. "You made her give them to you against her will."

The child scrunched up her face. "No!"

"Did you put magic in your voice?" The mother blinked away sudden tears. "When you asked your friend for the gonggi, did your words feel thick and sweet like warm honey in your mouth?"

"Mihwa didn't ask for the gonggi." She stomped her foot on the dirt ground. "Yeongja gave them to me."

With a gasp, the mother dropped the child's wrist to hide her shaking hands in her hanbok chima. To bewitch without words was a power a child this young shouldn't be able to wield.

"D . . . did you wish you could have it?" she asked her daughter.

"I wished I had one just like Yeongja's. Her stones are smooth and round. All five of them the same size." The child held her thumb up. "As small as Mihwa's thumb. They make the perfect gonggi."

"Wh . . . when you wished for one . . . just like hers," the mother stuttered, "did your chest feel hot like you swallowed a mouthful of steaming tea?"

"I don't remember." The child pressed her free hand against the center of her chest, her brows crinkled in thought. "Maybe. I . . . I think so."

It wasn't her fault. The child did not mean to bewitch her friend. It was the mother's fault for not teaching her about the darkness inside her. But the child was only four years old. Her small hand could barely wrap around the five little stones.

"I will find five perfect stones for you," the mother said gently.

"Round and smooth?" The child bounced up and down, her beautiful smile overshadowing the midday sun. "As small as Mihwa's thumb?"

"Yes." The mother turned the child by her shoulders and gave her bottom a pat. "Now be good and return the gonggi to Yeongja."

The mother watched the child return the gonggi to her friend, and the two girls hugged. This time, the child had caused little harm. But tonight, the mother must teach the child that she was capable of causing great harm. Because there was no violation deeper than rendering someone powerless—powerless to think, to want, to choose. There was no magic more depraved than bewitching someone and robbing them of their free will.

The child must never ruin herself. She must never repeat the mother's mistakes.

CHAPTER
TWENTY-THREE

"You have me alone, king father." I sketch a mocking bow. "Please say what's on your mind. And *do* use small words so my tiny animal brain can process it."

"I will tell you where Daeseong is hiding." He smiles even though I keep my face impassive. It's as though he can hear the pounding of my heart. "*If* you swear to leave the Kingdom of Mountains *without* my son."

"I will do no such thing," I hiss before I can stop myself. *No one* can make me leave Ethan.

"Do you not want him to claim his birthright?" The tyrant's eyebrows crest in a travesty of benign concern. "Do you not want to give him the *peaceful* succession he so desperately wants? With you by his side, that will never be possible. No shinbiin, even the worthless commoners of the Kingdom of Mountains, will accept a gumiho as their queen."

I hold back a startled gasp. *Their queen?* Ethan and I love each other, but . . . marriage? Is that where this was leading? I've been so busy hiding my love that I never thought about what would happen after I gave all of myself to him. *Marriage.* I would be his beloved wife. My heart melts at the thought, but . . . I would also be their hated queen.

"A king must take a wife," the old king says, as though he read my mind. "He must have a queen and an heir to strengthen the throne."

"Do you even hear yourself?" I say with forced derision. "*You* didn't have a queen, because you killed her. And *you* didn't have an heir, because you chased him away and would have gladly killed him, too, if you had the chance."

"*That* was my mistake, wasn't it? I lost my queen and heir, and lost the support of my people." He shakes his head morosely. "The love of one's people is fickle. They will turn on you at the slightest shift of the wind. The closer you remain with my son, the quicker he will lose the throne."

I *know* he's full of shit, and yet . . . wouldn't Ethan's ascension to the throne be that much smoother with a shinbiin queen at his side? He can ally with a powerful noble if he takes their daughter as his wife. *Shit.* The wily tyrant is messing with my head. He is full of poisonous manipulations. I cannot be shaken.

"Where is Daeseong? Tell me," I demand.

"Swear that you'll leave this kingdom—*alone*—and never return," he barters smoothly.

"Sure," I drawl without an ounce of sincerity. "Why not?"

His low chuckle makes nausea churn in my stomach. "I would need your blood oath, gumiho."

I suck in a sharp breath, the dank smell of the dungeon coating my mouth. "I'll give you my *word*. Unless you plan on returning the blood oath to swear you are telling the truth."

"I will," he says without hesitation, a creepy sneer curling his lips.

That is the *last* thing I expected him to say. And I do *not* like the look of that smile. This is a trick. I just don't know how it can be. If he swears by a blood oath to tell me the truth, he literally *cannot* lie. It means I can get the truth out of him without bewitching him. I shudder at the mere thought of drawing on that power. But I would have to swear to leave the Kingdom of Mountains and never come back. This is Ethan's home now. I want it to be my home too.

Every cell in my body rebels against leaving Ethan. He *is* my home. But there are a thousand human beings who might breathe their last if

I don't help them. The Mortal Realm, and the lives of over eight billion humans and beings of the Shingae, are in imminent danger. I can't put my desire—no, *need*—to be with Ethan ahead of eight billion lives.

I shake my head. I can't accept that. There must be another way. My eyes jump around the dark cell as a scream builds in my chest. *Please . . .* There *has* to be another way.

I can . . . I can use my dark power. I can stay with Ethan. I just have to . . . I just . . . *No, I can't.* I lock my knees to keep them from buckling—to keep my body from crumpling to the ground. I can't cross that line, even to be with Ethan. Because if I do, I would no longer be the person he fell in love with.

There's no use prolonging the inevitable. I am making this blood oath. I have no other choice—no choice I can live with. I have to leave Ethan . . . for now. But I *will* find my way back to him.

I stalk over to the prisoner and stop two steps away from him, then crouch to the ground. I let my incisors elongate and pierce the tip of my index finger. When blood wells on my fingertip, nearly black in the dark cell, I draw a half circle on the ground with it.

"I swear to leave the Kingdom of Mountains—"

"Tonight," the old king interjects.

"Wh . . . what?"

"You leave *tonight*," he snarls. "Or I tell you nothing."

I glare at him, my blood pounding in my head. *That's too soon.* But I swallow and resume my oath because the dark mudang must be stopped.

"I swear to leave the Kingdom of Mountains tonight and . . . never return," I rasp. "In exchange for the current and exact location of Daeseong and his human captives."

"I swear to give the gumiho the current and exact location of Daeseong and his human captives." The former king slices open his index finger with the sharp nail on his pinky and draws a half circle next to mine, finishing the circle. "In exchange for her leaving the Kingdom of Mountains *tonight* to never return."

The circle of blood bursts into fire, shining light on the tyrant's gleeful eyes, then it extinguishes in a heartbeat, leaving no trace of blood behind. I slowly turn my left hand over and stare down at my palm. And there it is. The crudely drawn blood circle imprinted onto the mound beneath my thumb. *Gods, what have I done?*

The tyrant holds up his left hand to me, showing me the identical imprint on his palm. "The dark mudang—"

"Say his fucking name," I growl, in no mood for games.

He snarls at my disrespect but continues through gritted teeth. "Daeseong is at the Santorini caldera."

"The Santorini caldera?" I blink at his sudden switch to impeccable English, the words sounding foreign coming from his mouth. "What the fuck is Daeseong doing at the Santorini caldera? Taking his dream vacation? Working on his tan?"

"Leave me, gumiho." The former king has that smug look on his face again, and my stomach drops like lead.

"He's expecting me." My voice is soft with wonder at my own stupidity. I gave the blood oath for nothing. "The dark mudang told you to send me there, didn't he?"

"You figured it out at last?" He chortles. "Gods, you're slow."

"He needs me there to move his plans forward. Tonight . . ." My knees give out, and I fall on my ass. "But *why?*"

"You can think about that on your way out," the tyrant bites out. "I cannot bear your stench a minute longer."

I grab the long end of the cangue and raise it toward the ceiling until the prisoner is dangling by his neck, his feet kicking in the air. It feels like he and the thick wooden cangue weigh nothing.

I vaguely register my extraordinary strength in the back of my mind.

He digs his hands into his neck hole to fight against strangulation. His face turns a mottled purple, and he gurgles weakly. I drop him to the ground.

"Is Daeseong planning to kill the humans tonight, king father?" I ask with impeccable manners. "Why does he need me at Santorini?"

The tyrant tries to laugh but ends up coughing and gagging instead, drool dribbling down his chin. "Do you think the dark mudang shares his plans with me? If you weren't a filthy animal, I would've been flattered at how highly you think of me."

"Tell me." I raise the cangue again until his ass lifts off the ground.

"I do not know," he yells, panic in his eyes. "He truly does not share his plans with me. I do *not* know."

I drop the cangue back to the ground. The coward is telling the truth. "What do you get for handing me over to Daeseong?"

"I told you. I'm the only thing standing between the Realm of Four Kingdoms and the Amheuk. The dark mudang said he'll spare this realm if I sent you to him. He promised that the eternal darkness will drown the Mortal Realm but nothing beyond it," he gloats. "I saved this realm from the Amheuk. Every kingdom will fall at my feet in awe and gratitude. *I* will be the King Foretold."

"And you believed him? The Gray Void already stands between the Amheuk and the Realm of Four Kingdoms. If Daeseong somehow finds a way past the Gray Void, then he and the Amheuk wouldn't hesitate to conquer this realm. *You* are meaningless in the equation." I cluck my tongue, remorseful that this pathetic male is Ethan's father. "You can save no one, not even yourself."

I don't wait for him to respond. I walk out of the cell and close the heavy door behind me. Then I stand in the quiet of the stone hall, blinking against the light. And even before I see that there is no one in the circular hall, I know that something has gone wrong.

"There you are," Hailey cries, running down the stairwell. Her shirt is torn at the shoulder like she broke free from someone trying to grab hold of her. Blood oozes from a thin gash on her chin. "We need to get out of here."

"Is Ethan okay?" I meet her at the bottom of the stairs and motion for her to climb back up the steps. "Is Jihun with him? What's going on?"

"Don't worry. They're both okay." Hailey glances over her shoulder. "But a general who remains loyal to the tyrant has attacked. Well, *loyal* might be an exaggeration. He's just looking out for himself because if the king loses power, he loses power."

My stomach drops. "How bad is it?"

"It's not *terrible*," she says. "Captain Ha managed to gather the rest of the generals and enlisted many of the high officials to back Ethan, with more and more joining his side as we speak. It's hard for anyone to deny that he's the rightful King of Mountains when he's forcing back a small army, wielding the legendary axes like they're part of his limbs."

"Hailey." I place a hand on her arm to get her attention. She looks down at me from two steps above. "I need to leave."

"Yes, we have to get to the royal audience hall. That's our rendezvous point." She starts to turn away from me to resume climbing the stairs, when I gently squeeze her arm to hold her attention.

"No, Hailey. I have to leave the Kingdom of Mountains," I tell her, my chest constricting. *And never come back.* "I have to get to the Mortal Realm. I know where Daeseong is, and I need to stop him before it's too late."

"We'll tell Jihun, then you and I—"

"No." I slice my hand through the air. "You can't tell anyone. You and Jihun are Ethan's royal guards. Stay here and do your sworn duty. Protect *him*."

"I can't let you go alone." She presses her lips into a stubborn line.

I take a steadying breath and summon the light of the Yeoiju onto my palm. Hailey falls on her butt with a gasp and crab crawls up the stairs before she catches herself. I offer her a small smile. She knows she's in no danger from me. I am her friend.

"Is that . . . ?" She gingerly gets back onto her feet.

"Yes." That much is true. The next part is the lie. "I figured out how to wield the power of the Yeoiju. I can stop Daeseong on my own. I'm the only one who can."

"Wh . . . what do you need me to do?" Hailey asks, two grooves appearing between her brows.

"We need to divide and conquer. I'll go kick the dark mudang's ass into the abyss, and you stay here and get Ethan securely on the throne." I shrug. *Easy peasy.* "I doubt that stray general will give you much trouble. He won't have the conviction to truly risk his neck."

I extinguish the light on my palm and hide my trembling hand behind my back. I might never see Ethan again. I might never see my friends again.

"Just help me find the gateway to the Mortal Realm in this kingdom," I say casually. "I need to find the Gray Void."

"Oh gods. How could I have forgotten?" Hailey takes me by the shoulders. "Sunny, you can't go to the Mortal Realm. Minju never got a chance to erase the word of power from your back. The Gray Void will destroy you."

"The rune has gone . . . quiet." I realize I'm not lying. "I've gone through some intense shit since I got to the Kingdom of Mountains, but I haven't felt the word of power flare once. Maybe it has something to do with my ability to wield the Yeoiju." But I don't believe the rune is gone, so I tell another lie. "Maybe the dark power couldn't survive alongside the gift of the Cheon'gwang."

"You can't risk your life on a *maybe*." Hailey shakes me a little.

"It's better odds than *impossible*." I pry her hands off my shoulders and grip them in mine. "I have to do this. I . . . no . . . *we* have no other choice. Please, Hailey."

"The Gray Void sits outside the walls of the capital in every kingdom," Hailey says in a sad, resigned voice. "I can take you there."

"Thank you." I give her a tight hug. "We need to go now."

"Ethan and Jihun probably made good progress toward the audience hall already." She climbs arduously up the stairs, as though her legs are weighed down with sandbags. "Hopefully, we'll be able to sneak out of the dungeon without notice."

It's a cute sentiment, but a short-lived one. Because as soon as we step outside the hanok, we come face to face with the royal guard who guided us here in the first place. And a dozen soldiers stand behind him.

"They're with the usurper," he shouts, pointing at us. "Seize them."

"Like hell you will, traitor," I shout, summoning my hwando, hilt-side down.

"You sneaky little rodent," Hailey yells at the same time, her crossbow materializing in her hands.

The traitorous guard stands back while the foot soldiers rush us. Hailey shoots three arrows in the blink of an eye, felling three soldiers. I spin away from a spear thrust at my chest—damn, they're going for the kill—and sink into a low crouch, slashing the soldier behind his knee. I drop another soldier with a shallow leg wound on my way up.

We lay out the dozen soldiers on the ground before the royal guard even has a chance to lower his arm, and the finger pointed at us crooks into a sad hook as he gapes at us. He tries to turn tail and run, but Hailey twists her wrist, binding and gagging him.

I grab him by the scruff of his neck and throw him into the dark hallway of the dungeon, closing the doors behind him. Even if he had the guts, he would never be able to find the tyrant, much less free him.

"Let's go." Hailey takes off in a sprint, and I follow close behind her. We edge along the palace walls until we come to an unmanned side gate. "The guards must've been called away. Hopefully, they were sent to assist the rightful king."

Once we're outside the palace grounds, she guides me through side streets and alleyways until we come to the main gates of the walled capital. A confused mob of people stands near the gates, with several grim-faced guards blocking their way.

"There will be no entering or leaving the capital until we receive further orders from the palace." One of the guards raises his voice to be heard. "I repeat, no one enters or leaves the capital until further notice. Anyone who tries shall receive no mercy. Now leave. Go on."

As we watch from the sidelines, Hailey's lips pinch in annoyance. "All I want is *one* easy thing. Just one. Is that too much to ask?"

"Yes," I deadpan, and my friend snorts.

"Okay." She raises her eyebrows. "Do you want to do this? Or shall I?"

"You got so dehydrated from your last bout." I purse my lips. "I'll take the lead."

"Aww." She presses a hand to her chest. "Are you sure?"

"I'm sure." With a smile, I become my gumiho.

Hailey clamps her hands around my neck with zero hesitation, and I make a beeline for the closed gates. With earsplitting screams, the people part like the proverbial Red Sea. The guards bravely stand their ground for a few seconds before diving out of our way with alarmed shouts. I rear up on my hind legs and ram open the giant, wooden doors with my front legs. Then I take us outside the capital and run until Hailey pats my head.

"Okay, you can put me down." She straightens and looks at me with a bemused expression when I stand before her in my human form. "I still can't get over how quickly you shift between your two forms. Do you just say *shift* in your head? And boom, you shift?"

"It's more like a sense of *being*." I do my best to explain. "When I *am* my gumiho, I become her. It's not so much a shifting of forms, but a shifting of consciousness."

"So you . . . shift?"

"All right, smart-ass." I laugh. "How far are we?"

"It's just around the bend and over that hill." Hailey hesitates. "I don't like this one bit, Sunny. I don't want to lose you."

"I don't want to lose you either." I taste salt in the back of my throat. "That's why I have to go. Because I don't want to lose any of you."

"I . . . I can't watch you go into the Gray Void." Her tears fall freely.

"That's okay." I sniff and rub my nose. "I want you to go back to Ethan anyway. Tell him I'll kick his ass if he gets mad at you for bringing me here. I would've come with or without your help. You just saved me some precious time and energy."

"Be careful, Sunny." Hailey hugs me, and I hold her tight. "Don't die."

"Ditto." I pull away from her and spin on my heels, because I can't keep my tears at bay. "Tell Ethan . . . tell him . . . I'll see him soon."

I become my gumiho and run toward the Gray Void, tears soaking the white fur of my face.

CHAPTER
TWENTY-FOUR

When I stand in the soft breeze of the open field, the Kingdom of Mountains feels both familiar and distant—a place that could've been home and a place I can never return to. I shift into my human body and watch the sun sink behind the verdant mountains, hoping it won't be the last sunset I see in either realm.

I summon the white light to my palm and stare at it in wonder. How am I able to wield the Yeoiju's power so easily? Well, I'm not exactly utilizing its full potential. All I can do is make a pretty white orb of light. Even so, confessing my love to Ethan and consummating that love unlocked something within me. Minju was right. The Yeoiju and I are intertwined. It no longer feels like a foreign object inside me, but something comfortable and welcomed.

The gateway to the Mortal Realm, a.k.a. the fucking Gray Void, looks perfectly innocuous, no different from the rest of the green field. But the air around it vibrates sporadically, and an odd energy comes off the area. I've felt that weird vibe somewhere else before . . . I frown and shake my head impatiently. I have things to do, places to be. I have no time to be a gi connoisseur.

I wipe my sweaty palms down the skirt of my hanbok and check to make sure my hwando is secure against my thigh. I bounce on my feet, shake out my arms, and stretch my neck, cracking a vertebra or two.

And I blow out three short breaths like I'm bracing myself to plunge into something unpleasant, which is very accurate. *Oh, how I wish I had some chocolate.*

Then I stand in the field until darkness blankets the mountains.

"For fuck's sake," I hiss. "Quit stalling."

With a sharp cry, I grip my wrist as unbearable pain suddenly pierces my hand. I stare down at my palm in the moonlight and horror fills me. Blood gushes from the mark of the oath, so fast that I fall to my knees on a wave of dizziness.

I fold in on myself. *Leave.* Agony wrenches through me. *Leave now.*

I have to leave. Whimpering from the agony, I crawl toward the Gray Void. I have to fulfill the blood oath. It won't stop hurting until I leave. Screaming through gritted teeth, I struggle to my feet, then I take off in a dead run.

Bone-chilling water swallows me whole. The icy liquid fills my nose and ears in an instant. I press my lips together to keep from breathing it into my lungs. My chest burns, and my eyes tear up.

The ice burns its way across my back, and fiery heat bursts from the ancient rune. I traded the pain of the blood oath for the pain of the Gray Void. A silent cry rips out of my mouth as my back arches.

The only saving grace is that air fills my lungs instead of the icy water I'd feared. But I already knew that. I hear Jihun's voice echo through my head. *Breathe, Sunny.* I suck in a lungful of air as I jerk and writhe.

The ice and fire coil round my spine, wringing me in opposite directions. I lose feeling in my legs. I know—I don't know how—but I know the two forces will tear me in half. I recognize the dark magic in the heat, but the icy cold doesn't feel right either. It doesn't feel like magic born of the Cheon'gwang. It's twisted and broken.

It hurts. It hurts so much.

Mother.

Ice pierces my chest like a long spear, skewering me. Fire punches through my stomach from the inside out. My body spasms uncontrollably. My limbs flap around, and my teeth clack together. Black edges around my consciousness, shrinking in until only a pinprick of awareness remains.

I shiver as ice coats me from head to toe. The fire is dying, turning lukewarm against my skin, until I only feel a vague warmth on my back. Then it's gone. Only the ice is left.

I'm cold. It's so cold. The sliver of my consciousness flickers, blinking in and out. The cold feels . . . off. It isn't good. It isn't only destroying the word of power and its dark magic. The icy cold of the Gray Void is also destroying *me*—drowning me in its despair.

My eyes burst open, and the thick gray fog reverberates around me, as though it is screaming. Then I hear it. The shrill wailing of countless stranded souls . . . their life forces cold and slithering. The magic of the Gray Void is born of han—grief twisted into something foul and unholy. Its magic is not darkness. It is light distorted. And I must not give in to it. I cannot.

Please.

I call on my Yeoiju, again and again. I whimper as the cold begins to seep into my heart, but I don't stop. I call on the light until it sings to me. The song is faint at first, then it grows stronger . . . and stronger. *At last.*

The Yeoiju is a part of me, so I let it fill me. I'm not afraid, because it *is* me. It cannot exist without me, because I am *it*. I know this in the depth of my soul. I don't falter even as it grows inside me because . . . I am not alone. Warmth surrounds me and seeps into me. The light shines from the center of my heart to the tips of my fingers and my toes. It spreads to every corner of my being. And I shine.

The shrieks of the stranded quiet. The icy cold of the Gray Void evaporates. A voice—or perhaps many—whisper.

Thank you.

I blink my eyes open to the night sky, the crescent moon casting a faint silvery light on the woods around me. I'm lying flat on my back, and literally every muscle in my body aches. Even the strands of my hair hurt. But I'm alive. I made it past the Gray Void. *How?* I don't remember any of it, except the freezing cold. Gods, I don't *want* to remember the freezing cold.

With a long groan, I push myself onto my elbows and painstakingly sit upright. I glance around me. Why does this mountain look familiar? I look around me again, my mouth hanging open. This mountain looks familiar because I'm in the Mortal Realm.

I realize with a jolt that my plan had been flawed. Even if I made it past the Gray Void, I had no way of reaching this mountain without being creamed into an unrecognizable blob. Jihun usually carried me between this mountain and the entrance to the Gray Void, high up in the sky. I have no idea how I'm still in one piece.

I get to my feet and peer at the tall mountain in the distance. Is it my imagination, or did the ominous looking clouds at the peak vanish? I give my head a sharp shake. I'm here, and I'm not dead. I can ponder all life's mysteries after I stop Daeseong.

"Fuck." I grab my hair in both fists. "I *really* don't want to go to Santorini."

Now, there's a sentence no one has *ever* uttered. In any other scenario, even *I* would've been thrilled to visit the stunning Greek island, salty skepticism be damned. There's just something *glorious* about the crisp white buildings with their blue domed roofs, set against the backdrop of the Aegean Sea. It calls to your soul . . . and tells you to put on a tiny bikini.

But in *this* particular scenario, I'd rather go anywhere but Santorini. There goes Daeseong ruining *everything* again. With a sigh, I squint up at the sky. It still looks like early evening. I have some time to kill. Not here though. No matter how familiar the mountain feels, I don't want to get mistakenly shot down by North Korean soldiers.

I find a shallow pond nearby and moon shift without hesitation. I step out on the other side without breaking my stride. I'm at the bottom of the mountain in the fishing town Ethan and I passed through a lifetime ago. I blink away the tears that burn at the back of my eyes. I'll see him again. I won't stop until I'm by his side, where I belong.

I hike up my hanbok chima and head toward town with determined steps. I need to lay low for a few hours until Santorini is dark enough for moon shifting. A PC bang, Korea's version of an internet café, will be the perfect place for that. I can research the ins and outs of the island while eating some first-rate snack foods.

But first, I need to get out of this hanbok. The rough fabric is scratchy as hell, and I sheepishly realize that I've been spoiled by the luxurious silk hanboks that Miok donned on me. Either way, this hanbok goes.

The owner of the small boutique gives me the side-eye when I walk in, but she is all smiles by the time I hand her the black card Hailey lent me. As she rings me up, I look down at my new outfit and feel a spark of happiness. A black tank top, a loose pair of gray-washed jeans, and a perfect black leather jacket to tie the outfit together. The boutique doesn't carry Converse, but I can live with the black combat boots the owner dug out for me from the back, even though the military look is *so last season.*

She hands me back my credit card, and I take it from her with a genuine smile. "Thank you. Have a good night."

"What about your hanbok?" the owner asks with wide eyes.

"You can throw it away." I open the door and look back at her. "I need to travel light."

I walk out into the teeming thoroughfare and breathe in the nighttime scent. The air smells of garlic, spices, and deep-fried goodness with an underlying trace of exhaust—which is all happy-making for this city girl. I eye a street vendor cooking up vats of spicy, chewy ddeokbokki and fish cake skewers in broth, and their next-door neighbor serving battered veggies, shrimp, and dumplings.

My stomach growls, but I pass by the food stalls in search of a PC bang. With powerful computers, high-speed internet, and food service, PC bangs are a gamer's dream come true. But I'm not planning on playing *League of Legends*. I need to figure out the exact time difference between here and Santorini so I can moon shift when both locations are dark.

I choose the most bustling PC bang in town and squeeze into an empty seat at the back. Nothing will keep me hidden from the Shingae better than a crowd of humans and their innate skepticism toward magic.

It's a full house, but someone promptly drops off a menu, and I eagerly bury my nose in it. I haven't eaten in more than twenty-four hours, and I'm starving. I couldn't bear to eat the jumeokbap that Hailey had packed for Ethan, Jihun, and me when we left for the Kingdom of Mountains. It reminded me too much of Hana. I push away my grief and focus on the menu.

"Jackpot," I say under my breath.

This PC bang has grilled pork belly—no wonder it's booming—and I am overcome with gratitude. The employee doesn't quirk an eyebrow when I order three servings of it. Emboldened, I add a cup ramyeon and kimchi fried rice as appetizers. I ignore the small voice that says this might be my last meal.

While I wait for my food, I discover that Santorini is six hours behind the local time here. That means I should wait until 3 a.m. here—making it 9 p.m. there—to moon shift. That gives me plenty of time to search for potential hideouts Daeseong might be using to keep the humans captive.

It only takes me a few minutes to stumble onto why the dark mudang chose Santorini of all places. *Son of a bitch.* Daeseong bragged about the depths of Heaven Lake being darker than outer space. We didn't understand the significance of that factoid until he went to hide in its dark depths when my Yeoiju nearly killed him.

I absently accept my ramyeon from the PC bang employee and slurp away. The Santorini caldera is 385 meters deep, and Heaven Lake is 384 meters deep. The sneaky bastard is staging our showdowns in places where darkness can survive the light of the Yeoiju. But that also means he's afraid. He knows he's not invincible. Now *I* just have to believe that.

The pork belly goes a long way in fortifying my resolve. I swear my Yeoiju hums happily with every juicy bite of grilled meat. I practically do the dishes for them when I clean off my plate, then I reach for my kimchi fried rice. I saved it for last because its spicy kick will cut the richness of the pork belly. I pop the sunny-side up egg on top and scoop up a perfect spoonful.

"Fuck me," I moan around my bite. The kimchi in the fried rice is just overfermented enough to be tart against my tongue—as it should be for this dish. I shovel in bite after bite, thinking of nothing but the joy of eating one of my favorite comfort foods.

But even my avoidance skills are no match for my concern for Ethan and my friends, and soon, the food forms a cement dam halfway down my esophagus. What if the tyrant's general overtook the audience hall? I see strong and stubborn Jihun throwing himself in harm's way to protect Ethan. I see noble and loyal Ethan pushing Jihun away to stop another person he loves from dying for him. Hailey fights with ferocious bravery, carrying out her sworn duty with all her heart. They're hurt. They're bleeding. They're . . . dying.

"It's not real," I mutter. "It's not real."

The best way I can help them is to stop Daeseong and maybe not die in the process. Even if I can't return to the Kingdom of Mountains, I'll find a way to help them. My stomach roiling with sudden nerves, I hurriedly pile all the dishes onto the serving tray and push it in front of an unoccupied computer. The PC bang employee clears away the empty dishes with an annoyed glance my way.

I read everything I find on Santorini with no particular focus. I hope my intuition will soon point me in the right direction. The island is beautiful, unforgettable, breathtaking, and many other evocative adjectives. I feel like I know every inch of Santorini, when the hair on the back of my neck stands on end.

This article is from two days ago. The Minoan archaeological site near the village of Akrotiri, one of the most popular tourist destinations in Santorini, has been closed with vague claims of structural instability. *Gods.* The kidnapped humans are there. I can feel it in my bones. Why there of all places?

I don't want to be responsible for the destruction of a prehistoric settlement dating back to around 4500 B.C. Human history has value. The history of all beings has value and is worth preserving. But what about the lives of a thousand human beings? Doesn't even a single life have more value than the preservation of the past? I fucking don't know. I'm not a philosopher or a scholar. I'm just . . . lost.

I know I have to think and plan, but I'm so tired. My soul is weary from the unending fear and worry of the last several months since Ethan found me at Roxy's Diner. In a way, I want to run headlong into this battle with the dark mudang—a nemesis who refuses to stay dead—just so it can all . . . end.

But I don't want it *all* to end. Not really. I want to end this nightmare so I can *begin.* I want a future with Ethan. I want to show him how much he means to me. I want to love him with everything in me.

I want to nurture the friendships I came by unwittingly but can't imagine losing. They are the family I chose, the family of my heart. I am not alone. Not anymore. I can't forget that. I can't forget what I'm fighting for—*who* I'm fighting for.

You're tired? Well tough. Take a fucking nap.

Wow, that is the best pep talk I've ever given myself. I set the alarm on my PC and slide down in the plush gamer chair. I cross my arms and tuck my chin to my chest. When I wake up, I'll go end that motherfucker once and for all. And make sure he stays dead this time.

CHAPTER
TWENTY-FIVE

After my surprisingly restorative nap, I settle my bill at the PC bang and retrace my steps to the small mountain. The medicinal spring near the bottom should get a good reflection of the moon. I'll shift from there.

I reach the mountain sooner than I wanted and stop in front of the seonangdang at its base. The tall, broad tree is decorated with strips of blue, red, yellow, white, and black fabric, which flutter in the breezeless night. Its life force, strong and wise, brushes against me.

"Hello, old friend." I put my hand on its trunk. The Seonangshin doesn't really reside in this tree, but nature is powerful and good in its own right. "Wish me luck."

With one last pat on its warm bark, I walk to the spring nearby. I stare blankly at the moon reflected on the surface of the water. Minutes pass by, and I shake my head to pull myself together. I summon my hwando and my sword belt, which I'd hidden in the woods earlier, and buckle the leather strap low and tight on my waist.

Picturing the famous Red Beach near Akrotiri, I step into the spring. My next step falls on crimson sand, surrounded by red-and-black volcanic cliffs. The Red Beach is stunning in the moonlight, and I inhale shakily, awed by its beauty.

My throat tightens and my eyes water, but I don't chide myself for being grateful for this moment. I let my gaze linger on the beautiful beach, hoping to come back with Ethan someday. I don't bite my head off for that sentimental thought either. As much as I hate to admit it, this is who I am now.

With one last glance at the Red Beach, I walk toward the cliffs that lead into the village. The night here hasn't reached its zenith yet, and I find the path to Akrotiri easily enough. But I could've missed the actual archaeological site if I hadn't done my research.

The ancient buried city is hidden from view with a bioclimatic roof, covered with earth to blend into the landscape. There are, of course, signs along the way, but I don't have the patience to read those even on the best of days. And today isn't exactly my best day.

The stark, dusty landscape is eerily quiet as I approach the ancient site. It screams, *It's a trap, you idiot!* But I focus on the underground city and search for the soft, steady flow of human gi. I stumble back with a gasp when I locate the faint trickle of their life forces. They're really here. All one thousand kidnapped humans.

Crouching low to the ground, I head for the entrance to Akrotiri. Two security guards stand between the ancient city and any would-be trespassers. I could easily sneak past them—the Jaenanpa already did with a thousand human captives—but they are two more humans in danger tonight. I knew I had a good reason for keeping the acupuncture needles on me.

I call on my gumiho's speed and pierce their pressure points with the needles. It's a little tricky getting past their uniforms, but I can't complain. It's a thousand times easier than paralyzing a powerful shinbiin king, even with his chest bare.

I move so quickly the security guards freeze with their bored expressions intact, and I carry them across the street to settle them beneath a sturdy tree. I slide their eyes closed and remove the needles from their torsos. They'll wake up tomorrow morning without a scratch on them, wondering what the hell happened. Unless the worlds end tonight. Then no one will ever wake up again.

On that cheerful note, I return to break into Akrotiri. I descend into the buried city and immediately clap a hand over my mouth and nose. The faintest trace of doksacho poisons the air beneath. The Jaenanpa is microdosing the humans with their signature poison to hold them captive, unconscious but alive.

Holding my breath, I tread soundlessly across the suspended walkway and find the first group of humans lying in the ancient ruins. I throw one over each shoulder and spirit them out to the open air. I lower them onto the ground and feel for their pulses. They're weak but steady. I get to my feet and stare down at them, grabbing my head with both hands. So I have to do this 499 more times? It's going to be a long night.

I transport captive after captive, knowing that Daeseong will arrive at any minute. My heart pounds against my rib cage from both exertion and dread. He must be watching, toying with me. But it doesn't matter. I have to save every life I can.

I stumble as I lay two more humans on the ground. I stretch my back with a groan, then wipe a forearm across my damp forehead. Growling in frustration, I tug off my leather jacket and throw it down next to them. How many of them did I get out? Fifty? Sixty?

"It is like watching an insect shrivel under a magnifying glass. Disturbing yet fascinating," an insidious voice says from behind me, close enough to make me jump.

But when I spin around, I find Daeseong standing yards away. As before, he looks like a Joseon-era scholar in his forties, but the pleasant, distinguished air about him is nowhere to be found. Instead, he exudes undisguised menace and chaos. My hand creeps slowly toward the hilt of my hwando.

"Yet, I find I cannot look away," he continues. "Alas, the Amheuk is not a patient master."

"What do you want with these humans?" I'm stalling, and Daeseong probably knows it. "Do you need to perform another blood sacrifice to release the Amheuk from its prison beyond the abyss?"

"If it were that simple, why do you think my master stayed imprisoned for over five centuries?" The dark mudang scoffs.

"Then why have you brought them here?" I sidestep away from the humans on the ground. "What do you want with them?"

"I might have led the Jaenanpa to believe a blood sacrifice was necessary to liberate the Yeoiju from its vessel." He lets loose a cackle that sends a chill down my spine, and my instinct screams at me to run. "Perhaps *necessary* was an exaggeration. The humans are more for my entertainment."

The dark mudang floats toward me, the moonlight illuminating the twisted smile on his face and the madness in his eyes. My steps falter as I remember that I destroyed the last of his sanity at Heaven Lake. I pray that it works in my favor . . . that he takes reckless risks only a psychopath would.

"You see, your suffering amuses me a great deal." He snickers as he draws closer. I unsheathe my hwando and widen my stance. "Would you like to know *how* you will suffer?"

"Nah." I raise my sword. "I'm not interested."

"We shall see how much longer you remain *uninterested.*" Daeseong grunts in annoyance.

I tighten my clammy grip around the hilt of my sword and hold my ground, fighting back my flight instinct. The dark mudang closes in on me, and I raise my hwando. I suck in a bracing breath, then . . .

He moves right past me.

"What the . . ." I frown and whip around in momentary confusion.

"Shit," I hiss. He's heading for the buried city. Or more accurately, for the roof covering it . . . and the 950 or so humans beneath it.

I don't pause to think. I have to stop him before he gets to the top of the roof. My gumiho breaks into a sprint, and the world blurs around me as I close in on him. He spins around as I take a flying leap and tackle him to the ground.

I slash his face with my claws. His skin gapes open, but no blood flows from the gashes. There is only darkness beneath his skin—a darkness so black that it is the absence of light. His wounds close as I watch with horrified eyes.

He backhands my snout so hard he knocks a whimper out of me and sends me flying. I tumble across the rocky ground before skidding to a stop in a limp heap.

That's going to leave a mark.

I stagger to a stand and launch myself at him again, my hackles raised. This time, I don't even get within tackling distance. With a flick of his hand, the dark mudang catapults me into the air. My stomach bottoms out as the wind whooshes past, and a silent scream builds inside me.

I don't know how far I'm flung, but his magic jerks me to a halt so abruptly that my teeth sink into my tongue. I grunt as the metallic taste of blood fills my mouth. I shake my head to clear it and glance below. Daeseong looks toy-sized from way up here. I'm at least a hundred feet high.

Not good. Not good at all.

"See what I mean?" He spins me around in the air. "So amusing."

I take a deep breath and hold it, bracing for the impact I know is coming. But Daeseong doesn't just drop me from ten stories high. He spikes me down.

I wrap my nine tails around my body, curling in on myself. The ground rushes up to meet me, and I crash into it with stunning force.

Everything goes dark and muted. Maybe the impact knocked my soul out of me, or maybe I blacked out. But the high-pitched ringing in my ears jolts me back to consciousness.

The numb daze of shock evaporates, and pain lances through me. I moan and writhe in the gumiho-sized crater around me.

Focus, Sunny.

Where is Daeseong? Did he kill the humans? *No.*

Even as I cough up blood, I try to stand. But . . . I can't feel my hind legs. Realization bolts through my head like lightning. The motherfucker snapped my spine.

I swallow my fear along with the blood gurgling in my throat. I claw at the wall of dirt around me with my front legs, trying to crawl out of the crater. The rough, packed earth digs into my nails as I pull my heavy body up, but after a few inches, I slide back down, twisted into an awkward angle.

It's no use. I can't climb out as my gumiho.

I shift into my human form and moan in agony, the pain sharper and the healing slower, but I drag my limp legs behind me and pull myself out of the crater. Then I stab my hwando into the ground and inch toward Daeseong in an army crawl.

I will not allow him to kill the humans. I will *not* allow him to usher in the Amheuk. He doesn't get to win while I have breath left in me.

"Oops." The dark mudang scoots back with sadistic glee.

Every time I crawl an agonizing inch toward him, he retreats a tiny step. He's taking away my hard-won ground but staying close enough to give me hope. The asshole is toying with me. Still, in my pain-ridden, destitute state, I'm devastated by every inch I lose.

I'll never reach him. *But you have to try.*

I growl, tears streaking muddy lines down my face, but I keep inching toward him. The rocky ground cuts my stomach through my tank top and scrapes the soft skin under my arms raw.

My healing power flares and flares against my wrecked spine, but it's not a simple stab wound it can easily mend. Sweat soaks my hair and face, and blood drips into my eyes from a head wound I hadn't noticed.

I can barely make Daeseong out in front of me. The unbearable pain saps me of my strength, but I don't stop moving. I don't give up. My stubbornness is my strongest superpower.

I could really use my bloodlust right now—where I feel no pain, only the strength of violence—but the arcane word of power is . . . gone. I can't sense it anymore. Something happened when I went through the Gray Void.

But I *can* feel my Yeoiju inside me. Its song is faint but there. Too bad I can only manifest a small ball of light with it.

"This is getting rather tedious, no?" the dark mudang says around a long yawn. "So much *crawling*. It is not as entertaining when you do the same thing over and over again, you know. It's like staring at a wiggling worm."

I crawl another inch forward, propelled purely by my desire to annoy him. I do it *over and over again*, grinning despite my agony.

His smug smile droops bit by bit until anger twists his face. "Enough."

Hehe.

Regrettably, I don't get to savor my tiny win for long. Because one second, he is a mere yard ahead of me, but the next second, he is floating above the rooftop of Akrotiri.

"No." My mouth moves to shape the word, but no sound comes out.

"Give me the Yeoiju." He raises his arms, mimicking the iconic pose of *Christ the Redeemer*. The mudang is taking his god complex to a whole new level. "Give it to me. Or every human beneath this roof will cease to exist."

Ah, it was all for me.

Daeseong tricked the Jaenanpa into kidnapping a thousand humans so he could threaten me with their lives. To force me to make the choice between giving him the Yeoiju and sacrificing a thousand lives to hold onto a power I don't even understand.

The fog of pain clears away as helpless fury burns inside me. I know why he lured me here. The dark mudang needs the Yeoiju to release the Amheuk. My Yeoiju is somehow key to both stopping the darkness and unleashing it.

But I won't be able to figure out the why or how in my sorry state. One thing at a time. I need to figure out how to keep the humans in the buried city safe *without* giving up the Yeoiju.

Think, Cadet Cho.

"Do you need time to think?" Daeseong asks, as though he heard Captain Seo too. "Do go on. I can keep myself occupied while I wait."

He telekinetically raises an unconscious woman from the ground—one of the humans I'd carried out on my shoulders—until she stands drunkenly on her feet. What is he . . . ? I reach a trembling hand toward her. *Please no.* Then with another yawn, he snaps her neck and lets her lifeless body crumple to the ground.

"No," I rasp in a weedy whisper even though I'm screaming in my head.

"Don't mind me." He raises the next human. I hear another sickening crunch, then the thump of a dead body dropping to the ground. "Take your time. I have plenty of humans to go through, conveniently in front of me. But once I run out of these toys, I think I shall tire of playing. Every human under this roof will die rather quickly."

Baring my bloody teeth, I drag myself toward the humans lying on the ground. A sharp cry rips out of me when the dark mudang raises a boy—he can't be more than five—onto his little feet.

"Stop," I cry and scrabble toward the child, my nails ripping and bleeding. "No, please."

"Very interesting." Daeseong cocks his head to the side and watches me in fascination. "You value a child more than an adult? I wonder why. While I hope we do not meet this way again, if there is a next time, I will have my underlings collect only the children."

"I . . . I'll give it to you." I plead with one hand outstretched. "Just . . . don't hurt the boy."

"Now that wasn't too hard, was it?" the dark mudang coos but doesn't release the child.

"Put him down. Look." I summon the orb of white light onto my palm. "I will give it to you."

Daeseong gasps and drops the little boy, alive and unhurt—not in response to my plea but because he has lost interest. He is much more interested in what he sees on my palm.

I'm thrust into the air again, and the pain in my back makes stars spark behind my eyes. I scream, and the white light blinks out.

"Where is it?" He wraps an invisible hand around my throat and lifts me higher off the ground. He squeezes as though he's going to rip out my voice box. "Bring it back."

But I can't breathe. It hurts so much. My eyes roll back.

He shakes me by the throat. "Bring it back!"

"Let her go." A deep, rumbling voice thunders in my head, and warm hands snatch me out of Daeseong's grip, taking him by surprise.

"You're okay, Sunny." Someone wraps their arms tightly around me.

"How is she okay?" The deep voice growls. "Her fucking back is broken."

"She's going to be okay." The other person, a female, speaks with calm certainty.

I drift in and out of consciousness as silver light glows around me. Slowly but miraculously, I hurt a little less and feel my legs twitching beneath me. As the pain recedes even further, I realize that Minju is holding me atop a dragon's back as we circle the sky above Daeseong.

The silver glow of the historian's healing spell gradually dims, and her arms slip from my body. Spurred by pure instinct, I catch her before she falls off Draco's back. The agony in my back has quieted to a deep ache, but I still hiss in pain when I bear the brunt of Minju's weight in my arms.

"Sorry, sorry." She comes to and quickly straightens away from me. "I'm fine."

"What are you guys doing here?" I demand, delayed shock jolting through me. "Ethan needs your help. *That* is your sworn duty as his royal guards."

"Jaeseok and Captain Seo went to his aid, but I'm not much use in a battlefield," Minju says quietly. "I hoped I could be of help to you here instead."

"And *I'm* not a royal guard." Draco glances back at me with their sullen dragon eyes. "I'm not even a suhoshin, so *I* get to decide where *my* duty lies."

"You're right, kid. Thank you. Both of you." I don't fight it anymore. I'm so happy they're here. *"Shit."*

My heart ramming into my ribs, I whip my head around every which way and see the dark mudang doing the same thing below us. "Why hasn't he shot us down?"

"Don't worry. He can't see us," Minju says. "The invisibility spell should hold for a few more minutes."

I sag in relief, then jerk back up.

"Daeseong is keeping the humans captive in an underground archaeological site down there." I grip Minju's arm. "He's threatening to collapse the roof and kill them all if I don't hand over the Yeoiju."

"Sunny, you can't . . ."

"I know." I squeeze the historian's hand reassuringly. "I need you to get those humans to safety while I distract Daeseong."

"I can peel the roof off and fly them out," Draco says.

"The humans are unconscious—" I begin.

"We got this, Sunny. You worry about Daeseong." Minju summons a short sword that looks eerily like my hwando in a sheath made of blue dragon scales. "Here. You're going to need this."

I nearly fall off Draco's back. "I . . . is that the sword of light?"

"What gave it away? The dragon-scale sheath?" the teenager says sardonically.

"Watch it, brat." I smack their back and reverently accept the sword of light from Minju.

"I'll go wake up the humans." Minju smiles guilelessly. "See you soon."

Before I can wonder at her premature farewell, the historian jumps off the dragon's back, drawing a yelp from me. But I belatedly remember that she's a seonnyeo as she flies gracefully down on her wings of wind.

"I keep forgetting you're the only one of us who can't fly." Draco snorts, and a puff of smoke comes out of their nostrils. "Big L."

"Shut up," I say, fighting a grin. They are a child after my own heart. Gods, I love them. "Now be a good dragon and fly us annoyingly close to Daeseong's head, so he doesn't see Minju sneaking underground."

"He's so creepy." It feels like an earthquake when Draco's enormous, serpentine body shivers beneath me.

"Once we catch his attention, I'm going after him alone." My voice is both urgent and stern. "Fly away as quickly as you can and go save the humans with Minju."

"But—"

"No *buts*." I lean close to their head. "Don't follow me, Draco. No matter what you see. You can't interfere. This is my fight. Understand?"

They stay stubbornly silent, but I stop pushing. I don't want to force them to double down. I just have to hope they'll listen when the time comes. *Since when do teenagers ever listen?* I push away the panicked thought.

Draco will listen. They have to.

CHAPTER TWENTY-SIX

True to our plan, Draco swoops toward Daeseong's head before pulling up at the last second. The dark mudang growls and swats the air in front of him as if at a pesky fly. It sends the dragon tumbling through the sky, and I hang on to their back for dear life until Draco finally rights themself.

"Land over there," I shout and point toward an open field opposite Akrotiri. They miraculously comply, and I slide down their back. "Now go. Save the humans."

When the teenager obediently flies away, I'm convinced my luck is changing. But my newfound optimism is extinguished when Daeseong turns to follow them.

"Hey." I wrap my lips around my fingers and emit an earsplitting whistle. When the dark mudang deigns to glance my way, I hold my palm out and summon a white light the size of a Ping-Pong ball. "Don't you have unfinished business with me?"

The dark mudang floats across the field toward me and my pretty light—away from my friends and the humans. Even if I can't defeat Daeseong, I will find a way to keep him away from Draco and Minju. I will find a way to keep them safe.

My Yeoiju hums in my chest, and the orb of light hovering over my open palm grows bigger than the width of my hand. The avaricious glint in Daeseong's eyes shifts into apprehension the closer he approaches, until he stops a few yards away, squinting against the light.

My little light . . . hurts him. Even the smallest, softest manifestation of the Yeoiju hurts him. Maybe I *can* stop him without letting it shatter me from the inside out.

"I see you have learned some new tricks since we last met, little fox." Another off-kilter smile rips across his face. "Show me what else you can do."

"When will you learn that I'll always, without fail, do the exact opposite of what you want?" I try to fist my palm to extinguish the light, but my hand won't move. Instead, my heart warms and vibrates with an answering light.

What the fuck is happening?

I gasp sharply as my head snaps back and my chest thrusts forward hard enough to arch my spine. My gi streams out of me into the floating orb, my arms thrown back from the force of the pull. The white light grows brighter and bigger as it siphons my life force.

I can't . . . move. I can't even blink.

This isn't paralysis. It feels as though my will has been disconnected from my body. The gift of the Cheon'gwang, *my ass*. The Yeoiju is *stealing* my gi.

But a quiet calm pacifies the fear shuddering through me. I *want* to give in to the Yeoiju's call. I want to pour my life force into it.

A shrill scream rends through the night, and I'm thrown off my feet. I crash onto my back, hard enough to knock the wind out of me.

Then everything . . . stops.

I blink, flexing my hand. I have control over my body again. The orb of light is gone. And the Yeoiju hums contentedly inside me, as though it's happy to be back home.

What in the ever-loving hell was *that*?

Then I remember I was in the middle of a conversation with a dark mudang hell bent on destroying the worlds. I struggle up to my elbows, expecting to find Daeseong coming at me with his figurative claws out, but he is nowhere to be found.

No.

In a panic, I scramble to my feet and spin in a circle. I do it one more time to make sure. He's gone. Gone *where*, though?

Minju. Draco. All those people.

"Shit." I sprint toward Akrotiri but don't get very far because I'm met by a swarm of humans, pulsing with dark, stolen magic. *Jaenanpa assholes.* "Get out of my way. I don't have time to play with you."

Unfortunately, they don't listen, and they come at me with angry roars of varying pitches. I shrug and draw my sword of light. Then I pause and blink down at it. It looks and feels exactly like my hwando. Don't get me wrong. I love my hwando. But I kind of expected the sword of light to be *extra*. I push aside the pinch of disappointment.

Don't knock it till you try it.

Luckily, a horde of maniacal shamans are storming me. I run straight into the mob, excited to try out my fancy new toy. I swing the sword of light over my head, wearing a razor-sharp smile, and slash my way through the first wave of bad guys.

The bastards kidnapped a thousand humans for what they believed would be a blood sacrifice. They don't deserve my mercy. Yet, even as I slice, jab, and pierce with lightning-fast attacks, I make sure none of their wounds are fatal. Maybe I'm not so ferocious after all.

Maybe I am good after all.

I search for signs of Daeseong, even as I work my way through the throng of corrupted mudangs. Is he in the buried city? Did he get to Draco and Minju?

A ball of fire barely misses my head by an inch.

I smell my burned hair before I see the ashes rain past my shoulder. I run one hand through my hair to find that I've been given a bob cut on half of my head. With my mouth gaping in shocked outrage, I glance in the direction the fireball came from. A scrawny, bespectacled blond in a loose T-shirt and khaki pants stands with another ball of fire in his hand.

"You lot can go make sure the captives don't escape," he barks to the other mudangs, inching toward me with a sly smile. "I can take care of this one."

Blondie must rank higher than the others, but not that much higher, because they grumble and glare at him even as they follow his orders. They probably suspect he wants to steal my magic for himself. And maybe he does.

"Did you torture a being of the Shingae to steal that elemental power, mudang?" I growl, my lip peeling back from my teeth.

"Oh, you mean this power?" He ignites a matching fireball in his other hand. "*Torture* is putting it nicely, but I deserve this power more than that kid ever did. I *earned* this power."

Nausea floods my stomach at his utter lack of remorse, at his absolute entitlement. When screams of terror erupt behind the sadistic mudang, I smile grimly. "The only thing you earned is the comeuppance you're about to receive."

With trepidation in every line of his body, the mudang turns around just in time to witness Draco roar into the night and land on top of a dozen Jaenanpa minions. Blondie stumbles toward me, but I push him back to the furious blue dragon and the terrified mudangs scattering in every direction.

"J . . . Jaenanpa." His voice cracks like a pubescent boy as he corrals every mudang within his reach. "Stand y . . . your ground. Do n . . . not be afraid."

I shake my head at the pathetic coward and sprint toward my friends. My legs wobble with relief that Daeseong hasn't gotten them.

"Hurry, everyone." Minju slides down Draco's back and urges the groggy humans with her to follow her example. "You have to go. Run toward that tree at the top of the hill. Stay down and keep each other safe."

I reach Minju's side. "How did you wake them up?"

"I brought some seungmacho, the antidote," she says, helping the remaining people down. "I figured the Jaenanpa would fall back on their favorite poison."

"You're a genius." I watch the humans—about a dozen of them—run for the hills. Then I turn a wary eye to the Jaenanpa surrounding Draco. "Minju, how many more do you have down there?"

"Too many." She rubs a tired hand across her forehead, leaving behind a streak of dirt.

"Leave the Jaenanpa to me," the dragon rumbles inside my head with barely leashed fury. "They poisoned my dad and bound him with dark magic before they ripped his power . . . his *life* . . . out of him."

"I'm so sorry, kid." My voice breaks. "What the Jaenanpa did to your dad was wrong and despicable. But taking a human life—no matter how much they deserve it—will leave a mark on you. It'll alter you forever, and not for the better."

"I . . . I can't stand by and let them hurt innocent people," they argue, but the edge of violence has faded from their voice.

"You can stop the Jaenanpa and protect the innocent *without* losing yourself." I pat their front leg—the only part of them I can reach. "I like you just the way you are. Okay, kid?"

"Bruh." Tears well in their beautiful cerulean eyes.

I want to reach up and catch the giant teardrop, but I shouldn't push my luck. The teenager has probably reached their daily capacity for non-angsty emotion.

"Well?" I smirk. "What are you standing around for?"

With a keening cry of determination, the dragon charges into battle. *Gods.* I'm so proud of that kid.

"What is it?" I spin toward Minju when she tugs on my arm. "Do you think Draco will be okay on their own? Should I help you rescue more of the captives?"

"Where is Daeseong, Sunny?" Minju asks urgently.

"I . . . I don't know." I'd been purposely not thinking about that.

"That beam of white light . . ." She looks across the field as though remembering it. "I could even see it from underground. Was that you?"

"I don't know." Maybe it started out as me, but in the end, it was the Yeoiju. A shiver of fear runs down my back. If I can't learn to control it, the Yeoiju will destroy me. It will destroy both of us.

"Daeseong must have run from the light. You have to go after him." Minju grips my shoulders and shakes me lightly. "Do you know where he could have gone to hide?"

"The caldera." I recall with a start. "He's at the caldera."

If I can stop the dark mudang once and for all, it doesn't matter if the Yeoiju destroys me. I remember the aching love in Ethan's eyes. And the warmth of my friends' loyalty and affection glows in my chest. The Amheuk will *not* touch them.

I cast a worried glance at Draco. While evading the Jaenanpa's dark spells in a graceful, sinuous dance, the dragon is taking them down with fire and might, leaving them injured but alive. But there are at least a hundred corrupt mudangs coming after them, and my stomach clenches with fear. Maybe I should've told them to just kill the bastards in one blast.

"Don't worry. I will help them," Minju says. "You must go, Sunny."

I know she's right, but that doesn't make it any easier to walk away from them while they're in danger. But I take one heavy step, then another, until I'm flat out running for the Red Beach. I need to moon shift to the caldera.

When I reach the beach, I stride into the moonlit ocean without pause. Then I step out onto the rim of an infinity pool and teeter on its edge, with my arms flailing. A quick glance around tells me that I'm at a luxury cave hotel, and I nearly tumbled down the stone steps overlooking the Santorini caldera.

After regaining my balance, I leap down to the walkway below the pool and head for the caldera. But when I get there, I don't feel the dark mudang hiding in the depth of the waters—its serene life force remains undisturbed. Then where is he?

Wherever he is, I have no desire to make my fight with Daeseong a tourist attraction. I hike up the island, guided only by moonlight. Away from the populated villages, Santorini lies asleep in a deep, lightless night. As I climb higher, the landscape grows stark and rocky, beautiful in its own way.

When I reach an abandoned church on top of the hill, the blue of its domed roof long faded to a sandy brown, I stop to admire the caldera stretching wide and open before me. Going by instinct, I summon the white orb to my palm, careful not to let it grow much bigger than a Ping-Pong ball.

I walk to the edge of the cliff and scan the curve of the caldera with the light outstretched in my hand. No, I need to look *through* it. I bring the orb to eye level and squint at it, searching for . . . something. I'm not sure what I expect to happen, but I'll know it when I see it.

I'm about to give up my experiment, feeling beyond ridiculous, when the orb suddenly becomes distorted as I move it past an outcropping near the bottom of the cliffs. I whip my hand back toward it, and the light of the Yeoiju undulates against the darkness. My stomach sinks. I found what I was looking for—I found Daeseong.

The light I summoned in front of Akrotiri wasn't powerful enough to hurt the dark mudang. It just frightened him. That's why he isn't hiding in the caldera. No, he is merely lying in wait for me.

Not giving myself time to chicken out, I shift into my gumiho and take a flying leap off the edge of the caldera. I half run, half slide down the steep cliff, sending rocks raining into the ocean. When I reach the outcropping, my eyes widen, recognizing an abandoned monastery I read about in the PC bang.

Tunneled into the face of the cliff, the monastery sits midway between the sea and the clifftop, making access from either direction precarious. I have no choice but to make the climb up. Out of breath from exertion and nerves, I skid to a stop on a narrow pathway that leads to the entrance of the monastery and shift to my human form.

With a squeak, I press my back against the cliff and cling on for dear life.

"You might as well come inside," Daeseong drawls before I can catch my breath. "You came all this way after all."

"What are you playing at, mudang?" I grit out.

"Akrotiri was getting a bit too crowded for my tastes. This peaceful monastery is a better place for us to chat, is it not?" He pauses. "Well? Are you coming in? Or do you want to stand on your tiptoes all night?"

I mutter a curse and step into the suffocating darkness of the man-made cave. I pitch an orb of light into the air. Daeseong is standing closer than I expected, and I take half a step back before I catch myself. On the plus side, I also catch him flinching ever so slightly.

"Don't worry." I smirk as my gaze skitters across the large hall, chiseled into a semblance of a room with four walls and a higher-than-expected ceiling. The two smaller pathways leading deeper into the monastery seem to have collapsed long ago. "It's just a regular old light orb."

"I'm not worried." Daeseong sneers at me. "I know you can't control the Yeoiju."

I decide not to tell him I have the sword of light now.

"If you're afraid of the little white light"—I step around him with my back to the rough wall—"then what are you going to do with the Yeoiju even if I give it to you?"

Never mind that I have no idea *how* to go about giving anyone the Yeoiju. All I know is that it would kill me to do it.

"No need to worry your little head over it." He snickers like he's impressed with his own witty retort. "This has been diverting, but we have much to do tonight."

With a flick of his fingers, he extinguishes my light orb. My eyes skip around the darkness as an ominous rumble rolls through the cave. The mouth of the cave collapses with a deafening roar, drowning out even the meager moonlight.

I swallow my gasp. Fear is the last thing I can show him.

"If we have so much to do, let's get on with it," I quip, even as panic skitters down my spine. Where is he? What is he doing? "I wouldn't want all your party planning to go to waste."

"You really are rather amusing." His laugh rings from every corner of the cave, even from the wall behind me. I can't hold back my shudder. "It would be a shame to kill you."

"Too bad I can't return the compli—"

I dig my nails into my throat, trying to loosen the rope of darkness tightening around it. With my air supply cut off, I can't hold my fear at bay. My eyes bulge and my legs kick under me as the noose lifts me into the air until the top of my head brushes the high cave roof.

He did something similar outside of Akrotiri . . . before he drove me into the ground. I'm not as high in the air, but he could always throw me down harder. I need to shift so I can bear the impact of the fall. My gumiho's back snapped, but at least I didn't die.

All thoughts come to a screeching halt as the darkness closes in on me like a physical wall. No, it's more like thick, wet clay molding against every surface of my body—even my eyes, mouth, nose, and ears. I'm suffocating, not from a lack of oxygen but from a lack of light.

Light is life.

I gag and gurgle as I struggle against the oppressive power, but I can't move an inch. I am encased in a hungry, unending darkness. I rein in my terror and call forth the light of the Yeoiju. I don't care if it's nothing more than a pretty white orb. I need . . . warmth.

Light sparks to life on my palm, but it doesn't stay long enough to warm my skin. The darkness suctions the white light from me like a powerful vacuum. *No.* I stop summoning the light and hold the Yeoiju tightly inside me. But a different light, the beautiful green of my gi, begins to trickle out of me.

"Do you recognize my true form?" Daeseong's voice echoes in my head. "Last time, I tried to blanket all of Heaven Lake, but I've been humbled by my mistake and learned from it. I realized I only need to swallow *you* to consume your light."

With my ears muffled by the dark, my pounding heart echoes deafeningly through my head, too loudly for me to think. My life force continues to leave my body, turning oily, oozing, and black in Daeseong's embrace. Tears well in my eyes, but they can't fall past the impermeable darkness that erases even the memory of light.

"No." The single word bursts out through my mind.

"How are you . . . speaking?" The darkness quivers around me in shock. "No matter. Soon you will not have much to say, telepathically or not. With every beat of your heart—with every life-giving pulse—you are surrendering your life to me. Do you want to live, little fox? Then give me the Yeoiju."

No, I say into his mind. *I am not giving you a fucking thing.*

It isn't enough to conjure a measly little orb. I need to call forth the living, breathing light that sent Daeseong running in fear. I have to summon the white light that nearly sucked the life out of me. If I'm going to have my gi siphoned out of me either way, I'd much rather give my life force to my Yeoiju than let the darkness have any part of me. My only wish is to take the dark mudang with me.

I stop listening to the frantic beating of my heart. I turn my back on the terror sinking its claws into me. I listen for the song of the Yeoiju at the core of my being. It starts as a pinprick of light, sound, and warmth. I don't know if I'm seeing, hearing, or feeling it—maybe all three—but it's *there.*

My body spasms in sudden panic. I can't control this power in my human form. But just as fast, I quiet, because my gumiho isn't strong enough to control it either. Nothing is strong enough, and my heart sings at the thought. My Yeoiju will defeat Daeseong. His darkness can't withstand my light.

I . . . let go.

The pinprick expands inside me, my gi flowing like a river into the orb. The light beams out of my chest, growing ever brighter. The tips of my fingers prickle as they evanesce. I realize the Yeoiju isn't sucking the life out of me like Daeseong's darkness was. My body isn't withering into an empty husk. It's *evolving*. I am becoming the light of the Yeoiju.

"S . . . stop," the dark mudang screeches. "You can't control the Yeoiju's power. Y . . . you will destroy this entire island, you evil, selfish girl."

I flinch and falter, but the Yeoiju doesn't. The light spills out of my eyes, mouth, nose, and ears, dissolving the darkness that was suffocating me. My arms and legs burst wide like a starfish as my chest thrusts forward, my back arching into a bow. The light pierces the darkness in a hundred different places, like starlight through the blanket of night, and Daeseong's agonized scream rings out.

With a menacing boom, the cave crumbles around us in a rain of boulders and jagged rocks and plummets into the caldera, tearing up the calm waters. But Daeseong and I, darkness and light, remain untouched, hovering in the air—weightless, formless . . . all encompassing.

The Yeoiju makes a sorrowful sound inside me.

"It's . . . okay. It doesn't h . . . hurt," I reassure it. "You can take the rest of me. We have to stop the Amheuk."

It keens again as my thoughts turn fuzzy around the edges.

There is another way. You are not alone. You must reach beyond you.

I smile sleepily. The Yeoiju sounds just like me.

"It's okay," I repeat as my arms begin to evanesce. First my wrists, then my forearms, and past my elbows . . .

"No," Draco bellows loudly enough to wake the dead—loudly enough to jerk me back to my consciousness.

Their serpentine body glistens exquisitely in the moonlight, every shade of azure, cobalt, and cerulean rippling across their scales. But the fire burning in their eyes is a deep, enraged indigo. *Uh-oh.* The dragon charges toward Daeseong and me. I think the dark mudang is in trouble.

"You fucking idiot," Draco shouts into my mind. "Are you *trying* to kill yourself?"

"Yes?" I answer vapidly.

"I hate you." The teenager sobs and slams through the sheet of darkness and light.

My life force crashes back into me, and I suck in a heaving breath—then another—and I fall toward the dark waters of the sunken caldera.

CHAPTER TWENTY-SEVEN

"Sunny," Minju shouts from somewhere, her voice pitched high with alarm.

I feel the rush of wind as she catches me midair. After a moment, she lands haphazardly at the bottom of the cliffs, struggling under my weight, and half drops me on the ground.

I moan against the pain in my back, the sharp, volcanic rocks digging into my skin. But I can't complain. The same rocks would have pierced and shattered my body if Minju hadn't caught me in the air.

Why was I falling through the air?

"Are you okay?" Minju taps my cheek. "Sunny, wake up."

My eyes shoot open. I try to sit up, but nothing happens. Why is my body not working? I can feel myself—limbs, digits, and everything else—so I'm not paralyzed. Then why can't I move?

"Draco?" I manage to rasp.

I hear their roar before Minju can answer. With my heart in my throat, I peer into the sky and see inky darkness coiling around the dragon's long body. Draco and Daeseong spin and churn against the night sky, forming a black-and-blue braid.

I try to get up again, but my body won't listen. "Why can't I move?"

"You're too weak from pouring your gi into the Yeoiju," she answers softly.

"Wh . . . why did it absorb my gi?" I feel . . . betrayed. I trusted the Yeoiju. I thought it was *good.*

"I'm not sure." Minju helps me sit up, and I lean heavily against her. "Nothing in my research even hinted at anything like that. The Yeoiju is supposed to empower you, not deplete you. There must be an element we're missing."

The dragon roars above me, and I nearly choke on my own terror.

"We don't have time to figure it out. Draco needs me. *Now.*" I glance up at the sky, desperation clawing at me. Fingerlike tentacles branch out from the dark coil and spread over Draco's scales like spiderwebs. "I need to help them. Daeseong is too strong. Please, do something. I have to go help them. Please."

This is all my fault. If only I had mastered the power of the Yeoiju . . .

"There is a way." She sits me up and looks me in the eyes. "No matter what happens, you must not pull away from me. If you do, you will endanger us both. Do you understand?"

"Okay." Trepidation runs through me as I hold my friend's grim gaze, but I look above me again. Draco is writhing against the twisting tentacles of darkness. I can't let Daeseong hurt the kid. "I . . . I understand."

Minju moves to sit behind me, with her palms pressed against my back. As she sings a haunting incantation, the silver and red of her life force flows and dances around us. Then her life force becomes an arrow in the night and comes right for me. I only have time to scream before the arrow of gi streams into my chest.

No, no, no.

My friend is transferring her life force into me. *Oh gods.* She might die if I don't stop her. But if I break away from her, we will both die. I can't save Draco if I die. They're just a kid. I can't let them die. I won't.

Silent tears stream down my cheeks, but I don't pull away from Minju. Her gi continues to fill me until strength returns to every inch of my body. I sit still until her silver-and-red life force wavers weakly, then stops flowing into me. Her hands slip off my back, and she collapses behind me.

"Don't you dare die on me." I scramble to my knees and tap Minju's cheek. I get a grip and focus on her gi. The red and silver of her life force flows softly over her prone form, growing stronger ever so slowly.

With one last touch on Minju's cheek, I push onto my feet and squint up at the sky, rage building in my chest. If the dark mudang hurts Draco . . . I reach for the sword of light, gritting my teeth, but my breath leaves me in a whoosh. I frantically pat my hip and the dragon-scale sheath—the *empty* dragon-scale sheathe.

"Draco, no."

My lungs stop working, and all the blood drains out of my body. I nearly collapse onto the ground again, my knees buckling, but I remain upright somehow. Draco took the sword of light. That foolish, reckless child plans to end the dark mudang themself. I focus on my outrage so fear won't paralyze me.

"If you get so much as a strand of your blue hair hurt, I'll whup your scaly ass with my nine tails." I shake my fist at the sky, where the dragon thrashes against the coil of darkness. "Do you hear me?"

I take my gumiho form, desperation and fury wringing my insides. I scale the cliffs with such speed that my paws barely touch the surface. When I see Draco and Daeseong careen toward an outcropping out in the ocean, I change course and push myself even faster, leaping and bounding toward the jutting rock.

I skid to a halt at the bottom of the outcropping. It's much too steep for my gumiho to climb. I shift to my human form and make the painfully slow ascent up the sheer cliff, searching for every minuscule crack and foothold needed to haul myself up to the peak.

With a labored heave, I hoist my body onto the top, then leap to my feet, expecting to see a blue, serpentine dragon facing off with a churning, oily darkness. Instead, Draco stands in their human form with the sword of light in their hand as the dark mass condenses into Daeseong's corporeal body. I stumble back, my hand rising to my throat.

"No," I shout. The dark mudang gives me a leisurely glance over his shoulder, a chilling smile stretching across his face. "No, please. Don't hurt them."

I shriek incoherently and sprint toward Daeseong, but I'm not going to reach him in time. I can't stop the dark mudang. My heart already knows this, and it rips down the middle. I can't save the kid. My soul already knows this, and it cries a sound of pure anguish. But my eyes refuse to believe the horror unfolding before me. I keep running faster than I've ever run.

With a ferocious battle cry, Draco—the brave, good child—raises the sword of light and charges toward Daeseong. The dark mudang's gaze never leaves my face as he lifts his arm and flicks a single, careless finger.

"No!" The shout rings in my ears before I'm aware my throat is tearing from the force of it.

Darkness ribbons out of Daeseong's fingertip and flies toward the kid, morphing into a spear. I can catch it—even if I have to throw my body in front of the spear. I will stop it.

I'm almost there, kid.

I'm close. The dark spear whooshes past me. My neck strains as I push myself to move faster. *Faster.* I leap into the air, my fingers straining to reach the kid. I'm so close . . . I can see every shift in Draco's expression as the spear pierces their chest and bursts out their back.

"N . . . n . . . no . . ." I choke on my scream.

Mouth gaping, Draco glances at their ruined chest. Their knees buckle, but they don't fall. They cry out in pain as the spear hovers in the air, holding them aloft through their gaping wound. Daeseong's delighted chuckle fills the night, but I don't spare him a glance.

"Draco." I reach their side and wrap my arms around their waist, trying to bear the brunt of their weight. "Hey, kid."

"Sun . . . ny." They look down at me with wide, stunned eyes.

"Yeah, it's me." I nod with a tremulous smile. They cough wetly, and blood dribbles down their chin. I wipe it away frantically. "You're okay. You're going to be okay."

I know the dark mudang is watching and enjoying himself, because my suffering *amuses* him. I don't give a flying fuck. He can watch all he wants. All I see is the kid.

"I don't w . . . want to die." Draco weaves back and forth on the spear of darkness, moaning weakly, and I hike them up higher against me.

"I won't let you." Tears blur my eyes. "I won't let you die, kid."

"G . . . good." They smile crookedly at me. *Gods.* They're such a beautiful child. But then, they gasp in pain and lurch forward. "Sunny, it hurts."

"I know." My voice breaks as I scramble to bear more of their weight. "It hurts me too."

Their head lolls back, and I stop breathing. Everything . . . stops.

I need to lie them down so they can rest—maybe hurt a little less. But I can't because of the spear skewered through them. The spear the dark mudang is holding aloft to prolong Draco's suffering. The dark spear that is part Daeseong.

I focus on the rage past the fog of grief until I can think clearly again. Draco needs me. There is so little I can do for them, but I will *die* to give them the briefest rest—to alleviate their pain even for a second. A steely calm settles over me, and I turn my gaze toward the dark mudang.

"You." My lips pull back, and my incisors elongate.

"Who? *Me?*" Daeseong hoots with mad laughter. "Are you sad your little friend is dying? Does the child's suffering *hurt* you? I so appreciate the dragon joining in the fun. We both know you care especially about the young ones."

I look away from the ranting psychopath and focus on the kid. The dark mudang's laughter dwindles, and his vitriol fills the air. He doesn't like being disregarded.

"Draco, sweetie." I look up at their handsome face and brush their blue locks out of their eyes. I gently take the sword of light from their limp grip. "This will only hurt for a second. Be brave for me, okay?"

I glance at Daeseong across the rocky terrain. He wants fun? I will deliver the fucking fun.

With a sharp cry, I bring the sword down on the spear of darkness, slicing clean through it. Daeseong screeches in pain and collapses. The darkness dissipates into the air, freeing Draco at last.

I carefully lower the kid to the ground. I grab their hand and bring it up to their chest, pressing it down on their wound. They bite back a whimper, gritting their teeth against the pain. Such a strong, brave child.

"Rest for a bit." My voice shakes no matter how hard I try to be strong for them.

Draco doesn't have much longer, and neither do I. Daeseong is no longer amused. The blow from the sword of light wounded him, but I don't know how quickly he will recover. I have to say goodbye to the kid before I lose the chance.

"You'll feel better when you wake up." A sob hitches in my throat.

"Liar." Draco pauses as a cough quakes through them, blood spurting from their mouth. "I'm not stupid, you know."

"You are many things—like a smart aleck and a thorn in my side—but stupid isn't one of them." I force myself to grin even as tears rain down my cheeks. "You are also brave, strong, and kind. And as much as it pains me to admit it, you are funny as hell."

"You have your moments, too, I guess." Their weak chuckle gurgles in their throat, but their expression turns earnest. "Sunny, I know I give you a hard time, but you know that . . . you know I . . ."

"I know, kid." I cup their cheek with my hand. "I love you too."

"I was going to say I don't *totally* hate you. Not *all* the time, at least." Their breath rattles in their chest. "But you do you."

"Brat." My laugh turns into a sob. "I'm so sorry, Draco."

"It's not your fault, Sunny." Their hand flutters at their chest, and I clasp it in mine. "But you *owe* me now. If you die, then I would've died for nothing."

"You're not going to die," I choke out.

"Are we seriously doing this again?" Their body jerks and spasms on the ground. I hold tighter to their hand, like I could keep them with me if I hold on tight enough.

"Th . . . thank you for saving my life, kid." I rock back and forth, cradling their hand against my chest. "I will save the fucking worlds for you. I swear it."

"I know you will, but promise me you won't die doing it," Draco says fervently. "Promise me you won't die, Sunny."

The night stirs around me. I swivel my head to glance over my shoulder. Daeseong is recovering. Slowly, he gathers the darkness into a tower of black violence above him.

I look down at the kid. I can't . . . I can't leave their side. I shoot another panicked glance behind me. I have to be by their side when they go . . .

"I . . . I promise." I bite my trembling lip and ruffle their hair. "Do you need me to pinky promise?"

"Shut up and keep your word. And when you save the worlds, you better give me some of the credit." They turn their gaze to the brightening sky. "Hey, Dad. Did you miss me?"

"D . . . Draco?" I'm shaking so hard that my teeth chatter.

"Don't be sad, Sunny. I didn't have to be alone anymore because of you. Thank you for being my family." Their eyes slide closed, a faint smile playing around their lips. "Now, go kick ass."

And they're . . . gone.

I swallow my scream. Daeseong may delight in watching my pain and suffering, but he will *not* witness my grief. My love for Draco, and the grief born out of it, is for them and them alone. I will not share a shred of it with the dark mudang.

Think, Sunny.

I glance over my shoulder to find Daeseong getting to his feet, massaging his wrist as though it feels a bit stiff.

Is that all?

That's all the sword of light did to him when I cut the dark spear in half? It took him a while to recover, but he looks as good as new.

That can't be right. No way did a flesh wound hold him off all this time.

Think.

From his agonized scream, I knew I wounded Daeseong, but I didn't know how or how much. I didn't care beyond the fact that I had bought myself time to say goodbye to the kid.

Draco.

I bite the insides of my cheeks. I will grieve them like they deserve once I kill the dark mudang.

Think, Sunny.

That wasn't a flesh wound. I must have . . . Did I cut the dark mudang's hand clean off? That has to be it. He must be massaging his wrist because he's getting accustomed to the feel of a new appendage.

Fuck yeah.

Daeseong is vulnerable to the sword of light. Its blade reaches beyond his skin and cuts into his essence. And it took him real time to heal—not mere seconds but *minutes*. That's why he didn't attack sooner. Because he *couldn't.*

The sword of light makes Daeseong as killable as me—not easy, but also not impossible. *That* is the power of the sword forged from sacrifice and hope.

Thank you, Samshin Halmeom. Thank you, Draco.

Now, I just have to wound him badly enough and quickly enough to kill him before he can heal himself.

I lean down and press a quick kiss on the kid's forehead. They're still warm, and it hurts so much that I claw at my chest, my nails breaking skin. I don't want to leave their side, but I have to do as they asked. I have to go kick ass.

I rise to my feet and stalk toward Daeseong, drawing an infinity sign in the air with the sword of light.

Think, Sunny.

I realize I was wrong. The sword might look like my hwando, but it does *not* feel the same. It's lighter in weight, but it takes more force to swing it, like the blade is *cutting* the molecules in the air, not just moving through it. With slow, deliberate movements, I familiarize myself with the weight and feel of the sword of light.

"You have the Gwangdo." The dark mudang watches me with sharp interest.

"We haven't named it yet." I offer him a vicious smile, shoving down my trepidation. "But the *Amheuk Killer* has a nice ring to it, don't you think?"

Daeseong doesn't answer. I guess he's done playing for the night.

He gathers the darkness into his hands and raises his arms to attack. But I don't give him the fucking privilege. With light-blurring speed, I leap into the air and come down on him, slicing my sword in a long horizontal line across his chest. I hear the hiss of burning skin even before the dark mudang stumbles back.

"This is certainly . . . interesting," he grunts, staring at the gaping gash in his chest. "I wasn't expecting a challenge."

"Nah." I shake my head. "I still don't see a challenge here."

I twist and spin, slashing the sword nonstop, encouraged by the black smoke seeping out of his wounds. He lashes out with bruising blows that slow me down, but I don't stop the onslaught of attacks. Not until my lungs burn and my limbs shake from fatigue.

At last, I leap back and admire my handwork with my head cocked to the side. The dark mudang looks like Frankenstein's monster before his creator stitched him together—a veritable patchwork of flapping, slashed skin. And black smoke oozes out of the gashes like dark blood.

"Cease," he booms and reaches out a dark tentacle to grab my sword arm.

I scream in pain as the darkness singes me to my bones. But I don't drop my sword. I've been told I have a stubborn streak. With a twist, I spin the hilt of the sword in my hand to switch to an underhanded grip and slash upward at the darkness wrapped around my arm.

The tentacle snaps back against Daeseong like a contracting rubber band, and he staggers on his feet. Baring his teeth in feral anger, he spreads his fingers toward me.

My breath catches in my throat as four shadowy arrows pierce me across my chest and shoulders, one buried in each end of my collarbone and the other two at the junctions where my shoulders meet my arms. My head spins, and I fall to my knees, stabbing my sword into the ground to stop myself from collapsing.

I feel the darkness suctioning my life—my light—out of me again, but this time it absorbs my gi through the blood pooling at my wounds. The Yeoiju is not a little pearl I could pluck out of me and hand over. Its magic lives in my very blood. The bastard is trying to absorb my very being.

I roar with fury. I swipe my sword across the row of dark arrows and scream in pain. Daeseong screams as well and stumbles to one knee, cradling his fingers against his chest.

I grab the broken end of a shaft and whimper as agony sears my palm. I grit my teeth and pull out an arrow. Cold sweat beads on my forehead and drenches my back, but I rip the rest of the arrows out in quick succession.

Blood soaks through the front of my tank top, making the fabric cling to my chest. My wounds are slow to heal as well, but I can't make myself care. *Draco.* I stagger to my feet and rush toward the patchwork mudang, the sword of light thrust forward.

"Enough," Daeseong says with eerie calm before the night is cloaked black. His voice worms into my mind again as the darkness surrounds me. "I have had enough of you, gumiho."

I tighten my grip on the hilt of my sword before I'm fully trapped. I *will* fight this. Draco did *not* die for nothing. Even so, despair seeps into my soul as darkness surrounds me. The only way I know how to fight this is to unleash my Yeoiju—to become the light. But I promised them I wouldn't die.

I'll try, Draco.

I summon the white light to my hand. My life force swirls inside me in a flurry of activity as though it's preparing to pour out of me at the first opportunity. I hold my gi in check and allow only a trickle to feed the light. The darkness will absorb the light if it's too small, but the Yeoiju will drain me if it grows too large.

You are not alone.

Why do I keep thinking that? I already know. No matter how alone I sometimes feel, Ethan and my friends will always have my back. They love me as I love them. So why?

"Are you trying that trick again, little fox?" Daeseong's voice slithers through my mind, cold and oily. "There is no need for you to die, you know. Just give me the Yeoiju. Let me absorb it from you . . . little by little. If you stop resisting, I can take the power from you without killing you."

I focus my bleary gaze on him as his lie worms its way into my mind. The Yeoiju has been nothing but a burden to me. If I didn't have the Yeoiju, my mother wouldn't have died protecting me. I never would have run from my home. I never would have lived without roots, alone and scared . . . always so scared. It ruined everything, and it could ruin everything again.

If I didn't possess the Yeoiju, it wouldn't have fallen on me to kill Daeseong and to stop the coming of the Amheuk. I wouldn't have had to put my life on the line again and again. And if I didn't possess the Yeoiju, Ethan wouldn't have to fulfill the prophecy. He would have no reason to kill me. We could love freely without the shadow of the prophecy dogging us, tainting our happiness.

"Think, little fox. You are a clever thing," the dark mudang entices. "Give me the Yeoiju and return to the arms of the King Foretold."

Ethan. I love you so much.

"No," I snarl, my will pulsating into the darkness. Even if I survive somehow, my life would be forfeit as long as Daeseong lives. If he ushers the Amheuk into the worlds, life itself will cease to exist.

Despair will not trick me into relinquishing hope.

My body spasms and twists. I didn't even realize I was breathing, but my lungs seize in abrupt panic. The light is expanding too fast. My gi rushes toward it like water past a crumbling dam. I . . . I can't stop it. The darkness tightens around me and crushes my chest with unspeakable force, trying to stop the light from exploding out of me.

Pain spears through me—the light pulling to arch my back, the dark pushing against it. Agony builds at the bottom of my spine, and I feel as though I'll snap in two. I whimper, but the light and the darkness swallow the sound like I don't exist. And I'm tempted to let them erase me. I'm tired. I don't want to fight anymore.

You must reach beyond you.

I did *not* just think that. That . . . wasn't *my* thought.

But understanding spreads through me as warm and serene as the white light. The Yeoiju is not merely a part of me. It *is* me. It can't erase me without erasing itself. It cannot exist without me because we are one and the same.

How did I forget? Or maybe I just didn't truly believe it until now. I am not alone.

Did I already know this? A memory flickers in the back of my mind—the cold void, the warm light—but it vanishes too quickly for me to catch it.

I focus all my energy on the nature surrounding me, and I see past the darkness. The stunning life forces of Mountains, Water, Sky, and Underworld—green, blue, silver, and red—radiate around me. The gi born of the Cheon'gwang undulate in the night, their dance more haunting and beautiful than the brightest aurora.

The Yeoiju and I, we need your help. My mind reaches out to the gi around me—to life itself. *Help us defeat the darkness.*

My eyes widen in astonishment. I understand now. The green of Mountains, the blue of Water, the silver of Sky, and the red of Underworld swirl together and converge until there is only one life force—the white gi.

The light inside me—the power of the Yeoiju—is the four life forces united as one.

The Yeoiju isn't a mere gift of the Cheon'gwang. It *is* the true light.

"Wh . . . what are you doing? What are you *doing*, beast?" Daeseong screeches as the light surrounds us. "You cannot defeat the powers of the Amheuk."

The white gi rushes into me, and the world around me snaps into clarity. It fills me with strength, and I summon the light of the Yeoiju to my hand with absolute control—with absolute faith. The light doesn't seek to explode from me, draining me, because I am not alone. I am strong. Both my gumiho and I. We are safe.

The darkness tightens around me and fights to extinguish my light. I welcome it with a smile. I can't have Daeseong plunging to the bottom of the caldera. I ease the gi into my sword of light, and the sword at last glows white with power. It is the Shin'gwangdo.

I raise the sword in a double-handed grip and bring it down with absolute certainty. Light rips through the darkness in a long, diagonal slash.

Daeseong screams—a sound of pure terror—and the darkness dissipates. I see the night sky of Santorini and the Aegean Sea before me again.

On the rugged outcropping where Draco lies still and small, the dark mudang stands before me in his corporeal form. Darkness oozes between his fingers as he presses his hand against the gash in his chest.

He can't run. He can't hide. I am too fast for him—too powerful.

"Do not think you have won, daughter." His face twists into a mask of hate, terrifying and wrong.

"I don't *think* anything. I *know* I won," I spit out even as a corner of my heart chills. *Daughter?* I won't let his Hail Mary mess with my head. "You lost, mudang."

"You think I am lying." His chuckle is indulgent until a hacking cough overtakes him, and thick, greasy darkness drips down his chin. "About your inevitable defeat. About you being my daughter."

"What I think is that you bore the shit out of me." I grip the hilt of the Shin'gwangdo in both hands and raise it horizontally above my head. Then I widen my stance and dip low on one knee, the other leg stretched long. "Do you really want to blabber nonsense so you could live another minute?"

I don't give him a chance to respond. I don't give in to the doubt and fear flickering in the corner of my mind. My human body doesn't just move as fast as my gumiho. It moves as fast as light. And I bury the glowing white blade of the Shin'gwangdo in the dark mudang's heart before he can blink.

I meet his stricken gaze and hold it as I withdraw the blade *slowly*, making sure the motherfucker hurts. Then I step back as he crumples to the ground.

It's done. It's over. Nothing else matters.

"Your mother was filth like you," Daeseong sneers, even as his eyes roll back.

"Shut up." I hate that my voice trembles.

"She bewitched me to fall in love with her, then she *stole* you from me," he hisses. "She ran from me, pregnant with *my* child."

"*Shut up*," I scream. He's lying. He has to be. He is *lying*.

I should chop his head off so he stops talking. So why don't I? The Shin'gwangdo shakes in my grip. Why can't I?

"You don't get to speak about my mother. Just *die* already."

"She hid you from me for eighteen years, but I found you," he rasps, his lips stretching into a dark smile.

Horrified laughter bubbles up my throat. Do I smile like that when I taunt people? I swallow the laugh and crush the thought.

"I *found* you." He coughs wetly before he continues, "Didn't I, daughter? And we both learned on that mountain that you are more like me than your mother. There is darkness inside you, Mihwa. Darkness born of me."

"You're lying." My legs give out, and I fall to my knees.

I have to think. What does he have to gain by lying to me in this moment? *To see me suffer.* He wants to see me suffer before he dies. He wants me to doubt myself. He wants me to falter. That's all.

"Your mother stole you from me," he babbles. He's delusional. He doesn't even know what he's saying anymore. He was already insane before I stabbed him in the heart. Now he's insane *and* dying. He doesn't know what he's saying. "She stole *my* Yeoiju from me."

Daeseong is not my father. He can't be. My mother said my father was a gentle, mild-mannered scholar. He died before I was born.

"The Yeoiju can reveal *everything*, daughter." Darkness spills from the corner of his eyes like tears. "That's all I ever wanted. Why is it wrong to seek knowledge? I only wanted to understand . . . everything."

I sit back on my ass with a thump.

Daeseong was a scholar before he became consumed by his obsession with magic and power. Had my mother been speaking in fucking metaphors? Did she mean Daeseong the scholar died when he became Daeseong the dark mudang?

My lungs tighten around every ragged breath. I would scream if I weren't hyperventilating. *Why, Mother?* She can't *do* this to me. She can't. It's not true. None of it is true.

"No," I mutter past numb lips. I grab Daeseong by the shoulders and shake him hard enough for the back of his head to bang against the rocky ground. "You are *lying*."

"Why the tears, daughter?" He cackles. "Sad to see your father die so soon after you have found him? Are you crying for me, daughter?"

I swipe my forearms across my eyes. Why am I crying? There's nothing to cry about. He is not my father. I have no reason to cry, because my father is not an evil megalomaniac.

Why should I cry? It's not like I stabbed my father in the heart. I'm not the daughter who killed her own father. I wipe away the unending tears streaming down my cheeks.

Seriously, why am I crying? I can prove he's lying.

Daeseong moans, and his eyelids flutter. *Oh gods.* He's dying. I don't have much time. My heart lurches, and wild panic slams into me. I have to hurry. He can't die until I get the truth out of him. And I will get it, even if I have to rip it out of him.

I grab him by his lapels and lift him until his eyes focus on mine. "You *will* tell me the truth."

I bare my teeth in a snarl as I wrench free the power buried deep inside me. Its wrongness jars me to the core of my being, but I don't stop calling on the power. The night grows darker as the white glow fades from the sword of light, and the gi of nature scatters away from me. And my chest fills with searing heat, even as my skin crawls with shame.

"Am I your daughter?" The words drip from my tongue as sweet and cloying as honey, my voice both sibilant and echoing. "Tell me the truth."

"Yes, Mihwa," he answers, obeying my command. "You are my daughter."

"You're lying," I shout, the honey still coating my mouth. "Tell me you're lying."

But it wouldn't mean anything because I would've forced him to say those words. Besides, it's too late for him to tell me anything.

Daeseong is dead.

My dark power sputters out, and I fall limply to my side.

I killed . . . my own father.

CHAPTER TWENTY-EIGHT

We lay Draco to rest, embraced by the blue gi of Heaven Lake. I have a feeling they'll get a kick out of being forever remembered as the Cheonji Monster. An empty smile quirks my lips.

"Sunny, we must delay no longer." Minju places a soft hand on my arm, and I flinch away from her. "We have to return to the Kingdom of Mountains. Our king needs us. Our friends need us."

But I don't have any friends. Not anymore. They deserve someone better than me. And Ethan? A sharp pain shoots through my hollow despair.

Ethan.

I can never face him again. I robbed Daeseong of his free will. I bewitched him. Sure, he was an evil monster, but in the end, I was no better than him. *No.* I am a *worse* monster than my father. Hysterical laughter builds in my chest, and I bite my cheeks to stop it from escaping.

I force myself to speak. "I thought you said you were no use in a battlefield."

"I lied, obviously." Minju blinks myopically at me. "My healing powers will come in very useful in a battlefield."

I nod distractedly. She needs to go. She can help them. As for me, it's a good thing I can never return to the Kingdom of Mountains. I clench my fist around the mark of the blood oath. This way I won't be tempted to beg Ethan for his forgiveness, because I don't deserve to be forgiven.

"Ethan is in good hands." I stare out at the moonlit lake, my body trembling. I haven't stopped shaking since . . . before. "He has the Sentinels at his side, as well as his royal guards from the Kingdom of Mountains. I'm sure they already subdued the loyalist general."

"You don't understand." Minju worries her bottom lip. "The Kingdom of Sky . . . General Bak . . . plans to wage a war against the Kingdom of Mountains. He might already have begun the invasion."

"What?" I surface from the depth of my self-loathing. "Doesn't he know that Ethan subdued his father?"

"The general . . . he doesn't care." The historian sniffs, looking down at her hands. "Jaeseok and I . . . the Order of the Suhoshin . . . we all tried to convince him, but he said he won't stop until he eradicates the tyrant's bloodline from the Realm of Four Kingdoms."

"But Ethan is his *grandson*," I gasp, horrified. Why is this happening? Why can't they leave Ethan alone?

"I know. First, his father. Now, his grandfather. Our king doesn't deserve this," Minju says with a sad shake of her head. "We hoped the Queen of Sky would stop the general, but she added more forces to his army instead. The queen must want vengeance for her sister as much as her father does."

"Wh . . . what?" I clasp my hand against my forehead. "The Queen of Sky is General Bak's *daughter*? The queen is Ethan's *aunt*?"

"Yes." Minju nods calmly. "There were rumors that he forced his younger daughter to marry the decrepit King of Sky so he could use her influence to conquer the Kingdom of Mountains. But the rumors died away when the impending war never came. I always thought the queen prevented the war. I don't know what happened to change her mind this time."

My heart twists with pain. *I'm sorry I can't be there for you, Ethan. I'm sorry I can't be the family you chose.* But he won't want me beside him if he finds out what I am. He won't choose me if he knows what I've done.

Despair claws at my throat.

"I can't go back." I let the numbness settle around me once more.

"Why ever not?" Minju cocks her head to the side.

"I made a deal with Ethan's father." The best lie is a half truth. I hold up my left palm, branded with the circle of blood. "I vowed never to return to the Kingdom of Mountains in exchange for Daeseong's location."

Even with the blood oath, I would've found my way back to Ethan. I wouldn't have given up on our love. But everything is different now. *I am different.* Ethan is better off without me. I can never go back to him. Then . . . where do I go from here? Back to my aimless, meaningless life, hiding from the Shingae.

"You can come with me to the Kingdom of Sky to convince the queen to withdraw the army," Minju says pertly.

"You're not going to yell at me?" I look at the historian with mild curiosity, but it doesn't matter. Nothing matters. I'm not going anywhere with her, whether she yells at me or not. Like Ethan, she is better off without me. All my friends are better off without me.

But what if they need me? What if they need the Yeoiju?

The dark mudang is dead. They'll be fine without me.

"I told you we mustn't delay." Minju frowns. "I will yell at you at a more practical time. Come now."

I let her grab my hand, and I step into Heaven Lake with her—not because I intend to return to the Realm of Four Kingdoms, but because I want to say goodbye to my friend before she leaves. I want to thank her for risking her life to save me. For giving me a chance to protect Draco even though I couldn't save them.

If it wasn't for Minju, I wouldn't have been there to hold their hand as they moved on to the next life. I swallow the useless tears tightening my throat. I should be grateful they died without knowing what I would become. At least I didn't die. I kept my promise to the kid.

We moon shift out onto the small mountain that leads to the entryway to the Kingdom of Sky. But the faraway mountain peak below the Gray Void looks more ominous than usual. I squint at it. What can it be?

Lightning illuminates the sky, and I gasp.

The eerie clouds surrounding the peak are gone. Instead, the sky beyond the mountain—the exposed entrance to the Kingdom of Sky— is webbed with tendrils of darkness.

"Minju?" I breathe. "What are we looking at?"

"The Amheuk . . ." She looks at me with horror in her eyes. "The Amheuk has breached its prison."

I don't bother asking her *how* as laughter bubbles up my throat. It doesn't matter how. All that matters is the darkness is free. I laugh until tears stream down my face.

"Sunny?"

How did I ever believe that I can choose to be good? What was I thinking? I *wasn't*, obviously. I laugh harder, out of control. I had been deluding myself all this time. The tears come faster.

I remember now. I remember *everything* that happened the last time I was in the Gray Void. I freed the stranded souls and dispersed their han.

I destroyed the Gray Void.

My Yeoiju and I destroyed the only thing that stood between the Amheuk and the Realm of Four Kingdoms—the defensive wall that would have stopped the eternal darkness even if it escaped the prison beyond the abyss.

I have unleashed the Amheuk into the Realm of Four Kingdoms.

ACKNOWLEDGMENTS

I'm so grateful to everyone who made this book possible.

To my agent, Sarah Younger, thank you for holding my hand through every bout of anxiety, big and small. And thank you for answering even my silliest questions with thoughtful care and sharing my enthusiasm for all the "brilliant" ideas I have. Most of all, thank you so much for propping me up when I can't stand on my own. You are my rock.

To my acquisition editor and fellow perfectionist, Megan Sakoi, thank you for keeping me honest. Let's overachieve the heck out of *King Foretold* and eat all the yummy cakes to celebrate. I'm so hyped for our partnership on the Realm of Four Kingdoms series!

To my developmental editor Charlotte Herscher, thank you for helping me make *King Foretold* the best book it can be. Thank you so much for answering all my questions so promptly and for helping me put my chaotic thoughts in order. And thank you for your endless patience as I made too-numerous-to-count last minute changes. Why does my brain think of things the moment I hit Send?

To my amazing beta reader Abigail Owen, thank you for putting so much time and energy into making *King Foretold* shine even brighter. Your insight and expertise were absolutely invaluable. I learned so much, and I'm so excited to put it to good use in my future books.

To my beloved family, thank you for believing in me and supporting me. I'm the happiest when I make you proud. My every success is our success because I wouldn't be able to do this without you. I love you guys so much.

GLOSSARY

- Amheuk: Ancient force of true darkness
- banchan: Side dishes served alongside rice
- bojagi: A cloth used for wrapping items
- bomo: A child's nursemaid
- bujeok: A talisman or amulet (often a piece of paper with writings and symbols drawn by a shaman) to bring either good fortune or protection. It can also be used to bring ill fortune to an enemy.
- Cheon'gwang: Ancient force of true light
- Cheonji: Heaven Lake, a lake that lies on the border between China and North Korea on Mount Baekdu
- chima: A skirt worn as part of a hanbok
- cup ramyeon: A bowl of ramen made in the Korean style
- dakjuk: Chicken porridge
- dangui: A jeogori with an elongated front panel
- Dangun: A manifestation of the god of Mountains; son of Hwanung and Ungnyeo
- darisokot: A rudimentary string bikini
- ddeokbokki: Rice cakes popular as street food
- dobok: A martial arts uniform
- dokkaebi: A goblin from Korean folklore
- doksacho: A deadly poisonous herb
- dol: A first birthday
- Donggul: Building where the Suhoshin trial is held, nick-named "the Cave"

- dopo: A long outer robe worn by Korean nobility
- gama: A traditional Korean litter or palanquin
- gat: A traditional Korean hat with a wide brim made of black mesh
- gi: Life force, commonly referred to as *chi* (based on the Mandarin pronunciation)
- Gojoseon: The ancient kingdom that evolved into Korea
- gonggi: Also known as *Korean Jacks*; a children's game played with small stones
- goreum: A ribbon of cloth tied on a jeogori
- gukbap: A Korean dish of soup with rice
- gumiho: A nine-tailed fox spirit
- gungnyeo: A lady-in-waiting for royalty
- Gwangdo: Sword of light
- haejangguk: A soup, often containing seonji, used to help cure a hangover
- halmeoni: An honorific meaning *grandmother*
- han: Grief perverted by resentment and vengeance into something that haunts the soul
- hanbok: Traditional Korean clothing referring to both women's (a cropped top and a floor-length skirt that ties at the chest) and men's (a top and baggy pants)
- hanji: A traditional Korean handmade paper
- hanok: A traditional Korean house, single-story, with a stone-tiled roof and curved eaves
- hwando: A short, single-edged Korean sword
- Hwanin: The god of the heavens
- Hwanung: The god of earth, son of Hwanin and father of Dangun
- in'eo: A merfolk creature in Korean folklore
- Jaenanpa: Faction of dark shamans whose primary purpose is to steal magic from beings of the Shingae

- jeogori: A traditional shirt that goes with the skirt or pants of a hanbok
- jeoseungsaja: A being of Underworld who guides the souls of the dead to the Kingdom of Underworld
- jimil: Inner court
- Joseon: The last dynastic kingdom in Korea (1392–1897)
- jumeokbap: Rice balls
- kimchi: A seasoned dish of pickled or fermented cabbage and other vegetables
- mudang: A Korean shaman
- noona: An honorific meaning *older sister*
- oppa: An honorific meaning *older brother*
- Samshin Halmeom: A manifestation of the Seonangshin in the form of an elderly woman
- sanggung: The most senior gungnyeo
- Sanshillyeong: Spirit of Mountains, another manifestation of the Seonangshin in the form of an elderly man
- sayak: A poisonous elixir used for capital punishment during the Joseon Dynasty
- seonangdang: Tree shrine for the Seonangshin used by humans
- Seonangshin: The god of Mountains
- seonji: Congealed animal blood with a sweet taste and dense yet crumbly texture
- seonnam: A winged angelic being of Sky (male)
- seonnyeo: A winged angelic being of Sky (female)
- seungmacho: An herb used as an antidote
- Shinbiin: Beings of the Shingae in the Realm of Four Kingdoms
- Shindansu: The Sacred Tree of Life
- Shingae: World of gods

- Shin'gwangdo: The newly forged twin to the Gwangdo, forged of dragon scales melded with sacred ashes from Samshin Halmeom
- Shinsan: The divine mountain
- Suhoshin: Guardians of the Shingae
- uinyeo: A medical nurse
- Ungnyeo: In legend, a bear that asked Hwanung to transform her into a woman
- Yeoiju: Pearl of Light (the last of the Cheon'gwang)
- Yongwang: Dragon King, the god of Water

ABOUT THE AUTHOR

Photo © 2025 Alice Kuo Shippee

Jayci Lee writes poignant, sexy, and laugh-out-loud romance featuring Korean American main characters. Her books have been featured in *Cosmopolitan, Entertainment Weekly, Hollywood Reporter, E! News, Women's World,* and *O, The Oprah Magazine.* Jayci is retired from her fifteen-year career as a litigator because of all the badass heroines and drool-worthy heroes demanding to have their stories told. Food, wine, and travel are her jam. She makes her home in sunny California with her tall-dark-and-handsome husband, two amazing boys, and a fluffy rescue.

Printed in Dunstable, United Kingdom